INNOCENCE BETRAYED

Kara Wyse lacked for nothing in her life, until her sheltered world is shattered when her father, arrested for debt, commits suicide. His legacy to Kara is poverty and the revelation that her mother, whom she believed dead, was expecting a daughter, Beatrice, when she ran off with her lover. Beatrice, brought up in poverty, is embittered when she learns of Kara's existence. She vows that Kara will pay for the wrongs she has suffered – Beatrice will take everything that was Kara's. Beatrice has been a thief too long to turn truly respectable, however, for lost innocence can never be regained.

INNOCENCE BETRAYED

INNOCENCE BETRAYED

by

Alison Stuart

Magna Large Print Books
Long Preston, North Yorkshire,
BD23 4ND, England.

British Library Cataloguing in Publication Data.

Stuart, Alison
Innocence betrayed.

A catalogue record of this book is available from the British Library

ISBN 0-7505-1830-8

First published in Great Britain in 1994 by Headline Book Publishing

Published in Large Print 2002 by arrangement with Darley Anderson

Magna Large Print is an imprint of Library Magna Books Ltd.

Printed and bound in Great Britain by T.J. (International) Ltd., Cornwall, PL28 8RW

To my brothers, Alan and Colin and dear John
– always remembered

Also to Mother and Chris – with love

PART ONE

The blood-dimmed tide is loosed, and everywhere
The ceremony of innocence is drowned.

W. B. YEATS, *The Second Coming*

Chapter One

'Education is wasted on women,' Abel Wyse proclaimed. He regarded his daughter with an imperial assumption that his will would be obeyed. His tone carried its usual contempt; resentment at the fact that his only child had been female and not a son.

'But this is 1903, Papa. Surely–'

'You are impertinent, daughter. This book is upon a subject no decent woman would even mention, let alone study. I am shocked, Kara. And disappointed in you.'

He pursed his lips into a line of censure and stared at a point above the honey-gold ringlets of his daughter's bowed head. He needed to lift his head an inch. At twenty Kara was the same height as his own five foot six. He could never look into her oval face with its high cheekbones and wide mouth without feeling acute distaste. If his trials on this earth were not great enough, the bane of his life had to be the image of her mother.

Absently, he noted the slim figure impeccably attired in white muslin. The trumpet-shaped skirt with its pleated folds at the back swept the floor in a short train. The lace collar of her blouse demurely circled her throat, emphasising her virginal purity. Her hair was worn in a powder-puff style, and long pearl and opal earrings framed her face. No one could say that Abel Wyse spared the pounds where his only child was concerned. His daughter lacked for nothing. Only the finest material ever graced those slender shoulders. And how did the chit repay him? By defiance…

Long lashes shielded her violet-blue eyes from his glare. How dare she flout his commands? He waved the offending book, Charles Darwin's *Origin of the Species,* at Kara. With satisfaction he noted that she looked chastened.

'You are to be betrothed tomorrow,' he declared. 'I will not be shamed. You will go to your husband knowing your place. Your future role is as your husband's hostess, to keep his house in good order and bear his children.'

The gaslight hissed behind its cut-glass shade. Its bluish light was reflected in the polished, heavy mahogany furniture which cluttered the room. A large potted palm and aspidistra dominated the two walls each side of the bay window. The maroon velvet curtains were drawn to shut out the bleakness of the Essex fog sweeping in from the Thames estuary, and a fire burned in the black marble fireplace. But even the deep resonant ticking of the grandfather clock in the corner could not make this room seem homely. It was devoid of love. Censure and recrimination had long ago seeped into the dark green silk wallpaper and the brown paintwork. It had overridden the veneer of luxury and wealth so ostentatiously displayed.

With the preciseness that governed all his movements, Abel placed the book on the overcrowded sideboard where crystal bowls and vases jostled with ornate silverware and porcelain figurines on the embroidered and tasselled cover. He had not raised his voice throughout the reprimand. There was no need. He was the supreme head of his household and within its walls his word was law.

Kara kept her head bowed so that her father would not see the anger and resentment in her eyes. Her fists were clenched tight behind a ramrod-straight back. Her erect figure was considered by Papa as the necessary deportment for a wealthy merchant's daughter. It had been obtained by having a blackboard strapped to her back daily for three hours. Inwardly she seethed, her mind rebelling at being unable to make any decisions of her own – even as to what books she should read. What was so terrible about reading Darwin's theories on the evolution of the species? She could understand Papa being displeased if he had caught her reading the poems of John Donne, Lord Byron or even Shelley. He would most certainly view the beautiful, sensual prose as an immoral and corruptive influence. The secretly purchased copies of those poets' works were hidden under a floorboard in her bedchamber.

She had seen marriage to Ernest Holman as a way to escape her father's tyranny. Now she could feel the jaws of a trap closing. Would there be any escape? Would marriage give her the freedom to exercise her mind as she desired? How could she bear it if she must continue to be a beautiful doll, elegantly dressed and mannered, a showpiece to offset the grandeur of man's achievements and pride.

She mastered the rebellion burning in her breast. Queen Victoria had been dead for two years, after ruling an expanding Empire for over sixty years. Yet women were still regarded as unfit to govern their own lives. It was unjust. Since the beginning of the last century, Elizabeth Fry had been fighting for prison and social reform. Florence Nightingale had triumphed over prejudice to revolutionise hospitals. The intrepid Mrs Samuel Baker had accompanied her husband in his quest to discover the source of the Nile. Even so, the domestic world of England was ruled by men who jealousy guarded their supremacy. Any woman attempting to break the mould of convention that had encased them for centuries met with prejudice and ridicule. Some men saw insubordination, or a will to be independent, as bordering upon insanity. They had gone so far as to commit such unnatural daughters to Warley mental asylum, until God saw fit to bring them back to their senses.

More than once, after a clash of wills, Papa had threatened her with the same fate. It wasn't a bluff. He was a true Victorian, a rigid disciplinarian. He upheld the views of morality and conduct instilled in him by his tyrannical grandfather. He was not a man to bend to progress or change. In his eyes only men were important – women were their chattels.

'Summon the servants for prayers, Kara,' he ordered, picking up the family Bible from its table by the firescreen. His narrow face with its wide greying whiskers and prim narrow moustache added to the hauteur of his expression. His thinning grey hair was parted in the middle and slickly oiled so that not a strand fell out of place. 'Because of your wilful disobedience, we will now be dining five minutes late.' His tone implied that the interruption to the routine of his day was as great an anathema to him as his daughter's fall from grace.

Kara pulled the old-fashioned petit-point bell-rope with its large golden tassel, and heard the bell's faint ringing in the servants' quarters at the foot of the stairs.

'You will pray for temperance and guidance,' he informed her coldly. 'Most of all, you will pray for forgiveness for being an unnatural and disrespectful daughter. Clearly, you have no regard for the commandment: "Thou shalt honour thy father and mother".'

Her nails dug into the palms of her hands to control her seething anger. You can only honour those you respect, and it was years since she had respected Papa. You cannot respect a narrow-minded bigot. A man who sought to crush your will and would have you speak only words imitating his opinions. You cannot respect a man who, though he despises you, was so possessive he would not allow you friends. The daughter of the owner of Essex's largest haulage company, with a score of wagons and drivers at his disposal, could not be tainted by the company of lesser mortals. There were few families in Brentwood that Abel Wyse regarded as his equal.

Kara was a virtual prisoner in her home.

Perhaps if her mother was still alive she would have had more love and freedom. But Florence Wyse had died when she was four. She was only allowed out to church on Sunday, and twice yearly she was taken to London by Aunt Ethel to purchase clothes. Since leaving Miss Kate Bryan's private High School for Girls as their star pupil when she was fifteen, none of her old school friends was permitted to call. Neither was she allowed to visit them. Once a month she could spend an afternoon in town, chaperoned by her maid, Jenny. Thank God for the open-mindedness of Jenny. Without those monthly visits she would have gone mad. That was when she purchased the books she craved to read, spending her small allowance intended for fripperies on something worthwhile instead. Life had been less restrictive since Abel had permitted Ernest Holman to call once a week. Ernest had recently inherited his father's bank and was considered a fitting suitor for Abel Wyse's only child.

Last week Abel had permitted Kara to attend a musical evening with Ernest at the Church Hall. They were chaperoned by his married sister Imelda and her husband. The taste of freedom, however small, had made her hunger for more. There was an exciting world outside her home. She longed to taste and experience more of its splendours. Surely that was not so terrible an ambition?

She would pray as Papa instructed, but not for temperance or humility. She would pray for independence and for the chance to make something of her life. No, that was wicked. Years of being forced to bow to Papa's will could not be erased so easily. She would pray to be a good wife to Ernest. Tomorrow they would be betrothed and a June wedding was planned. Ernest was not like Papa. He was not a tyrant. He loved her. In the six months of their courtship, she had learned that her will was the stronger. With a smile and gentle persuasion, she could overcome his reservations and make him agree to her wishes.

She had glimpsed an opening door to her cage. Although Ernest had been Papa's choice, she had been delighted on being introduced to find him a handsome and agreeable young man. By the third meeting she was confident that, once married to him, her life would be different. But would it? The nagging doubt gnawed at her mind with unremitting persistence. Would marriage be the exchange of one cage for another?

She would feel no regret at leaving this house. A house without love, without even a photograph of her Mama. Compared to the few other houses she had visited, the lack of photographs in hers was the most singular difference. Those others had been crammed with family photographs on every available surface. What sort of an unfeeling monster – for that was how she now viewed Papa – did not even keep a photograph of the woman he had married?

Kara took her place at her father's side as the six servants filed into the room for the second prayer-reading of the day. Her stare fell upon Keech, her father's valet. He was obsequious, with a small waxed moustache and oiled thinning hair. He had informed Abel that Kara was reading Charles Darwin's book. He never missed a chance to ingratiate himself with his master.

Papa began to read a passage from the Bible. As his voice droned piously on, Kara's attention wandered to the other servants. All looked tired. She felt a stab of guilt that her engagement dinner had given them so much extra work. Mrs Middlewich, the cook, had a smudge of flour on her podgy cheeks, and where she had removed her apron there were several spots of sauce and fat on her grey dress. As usual her grey hair escaped untidily from her linen cap. It surprised Kara that Papa allowed such a slovenly servant in his house, but then no cook in Essex could rival Mrs Middlewich's light pastry, or her special sauces.

Kara noted with dismay that, as the servants rose from their knees, Nanny Brewster was leaning heavily upon Seth Ford's arm. Seth's young freckled face was full of sympathy as he helped the old woman, a lock of his rusty-coloured hair continually falling over his brow. He was the general workman and groom for their one horse-carriage. Arthritis had shrunk the once rigid-backed Nanny to a bent figure, her joints painfully swollen. Kara controlled her impulse to plead with Papa that Nanny be excused the twice-daily climb up the stairs from her tiny room behind the kitchen. It was years since Kara had needed a nanny. When Papa had voiced his intention of dismissing Brewster, Kara had pleaded with him to keep her employed. Kara's mother had died when she was four, and Nanny Brewster had given her the love denied her by her cold-hearted father.

'My home is not a charitable institution,' Papa had declared when Kara pleaded with him on Nanny's behalf. 'Whilst Brewster remains active and can continue with minor tasks of sewing and ironing, she may remain. Otherwise she must go to the workhouse.'

The thought filled Kara with alarm. Nanny was almost sixty and her swollen and twisted fingers were making it difficult for her to continue with her sewing. The old woman exchanged a look with Kara, and she saw the fear of dismissal bleak in her eyes. The workhouse was the terror which haunted every ageing servant. Nanny would not end her days there, Kara vowed. She would insist that she come to live with Ernest and herself when they married. Kara would look after her.

Downstairs the talk was all of the betrothal tomorrow. Jenny Maddox held court as she pressed the flounces of her mistress's silk petticoats. She wrapped a cloth around her hand and picked up the flat iron from its stand by the range. To test its heat she spat on it, before continuing her work and her gossip.

'It will be like a morgue here once Miss Kara is wed,' she complained.

'Less work for you,' Seth Ford declared as he held up a silver spoon he was polishing, and squinted at it short-sightedly to ensure no tarnish remained on its handle.

'And what work will that be?' Jenny groaned. 'Maid of all work – from lighting the fires at five in the morning, to scrubbing the kitchen floor at ten at night. The day Miss Kara weds I'm giving notice.'

'Don't let old Gerty hear you.' Seth looked over the round spectacles perched on the end of his freckled nose. 'She'll sack you on the spot for disloyalty and no references…'

'I'm not afraid of Mrs Gertrude Reeves,' Jenny said, but looked over her shoulder to ensure that the housekeeper was not in sight. 'She's an old witch, and too fond of using that birch rod of hers.'

'Spare the rod and spoil the child,' Mrs Middlewich said spitefully whilst rolling out a vast round of pastry for her famous apple and cinnamon tartlets. 'You've put on your airs and graces since Mr Wyse promoted you to lady's maid.'

Jenny replaced the iron on its stand and picked up the reheated one. 'But he didn't get a maid to replace me. So I still have to set the fires each morning and polish the furniture every day. I do the work of three maids, and don't think I don't. You'd think a man of Mr Wyse's standing in the town would employ more servants.'

Seth winked at Jenny, whom he was soft on, and attacked a blackened fork with renewed vigour. 'How many months' wages does he owe you? I've not been paid since last Lady-day. And I know that both the butcher and the grocer were loath to deliver the orders for tomorrow's banquet. It wasn't until I mentioned that Miss Kara was about to be engaged to Mr Holman that they supplied us. Mr Wyse ain't paid any tradesmen for months.'

'That's the way of gentry,' Mrs Middlewich stated flatly. 'Keeps the servants and the tradesmen in their places by being behind with their wages and bills. He'll feast his guests as though they were visiting royalty. Look at the fine trousseau he provided for Miss Kara.'

'Five hundred pounds must have been spent at the dressmaker's alone,' Jenny added. 'Only the best is good enough for Miss Kara.'

'Guilt money.' Mrs Middlewich nodded sagely, setting her several chins wobbling. 'Never showed the poor mite a day's affection in her life.'

'Gossiping about your betters again, Mrs Middlewich.' The high-pitched voice of Mrs Reeves froze the conversation. The housekeeper stood in the doorway in her black gown, the heavy chatelaine jangling from her waist. 'If your hands were as agile as your tongues, there would be twice as much work done here.'

'And talking of work needing to be done, where's Keech?' Seth scowled at the housekeeper. 'Cleaning the silver were supposed to be his job today. Stuck-up runt thinks himself too good to soil his hands. If he's skived off to the pub again I'll…'

'That's enough of such talk,' Mrs Reeves cut in. 'Mr Keech is not answerable to you, young man.'

She would not let the lower order of servants deride Mr Keech. A valet was far superior to a general manservant. Servants should know their rightful place in the hierarchy of things. She looked pointedly at the corner of the large kitchen table. A silver salver laid with a Crown Derby tea-set and Georgian silver teapot awaited the hot water from the boiling kettle. Mrs Reeves selected the timepiece which hung from her chatelaine and tutted as she regarded it.

'The hot water should be in the teapot and the brew mashing by now,' she ordered. 'What can you be about, Middlewich? Mr Wyse will be most displeased if his tea is served late. Move yourselves, all of you. In precisely two minutes Mr Wyse will be ringing for his afternoon tea. And is that fruit cake I see on the plate? Today is Friday. On Fridays, Mr Wyse has chocolate cake. Wednesday is his day for fruit cake.'

'Haven't I enough cooking to do this day without making an extra chocolate cake?' Mrs Middlewich didn't even bother to look at Mrs Reeves as she continued pressing the cutter into the pastry. She knew her services were too valuable for Mr Wyse to dismiss her. No one could prepare Angels on Horseback the way she did, and it was Mr Wyse's favourite dish. 'Send my regrets to Mr Wyse,' she continued sarcastically. 'For once he must have the fruit cake. If I'd been given the two extra kitchen maids I requested should be hired from the agency, I would have had the time to cook his chocolate cake. I can't do everything.'

Mrs Reeves drew in a sharp breath, then thought better of reprimanding the cook. Instead she turned her displeasure upon the maid. 'God help you, Jenny, if the table is not already laid. Must I supervise everything?'

'The table is laid, Mrs Reeves.' Jenny scowled at the departing figure of the housekeeper. Bossy old bat! She never soiled her milk-white housekeeper's hands by doing common work. If ever there was a woman who had notions above her station, it was Mrs Reeves.

Gertrude Reeves suppressed her irritation at the laxity of the servants. At least Mr Wyse's tea would not be late. She smoothed a hand over the tiny pintucks on her flat-chested bodice. Mr Wyse was particular about his time-keeping. She admired that in a man. In fact she admired everything about Mr Wyse. She had been his housekeeper for sixteen years, ever since his wife had died, and for fifteen of those years she had been secretly in love with him. No detail was too small for her to oversee for his comfort. Not that he noticed.

A sigh escaped her and she rebuked herself. Mr Wyse was too important a man to notice a servant, even a housekeeper. She patted the smooth line of her brown hair under her widow's cap. She was forty-eight and had been a widow for half her life. Her marriage had lasted three months – three blissful months when she had discovered the pleasures to be experienced in the bedchamber. She had never expected to marry, knowing that her thin body and long face were plain in the extreme. Sam, a merchant's clerk, had taken lodgings with her widowed mother. They had married a year later. Then Sam had been killed when two wagons collided in the street; a load of timber had fallen on the pavement, crushing him as he walked to work. Twenty-four years was a long time for a passionate woman to sleep in a lonely bed, and with each passing year her frustration made her more embittered.

Her lips narrowed. She had spent the afternoon working on the household accounts. So many of the bills had remained unpaid. When she had gone into Mr Wyse's study to ensure that it was tidy for when he returned from work, his desk was open. On it were the dressmaker's, shoemaker's and milliner's bills from London. She had been aghast at the figures on the accounts. How could Kara be so selfish to spend so lavishly? Didn't she know how straitened Mr Wyse's haulage business had become since he had lost so many contracts to the railways?

Kara pounded the keyboard of the piano, a wildness entering her playing as she began to breathe harder. The music absorbed the tumult in her mind, echoing her subconscious rebellion. Through her playing, the years of resentment at her confinement and defeated hopes poured out of her in the only way she could express them. She was supposed to be practising the complicated pieces Papa had chosen that she perform for their guests tonight. Such entertainment always had to be a complicated piece. Her skill was something to be paraded and displayed to the glorification of Abel Wyse. At such times she felt like a pet puppy dutifully jumping through hoops.

The music her father had chosen bored her. She played a new favourite, a piece by Rachmaninov she had recently discovered. It was wild and passionate. As she played, her yearning for independence overpowered her. Her figure encased in the stiff confining corset, ensuring that her waist was the required seventeen inches for a gentlewoman of fashion, made her labour for breath.

A discreet cough instantly stilled her hands. Jenny bobbed a curtsey. 'Time to dress, Miss Kara. Your guests will be here in two hours.'

A nervous glance at the French gilt and enamelled clock under its high glass dome on the mantelpiece halted the fear which made her heart pound. Papa would not return for another fifteen minutes. Jenny had warned her in time. The last time Papa had heard her playing with such abandon, he had locked the piano for several weeks as punishment.

'Thank you for reminding me, Jenny.' Kara smiled warmly. There were dark circles under the maid's eyes from the long hours she worked. The maid's real name was Camilla, but Papa had declared that it was an unsuitable name for a maid, and insisted she change it to Jenny. Kara resolved to buy her some hair ribbons when next they visited the shops. At twenty-eight, Jenny was the closest in age to Kara in the household. Though Papa was quick to stamp out any hint of familiarity between the two women, Jenny had become Kara's confidante. Without Jenny keeping secret her purchase of books, Kara's life would have been even more onerous. In return she kept secret that Jenny and Seth were planning to marry. Papa would dismiss them both for daring to conduct a courtship under his roof.

Kara stood up and sighed. 'I must look my best for our guests this evening. Papa expects it. He has spent a fortune to ensure that I will look like a fairy doll for the occasion.'

Dressed in pearl-coloured silk, the tight bodice edged with pearls and pink flowers, Kara did feel like a fairy doll. Her creamy shoulders were displayed above the low neckline. Her dark gold hair had been swept high on to her head and studded with pearl stars. About her neck was a triple strand of pearls, her betrothal present from Papa. As she stared at her figure in the long cheval mirror, a blank mask settled upon her face, and her violet-blue eyes glazed with dislike. The fairytale image was so far removed from how Kara truly saw herself, it was like looking at a grotesque caricature of how Papa believed his daughter should appear in public.

She turned from the mirror and picked up her ivory-handled fan. Was it unnatural to resent rich clothes when, according to Mr Dickens' novels, there were so many starving and wretched people striving to survive in a cruel and bleak world? Times had changed little for the poor since his novels were written. Yet what did she truly know of the world outside the protection of her father's home? Next to nothing. Because Papa had decreed that she should not. Whatever information she had gleaned from the newspaper when it was discarded by her father had been done in secret. Seth would rescue it before it was used to wrap kitchen scraps, and Jenny would bring it to her with her morning tea at seven each morning. The news she read was always a day late, but it kept her abreast of events in the world.

Often, after laying the paper aside, she would feel restless. Women suffragettes were demanding the vote. The duchess of this or that was working on a committee to help the poor or needy. She felt so useless. The only charity work Papa permitted her to do was embroidering tray-cloths for the church bazaar. She was capable of so much more than that. If, as Dickens wrote, there were young children forced to work in horrible sweat-houses, widows striving to bring up several children on a pittance, and cripples, the sick, ailing and homeless begging on the streets, she wanted to do something worthwhile to help them.

There was a knock at the door and Jenny entered. 'The Holmans' carriage has just pulled up. Mr Wyse is expecting you to greet your guests.' The maid's eyes shone as she regarded her mistress. 'You look beautiful, Miss Kara. You must be the happiest woman alive tonight. Mr Holman is such a handsome man. Just think: in three months time you will be his wife.'

Kara inclined her head in acknowledgement, but as she began to descend the stairs and saw Ernest talking to her father, she felt no wild leaping of her heart. As though sensing her presence, Ernest looked up. His handsome face lit with pleasure. A glow spread through her. Never had Papa shown any appreciation of her appearance.

In his black frock coat, white winged collar and white tie, Ernest cut a dashing figure. His flaxen hair with its cap of unruly curls was endearingly boyish, and his narrow side-whiskers gave maturity to his smooth classical features. The only imperfection to this tall, slender Adonis was a small chin, which some might call a sign of weakness.

'My dear,' Ernest said as she walked across the black and white marble floor to his side. He took her hand and raised it to his lips. 'You look magnificent – a vision of beauty to steal any man's heart. I am the proudest man in England this day.'

Her doubts dissolved concerning her future marriage. Ernest adored her. All he wanted was to make her happy. He would never shut her away from friends and new interests. Her smile was dazzling as she held his tender gaze. 'I want only to make you happy and be a good wife to you, Ernest.' She meant every word.

A blush spread across his cheeks, heightening the paleness of his flaxen hair. 'Mama is impatient to meet you. I know you will adore her, as I adore her, when we live together after we are married.'

The first alarm bell began to ring. Were they not to have their own house? Kara silenced it. 'I, too, am impatient to meet your Mama. You have spoken so often of her. I am quite in awe of this paragon.'

He laughed, too enchanted with her appearance to heed the irony in her voice. They entered the saloon where the guests were assembled.

'Kara, this is dear Mama.'

The paragon turned from talking with her daughter Imelda, and fixed grey eyes coated in frost upon Kara. The smile froze upon Kara's lips. Absently, she noted the coiffured grey hair adorned by a dainty lace cap. Rubies like droplets of blood dripped from her ears and neck. Kara's flesh turned to ice beneath that stare. It was the most hostile she had ever encountered. Augustina Holman hated her future daughter-in-law on sight. The glittering intensity in that icy glare was as clear as a beacon. *Ernest is my son, my possession,* it warned. *I never yield what is mine.*

The alarm bells sounded with all the urgency of a horse-drawn fire-engine clanging through the streets. Disillusion was so acute that for a moment Kara felt the room beginning to slip away from her. The edges of her vision blurred. Terrified that she would faint, she drew a steadying breath. She would never show weakness before Mrs Holman. Her chin lifted and her eyes sparked her answering challenge.

Ernest is yours now, but on the day we wed he will be for ever mine – if I want him.

But did she want Ernest upon those terms?

The evening passed in a haze for Kara. People fussed over her and admired the diamond cluster ring Ernest had presented to her. It was rather too ostentatious for her taste, rather like something Papa would have bought to declare his possession.

Stoically throughout the evening, Kara performed the role expected of her. Her smile was never brighter, her piano playing faultless, her wit surprising even herself by the laughter it raised. Once she even caught a glint of satisfaction in Papa's eyes. She charmed everyone. Everyone except Augustina Holman.

It was a small consolation that Ernest never left her side, though he repeatedly praised his Mama. Before the meal was over, his adoring gaze had begun to irritate her where once it had captivated.

The first blackbird burst into song, heralding the start of the dawn chorus. Kara lay rigid and wide-awake in her bed, staring at the pale yellow wallpaper. The engagement ring on her finger felt like an iron manacle. She had not slept all night. With each passing hour, her certainty had grown that she did not want to be Ernest's wife. She would not exchange one house where she was despised by her Papa for another where Augustina Holman would regard her as a rival to her son's affections.

Yet how could she break the engagement without creating a scandal? Disgrace fell upon a jilted bride, even if she had done the jilting. A betrothal was regarded as being as binding as a marriage contract. Papa would never agree. Before retiring he had triumphantly proclaimed that Ernest had agreed to become his partner in his haulage business.

'Papa, surely that is not necessary?' she had queried.

'What is necessary or unnecessary in matters of business is none of your concern,' he had answered crushingly. 'I would not see all I have laboured for reduced to nothing because I have no son. Ernest is to become my son. He will continue my business when I retire. It is agreed that one of your sons will inherit my company.' He had subjected her to an imperious glare. 'Sons, Kara. That is what marriage is all about. Producing sons. Do not fail Ernest. Do not fail me.'

His words hammered into her mind like nails into her coffin. She saw her dream of independence and freedom evaporating like morning dew. Kara's fists screwed tight. I won't let it happen, she vowed.

Her defiance began by missing morning prayers. Expecting Papa to order her punishment for laxity in her devotions, she was surprised when Jenny returned. The maid was smiling.

'Mr Wyse said you must rest. He declared your indisposition was only to be expected. A young lady does not become engaged every day.'

'Papa said that?'

'And not in his usual cutting way.' Jenny voiced her own surprise. 'Come to think of it, the master was in an exceptionally good mood. The like of which I've never seen before.'

The news was worse than any punishment. Papa's good mood was a result of her engagement. Clearly nothing she said or did would stop her marriage to Ernest. But that wouldn't stop her trying.

Chapter Two

Abel Wyse tapped his chin as he regarded the huge arrangement of flowers delivered by the florist. They were for Kara from Ernest. A fresh arrangement had arrived every day for his daughter since he had agreed to their engagement. Holman was besotted with the girl. Abel permitted himself a rare smile. The match was better than he had dared to hope for. At least if he had to suffer a daughter as his heir, he had been fortunate that she was not unattractive. There had been several suitors who had approached him. Holman had been the wealthiest.

He picked up the pile of bills delivered from the London dressmaker's. Ethel as usual had been more than extravagant in meeting her niece's requirements. He winced at the size of the lingerie account alone. He put the accounts aside. Appearance was everything. He did not begrudge providing for his only child. A frown furrowed the lines on his brow and his eyes hardened with bitterness. Yes, Kara was his only child – his only daughter.

At least by winning Holman's interest Kara had not failed in her duty. Years of resentment smouldered in his veins. He could not see that Kara was so like him in many ways. Instead of hidden strengths of character, he saw defiance. Rather than acknowledging her keen intellect, she saw it as obstinacy. Her uncowed and fierce determination was to him merely stubbornness and wilful disobedience. Qualities he would have praised in a man and which would make him proud of a son were regarded as unfeminine, if not verging on the indecent, in a daughter. Courage was expected of a man. In a woman it was immodest. Any show of independence, or an inquiring spirit, was abject wantonness.

Abel did not regard his opinions as unreasonable. His mother had been an invalid after falling in the snow and breaking her hip. Until her death several years later, she had constantly complained of her fragile health and the pain she suffered. It had left him with the idea that women were definitely the weaker sex. If they were family, they must be pampered. That was a man's duty. Women needed careful nurturing in order to fulfil their duties in serving a man's every need. His sister, Ethel, was the perfect example of womanhood. She dressed impeccably, her home was well ordered, and she had given Bertram five sons besides three daughters.

Thoughts of his sister's family life soured Abel's expression. His own had been disastrous. Why couldn't his wife Florence have been more like Ethel? Memories brought a return of the anger and pain. Even after sixteen years, thoughts of his marriage made his fist bunch with fury.

In the following month, the house closed in on Kara like a prison cell. Her only relief was four visits from Ernest, who had been allowed to take tea with her with Mrs Reeves in attendance. Any pleasure in Ernest's company was spoilt by the housekeeper's sour vigilance. Strangely, he had not visited this week, neither had he sent word.

For the first time since her engagement, there was no fog, and the late April sunshine lanced palely through the heavy lace curtains and velvet drapes. Tall ferns in every window further obscured the daylight. Every room was oppressive and gloomy. Kara was desperate to get out of the house into the sunshine. Her restless glance fell upon several glass domes filled with stuffed birds and woodland animals. She hated the thought of their destruction for the sake of fashionable adornment to their living room. Often she felt she was just another ornament for Papa's home, kept under glass and expected to be a dumb captive.

Her clenched fist beat her side as she paced the dismal room. She needed to think. But it was impossible to do so here. Papa's will and influence permeated the dark papered walls and heavy furnishings.

She encountered Mrs Reeves in the hallway. She was giving Jenny her instructions for the morning.

'I require my maid's services this morning, Mrs Reeves,' Kara announced. 'I have some purchases to make. Jenny will accompany me.'

Immediately the older woman's back stiffened. 'It is not your usual day to go abroad, Miss Kara. Mr Wyse made no mention of you going out. He'd not like it. Especially now that the soldiers have returned from the Boer War. The Essex regiment is back at Warley barracks. The town will be full of soldiers. It would not be seemly.'

'I will be no longer than two hours. It's Papa's birthday next month. I've a special gift planned for him and it must be a surprise. You know how he questions me about where I have been?' Kara glibly improvised. Mrs Reeves was Papa's spy, and would inform him she had left the house without his permission. 'I wish to buy Papa something special as he has been so generous with my trousseau,' she coerced. 'It may be necessary to order his gift, and I would be assured that it arrives in good time.'

Kara saw the conflicting emotions warring on Mrs Reeves' face. The woman slavishly enforced all Abel's wishes, but to refuse her request would be churlish in the extreme.

'Two hours seems excessive. Take care you are no longer.' Mrs Reeves regarded her sternly. 'It is most irregular. Mr Wyse insists that you observe his wishes. A dutiful daughter's place is in the home.'

Kara was careful to speak meekly and keep her expression demure. Inside she was raging. 'Two hours only, I promise.'

'If you are late, I must inform Mr Wyse that you have flouted his ruling.' She turned to Jenny and, seeing the pleasure on the maid's face at escaping from her work, added spitefully, 'You will still complete the tasks I set you. You'll just have to work harder when you return.'

Kara felt a pang of guilt as the housekeeper left them alone. 'I'm sorry, Jenny. I've made it worse for you.'

'To escape the old dragon's tongue for two hours I'd do double the tasks she set me. After being brought up on a farm I hate being shut inside on a sunny day.'

They left the detached redbrick house in Priests Lane, walking along the tree-lined road towards Shenfield Common. The few houses stood in their own grounds, their fronts obscured by tall privet hedges or trees. Living in Priests Lane added to Kara's sense of isolation. Two young woman giggled as they wobbled along the poorly made-up road on their bicycles.

Kara suppressed her envy. She would love to own a bicycle of her own. Papa had almost exploded when she asked for one.

'Only a loose woman would cavort about in such a manner,' he had raged. 'I cannot believe that my daughter would wish to expose her ankles in the street for all to see, like a common trollop.'

Even a horse was now denied her. Until she left school she had had her own pony, and Sam had accompanied her riding every afternoon. When she was fifteen it had been sold. Papa had announced that it was too dangerous for her to ride abroad with the army barracks so close to town. There were so many pleasures Papa disapproved of.

Upon reaching the mill pond at Shenfield Common, Jenny produced some bread she had taken from the kitchen to feed the ducks. Kara smiled absently at the ducks' antics as they squabbled and gobbled up the bread.

On their return along the Ingrave Road, Kara noticed a young flowerseller near the gates of the redbrick building of Brentwood Grammar School. The shivering figure was barefoot, her woollen shawl was full of holes and her skirt and blouse ragged. A bony shoulder showed through a rent, the flesh grey from never having been washed. There were goosebumps on her flesh from the cold, and her bare toes were red and swollen from chilblains. The girl continually wiped her streaming nose on the back of her hand. When she coughed, the hacking sound shook her frail body.

Feeling uncomfortably overdressed in her beige woollen suit with its tight-fitting bolero jacket and brown velvet cape, Kara dropped a shilling in the dirty hand and waved aside the proffered posy.

Kara's steps quickened with resolve. The walk had cleared her mind and set a path for her future. She had allowed Papa to dictate the terms of her life for too long.

She cut through the back streets of terraced houses to where her father had his haulage company. Stopping at the corner, she watched a red wagon with gold lettering drawn by two shire horses clatter into the yard.

Kara paused, staring up at the company's high wrought-iron gates, which stood open. In gilt lettering across their top were the words, 'Wyse and Son, Haulage Company'. Only there was no son. There was only a daughter about to be bartered in marriage to provide the sons of the future. The 'and Son' on the lettering dated back to her grandfather's time. It had been displayed throughout his lifetime in the assurance that Abel would inherit.

Why had Papa not changed the lettering? Stranger still, in his obsession to have a son, why had he not remarried?

For a moment Kara's courage faltered. She was determined to face her father without delay – to beard the lion in its den. Her stomach clenched with dread. Papa would be furious. The consequences were bound to be unpleasant, but she refused to go meekly to the slaughter. She knew that he could force her to marry Ernest, that he could force her to marry a man who was ugly and cruel, if it suited his purposes. Was she foolish to rebel against the convention which had governed women's lives for centuries? Here Abel Wyse was still a tyrant ruling his business empire. Precluded by her sex, she had never been a part of that world. She had never been brought here as a child to see the horses – even though she had pleaded many times to be allowed to do so.

Though she had never visited the yard, Kara was surprised to see a dozen drivers standing in a group talking in heated tones. At this time of day she had expected them to be on their deliveries. Several of their heads were turned to look up at a stone building where wooden stairs led to an open doorway. That must be where Papa had his office. Outside the door, two policemen in dark, brass-buttoned uniforms and top hats appeared to be standing on guard.

Alarm quickened Kara's heartbeat. The atmosphere in the yard was palpable. Something was wrong. Had something happened to Papa? She hurried forward, her gaze fixed upon the open door at the top of the stairs.

As she reached the iron gates there was an outbreak of angry shouting from the office. Recognising her father's voice, Kara halted. There was something in his tone which chilled her to the marrow. It was inconceivable, but Abel sounded afraid.

This was not the time to confront him about her marriage. On the point of turning away, she saw four men appear on the verandah at the head of the stairs. Two were policemen, another was a red-faced man who continued to shout abuse at the fourth figure. Surely that bowed, stoop-shouldered figure could not be her father? But it was. From the way two of the policemen were holding his arms, it looked as though he had been arrested.

Kara felt her knees buckle and snatched at Jenny's arm for support.

'Blimey, it's the master,' Jenny said, shocked. 'The peelers have nabbed him. I don't believe it.'

'Be quiet, Jenny.' Kara drew the maid back around the corner and out of sight of the yard. She was convinced there had been some dreadful mistake. It would humiliate Abel to know that his arrest had been witnessed by his daughter and a servant. 'Papa must not see us. I'm sure he'll return home this evening as usual. This is a misunderstanding.'

'It didn't look like no misunderstanding as far as that other man was concerned,' Jenny stated. 'If ever a man looked like he had right on his side and had just seen justice done, it were him.'

'No, it's a mistake. Come away. Papa must not see us.'

They flattened themselves against the side wall of a row of terraced houses as a crowd began to gather, drawn by the shouting.

'Ain't that old Wyse?' a bearded coster yelled as he pushed his fruit barrow closer.

As the crowd surged forward to view the scene, Kara was jostled and pushed into view of the haulage yard. The man who had accompanied the policemen remained in the yard with two constables. Her father was being shoved into a closed carriage waiting outside the gates. As it drove away, Kara saw that the man in the yard was shouting at two grooms to spend the night in the yard with the horses. The policemen were urging the protesting drivers from the premises. Stunned by the rapidity of events, Kara stayed long enough to see the two huge iron gates drawn together and chained. The officer in charge affixed some kind of seal to the padlock.

Kara couldn't bear to watch. She fled as fast as her long heavy skirts permitted. A group of soldiers, loitering outside a tavern, whistled and cat-called as she passed. Two of them stepped on to the pavement to detain her. From the purple and pink facings on their tunics she knew they belonged to the 'Pompadours'. The First Essex Battalion, so named because of those facings.

'Let me pass, gentleman.' She kept her eyes lowered, feeling no fear, just concern for what had happened to her father. Side-stepping, she tutted in annoyance when both men did the same to remain standing in her way.

'What's yer 'urry, darlin'?' a cockney voice taunted.

Jenny stepped forward, her hands on her hips. 'You get out of Miss Wyse's way. She's a respectable woman.'

An officer passing on horseback reined in. 'Let the lady pass, men,' he ordered, and the soldiers hastily moved aside.

Nodding a curt thank-you to the officer, but without looking at him directly, Kara hurried away.

The captain watched her trim figure; the unconscious sway of her hips was an appealing sight. In her haste, she had lifted her skirts, tantalisingly revealing the trimmest ankle he had seen in a long year. His interest quickened. He had heard her maid's admonition to his men: so that was Abel Wyse's daughter. Reputedly one of the wealthiest heiresses in the county. A pity he'd just come from resigning his commission. After the Boer War, he'd had enough of killing and the stifling heat of hot countries. Besides, there was no money to be made in the army, though he had always managed to keep abreast of his debts, usually by gambling. Just his luck that during the ten years he'd been stationed at Warley barracks, when not upon foreign service, he'd never met the lovely heiress. A pretty face and riches were few and far between. Captain Zachariah Morton rubbed a finger across his dark moustache and grinned. Once he lived in London there'd be wealthy debutantes aplenty to ply his charms upon.

Back at Priests Lane, Kara was shocked to find the place in chaos. Three carts were outside her house, and the most valuable pieces of furniture were already loaded on them. A crowd had gathered outside and, at Kara's approach, began jeering and shouting for news.

Fears for her father multiplied. She had seen the bailiffs at work before, and knew the shame a family suffered at having their possessions seized against a debt. But Papa was not in debt. He couldn't be. He was a rich man. How dare they treat her family in this manner?

Ignoring the cries, Kara pushed her way through the people. So great was her anger that she did not notice the purse lifted from her pocket, or the silver brooch deftly snatched from the front of her cape.

A short man with an immense waxed moustache barred her entrance.

'No one's to go inside,' he proclaimed officiously.

'This is my house. I am Kara Wyse.'

He grunted, looking her up and down in such a disdainful manner that Kara was tempted to slap the insolence from his face. She controlled her impulse. A show of temper would not solve anything.

'Woman here says she's Kara Wyse,' the man shouted over his shoulder. 'Where's the housekeeper?'

Mrs Reeves appeared. Her eyes were red and she was sobbing into her handkerchief.

'Is this your mistress?' the man demanded.

Mrs Reeves nodded. Then, bursting into a fresh wave of weeping, she sagged down on to a chair in the hall.

Kara pushed past the officious man, her voice cutting. 'This is my maid. I trust you will not object to her entering my house?'

'Won't be your house much longer,' he snapped, nastily. 'You've got a week to find yourself somewhere else to live. I'd say that's generous, given that Mr Wyse owes ten thousand pounds in debts.'

'That's not possible,' Kara gasped. She could not fully take in what was happening. It could not be possible that she was about to be made homeless. 'I've only just become engaged to Mr Ernest Holman. He is my father's business partner.'

'Not any more, if what I've heard of this morning's events are true. Wyse was able to run up so much credit these last few months on account of the prospective marriage. It's all over town that Holman pulled out when the extent of Wyse's debts were known.'

Kara still found it impossible to believe. How could Papa owe ten thousand pounds? He was a respected and prominent businessman, a town alderman. Once a month he read the lesson in their parish church. What did the man mean, Ernest had pulled out? Out of what? Their marriage? His business partnership?

A heavy-set man in a leather apron pushed past her carrying the French gilt and enamelled clock under its high dome. Instinctively, she put out a hand to stop him.

'That was a wedding present to my great-grandfather.'

'Sorry, miss. It's the property of Mr Wyse's creditors now.'

She turned to a tall policeman who was standing, ill-at-ease, in the hallway. 'Surely they cannot just take our possessions in this way?'

He cleared his throat. 'Writs have been issued and the goods to the value of the debts are to be impounded to repay the creditor.'

'But this is my home,' Kara said stupidly, still unable to grapple with the enormity of what was happening.

The policeman scratched his thick side-whiskers. He was middle-aged and his round face was not unkindly. 'It's only because of Mr Wyse's standing in the town that you've not all been put on to the streets today. I'm sorry, miss. I've got daughters of my own. I wouldn't like to see any of them in such straits. But the law must be obeyed. The house is now the property of the bank.'

The bailiff preened his flamboyant moustache. 'There's a score or more creditors on Wyse's back.' He laughed cruelly. 'Not so wise after all, it seems.'

Kara ignored the rude and obnoxious man. At least the policeman had some sympathy for her plight. 'Where has Mr Wyse been taken?' she asked, her voice shaking with shock.

'He's at the police station, answering questions.'

'My father isn't a criminal. They can't lock him up. Can I visit him?'

He looked at her pityingly. 'The gaol is no place for a gentlewoman.'

'I will not abandon my father. There may be things he needs.'

The policeman sighed. 'To see your father in gaol will only upset you, miss. Like as not, he'll be home before supper-time.'

For years Kara had believed she hated her autocratic father. Now that he was in trouble, she could never desert him. The ties of blood and duty irrevocably bound them. She knew nothing of money matters, but surely with a large house, and the haulage company with its storage sheds, wagons and horses, Papa would have no trouble raising the money to settle his creditors.

The alternative was unacceptable to dwell upon. Everything the family possessed would be sold. If the debts could not be settled in full, Papa could face imprisonment.

Kara went to the writing bureau, only to find that it had been removed, its contents scattered on the bare floorboards of the parlour. The Chinese carpet, grand piano and the silverware had also gone. All that remained of the furniture were two footstools.

Dazedly, Kara picked up some writing paper and a pen from where they had been thrown on the floor, and wrote a note to Ernest, asking him to call on her that evening. All thoughts of ending their engagement had left her. She needed to speak with him as a friend. If by marrying Ernest she could save Papa, then she would put her reservations aside. In this, duty must come before personal happiness.

The missive written, she gave it to Jenny to deliver, then went to speak with the servants. They had the right to know what was happening. The servants, apart from Mrs Reeves and Keech, were seated around the kitchen table looking stunned.

They rose to their feet as Kara entered.

'What's going to happen to us?' Nanny Brewster croaked.

Mrs Middlewich turned on her. 'It will be the workhouse for you. I'm off to Mrs Wilmott's house. She's been trying to get me away from Mr Wyse for years. Little good my loyalty did me. I've three months' wages owing.'

Kara sighed. 'There will be no workhouse for Nanny Brewster, and you will all be paid. Even if I have to sell my gowns. I suppose I shall at least be allowed to keep them.'

Kara looked around the kitchen. It was an alien world to her. Papa did not permit her to set foot in the servants' quarters, except to visit Nanny Brewster, whose room was at the foot of the stairs.

Mrs Middlewich snorted, and pointedly removed her large apron from her stout waist. 'Send my wages to the Wilmott house. I'll be making my claim along with the other creditors. I'll not be cheated out of what's owing to me.'

The woman's nasty tone stung Kara out of her shocked state. Her violet eyes blazing with fury, she rounded on the cook. 'I've given my word that you'll be paid, Mrs Middlewich.' Her tone was thick with contempt. 'Mrs Reeves will give me a list of all salaries owed to the staff. When I give my word, I keep it.'

Nanny Brewster limped forward and held out her gnarled hands to Kara. 'This is a sad day I never thought to see. Don't you go worrying about me; you have troubles enough of your own.'

Kara put her arms around her old nanny and hugged her. 'I won't let you end your days in the workhouse. There must be something I can do.'

The woman's rheumy eyes regarded her tenderly. 'You've a kind heart. That you care what happens to me I shall always treasure. You must look after your own needs now. You had best keep an eye on those men upstairs. You don't want them going through your possessions without you being present. Though I fear it's likely they'll take your jewels.'

Kara gave Nanny Brewster another hug before leaving the kitchen. She approached the policeman, having no wish to discuss any personal details with the bailiff.

'What possessions, if any, will I be allowed to keep? Am I to have only the clothes I stand up in?'

'There's creditors in London,' the bailiff interrupted. 'They either want paying for the goods purchased last month, or the goods returned – unsoiled of course.'

'Please inform them that the items of clothing which have not been worn will be carefully packed and returned to them,' Kara said stiffly.

Mrs Reeves, who had remained swooning in the hall chair, recovered her wits. 'I cannot believe it. Mr Wyse is a good man. Oh, the shame of this day.' Her voice began to rise with indignation. 'The shame of working for a common debtor. I shall be leaving this house of disgrace at once.'

Kara eyed her narrowly. The woman was a hypocrite. So much for the false affection she had harboured for her father. She had turned on him as spitefully as his creditors had done. She had expected more loyalty from the housekeeper.

It was dark when Kara heard her father return. Both Mrs Reeves and Mrs Middlewich had packed their bags and left. Like rats leaving a sinking ship, Kara thought with disgust.

Kara ran downstairs, following her father into his study. He had paused to stare stupefied at the room stripped of furniture, paintings, and the books which had lined two walls. With a groan he sank down on to the window-seat. His head rested on his hands and his shoulders were slumped in dejection. He did not look up.

'Papa!' she said gently.

He shuddered and, wiping a hand across his face, rose slowly to his feet, but he kept his face averted from her.

'Are you hungry?' she asked. 'Shall I fetch the cold supper which was prepared for you?'

'Good God, woman! Do you think I can eat?' His voice was a faint echo of his usual bellow. 'Leave me. Tomorrow you will go to your Aunt Ethel at Gidea Park. Though what she will say when she learns of my shame…' A tortured sigh followed his faltering words. 'I'm ruined.'

Kara could not believe the transformation in her father. Could only a few hours in prison so completely break a proud man's spirit? His shoulders were slumped and his necktie and shirt were crumpled. His oiled hair was in wild disarray, where he had run his hands through its thinning strands. But worst of all was the greyness of his complexion and the stark despair in his red-rimmed eyes.

'Tell me what I must do. I want to help you, Papa.'

'What can a woman do?' Even his sarcasm had lost its strident edge. 'Leave me. I would bear my shame alone.'

'I never thought to see you surrender to self-pity.' The words were out before she could stop them. Her father's head shot up in affront and she braced herself against his fury.

It did not come. He seemed to shrink even further into his bones. Before her eyes he was changing to an old and defeated man. 'Even you revile me. I am finished. Ruined.'

'Papa, you mustn't speak that way.' Kara grew alarmed. 'The house and the business can be sold. We can live quietly. You can start afresh. When I marry Ernest…' The words stuck in her throat, but she forced them out with false enthusiasm. 'Ernest will not permit–'

He laughed bitterly. 'Ernest has broken off the engagement. Or rather that harridan of a mother of his did so. She wears the trousers in that house. Can't have the Holman name linked with that of a debtor. What the old harridan couldn't stand was that Holman was besotted with you. She had my affairs investigated. Then purchased my outstanding mortgages and loans from other banks. She is my principal creditor.'

Kara was too shocked to answer. Wide-eyed she stared at her father's haggard face. The change in him appalled her. Pride warred with the years of resentment she had harboured at his strict discipline. That autocratic ruling had come from a different man than the one before her now. Loyalty and anger rose like a phoenix out of the ashes of her resentment.

'How dare Mrs Holman treat you so shabbily! She's wicked. Evil! Ernest loves me. I shall speak with him.'

She paced the study in her agitation, the navy velvet train of her nightrobe billowing out at her furious pace. She spun round to discover her father staring at her in astonishment.

'Why weren't you a son, Kara?'

Something snapped in her. She had tried to be a dutiful daughter – to revere him as she should. Her anger burst from her. 'Why did you let it matter so much to you? I couldn't help being born a woman. At times I resent that fact as much as you. I hate being pampered and treated like a feeble-minded imbecile. I hate being dressed to look like a doll, and being expected to act meekly and never speak my mind. Papa, don't dismiss me as unimportant because I'm a woman. Whatever must be done to free you from this debt, I will help you. I may not be the son you wanted, but your blood runs in my veins. I am as much a part of you as I am a part of my mother.'

'Do not speak of her.' Abel backed away. 'She betrayed me.'

'Because she did not give you a son.' Kara was beyond caution, so great was her outrage at his continued contempt for her sex. 'You are more worthy a man than to speak so ill of the dead.'

He recoiled as though she had struck him. 'Florence is not dead.'

'What was that you said?'

'Your mother is not dead.'

'Then where is she?' Kara demanded in astonishment.

He did not answer, his body frozen in an attitude of despair.

'Papa, you cannot tell me that Mama is alive. Then say nothing more.'

'Florence is dead to me,' his voice cracked with pain. 'I am ashamed, not only of the debts which have brought me here, but also of how I treated her.' His lips clamped shut.

Kara bit her lip and clenched her hands tightly together to stop screaming out. Could this be true? If so, where was her mother? There was such anguish in his eyes that she held back her demands for the moment.

A bleakness settled over his austere features. Finally he added, 'I have failed you. It was my duty to provide a dowry and find a husband for you.'

'No, Papa. Those things don't matter.'

He smiled thinly. 'You are a good girl. Perhaps I was too hard on you.' His eyes glazed with remembered pain. 'So many disappointments. But bankruptcy humbles a man. Makes you realise that you're not invincible. I will end my days in prison. The business – the house – are both heavily mortgaged. There is not enough money to pay the creditors. There is only shame and humiliation ahead for me.'

'That is your pride speaking,' she said softly. 'The money will be raised to pay your debts.'

'Child, my debts are ten thousand pounds,' he said disparagingly. 'Where would an innocent like you get such an amount?'

'So much. How is that possible, Papa?'

'You question me?' He rounded on her, his expression autocratic.

'In the circumstances, have I not that right?' She faced him without flinching. Even now he would make her appear in the wrong, when all she wanted to do was help him. 'My life will also be affected by this.'

He looked at her fiercely. When she continued to hold his glare, his gaze slid from hers and he sighed. 'Over the years I've been losing business to the railways. Then there were several bad investments which depleted my capital. With no son to carry on the business, I lost heart. I became careless. Borrowed incautiously. The debts just mounted.'

'You had a daughter, Papa. I would have done anything for a chance to learn your business.'

He stared at her aghast. 'A woman running Wyse Haulage. What nonsense!'

Kara's eyes glittered as she struggled to master her growing anger. Her chin lifted as she rode the blow to her pride. 'I could not have made a worse mess of it than you, Papa. Why was I always so unworthy in your eyes? It was your loss that you saw me only as a woman, and therefore useless in your eyes. I've a sharp mind and the will to succeed in life, independent of any man.'

She braced herself for one of his withering rebukes. It never came. Instead he stared at her in stunned silence. The despair in his eyes wrenched at her heart. The proud always fell so much harder than the meek.

'I did not mean to condemn you,' she consoled. 'We can make a new life for ourselves. We can leave Brentwood and live where no one will know you.'

'It is my punishment,' he said hollowly, 'for abandoning Florence when she begged my forgiveness. Her disgrace was no greater than mine is now.'

'Perhaps it is not too late to put matters right,'

she suggested, and found herself expectantly holding her breath. 'Now I know Mama is not dead, I want to see her.'

Excitement was growing in her. Her mother was alive! She assumed that Florence Wyse must have done something shameful. It did not matter. Her mother was alive and she wanted to meet her. That was her right.

'Where is Mama?'

'The last I heard she was in London – where I do not know.' He rubbed a hand across his chin and a shudder went through his body. The stare he turned on her was haunted with pain. 'Your mother was a whore, Kara. I turned her out of my house when I learned that she had a lover – a common soldier from the barracks. She had the audacity to write to me some years ago asking for money. She said she wanted it for her child. A child she proclaimed was mine, born six months after I banished her from my home. It was another girl. I did not trouble to reply to the letter.'

Kara stood up. This second shock of the day was far greater than the first. She had begun to feel sympathy for her father, and now he had destroyed it.

'You sent my mother away. How could you? To what life did you condemn my sister?'

He pulled himself to his full height at her accusation. 'Florence's second child was no child of mine!' The familiar sarcasm was back in his voice. 'You know nothing of the circumstances, and I will not speak of them. They are unsuitable for an unmarried woman to hear.'

'How can anything concerning my mother be unsuitable for me to hear?' Kara snapped. She was sick of his double standards and hypocrisy.

Abel rose to his feet and turned his back on her. At her condemnation his hostility towards her returned. 'Leave me to my shame. Your future is secure. I made certain of that. My solicitors, Tennent, Tennent & Son of Chancery Lane in London have in their possession your grandmother's jewels. They were bequeathed to you in her will. If they are sold and Mr Tennent invests the capital for you, they will provide you with a modest income throughout your life.'

'I'd rather meet Mama than have the security of Grandmama's jewels.'

When he turned to face her, his lips were pursed in disdain. 'You are all your mother's daughter. You have her wilful, wanton streak.'

He sighed raggedly. 'Go to bed, Kara.' He looked at her for a long moment. His mouth had turned down and his eyes and cheeks seemed to have sunken into his skull. He looked an old and wizened man, his pride broken.

Chapter Three

Too keyed up to eat breakfast, Kara left the house in Priests Lane early the next morning with Jenny accompanying her. She left before her father had made an appearance. He would stop her if he suspected her plans.

The High Street was busier than she expected. The shops were already open, many displaying wares outside their doors, or on trestle tables, to catch a pedestrian's eye. As Brentwood's town-hall clock struck eight-thirty, she looked up at the building with its two imposing columns flanking its doorway. Ernest's bank would not open for half an hour. She hoped he would arrive before that. She was determined to get him to stop his mother foreclosing on her father's loan. All Papa needed was a few months and he would be able to pay, she was certain of that.

The Holman bank was near the Hunter monument – the stone obelisk set in the centre of the High Street which commemorated the martyrdom of William Hunter, who had been burned at the stake in 1555. Kara paced the pavement, lost in her own thoughts and the confrontation ahead. Gradually she became aware that several acquaintances had crossed the street to avoid greeting her. They all attended church twice on Sundays. So much for Christian compassion. Clearly they did not practise the Christian charity they professed to believe in.

At hearing the chug of an automobile approaching, Kara saw the green and black motor car driven by Ernest's chauffeur pull up in front of the bank. As Ernest stepped on to the pavement and noticed Kara, his face paled, then flushed scarlet.

'So it is true what Papa told me,' she said scathingly. His guilty look, like a child caught with his hand in the sweet jar, angered her. Forgetting her good intentions to placate him and win him to her side, she flared, 'You haven't enough backbone to tell me to my face that our engagement is off. That was despicable.'

'This is not the place to discuss the matter.' His arrogant tone did not hide his embarrassment. His stare darted along the street, nervous that some passer-by would overhear.

'I'm here because you ignored my letter,' she voiced her disgust. 'How could you go against your word and back out of your partnership with my father. Am I not owed an explanation?'

'You had better come into my office.' His face remained red as he caught several people watching them with open curiosity. The scandal of her father's ruin was all over Brentwood. Refusing to meet her accusing glare, Ernest inserted the key in the lock and ushered Kara into the bank.

'Your maid will remain here.' He indicated a chair. Two bank tellers behind the counter looked up, startled at seeing Kara with the manager. Ernest glared at them. 'I want no interruptions.'

He led Kara into his office and closed the door. He removed his long coat and top hat, his expression stern as he regarded her. In that moment she saw in him all the arrogance of her father at his most belligerent, and her anger burst out. She was not one of his employees or a servant. How dare he look at her as though she was in the wrong for coming here, especially after the infamy his family had worked?

'Quite frankly, Kara,' he said pompously, 'I'm amazed that you can conduct yourself in this manner.'

'Don't take that attitude with me, Ernest.' Her head tilted and her violet eyes glinted dangerously. 'Am I at least not owed an apology for your conduct? Last week my home resembled a hothouse, there were so many flowers from you professing your undying love. Your affection withered as fast as the flowers at the first hint of censure from your Mama.'

At her domineering manner, a change came over him. 'My regard for you has not altered, Kara.' With a harsh groan he reached for her hands and went down on one knee. His expression showed the indecisive emotions warring within him. 'I'm wretched. But I have my business to consider. If my name is linked with a bankrupt, I, too, could be ruined.'

Kara wrenched her hands free and stepped back. 'Get up, Ernest, you look ridiculous. Papa would not be in this mess if you had stood by your partnership agreement. Your mother was the one who purchased Papa's mortgages and then foreclosed on them.'

At the accusation, his eyes glazed with affront. He stood stiff, his manner again cold. 'Have your wits gone begging? Where did you hear such an outrageous story?'

'From my father. The bailiff enforcing the foreclosure told him the name of his chief creditor. Your mother could not abide sharing her son's affection. I saw it at our betrothal. She ruined Papa.'

'That's wicked and unjust!' Ernest thrust his thumbs through the fob chain which was draped across his burgundy waistcoat. His dark frock coat and high starched shirt collar made him look imposing, but he did not impress Kara.

'Then prove me wrong. Confront your Mama. Or at least stand by your business agreement with Papa. That's what an honourable man would do.'

'I object to your tone, Kara.' His gaze shifted from her forthright glare and there was a petulant droop to his mouth. 'This is most unlike you. Clearly Mama was right about your unladylike qualities. You have the tongue of a shrew.'

Kara's eyes narrowed. She leaned forward, putting her hands on his desk. To control her anger she pitched her voice low, but it lost none of its condemnation. 'If you were half the man I had believed you to be, you would have supported Papa. And if you loved me, you would have married me, even if I came to you penniless.'

She drew out of her pocket the diamond ring he had given to her. 'This is your property.'

He stared at it and then up at her face. His weak chin trembled and his eyes were tormented. 'I do love you, Kara. I can't sleep at nights for thoughts of you. But Mama ... I owe her so much. She could not have done this to your father. I would have known if the bank's money–'

'She used her own money, not the bank's. She obviously didn't want you interfering with her plans.'

'I will not listen to this. Mama's concern was for the bank. If it became knowledge that I was your father's partner when his debts became known, there could be a run on our money. The bank could fail.'

He recovered himself with a start, resorting once more to pomposity. 'You are upset. Naturally. This scandal will pass. I had meant only to postpone our wedding. We can continue to see each other later in the year.'

She stared at him incredulously. He was a worse hypocrite than her father.

Blithely, Ernest went on. 'Mama knows what is best for the bank. She guided Papa until he died last year. She feared that I would lose my inheritance if I remained your father's partner. These are lies you have been told. Mama would not … could not … Mama is–'

'A jealous and vindictive woman.' Kara was merciless in her disgust. 'I came here to appeal to your sense of justice, but you are too tightly bound to your mother's apron strings. No honourable man would turn his back on the woman he loved, or allow her father to be destroyed by petty jealousy.'

His expression was one of sulky outrage. 'I'm shocked you can speak of dear Mama that way. Mama was right. You are headstrong and unsuitable to be the bride of a bank manager.' Turning away, he shuffled the papers on his desk. His pouting stare was that of a spoilt child. 'Keep the ring,' he added churlishly. 'It is, I believe, the right of a jilted bride.'

Kara was tempted to throw it at him. Her fist clutched the large diamond cluster so tightly that it cut her skin. She opened her palm to look at it. She had never liked its showy magnificence, but it was worth a great deal of money. In her straitened circumstances she would be foolish to throw it away. She would sell it and use the proceeds to pay off some of her father's debts.

Walking to the door, she waited for Ernest to open it for her. As he did so, her attention was drawn to a policeman talking to the clerk. It was the same man who had been at her house yesterday. He looked ill-at-ease upon seeing Kara.

'Miss Wyse, a servant at your house said you were here.' He looked at Ernest. 'Could we go into your office? Perhaps Miss Wyse's maid could also accompany us.'

Something was wrong. Fear clutched at Kara's throat. She stared at the policeman. Beneath his high hat, his face was taut and pale. Returning to the office, the sound of her rapid heartbeat drummed in her ears as she awaited, dreaded, the policeman's words.

'Is it Papa?' Kara asked tremulously.

He nodded. 'I'm sorry to inform you, Miss Wyse. There's been an accident... Your father is dead.'

A trembling seized Kara's body, and she put a shaking hand to her mouth, fighting to keep control of her senses. 'How? What happened?'

'His manservant heard a shot shortly after you left the house. Your father... He was cleaning his shotgun and it went off.'

Blackness, like a giant cormorant with wings outspread, swooped down around Kara. She fought it, drawing great breaths to stop herself from fainting. Dear God! It was suicide. Papa had killed himself because he could not face the shame of his ruin. She regarded the policeman, knowing that to spare her pain he had been diplomatic. 'Will others view it as an accident?'

He cleared his throat. 'The inspector has to make inquiries. The doctor has been called, and of course the vicar. Your father was a respected member of the community. A churchwarden and an alderman.'

'My darling,' Ernest said, ignoring the policeman and taking her into his arms. 'I'm sorry for all I said. You've been under a great strain. But I will stand by you. Of course we shall marry. Everything will be all right. I'll look after you.'

His words acted like a catalyst, and Kara held her body rigid in his embrace, her faintness receding. 'Take your hands off me, Mr Holman. My father's death is on your mother's hands. I hope you both burn in hell.'

Her face pale, she kept her head high as she walked from the bank. She was trembling inside and was grateful for Jenny's arm to lean upon. A numbness settled over her as she entered the bare house. Outside in the road was the undertaker's closed wagon, the doctor's automobile and the vicar's bicycle. They greeted her sombrely, standing in the hall, for there were no chairs left for them to be seated on.

'A terrible tragedy, Miss Wyse,' the undertaker consoled. 'I will make the arrangements at once. I understand you will be leaving Brentwood to live with your aunt.'

'Very tragic,' the vicar added. 'Cut off in the prime of his life. He will be greatly missed. My condolences, Miss Wyse.'

Kara nodded mutely and looked at the doctor.

'Are you satisfied it was an accident?' she said candidly. She did not need to add that a verdict of suicide would be an even greater scandal to live down. Worse, suicides were not usually allowed to be buried in holy ground. Papa had always expected to be laid to rest in the family tomb, the ornate, sculptured edifice erected in the church by Abel's grandfather.

'We understand that Mr Wyse suffered a severe shock yesterday,' replied the doctor, a close friend of Abel's. 'In the circumstances, he must have been distracted when he cleaned his shotgun. There was to be a clay-pigeon shoot in the grounds of Thorndon Hall next weekend. Your father was a keen shot.'

'Mr Wyse was a truly God-fearing man,' the vicar emphasised. 'Over the years his donations to the church, and its charities, have been substantial.'

Kara swayed, the strain beginning to tell on her. The doctor took her arm to steady her. 'I will prescribe a sedative for you, Miss Wyse.'

Kara shook her head. 'No. That will make me sleepy, and there is much to be done. How soon can the funeral be arranged? Circumstances dictate that it must be a simple affair. As you see, it is not practical for me to stay in Brentwood. I think a brief service would be fitting, with Papa buried in the family vault. If that is possible?'

The vicar nodded. 'Tomorrow at nine in the morning, if that is convenient to you, Miss Wyse.'

'Yes.'

The remaining formalities were completed with tact and surprising ease. Kara sent Seth out to sell her engagement ring at a jeweller's. It brought in enough to pay for the funeral and her fare to London, with some in reserve. Seth was then sent to ride to Aunt Ethel's and Uncle Bertram's at Gidea Park to inform them of the events of the past two days.

Kara was still dazed from shock as the funeral entourage left the house the next morning. From the moment of Aunt Ethel's arrival, she had been bombarded with questions. She had answered them to the best of her ability. But when mention was made of her returning with them to Gidea Park, she evaded the issue. She wanted Papa decently buried before she confronted her aunt with her plans.

There was no time, or money, for Kara to procure proper mourning clothes. She had searched through the attic, the contents of which had been ignored by the bailiff. Two trunks had held women's clothes. Kara judged from the enormous full skirts that they must have been made to be stretched over a wide crinoline and so must have belonged to her grandmother. Amongst these were several black crepe dresses her grandmother would have worn when her brother died in the Crimea. Kara had no skill at dressmaking, but Jenny's sister had married a draper and lived in the town.

'Jenny, would your sister restyle these mourning gowns? I have little money, but she is welcome to all the old dresses. They have been beautifully kept. The silks and velvets from the enormous skirts alone should provide your sister with material for future gowns.'

'Sis is never one to turn away a customer. She's seven kids to feed, and the draper's is only a penny store when all's said and done. I'll call on her right away. That's if you don't need me for anything else.'

'There's little to be done here. I must have a dress for the funeral.'

Jenny's sister took Kara's measurements and promised a gown would be ready for Jenny to collect in the morning. She had also agreed to adapt two others for Kara's wear which would be ready in two days. A daughter was expected to wear mourning for a year after a parent's death.

The funeral procession was the grand affair that Abel Wyse would have wished. Uncle Bertram had countermanded Kara's instructions to the undertaker and declared that no expense was to be spared. He agreed to settle the account. Family pride demanded that the rumours be scotched of any hint of suicide. Abel was to be buried in the manner of a prominent and respectable citizen of the community.

As chief mourner, Kara walked directly behind the glass-sided hearse, with the carriage-horses bedecked with black ostrich feathers. Even the weather seemed inappropriate. The bright April sunlight was unseasonably hot. The light breeze carried the strong smell of malt and hops from Hill's and Fielder's local breweries. Behind Kara walked Aunt Ethel, in rustling black taffeta, a lace veil draped over her cartwheel hat to hide her face. She was sobbing into a black silk handkerchief and leaning heavily on her husband's arm, her stout body increased by the six-month pregnancy of her ninth child. Beside them walked the four eldest of their children. Following them were the remaining servants from Priests Lane.

Throughout the walk, Kara kept her eyes riveted on the cross of flowers on top of the black-draped coffin. Dimly, she was aware of men removing their hats as the coffin passed, and of the silence which momentarily stilled the roadside gossip.

As they passed Wilson's Corner, Kara heard a strident voice raised from a customer leaving Brentwood's largest store. Her gaze was drawn to Augustina Holman, who spoke loudly to a female companion. 'It was a lucky escape my Ernest had. He was deceived as to his financial expectations from the marriage. The daughter is a pauper now. And the scandal...'

Kara kept her head high and ignored the remark, though her blood ran hot with indignation. Mrs Holman's spite had ruined her father and led him to take his own life. The woman did not even have the decency to show reverence to the dead.

The rest of the procession and service was a blur to Kara. The coffin was lowered into the vault and the vicar spoke words of condolence and sympathy, none of which she recalled. On their return to the house, she wandered into the empty room which had been her father's study and stared bleakly at the space where his desk had been. Uncle Bertram, his usually round, ruddy face bleached of colour, tweaked his handlebar moustache before putting a hand on her shoulder.

'This is a terrible day, my dear,' he said, gruffly. He had removed his top hat and his balding head showed through the thin strands of oiled, greying, blond hair.

Kara sighed. 'Papa was so proud. Thanks to you, he at least had a decent burial. I can't believe it's all gone. The yard. The house.'

'You must not worry your pretty head about such matters,' he consoled. 'I shall deal with everything. I'm about to visit the yard and see what – if anything – can be salvaged from this affair, once the creditors have been paid.'

Kara resented his patronising tone. 'That will be dealt with by Papa's solicitor,' she reminded him.

Aunt Ethel was weeping copiously as she joined them. She dabbed at her eyes with her handkerchief. 'The shame of it. My brother a suicide. Oh, the shame of it.'

Ethel's wails became louder as she gazed around the room stripped of furniture and valuables. There had been no money to drape the rooms with black crepe, as was customary when a family was in mourning.

'All Mama's beautiful silver, given to her as a wedding present, is gone. The Chinese vases sent to her by her brother the sea-captain – gone. The French clocks were worth a fortune. All gone. Family heirlooms which have been handed down from generations ... stolen from us.'

Kara did not miss the possessions. Her childhood had been miserable in this oppressive house. She would not miss it, nor would she want any reminders of it when she left.

'Not stolen, Aunt. Taken against Papa's debts.'

Ethel shuddered, gathering herself up for a fresh burst of wailing.

'I would spend a moment alone in the garden, Aunt,' Kara said, seeking privacy to come to terms with the change in her life. She was surprised that, now he was dead, she did grieve for her father. He had not deserved his end. But even so, she could not forgive him for sending her mother away, nor for the lies he had told her all these years.

Resting on the wooden seat which circled an old chestnut tree, Kara leaned her head back against the trunk, the sunshine playing over her upturned face. Her thoughts were upon the future. Now her father's tyranny was at an end, she was determined to be in control of her life. As plans shaped in her mind, she shrugged off her grief. There was assurance in her step when she returned to the house. First she must confront and overcome the prejudices of her aunt and uncle.

As she entered the hallway, she heard Ethel's shrill voice ordering the servants to leave the house by tomorrow morning.

'Aunt Ethel,' Kara said firmly. 'It is not your place to command my father's servants. Seth and Jenny have not found new employment and, until the house is repossessed, I will not have them cast on to the streets.'

Her aunt had not even removed her hat and cape before taking over the household. The thick black veil was thrown back from her face and, when she turned to regard her niece, her heavy features were pinched with outrage.

'I cannot believe I have just heard such disrespectful words from a niece of mine.' Her pale grey eyes regarded her with unblinking, owl-like intensity, and her small, prim mouth was compressed with censure. 'You will apologise at once.'

'I meant no disrespect, Aunt Ethel. I was concerned for the welfare of loyal servants.'

'You are insolent. As your guardian, until you marry, you will do as I bid. Though who will wed you now, with this disgrace attached to your name and no dowry, I can't imagine! Still, it is my duty to my brother to take you in, and provide for you – penniless though you now are. No one can say I have ever shirked my duty.' There was no warmth in her manner. She had never approved of Kara's wilful spirit.

'Since you take such pride in your learning,' her aunt continued, 'you will be governess to your younger cousins, who have not yet started boarding school. Also you can assist Nanny with the infants.'

Kara knew her aunt's capacity for interference, and was determined that she would not exchange one tyrannical household for another. Two strong wills clashed in opposition.

'I appreciate your offer, Aunt Ethel, but you could only become my guardian if I were an orphan. Papa told me that Mama is still alive. I am going to London to find her.'

Ethel paled. 'I forbid it. Florence was a wanton

who shamed us all.'

'She is still my mother,' Kara persisted. 'You make her sound evil. I will not believe that.'

'She ran off with a lover. She abandoned a good man, leaving him to bring up a child alone. If that is not evil, then I don't know what is.'

Had her mother been miserable living in a house without love? Kara knew she herself could never have endured such a marriage. Her soul rebelled at the thought. There was no point in antagonising her aunt unnecessarily, though, so she kept her opinions to herself.

'It changes nothing,' she added resolutely. 'Papa said I also have a sister, born six months after Mama left.'

'Half-sister possibly,' Ethel sneered. 'The brat is a by-blow, fathered by her lover.'

Kara refused to acknowledge that her mother would have lied. All her life she had dreamed of having a sister, someone she could confide in and share her dreams with. Besides, Papa had spoken of Florence approaching him for money. Her mother must have been in dire circumstances to have asked Abel Wyse for money. And he had rejected her plea. Had Florence been imprisoned for debt? Was she ill? Starving? Homeless? Each thought became more horrific than the last. She had to find her mother and sister. She would sell her grandmother's jewellery and plan a future for them all. First she had to know they were safe and well.

'I'm going to London. Since you're not my guardian, you can't stop me.'

Ethel digested this information for several

moments in ominous silence. She had always prophesied that Kara would come to a bad end. The girl was an ingrate, and she wasn't fooled by that meek and demure look either. She was a deceitful baggage. Hadn't she found several novels in her bedchamber, all by authors forbidden by Abel? The girl was giddy-witted to think she could manage alone. Just let her try. She'd soon come running back with her tail between her legs. Ethel had no time for uppity women who thought they knew it all. Especially brazen chits who did not know their place. Insolence was something she could not abide. It might be carefully erased from her niece's expression, but it was there in the set of her shoulders, the tilt of a determined chin.

'Don't think you can come snivelling back to a decent household when you have thrown my generosity in my face,' Ethel said with withering disdain. 'You will come to Gidea Park and live with us, or forget you have an aunt and cousins. I'll not have my children tainted with your wanton flouting of convention.'

'I'm sorry you feel so strongly, Aunt. But I've made up my mind.'

'Then you'll end up on the streets, the same as your mother. You're no niece of mine.' She picked up her reticule and headed for the front door, her voice rising. 'You are just like your father. He would never listen to advice. Bertram has been warning Abel for years to cut his losses at the yard. To modernise and adapt to change. But Abel was convinced he could beat the competition of the railways. Arrogance brought him to this pass. He should have listened to Bertram. Abel only has himself to blame. Yet it is us who must bear the shame. How will I ever hold my head up in Gidea Park again?'

The door banged behind her departing figure and Kara sighed with relief. Life with Aunt Ethel would be intolerable. The woman could never accept anyone's opinion if it did not coincide with her own. She always thought she was right. She governed her own household in a bullying, bombastic manner. She was so puffed up with conceit that she disregarded other feelings when delivering her sarcastic and narrow-minded judgements upon those she considered her inferiors.

A moment's qualm made Kara's heart race with panic. What had she done? She was now a woman alone and without protection. What did she know of the real world outside the sheltered prison created by her father?

Her fear dispelled. Whatever trials lay ahead she would overcome them. She would survive, no matter what the cost. Once she had set her mind to a course she would not be turned from it. The servants would be settled in a few days. Then she would leave for London and visit Messrs Tennent, Tennent and Son. Her father's solicitors would give her the advice she needed to manage on the income provided by her grandmother's legacy.

She summoned the remaining servants together. The money she had received from the sale of her engagement ring would settle their wages, and provide her with the necessary money to support herself for a few weeks ahead. Seth had just returned from accepting another position and would leave tomorrow. Jenny had been taken on by an agency who promised to find her work before the week was ended. Keech, her father's valet, had fled the house after being the one to discover Abel's body. He had not been seen since. Kara suspected that he had taken several pieces of her father's jewellery. His signet ring, gold cufflinks and fob watch were later found to be missing. Unwilling to face another police inquiry, she did not report the theft. That just left Nanny Brewster to be considered.

Kara turned to the old woman who sat in a rocking chair by the kitchen range.

'Seth inquired at the workhouse for me,' Nanny Brewster said with dignified grace. 'There's no need for you to worry about me, Miss Kara.'

'You're not going to the workhouse,' Kara replied sternly. 'The vicar mentioned after last Sunday's service that the Widow Grafton was looking for a lodger and companion. I will pay the rent at Widow Grafton's until Michaelmas Day in September. Together with the wages you have owing, you should be able to live comfortably until I send more money then. If anyone has deserved a pension from this family, it is you. I will not fail you.'

Tears rolled down the old lady's cheeks and she gripped Kara's hand, too choked with emotion to speak. Her gratitude shone in her eyes. Kara smiled warmly: Nanny Brewster had been the closest to a mother she had known, and she would not see her wanting.

Later she returned to speak with Nanny Brewster when the old woman was alone in her room. The bailiffs had even been here, and had left only the bed and a scratched chest of drawers. The woman's few possessions had been untouched. A china rose bowl. A print of a woodland scene and a photograph of her brother and sister in a wooden frame. It wasn't much to own after sixty years of hard work.

'I intend to live in London and try and find my mother and sister,' Kara explained. 'I shall visit you whenever I can.'

'So Mr Wyse finally told you of them, did he?' Nanny Brewster said heavily. 'It was wicked the way he treated that dear woman, but she never would have a word said against him. She blamed herself for being a bad wife. She said she deserved all she had suffered for abandoning her elder child.'

Kara's heart clenched with excitement. 'Have you met with my mother since she left?'

'Yes, I kept in touch over the years.' Nanny Brewster nodded. 'I've never been allowed to speak of her before – on your father's orders. I was her Nanny before I was yours. When she learned she was expecting you, she insisted I joined the household. It broke her heart to leave you when he threw her out. She knew he did not care for his daughter. He kept you from Florence to punish her.' Her face grew sad and Nanny Brewster broke off to stare at her hands, her eyes haunted by unhappy memories. Then her features brightened and she reached forward to open the top drawer of the chest. She peeled back several layers of cotton underwear and lifted out another photograph in a tortoiseshell frame.

She stared at it for a moment, then held it towards Kara. 'This is your dear mother. It was taken before she wed your father.'

An ache of longing filled Kara's breast as she stared at the sepia portrait. 'I do look like Mama.'

'You also have her temperament. She always sees good in people. Though that can sometimes be a failing.'

'How came you to meet Mama again?'

'As you may remember, when my sister was alive I used to spend a few days with her every June. She lived in Stepney. She died last year. We always took the omnibus to Oxford Street to wander around the new department stores. Not that we could afford to buy anything. But it was a treat to see all the lovely things they had for sale. It was in Oxford Street I saw Florence. Poor lass was trying to make a living by selling flowers.' Her rheumy eyes scanned Kara's face. 'Have I shocked you?'

Kara shook her head. 'Poor Mama. Reduced to such straits. Papa had much to answer for.'

'Aye,' Nanny Brewster said sharply. 'Florence was embarrassed when I recognised her. I was so overcome I burst into tears. She looked so frail. My sister went off and I stayed talking to Florence for an hour or more. She wanted to know everything about you. She missed you so much. She loved you dearly.'

She lapsed into silence, her expression softening as she reflected on those memories. Kara needed all her willpower to curb her impatience.

Nanny was getting on and was given to rambling and long silences.

'And then,' Kara finally prompted.

'That was in 1889. She'd been away for three years. You were seven. After that we met every year, on the second Tuesday in June. She gave up the flower-selling soon after that. I don't know where she worked. She never spoke of her life. We meet each year now by the flower-seller near the bandstand in Hyde Park. With my sister Martha dead, and my legs so bad this year, I didn't think I could make it. You go in my stead. Miss Florence will be so pleased. She's never forgiven herself for leaving you behind. She's never stopped loving you.'

Kara brushed aside a tear at the suffering her mother must have endured. She was consumed with the need to find her.

'Of course I'll go, if I haven't managed to find her before then.' Kara's throat worked with emotion. 'Why didn't you tell me this before.'

'I wanted to, believe me. But it was more than my job was worth. Florence Wyse's name was forbidden in this house.'

'Why did she leave Papa? Was it for a lover? Was she unhappy here?' The questions spilled out, Kara was so eager to learn all she could about her mother.

'There was a man – a soldier. They met secretly in the town, but I swear he was not her lover. Not before your father threw her out. They were seen together by your aunt. She never liked Miss Florence. She could not dominate her, you see. She has a strong will. That's why she's survived.

Others, thrown into a life of poverty after being cosseted all their life, would not have lasted the first winter. Like you, Florence is a fighter. Your aunt could not wait to tell Mr Wyse. He employed a man to follow Florence whenever she left the house. One afternoon, when she returned from meeting the soldier, she found her bags packed. Mr Wyse ordered her from his home. But it was all innocent. Your mother may have been unhappy in her marriage, but she was no adulteress.'

'Poor Mama. She must have been terribly miserable. What happened after she left Brentwood?'

Nanny Brewster shook her grizzled head. 'She would never talk of her own life. If I questioned her, she always made an excuse to leave. At our meetings she was desperate to hear news of you, and she would tell me of Beatrice, your sister. In recent years that girl has been a constant worry to Florence. But I could see Florence's life was hard. Over the years she became so thin, her eyes weary from the burdens of her struggles. Each year she wore the same dress which got shabbier and shabbier.'

'Then I must find her,' Kara vowed. It would be her first goal on reaching London. She would make everything up to her mother. And sixteen years of poverty was a lot to make up for.

Chapter Four

Kara's first idea of travelling to London by train was discarded as she would also have to transport four trunks containing her possessions. The problem of expenditure was another worry. To hire a carter for a day was costly, and would greatly deplete what little was left of her money.

Seth had the answer. 'I've got an older cousin, Henry Wicken,' he advised. 'He works for Bradshaw's, a rival haulage firm to Wyse's. His deliveries take him to London every Thursday. There'll be room on the cart for your trunks.'

'I'd appreciate that. I was concerned about transporting my trunks across London. I've an appointment with the solicitor at two o'clock. Would it be possible for your cousin to meet me after he's unloaded, and take me to lodgings? I'll pay him for his time.'

'Henry will do that gladly. He don't trust London folk. He'd insist on seeing you safe.'

Kara left Brentwood early the next morning. She had no regrets at leaving her home town, but as she stepped on the buckboard of the cart she felt her stomach clench with nerves. Henry Wicken was a stocky man and wore a stained leather jerkin and scuffed brown corduroy trousers. He had a lined, tanned face, and his dour expression was far from reassuring.

'Sorry business about Mr Wyse,' he said as he

picked up the reins. 'Chancery Lane is it you're going to?'

'Yes.'

'My delivery is at Holborn. It don't take me more than an hour to unload. I'll take you to your lodgings after your meeting. Bad place London. I wouldn't leave a woman alone on the streets.' He pulled his cap down over his greasy greying hair and sniffed his disapproval. A shaggy grey moustache hid his mouth as he spoke. 'Full of pickpockets and rogues is London. Wicked thieves everywhere. Don't you trust no one.'

After those few words of advice, which filled Kara with apprehension, he lapsed into an uncommunicative silence. He ignored her presence, intent upon guiding the two horses through a flock of geese being herded to market.

Absorbed by her own plans for the future, Kara was grateful for his silence. The weather had changed again and, as they plodded along the Essex lanes, dark clouds threatening rain hung heavy in the sky. Traffic was light on the London road and only a few carts passed them on the first part of the journey. At one point, a noisy, open-top motor car chugged past, forcing Henry to pull over on the road. He scowled and shook his fist at the begoggled driver.

'Devil's wagon. God never meant us to travel at a dozen miles an hour. Don't know what the world's coming to.'

Kara bowed her head and hid her grin. Papa had never considered owning a motor car, though many merchants possessed one. His money had been in horse-drawn carts, and he'd disliked change. Perhaps if he had been less intransigent, his business would not have been ruined by the railways.

When they approached the fields on the outskirts of Bethnal Green, Kara saw that a fairground and large circus tent had been set up. There were dozens of brightly painted covered wagons. She stared in amazement at those depicting the world's fattest man, Salome the bearded lady, and Prince Rudolfus the fire-eater. She had never seen a circus before. Papa had considered such entertainment vulgar.

Caged lions roared in the background, and the fairground children ran shouting through the milling performers. Fascinated, Kara watched a procession begin to form as the acts prepared to ride through the streets to attract customers for their next performance. A painted elephant was in the lead, and behind him a man in multi-coloured trousers and clown's make-up strode about on tall stilts.

'Could we stop awhile?' Kara asked.

'Not safe to stop near circus folk,' Henry Wicken declared grimly. 'Wicked thieves, one and all. They'll have your trunks out of the cart and hidden away before you can bat an eyelid.'

'Surely not!' Kara said, appalled.

'They ain't much better than vagabonds. Don't you trust them. Wherever the circus go they attracts a crowd. A crowd attracts pickpockets. 'Tis wicked. Wicked.'

Kara began to suspect that Mr Wicken was obsessed with what he considered the evils of poverty and vagrancy. He was suspicious of anyone who was not in conventional employment. Or was London the disreputable and wicked place he declared? Disappointed that they did not halt, she craned her neck for a last look at the colourful, bustling campsite.

Their pace slowed as they reached the notorious Ratcliff Highway. Henry Wicken snarled at any ragged urchin who dared come close to his cart.

'One of the worst rookeries in London, this,' he said with a grimace.

'Rookery?' Kara questioned.

'That's what they call a district inhabited with whores, thieves and rogues. Hardly a night goes by without some foul murder. A dozen or more die from starvation every week. Not that there's so many of these devil's dens left standing now. Most have been pulled down in the last forty years. Only small pockets remain. The villains retreat into smaller, concentrated communities. But the evil remains. Regular Gomorrah is London, Miss Wyse.' He sniffed and rubbed his sleeve across his hooked nose before continuing in a harsher tone. 'There are other rookeries just as evil, not a stone's throw from Westminster Abbey and the opera house at Covent Garden. Sneak-thieves and beggars abound in the dark alleys behind Leicester Square, the Haymarket and Regent Street. You keep to the main thoroughfares if you venture out on foot. Take a wrong turning and you'll end up abducted and sold to some trugging house. I don't mean to talk indelicate to a lady like yourself, Miss Wyse. But you should be warned.'

He shot her a sour but well-intentioned glare, and chewed the edge of his moustache for some moments before adding, 'I doubt you've heard of such places. Don't you trust no one. There's folk always on the look-out for an unsuspecting woman coming to London from the country. If they realise you've no one to protect you, they'll use every trick they know to get you into their clutches.'

Kara shivered with growing unease. She was beginning to wonder if she hadn't made a grave error in coming to London.

They were caught up in the steadily mounting traffic. From out of the side turnings, a group of beggar children appeared and surrounded them.

A scrawny boy with sharp, dirty features and a battered top hat set back on his head shoved out his hand. 'Giv'us a penny, missus. Jus' a penny. I ain't eaten fer two days.'

'Me neither,' another equally filthy and ragged wretch of indeterminate age whined. 'Jus' a penny, missus.'

'Poor dears,' Kara said, her hand going to her purse.

Mr Wicken's hand on her arm stopped her. 'Take no heed of them damned beggars,' he snarled, jamming his cap further on to his greasy hair. 'They'd steal the nails out of their own mother's coffin, given half the chance. Don't you trust 'em, Miss Wyse. Wicked thieves to the last man, woman and child.'

'But they're only children, and they look so cold and hungry. I've a few spare pennies for them.'

'Don't make a move to your purse. That's what they're waiting for, to see where you keep your money. Whilst you're taking pity on one miserable wretch, his companion is filching your valuables behind your back.'

Reluctantly Kara heeded his advice, but her conscience tugged that her few pennies could have given them a decent meal that night.

'They'd not get to keep your money,' Henry Wicken announced. 'It goes straight to their parents who spend it on gin. I've heard stories about the villains of London which would make you gasp at the depravity of mankind. I wouldn't repeat them to a gentlewoman like yourself, Miss Wyse. But don't you trust them. Don't you trust not a one of them.'

'You make London sound a terrible place, Mr Wicken,' Kara said, repressing a shudder.

'Satan's lair. And you such an innocent young woman. You must be very careful. Don't take any lodgings unless your solicitor recommends them. Not that a solicitor – some middle-class old codger with his head filled with property contracts and death duties – can advise you how to survive in this devil's warren. The criminal underworld thrives in those foul tenements and alleyways.'

'How do you know so much, Mr Wicken?'

'I'm a Godfearing man. A missionary, so to speak. The nights I have to stay in London I sees it as my Christian duty to preach to these ungodly wretches. Often all I get is abuse, or even a beating for my pains. There ain't no law which can touch any in those rookeries. The peelers steer clear of such haunts, unless they want their heads broke. Many a criminal takes to his heels and hides there.'

'Then your missionary work is commendable that you risk your safety,' she said, understanding his fanaticism. He had probably seen the worst such districts could throw up.

He sniffed, turning aside her compliment. 'You heed my words. Don't trust no one.'

'I shall certainly remember,' Kara answered as another shudder gripped her body. She steeled herself against her growing fear. If she wanted to find her mother and sister, she must live in London. At least now she was aware of the dangers.

A glimpse down a dark alleyway, where the leaning houses almost touched at the rooftops, revealed a poverty-wracked world she had never suspected. Infants ran barefoot, or whined at their mothers' aprons, eyes large in half-starved faces. Women and men in tattered clothing lounged in doorways, hair straggling and unkempt, faces grey from never having felt the touch of soap. She could smell noisome gutters filled with rotting garbage and urine from emptied chamber-pots.

She had always thought of London as the golden city. The centre of commerce. A pleasure-loving place, where the gentry spent the season away from their country estates, revelling in the entertainments it provided. It was clear to her now that it was also a place of squalor and appalling poverty. Scores of costermongers, in their caps and cord trousers, bright kerchiefs tied jauntily about their necks, sold their wares from barrows on the Ratcliff Highway, adding to the congestion of traffic entering the city.

Kara was relieved when the squalor of the Highway changed to the bustle of Aldgate. The cobbled road was crushed with omnibuses with their bright lettering. They fought for passage with hansom cabs, motor cars, and carts of every description. Even an occasional elegant brougham or chaise could still be seen. An urchin darted into the road ahead of them, narrowly missing death as he scooped up the steaming pile of excrement just deposited by a horse pulling a brewer's dray.

The noise was deafening. Kara had never seen such a vast number of people. Everyone seemed to speak at a shout: the costers to sell their wares; pedestrians to be heard above the rumble of traffic. Through a gap in the houses, Kara saw the four central turrets of the great keep of the Tower of London. At the next corner she glimpsed the masts of sailing ships crowded in St Katherine's dock. On their approach to Cheapside, the breeze carried the stench of fish from Billingsgate market, the putrefying flesh from slaughterhouses, or the sour smell of tallow from the candlemaker's alley. As the thoroughfare broadened into Cheapside, Kara's ears were deafened by the constant shouts of the streetsellers crying out their wares. Here women shoppers filled the pavement in their sweeping skirts and wide cartwheel hats, and were accompanied by elegant men in frock coats and tall hats. Apprentices in their aprons and caps ran errands for their masters; clerks in dark suits and bowler hats emerged from the chop-houses having partaken of their lunch.

They passed St Paul's, its great dome like a celestial crown rising to the overcast sky. In the cathedral yard, bookstalls and shops had for centuries held pride of place. Further on, Kara shivered at the sight of the gatehouse of Newgate prison. Ice coated her spine; unaccountably she felt a sense of foreboding as they passed the most notorious of England's gaols.

The cart rattled along Fleet Street and finally approached Chancery Lane. Henry Wicken stopped outside a high gabled greystone building fronted by gilt-topped iron railings. 'I'll be back in an hour or so. The cart will be in the inn yard down the road.' Mr Wicken nodded in its direction. 'Your trunks will be safe there. When your meeting is finished, send a clerk to the inn to find me.'

Kara hesitated briefly on the steps of the offices of Tennent, Tennent & Son before lifting the lion-headed knocker to enter. She felt that she was about to step into an abyss – the uncertainty of her future was a bottomless pit, waiting to swallow up a foolish woman bent upon controlling her own destiny.

Five minutes later she was shown into Richard Tennent's office. Her palms moistened with nervous heat. Would a staid lawyer ridicule her plans? Did he have the power to send her back to her aunt at Gidea Park? Unconsciously she squared her shoulders. Never again would a man hold sway over her life as her father had done.

The solicitor's office was dark and dingy. Two of its walls were stacked with shelves holding rolled-up papers; a third wall held an oak bookcase filled with leather-bound legal books. A blue and red Indian carpet covered the floor, its edges piled up with more ribbon-tied papers. A large desk was in front of the sash window and, as Kara was announced, a man stood up to greet her.

'Miss Wyse, I am so very sorry to learn of the circumstances of your father's death.' His voice was attractively deep and husky, but his slim figure and face were in shadow. 'Please be seated.'

He moved quickly to clear a chair of further papers. 'Please excuse the clutter. It's not often a woman seeks our services. I had expected to deal with your uncle.'

'I prefer to manage my own affairs in future.' Her tone was sharper than she intended, instinctively defensive against any male who would seek to place her in a subservient role.

He remained with his back to the light and studied her before speaking. 'My comment was a casual one, not intended to offend, Miss Wyse.'

She relaxed.

He stepped forward and offered her his hand. The firm grip was brief. When he moved to the corner of his desk to pick up a large file, the light fell across his features. Though his angular face was austere, it was softened by the lock of dark hair which fell forward over his wide brow. To her surprise Kara saw that he could not be in more than his late twenties. She had expected her father's solicitor to be much older.

Seeing her puzzlement, he smiled and raised a fine curved brow. 'I'm the son in Tennent, Tennent & Son. My father died six months ago.'

'Then we have a shared grief in common, Mr Tennent.' She folded her hands in her lap, her fingers interlocked as she battled to overcome her nervousness.

Richard Tennent flicked through the file, saying, 'These are your father's papers. I fear there will be little, if anything, left of his estate once the creditors have been paid.'

'Will I be responsible for any of my father's debts?'

He regarded her for a long moment in silence.

'Mr Tennent, I would appreciate you being completely honest with me,' Kara said brusquely. 'The facts may be unpalatable, but I will not fall into hysterics. I'm not afraid to face the future alone. I've no intention of living with my aunt and uncle, to be regarded as a poor relation, the unpaid governess of their children.'

'You cannot mean to live alone, Miss Wyse.' His shock was evident in his voice. 'A respectable gentlewoman must take precautions to preserve her reputation.'

'My reputation is of the greatest concern to me, Mr Tennent.' She eyed him levelly. 'So is my intention to support myself in an independent fashion. Though I am aware that I need guidance: Papa insisted I lead a very sheltered life. I expect he was well meaning, but I regarded such strict constraint like a prison sentence.'

When he did not immediately speak, she felt

her temper begin to rise. She had been foolish to expect a strait-laced solicitor to understand. 'So am I responsible for Papa's debts, or not?'

'I'm afraid that you are.' He made a steeple of his fingers and tapped them thoughtfully against his jaw. Beneath the narrow flare of his side-whiskers, the faint shadow of his beard line on his clean-shaven cheeks accentuated the strong line of his jaw.

Her chin lifted and a challenging light entered her eyes as she continued in a firm voice. 'Papa told me that I had been left some jewellery by my grandmother. I will sell this, but I need advice upon how to invest the money. I intend to live in London. Before my father died, he told me that my mother was not dead, as I had been led to believe. She is living in London. Apparently I also have a sister. It is possible that they are living in impoverished circumstances. I intend to find them, but I've no idea how to go about such matters.'

'Admirable sentiments, Miss Wyse, but for a woman who has, by her own admission, led such a sheltered life, this course would be fraught with danger.'

Kara bristled again, suspecting ridicule. 'I'm aware of that. I'm not afraid.'

He continued to study her, his hazel eyes grave. 'It would be in your best interests to return to your aunt at Gidea Park. I will instruct a man on your behalf to find out what he can about your mother and sister and keep you informed.'

Kara stood up, her body tense. 'Do not patronise me, Mr Tennent. I am aware of the dangers a lone woman faces. I may be innocent, but I'm not a fool. If men but realised it, women are not the giddy-headed simpletons they would make of us. We are capable of rational thought, and some of us are capable of greatness.'

'And you believe yourself such a woman.' A glitter brightened his eyes as he regarded her sardonically.

Suspecting mockery, her years of frustrated ambition burst out. 'I would not be so conceited as to expect greatness. I would be worthy – I would contribute something to this world other than just rearing children.' Her eyes darkened dangerously and her face was flushed. 'Why should it be only men who enforce law reform, build business empires, or are driven to conquer continents? Why should not a woman also be allowed to study the secrets of the universe, or make her mark upon the world?'

Richard Tennent sat dumbfounded, listening to her impassioned outpourings. It struck a chord in him. He had expected this day to be no different from any other. The monotony of a solicitor's life often drove him to distraction. Her words echoed his frustration. He was bound by duty to the family company. Whilst an undergraduate at Oxford he had longed to join one of the Geographical Society's expeditions to Africa, South America or the Far East, to learn more of the cultures of ancient tribes. Archaeology was a hobby which had grown with the passing years. The idealist in him wanted to pursue it, but duty tied him to a desk in London.

He had never heard such sentiments from a

woman. As she was speaking, he studied her oval face framed by the large black hat and veil. Her mourning clothes enhanced the perfection of her creamy, unblemished skin. She was not beautiful by the accepted standards of the day. Nevertheless, her high cheekbones, delicately winged, honey-blonde brows and wide full mouth were striking. Her blue eyes, which darkened to violet when she became angry, sparkled now with a formidable determination. From her slender figure emanated an aura of courage and fortitude, which detracted nothing from the soft femininity of her graceful movements. There was also, in the set of her chin, a stubbornness of character which would be her greatest asset in life, or her greatest downfall.

He felt an empathy with Kara Wyse's desire to succeed. His own dreams remained dormant, stifled by the weight of family responsibilities. His father's death had crushed his present hopes of travel and exploration, but it had not destroyed the desire. Duty had forced him to administer his father's clients' legal affairs. Tennent, Tennent & Son was one of the leading solicitors in London. It had been in existence since his great-grandfather and his brother had started the firm in 1823. When his father died, Richard had felt the trap closing. He was the only surviving male Tennent to carry on the business. Many of the trusts they administered were so complicated that it would have been dishonourable to betray so many generations of clients. His interest had always been in the criminal side of law, not probate. That again was at present denied him because of family commitments.

'Please sit down, Miss Wyse,' he said with authoritative crispness. 'I meant no offence by my words. Your father was a valued client of this firm for many years. I would be failing in my duty to him if I did not warn you of the dangers involved in living alone.'

Kara sat down, though he could see from the compressed line of her lips that she was still on her guard. Clearly she could not be swayed from the plans she had made. He returned to the matter in hand. 'The jewellery, as valued, will not provide you with a vast fortune. If the money from the sale is invested, it could bring you in a modest income and enable you to live well until you marry.'

'I do not see marriage as the ultimate goal in my life, Mr Tennent.' Kara controlled her exasperation. 'My father's bankruptcy and manner of his death make me socially unacceptable to many families of my class.'

Richard shifted uncomfortably. The woman was uncommonly forthright. Still at least she was a realist. He had read in *The Times* the announcement of her engagement to Ernest Holman. The following week the declaration that the marriage would not take place had appeared. He studied her more closely. In a week she had lost her father, her home and her future husband. Her secure world had crumbled. Yet she sat unflustered, accepting the blows fate had dealt her with dignified calm. Beneath that outward demureness, he sensed an undercurrent of unawakened sensuality. A passionate and headstrong nature in a woman usually led to one thing – tragedy.

'I have no training, Mr Tennent,' she continued in a low, persuasive voice. 'And though my father deemed that a woman needed only a rudimentary education, I have a good head for figures. I have a mind to invest some of my income in a business.'

'Of what nature?'

For the first time since she had entered his office, he discerned a chink in the armour shielding her emotions. She sighed and bit her lip. 'I have no experience of such matters. I had an idea to run a bookshop. That would be a respectable occupation. Though I realise that first I should work in one for a few months to learn the trade. I would also need introductions to publishers to study their lists, and to research the market to learn what are the most popular sales. I would specialise in women's fiction and subjects of interest to them. All too often bookshops ignore the needs of their women customers.'

Again she surprised him. This was no harebrained scheme, but carefully thought out. Her father had been a valued client of their firm, and he felt some responsibility towards this proud and determined woman. Her refusal to give in to adversity was a quality he admired.

'It would not be impossible, Miss Wyse. Though it would be important to find the right establishment, which may not be so easy,' he cautioned, and was saddened to see the disappointment on her face. 'You could, of course, seek employment at a library.'

'But there I would not learn how to run a business efficiently, or make the necessary contacts within the trade.'

Like a dam bursting, she began to pour out her thoughts and plans for the future. He listened intently, rarely interrupting, except to ask a question to clarify a point. Finally Kara came to a halt and laughed softly. 'I fear I've run on. Thank you for listening to me. No one has taken any of my ideas seriously before. Do you think they could work?'

'I think anything you set your mind to achieve, Miss Wyse, you will achieve.' Admiration warmed his voice.

Kara glanced at her wrist-watch. To her dismay she saw she had been here for almost two hours. Outside, the threatened rain was slashing against the windowpanes in a downpour. 'Forgive me, I have taken up a great deal of your time. May I call upon you again for advice, Mr Tennent? You have been most understanding. Many men would have sneered at my pretensions to lead my own life.'

'But you do not see them as pretensions, do you?' He smiled. 'I would help you in any way I can.'

She relaxed, feeling at last that she had met someone who understood her, who would help and not hinder her plans for the future. 'I appreciate that, Mr Tennent. Could you recommend a suitable house where I could take lodgings?'

He had risen to his feet and she saw that, although his build was slim, it was wiry, and there was an athletic power in his assured movements. It surprised her. She had always imagined lawyers to be stoop-shouldered from peering over legal documents for hours on end, their manner pompous towards anyone with less learning. Richard Tennent was nothing like that. His manner was kind and sympathetic, in a way that made her feel that her idea was not a foolish dream. Now, as he regarded her gravely, she found herself holding her breath, eager for his approval.

'This is not the weather to go searching for lodgings, Miss Wyse. From what you have told me, your funds until the jewels are sold are limited. My wife and I would be honoured to have you as a guest in our house.'

'I could not expect so much from you, Mr Tennent,' Kara said, bewildered. She was momentarily wary of his intentions. Henry Wicken's warnings to trust no one made her hesitate. 'Neither can I believe that this is a normal service you offer to your clients.'

His expression remained serious. 'No, it is not. But I would not see a young gentlewoman cast adrift on the London streets. Your circumstances are exceptional. But in fact you will be doing me a service. My wife is an invalid. One of her greatest pleasures is reading. My mother lives with us, but she is set in her ways. She is not always sympathetic to Elizabeth's frail health. She is very involved with her charity work. For Elizabeth, even briefly, to have a companion who shared her interests would lighten the burden of her illness.'

Still Kara hesitated. It was a generous offer and

kindly meant. But she did not want to be beholden to anyone. Yet the sky was ominously dark and the prospect of finding lodgings and employment, as well as trying to find her mother and sister, was daunting.

'Please, Miss Wyse, do consider my offer. At least for a few days until you become accustomed to life in London. It will take me some weeks before your father's estate is in order. I must contact all the creditors to learn the full extent of his debts.'

Kara's eyes snapped with a brittle fire. 'My father's chief creditor was Holman's Bank. Mrs Holman purchased his mortgages and bills of credit, then foreclosed on him.'

'Ernest Holman's mother did that?' Richard's voice was thick with outrage. 'But you were to marry her son.'

Kara slapped her gloves into the palm of her hand, her tone contemptuous. 'She resented the affection her only child held for me. She vindictively set out to ruin my father. I wish there was some way of making her pay for her spiteful actions. They cost Papa his life. If my fiancé had more backbone, he would have stood up to her.' Pride laced her voice, warning him that she wanted no pity or sympathy.

Richard admired the proud, determined woman. He knew the type of matriarch who would emasculate their sons to keep control over their lives. Kara Wyse deserved better than a spineless weakling who could never have made her happy.

At seeing the emotional strain on her face,

which she was valiantly trying to mask, he resolved that Ernest Holman would sign over any remaining debts. Threat of breach of contract should be enough to win for Kara a decent settlement out of court.

'Your grandmother's jewels are deposited at my bank. Tomorrow I shall arrange their sale, if you wish. I will also start making inquiries about both your family and investing your capital.'

Kara nodded. Her expression lost its tautness as she smiled her gratitude. The change in her startled him. He'd been wrong to think her features merely striking. Now they were radiant – unforgettable – with an unconscious sensuality uniquely her own.

Despite all Kara's desire to be independent, it was a relief to have the immediate burdens taken from her. 'Are you sure your wife, or mother, will not object to another female in their house.'

He shook his head and gave a dry laugh. 'Mama will be delighted to have more time to spend on her charity work. And Elizabeth will welcome you with open arms. She sees so few people.'

She smiled warmly. 'Then it would be churlish of me not to accept. My trunks are with a carter who is awaiting me at the inn along the road.'

Richard Tennent strode to the door. 'A clerk will give him my address in Belgravia to deliver your trunks.' He excused himself and left the room to speak with one of the four clerks in the outer office.

Kara had a moment's doubt as to whether she had been wise to accept his offer. There was something about the way he looked at her, with such penetrating intensity, which disquieted her. No, disquiet was not the right word. She found his easy manner likeable, and felt she had met someone she could trust and confide in. But he made her feel different, more conscious of herself than other men of her acquaintance. Perhaps because he had taken her seriously. She wanted his approval. Her heart had raced faster as he had raptly listened to her plans for the future.

Richard Tennent returned before she could analyse her emotions further. What did she know of the man, or his family? Was it safe to trust him? Henry Wicken's warnings had made her aware of her unworldliness.

Chapter Five

'Everything is arranged.' The warmth in Richard Tennent's hazel eyes banished the sardonic gravity of his features. 'I am sure you and my wife will become good friends.'

Kara answered with a smile. She had to trust her judgement, and she did not believe that Richard Tennent was a dishonourable man. The chill fear of uncertainty which had settled over her since her father's death began to fade. She would not have to face the world alone. Richard Tennent would prove a valuable ally.

As they sat side by side in the hansom cab, Kara felt a nervousness which she had not experienced on the journey with Mr Wicken. Then her goal had been merely to reach London. Now that she was here, the events of the next few weeks would change the course of her life. It was both daunting and exciting, and she was relieved that she would not have to face it alone.

'What information have you about your mother's whereabouts, Miss Wyse?' Richard Tennent asked as they pulled away from his office.

She told him about the annual meeting her mother had with Nanny Brewster. 'But that's nearly nine weeks away,' she finished despondently. 'There must be something that can be done before then.'

'Short of engaging a man to make inquiries – and that could take time – there is nothing.'

Kara sighed and struggled to control her impatience. 'I would have suitable lodgings to bring my mother and sister to, if they are living in poverty. If I'm to support us all, I must be earning some kind of income.'

'I have been wondering about that,' Richard Tennent said. 'One of my clients is a recently bereaved widow who has a young family. Her husband owned a stationery shop. Since his death, her manager began stealing from the business. He was arrested last week. Mrs Henshawe, the widow, needs the income from the shop to support her family, but she has no business acumen. She is distraught and is thinking of selling the business. I advised her against it. To do so would leave her with only her capital to live upon. With four children to raise and educate, she could find herself in very reduced circumstances in a few years' time.'

He leaned towards Kara, his tone enthusiastic. 'It could be the ideal solution. The shop occupies the basement and ground floor of the widow's large house. The expenses of running it are rapidly draining her resources. Until now she has been loath to take in lodgers. I think she may lease a floor of the property to you if you become partners. Such an arrangement would safeguard your reputation.'

'I'm not sure, Mr Tennent. I did rather have my heart set on a bookshop. I know nothing about stationery.'

'The shop premises are large. Part of it could be converted to sell books. That could be a condition of your partnership.'

The idea appealed to Kara. 'It seems too good to be true,' she said, her heart pounding with excitement. 'But what of my father's debts? Won't I have to use the money from the jewellery to settle them?'

Richard was impressed that she wasn't allowing her excitement to cloud the main barrier to her success. 'I shall ensure when the house and business is sold that you get a fair price. The Holman family were responsible for your father's ruin. They are the chief creditors. Ernest Holman jilted you. You can sue him for breach of contract; for, say, the amount of your father's debts. I expect they will settle out of court to avoid a scandal.'

'The Holmans should pay for what they did to my father rather than what they did to me. I'm just relieved I'm not to marry Ernest. He was Papa's choice. Nothing would hurt Augustina Holman more than to lose so much money. If the case can be settled out of court, I want my father's debts and name cleared.'

Under Richard Tennent's piercing regard, Kara hesitated. She did not want to dwell upon the spite of the Holman family. She wanted to look to the future not the past. 'Tell me about Mrs Henshawe's shop. You make it sound so easy.'

'First we have to convince Mrs Henshawe that it is in her interests,' he warned. 'Mrs Henshawe is set on selling the shop, and your capital would not stretch to buying her out. She shies away from business responsibilities. They confuse her. All the business administration will fall on your shoulders. It is no little task.'

'Where are these premises?' Kara schooled her voice to remain calm, but the prospect of expanding a stationery shop to sell books caught her imagination. She already saw the possibility that, in a year or two, she could buy further premises. Why should she not start a chain of such shops? She pulled her thoughts up short. One step at a time. There were still her father's debts to settle. Neither did she want Mr Tennent to think she was too eager. That would be unbusinesslike.

'The shop is in a less developed part of Oxford Street, but still close enough to the new department stores to attract passing customers. If Oxford Street develops as I believe it will, the property and land will increase tremendously in value. It is an investment she should not dispose of yet. A partnership would seem the ideal solution for both you and Mrs Henshawe.'

Kara felt her cheeks begin to flush at the prospect of the venture. 'I would like to meet Mrs Henshawe to discuss it. It would be of paramount importance that we liked each other, or it would not work at all.'

'I have no doubts that you and Sophia Henshawe will get on famously,' he said, admiration shining in his eyes. 'You strike me as a remarkably determined woman.'

'It is worth considering.' Kara refused to commit herself further until she had seen the shop and met her prospective partner. She was attracted to the idea that Mrs Henshawe would not be directly involved in running the business. She wanted to make a success of it on her own. 'When can a meeting be arranged?'

'There I must disappoint you. Mrs Henshawe left yesterday to take the waters at Bath. She will not be returning for a month. But tomorrow we shall visit the premises. The shop is closed as a new manager has not been engaged. I have a key in Mrs Henshawe's absence.'

'In the meantime I shall look at any other options which may present themselves,' Kara said decisively. 'I've no wish to waste a month waiting upon Mrs Henshawe's decision which may not be favourable.'

A pulse beat along Richard Tennent's jaw. Kara felt a stab of disappointment. Here was another man who seemed to resent her making her own decisions. Then she saw that it was not anger, or censure, but that he was struggling to contain his amusement. Again, she was struck by the change in his austere features, and she realised that he was an extremely attractive man.

'Patience is not a virtue of yours, is it, Miss Wyse?'

She shook her head and laughed. 'I fear not. But I will not make a hurried decision merely because I am eager to get my own business started.'

They had reached Belgravia. The hansom cab turned into an elegant Georgian square of four-storeyed, sandstone properties and halted.

'This is my home, Miss Wyse,' he said, alighting, and held out a hand to assist her. His touch was firm on her elbow and, as she stepped on to the pavement, their gazes held. Before he released her arm, her heart gave an unexpected flutter. 'Any decision you make now is too important to your future to be hurried.'

'I am prepared to be guided by you, Mr Tennent.' The way her body was reacting to his nearness disconcerted her. He was too attractive for her peace of mind. He was so unlike her pompous father, her strait-laced Uncle Bertram, or the weak-willed Ernest, who until now had been the only men of any significance in her life. If she was to stay in his house, she must quash any sign of an infatuation before it could take root. And instinct told her that it would be all too easy to become infatuated with the charming and intellectual Richard Tennent, who treated her as an equal.

His eyes crinkled at the corners and she felt a bond of mutual respect form between them.

The house was part of an imposing terrace. Three steps flanked by Corinthian columns led up to the door which was opened as they ascended.

A grey-haired, haughty-featured butler greeted Mr Tennent. 'Mrs Tennent is in the blue room, sir,' the butler informed him.

'Siddons. This is Miss Kara Wyse. She will be staying with us for the time being. Inform Mrs Lane to have the green bedchamber prepared for her, and Mary will attend her as her maid during her visit.'

'Very good, sir.' Siddons's imperious stare flickered over Kara and, from the quality of her mourning clothes, did not find her wanting.

'Mrs Lane is our housekeeper,' Richard Tennent explained, then surprised Kara by adding, 'an estimable woman, but rather prim and short on a sense of humour.'

Kara would not have thought that a solicitor would consider a sense of humour a necessary attribute; rather the opposite in fact. As she followed him up the thickly carpeted stairs to the first floor, she noted the richness of her surroundings. Silk wallpaper in pale gold lined the walls. The panelled doors were painted white, their carved moulding picked out in gold leaf. Several bronze sculptures of figures from different cultures were mounted on pedestals, and two half-size marble statues of bare-breasted Greek goddesses stood in separate alcoves.

'What beautiful sculptures,' she could not help observing.

'I purchased them while excavating in Italy,

Greece and Mexico during summer breaks from university.'

'You are an archaeologist as well as a solicitor?' she asked, intrigued.

'I read law at university. Archaeology is more a hobby which study when I can.'

She paused, looking at the statues with deepening interest. 'I envy you your travels. Mr Tennent. You must have found such work fascinating. What does that half-man, half-bird statue represent?' It stood about two foot high.

'One of the Inca gods. It's from Mexico. A fascinating culture. Once it was my intention to return to South America and search for one of their lost cities.'

'What stopped you?' She checked herself abruptly. 'I'm sorry. How rude of me. You are waiting to introduce me to your wife.'

'You are interested in archaeology, Miss Wyse?'

'I find the ancient cultures fascinating. But Papa did not really approve. He frowned upon paganism of any sort. He burned two books he found of mine on Greek mythology and Egyptology. I was furious.'

'I have books on those subjects, and many more. You must make full use of my library whilst you are with us.'

'Thank you.' She smiled radiantly, delighted that he was so knowledgeable on subjects which interested her.

Kara was led into a sumptuously furnished parlour. An intricately patterned Persian carpet covered the floor, and the ruby wallpaper was almost hidden by a score of original oil and watercolour masterpieces. She restrained her first impulse to examine a Gainsborough and Turner more closely.

Mr Tennent had crossed to a day bed set before the fire. 'My dear, I have a visitor for you. A Miss Kara Wyse. She is a client whose father has recently died. She has come to London to settle his affairs.'

There was the soft rustle of silk as the figure reclining on the day bed sat up. Kara moved forward hesitantly and studied the woman who was smiling adoringly up at her husband. When she turned to face Kara, she was struck by her exquisite but delicate beauty. She was no more than a couple of years older than Kara. Dressed in pale pink edged with cream lace; with her silvery-blonde hair, vivid blue eyes, and heart-shaped face, she was like a fairy doll. The image was enhanced by a porcelain-white complexion which showed her frail health. She extended a slender hand to Kara.

'I am so sorry to hear of your father's death,' she said in a soft, musical voice. 'How very brave of you to come to London on your own.'

Kara smiled. 'It was not bravery which brought me here, but necessity.'

'Where are you staying? Have you relatives close by? I get so few visitors, I would…'

'My dear,' Richard Tennent interrupted gently. 'Miss Wyse is alone in London. I have invited her to stay with us. I am sure you will enjoy each other's company.'

Elizabeth smiled tenderly at her husband. 'Richard, you are always so thoughtful. Of course she must be our guest. It will be wonderful to have a woman my own age in the house.'

He stepped back and stood by the fireplace, looking down at his wife. There was affection in his expression, but Kara was aware of a tension in his figure that had not been there until they entered this house. He unfastened his black frock coat, his hand resting on his slim hip, and displayed a dark green and silver brocade waistcoat. The elegant but flamboyant waistcoat was at variance to her general impression of solicitors. Clearly Richard Tennent was not a man to put into a category. His broad shoulders and long, loose stride were certainly athletic, as she had earlier observed. She could imagine him more in the role of an explorer and archaeologist than a solicitor.

Again she was conscious of his handsome and commanding presence as he addressed his wife. 'Miss Wyse can only stay to keep you company if you promise not to get too excited. Your visitors are restricted because you know how easily you succumb to one of your attacks.' He looked at Kara. 'My wife has a nervous disorder which affects her breathing. It's important that she does not get over-excited.'

'You fuss so, Richard,' Elizabeth said, but from her expression clearly enjoyed her husband's concerned attention. 'Come sit by me, Kara. I may call you Kara, may I not? Such a pretty name. And unusual. You must tell me all about yourself.' She spoke quickly, her eyes bright with a childish excitement.

Richard strode towards the door. 'I will leave

you two ladies to become acquainted. I have some work to finish in my study.'

Elizabeth's adoring gaze followed her husband's departure from the room. As the door closed behind him, she sighed softly. 'He's such a wonderful man, and so understanding. I'm a poor wife. My illness makes me so frail. And Richard is such a vigorous man. So full of energy. He used to run at Oxford you know. He's got dozens of trophies for athletics and other sports. I'm so proud of him. Richard is so clever. He'll sort out all your problems.'

Kara smiled. It was obvious that Elizabeth was very much in love with her husband.

'Have you journeyed far to London? Where do you come from?' Elizabeth began to fire a barrage of questions as Kara sat down. 'Have you no relatives at all to deal with your father's estate? How dreadful to find yourself alone.' Elizabeth took Kara's hand, squeezing it in sympathy. 'I see no ring on your finger. But you are so pretty there must be a fiancé. Is there no fiancé to care for you? Richard will help you. He's such a tower of strength. How long are you staying? Oh, you must tell me everything, I know we will be such good friends, I feel it.'

Kara laughed. 'Which question shall I answer first?'

'Oh, I'm babbling again. So silly of me.' Elizabeth looked stricken. Her eyes were overbright and she was breathing heavily as she went on. 'I always do that. You will think me empty-headed. I don't mean to prattle so. It sometimes annoys Richard. Though the dear man never shows it.'

'I think you are charming,' Kara said truthfully.

To her alarm she saw Elizabeth begin to draw great gulps of air, her face becoming pinched as she fought for breath. 'My salts ... on the table... So silly ... of me... Please.'

'Don't talk,' Kara said, reaching for the smelling salts and wafting them under Elizabeth's nose. The breathing remained erratic. Kara heard a strange wheezing in the woman's chest, and her face now looked frighteningly transparent. Alarmed, she said, 'I'll fetch your husband.'

'No,' Elizabeth gasped. 'Please ... no. It eases.' She lay back on a cushion with her eyes closed. Gradually her breathing was returning to normal. 'Do not tell ... Richard. He worries so... So silly of me...'

'Are you sure you are all right? Should a physician be called?' Kara asked, worried at the woman's pallor.

Elizabeth lifted a hand in denial. 'My cordial is on the table. It will strengthen me.'

Kara poured the sweet-smelling liquid into a glass and pressed it to Elizabeth's lips. After a few sips her colour began to return and she opened her eyes, her breathing almost normal.

'I get so nervous meeting new people. So silly of me. Especially as I like you.' Her lips quivered and her eyes were large and pleading.

Kara smiled, feeling protective towards this beautiful, fragile woman. 'I think you should rest. Mr Tennent mentioned that you like reading; shall I read to you for a while?'

Elizabeth lay back and, closing her eyes,

nodded. 'I would like that.'

It was obvious the charming creature was used to being pampered, but Kara spent a pleasant hour in Elizabeth's company before she changed for the evening meal. Yet despite all Elizabeth's appealing charm, she suspected that she was capable of using her ill-health to get her own way.

'I cannot believe that you are serious in entertaining the idea of opening a bookshop and engaging in common trade.' Mrs Irene Tennent peered at Kara through her lorgnette with piercing grey eyes. Richard Tennent's mother was short, her plump figure squashed into tight corsets and dressed in widow's weeds. Even so, she was an imposing figure. 'I met Abel Wyse once when I called into the offices to see my husband. A very moral, imposing man. I cannot believe he would approve of his daughter entering trade.'

She spat the word 'trade' out with all the contempt of those of the professional middle-classes for those in commerce.

'My father owned one of the largest haulage companies in Essex.' Kara curbed her antagonism at the woman's rudeness. 'He was not ashamed of it. However, you are right, he would not approve of my plan. He would not approve of any woman who tried to succeed in a male-dominated world.'

'But only women in the lower orders work,' Irene Tennent continued with cutting disapproval. 'Now if you were to open a Ladies' Academy, that is a respectable occupation.'

'I would die of boredom,' Kara said, keeping a firm grip on her sliding temper. Clearly, Irene Tennent was a woman who believed her own opinions were the only ones which mattered. Kara disliked such dogmatic narrow-mindedness.

'Mama, Miss Wyse's intention of opening a bookshop is perfectly respectable,' Richard Tennent remarked. There was an edge to his voice whenever he addressed his mother, although his manner was always courteous and polite.

'It borders upon the unseemly.' Irene Tennent lifted her lorgnette to appraise him. 'I am surprised that you invited this woman into our house when she has shown views which flout convention so openly. You'll be telling me next that she's one of those dreadful suffragettes.'

Kara had heard enough. Putting down her napkin, she stood up and faced Irene Tennent, her cheeks flaring with angry colour. 'I admire the women who are campaigning for votes for women, though some of them are too militant in my view. Unless women believe themselves equal to men they will always be treated as inferior. I cannot accept that we are less intelligent or capable of governing our lives.' She turned to Richard who had risen to his feet when Kara did so, and saw he was tight-lipped with disapproval. Her heart lurched. It hurt that he was condemning of her. 'Your offer of hospitality was most generous,' she said, stiffly. 'I will retire now and leave first thing in the morning.'

'Richard, make her stay,' Elizabeth pleaded.

'Miss Wyse, you must forgive my mother. She speaks as she finds,' Richard apologised. 'She does not always realise how offensive her remarks can be.'

'I will not stay where I am not welcome.'

'You are most welcome here.'

He looked at his mother, and for a long moment their wills clashed in silent contest. A glow of expectancy spread through Kara. It was not her he had been censorious of, but his mother's conduct. Yet would he back down under his mother's disapproval as Ernest had done? Richard Tennent showed no sign of relenting. To Kara's surprise, Irene's steely glare lowered from her son's and she pursed her lips in a prim line.

'Miss Wyse, I am an old woman, set in my ways. I tend to expect people to take me as they find me. I meant no offence by my comments. Since Richard has invited you into our home, you are very welcome to stay for as long as you wish.'

'And will you take me as you find me, Mrs Tennent?' Kara could not resist the gibe. She saw Richard's mouth twitch as he struggled to contain his amusement and added pointedly, 'I may have to support myself by entering into trade, but I hold honour and integrity high.'

Irene Tennent inclined her head in acknowledgement of her remark, and then proceeded to monopolise the conversation by speaking of the charity work she had been involved in that day. Her favourite institution was the rescue of fallen women, especially unmarried mothers, who entered a hostel to await the birth and offered their babies for adoption.

Aware that she had caused dissent amongst the family, Kara sought to alleviate it. 'Mrs Tennent, I'd like to visit this hostel. If there is any way I can help, I shall willingly do so.'

'You are most kind.' Mrs Tennent barely mellowed. 'We never turn away helpers. Though in my opinion...' She drew a deep breath, preparing to expound further.

Richard cut in briskly. 'I doubt Miss Wyse will have much time to help you,' he informed them. 'She has much to learn before she can manage her own business. I will be arranging meetings with accountants, buyers and shop managers to advise her.'

Irene Tennent's overbearing manner, which sought to dominate people to her will, was beginning to grate on Kara's nerves. Elizabeth was clearly in awe of her mother-in-law. The over-brightness in her eyes and the rapid rising and falling of her breasts revealed her agitation. Grateful for the solicitor's intervention, Kara said, 'I did not expect you to give so much of your time, Mr Tennent. How can I repay you?'

His eyes crinkled at the corners as he regarded her seriously. 'By succeeding, Miss Wyse. Too few of us are free to explore our goals.'

Again a tautness was apparent in his voice which was at odds with the courtesy of his expression. There was a sharp gasp from Irene Tennent and Kara felt the tension in the room crackle like electric static.

'I thought you'd seen sense and put your nonsensical notions of studying ancient tribes behind you, Richard,' Irene snapped.

'I've not forgotten my duty,' he returned smoothly, but there was bleak hunger in his eyes.

Richard Tennent was certainly not all he at first appeared, and Kara was fascinated. A quiver of expectancy sped down her spine as she held his level stare. Then Mr Wicken's words were loud in her mind. Don't trust anyone. There were tensions in this family she did not understand. She thrust them aside. She did trust Richard Tennent. Though she could not banish the sudden thought that any threat he might present to her would be of a far more subtle and dangerous nature. But that was absurd. His wife clearly adored him and their marriage seemed a happy one.

'Now you've seen the premises and had time to consider the proposals I suggested,' Richard said, 'shall I write to Mrs Henshawe to arrange a meeting?'

It was five days after she had moved into his house, and they were in his study after dining. Elizabeth had gone early to her bed and his mother was spending the evening with friends.

'The shop is perfect. There's plenty of room for expansion to sell books.' Kara tried hard to contain her excitement, but it was impossible. Her face glowed and her eyes had taken on a luminous brilliance. 'There's a lot of unnecessary clutter in the shop. If it's properly displayed on shelves it would give us more space. And from what I saw of the property, if Mrs Henshawe is prepared to lease me the upper floor to live in, I would be delighted with the arrangement.' Her expression sobered. 'Though of course it depends on how Mrs Henshawe and I get on when we meet, Mr Tennent.'

'Isn't it time you called me Richard? You call Elizabeth by name.'

She smiled and was discomfited by a rush of heat to her cheeks. Turning away so that he would not see it, her gaze fell upon a glass trophy cabinet which was crowded with silver cups and plaques.

'Elizabeth said you ran at Oxford. Are all these cups yours?'

'They belong to another life.' The heaviness of his voice made her turn to face him.

'It seems a pity that you have put such success behind you, Richard.'

'Like many of my friends at university, I enjoyed sports of all kinds,' he said dismissively.

'But that part of your life was important to you,' intuition prompted her to add.

'At one time. As were other interests which were put aside when duty had to be honoured.'

'The archaeology?'

He nodded. The soft hiss of the single gaslight and the crackle of the log fire were the only sounds in the room. She was burning with curiosity. When he did not elaborate she persisted. 'Do you regret your decision?'

He lifted his head and shot her a chilling glare.

'I'm sorry, that was impertinent of me to ask.'

'I had little choice. I had once hoped to spend several months in Mexico, excavating Inca ruins. But my father became ill. The previous year Elizabeth had miscarried. She was still very ill.

Her breathing attacks were getting worse. For a time it seemed she might die. How could I leave England when my family needed me?'

'You made the noble choice. The only one an honourable man could have done. But...' She hesitated, wondering if he would be offended if she continued. When he lifted an inquiring brow, she added, 'But you must wonder what that other life would have been like. To visit such exotic lands and discover some new knowledge about those ancient people – that would be quite something.'

'It would be quite something indeed, Kara. I had a feeling you would understand,' he answered, his voice low and intimate.

They did not move, but Kara found it impossible to drag her gaze from his darkening hazel eyes. The lock of brown hair which he could not seem to restrain flopped over his brow. Inexplicably, she wanted to brush it back with her fingers. Her breath caught in her throat at the intensity of his regard and her mouth became dry. She swallowed, feeling her skin tingle with awareness of his closeness. Light-headedness assailed her, and for a moment she felt her body inexorably drawn towards him.

With a start she caught herself in time. What was happening to her? An ache settled over her heart and she realised with both wonder and dismay that she was falling in love with Richard Tennent.

'You must write to Mrs Henshawe at once.' She forced brightness into her voice, praying it did not betray the tumult of her emotions. 'It is unfortunate she does not return from Bath for another three weeks.'

'If you are so impatient, I could arrange for us to take the train to Bath and visit her there.'

She was tempted. He stood now with one leg bent and his hand resting on the black marble mantelpiece. The firelight flickered over the contours of his lean face and he smiled, revealing white, even teeth. His athletic figure was poised, threateningly male and commandingly handsome.

'I will wait until Mrs Henshawe returns.' She was amazed at the coolness of her tone, for her heart was pounding wildly. 'She will not wish to be troubled with business matters whilst away.'

The intensity of her emotions frightened her. She did not want to fall in love with Richard. How could she? He was married, and more particularly he was the husband of a woman she regarded as a friend.

Chapter Six

The next few weeks became a bitter-sweet torture for Kara. In an effort to keep her feelings for Richard at bay, she took pains to avoid his company whenever she could. It was virtually impossible. He had arranged several meetings for her with advisors about her business venture. He escorted her everywhere. Although grateful for his attendance and advice, with each day her affection for him became stronger, throwing her into constant turmoil.

Then Richard received a letter from Mrs Henshawe, informing him that she had broken her arm and would not be returning to London for another month.

'I cannot impose on your hospitality for so long,' Kara said at dinner that same evening.

'But you are not imposing,' Elizabeth hurriedly assured her. 'We love having you here. Don't we, Richard?'

'How could we manage without your piano recitals each evening?' he said gently, teasing. 'It is so long since Elizabeth has been well enough to accompany me to a concert or the opera. Your playing gives us great pleasure.'

'Papa was not a music-lover. He had a low opinion of opera. He said that most of them were indecent displays of passion, unfit for female ears.'

'Then you must come with us to one, mustn't she, Richard?' Elizabeth declared. 'It's been weeks since my last attack.'

'That would be wonderful,' Kara replied, her face glowing with excitement. 'But would it be seemly? It's so soon after my father's death.'

'His death freed you from his restraint,' Richard said softly. 'You came to London to put your past life behind you. If you would enjoy a night at the opera, I will arrange it.'

Irene Tennent put her fork down with a clatter. 'One must observe a decent mourning period.'

'Even if it is hypocritical?' Kara said crisply. 'My father did not want my love. I was a disappointment to him. He resented my existence.'

She still had not spoken to Irene, or Elizabeth, about her mother or sister. Although she would have liked to confide in Elizabeth, she sensed a strong moralistic trait in her friend. Elizabeth would see her mother as a wanton for deserting her marriage, and she did not want to put a strain on their friendship.

Irene sniffed her disapproval. 'One must respect the dead. He was your father, Kara.'

Kara wrestled with her conscience. The prospect of visiting the opera was too enthralling to resist. She turned to Richard. 'I know it's wicked of me, but I would love to accompany you.'

'I do not countenance such disgraceful neglect of duty, and disrespect to a parent,' Irene announced, her stare condemning.

'Mama, with respect, you did not know what Mr Wyse was like,' Richard said. 'He repressed Kara when he was alive. Why should convention dictate that he continue to do so from the grave?'

'He was your father's client.' Irene glared at her son. 'He deserves your respect.'

'No man deserves another's respect without reservation. It is something which is earned,' Richard stated.

'Perhaps I should wait until my mourning period is over,' Kara said to halt the tension building around the dining table.

Richard regarded her with enigmatic severity. 'You must do as you think best. Just because our late Queen wore her bereavement like a talisman, and shut herself away from the world for years, does not mean we all have to be so fanatical.

Times have changed.'

'And not for the better,' Irene interrupted. 'In my day we knew our duty to our parents.'

Richard ignored his mother's outburst. Leaning towards Kara, who had paled at Irene's attack, he taunted. 'Are you frightened by malicious gossip, Kara? Your life is your own now to do as you will. How can it harm anyone by you attending the opera?'

His reasoning echoed her own sentiments too much to be denied. 'I would very much like to attend such an entertainment.'

'Then it's settled,' Elizabeth said, clapping her hands with pleasure.

'I shall not be a part of such a gathering,' Irene said stiffly, clearly furious that her opinion had been ignored. 'And really, Elizabeth, I thought you had more decorum. Miss Wyse's presence in this house has had an unsettling influence on both you and Richard.'

She turned to Kara, disapproval thinning her lips. 'Respect for our parents in life, and death, is not cast aside by decent society. I can no longer condone your visiting the charitable institutions where I serve on the board. Those women are too easily led astray. I consider you a bad influence upon them.'

Kara bit her lip to stop an angry retort. She had been deeply moved when helping in the soup kitchen for the poor, or visiting the home for unmarried mothers.

'Isn't that rather petty, Mama?' Richard said sternly.

Irene reddened, her face stiffening into a mask

of outrage. 'You take that woman's side against your own mother,' she shrilled. 'Elizabeth no longer cares for my company now that this woman has become her friend. And she's resurrected your interest in the ridiculous expedition you had planned to Mexico.'

'It is not a question of taking sides,' Richard returned. 'Kara is interested in the things which interest both Elizabeth and myself. You have never been. You are too wrapped up with your charity work to consider the needs of your own family.'

Kara had heard enough. She knew that Irene had never approved of her staying in the Tennent house. Now it looked as if her stay had spread discontent in this family. Appalled, she stood up.

'Mrs Tennent, if I have offended your sensibilities, I apologise,' she said crisply. 'I will not be the cause of family dissent. Tomorrow I shall engage a maid and have my possessions moved to the Adelphi.'

'I will not hear of it.' Richard rose and came to her side. 'Besides, my mother has expressed a wish to visit an old friend of hers in Richmond. She never liked to go before, as it would mean leaving Elizabeth alone for so long each day. With Kara here, Mama could now write to Lady Wynbourne and stay until the end of the month.'

Irene's knuckles whitened over her dessert spoon, her voice strained. 'That will suit me admirably.'

Kara felt guilty that mother and son had quarrelled. Irene had lapsed into a sullen silence, but her body was taut with indignation. In the weeks since her arrival, Kara had witnessed many such confrontations between Richard and his mother. The woman was a matriarch who could not abide her wishes flouted. She had succeeded in subjugating Elizabeth, but Richard, with courteous resistance, refused to be dominated.

'Mama has been talking of visiting Lady Wynbourne for months,' Elizabeth said with a strained smile. 'I hate to be a burden on her. So silly, this illness of mine. And of late I have been feeling so much stronger. Especially since Kara has insisted that we take a carriage drive each day. We often stroll through Hyde Park. I never feel tired in her company. Please stay, Kara. With Irene away, I'd be so lonely. I'm sure I'd become so dejected I'd decline.'

'You must not use your illness to make Kara think she must stay,' Richard said firmly.

'Oh, I would never do that.' Elizabeth was all wide-eyed innocence. 'But when I am lonely I do have more attacks. Please, Kara, don't speak of leaving us until your business affairs are settled.'

'In that Elizabeth is right. I won't hear of you leaving until your business arrangements and your father's affairs have been settled,' Richard added, considering Kara over the top of his wine glass.

His eyes smiled at her. The warmth of his regard bathed her in a golden glow. His approval was the only one which mattered to her. She had been starved of affection too long to want to move to lodgings where she would live alone.

Richard continued, 'Mrs Henshawe returns on the fourteenth of June. You have many important matters to settle before then.'

Kara nodded. The date of Nanny Brewster's and her mother's reunion was rapidly approaching. The man Richard had employed to track down Florence Wyse had discovered nothing. She felt her hands break out in nervous perspiration and a stifling weight of panic press into her chest. What if her mother had moved out of London? Or was too ill to come?

'There is still much to be done to prepare yourself for your new life,' Richard went on. 'Next week there are meetings with publishers' representatives. We must also visit the most prestigious bookshops in London to analyse their stock.'

'But am I wasting my time and yours, Richard?' Kara gave in to a rare moment of depression. 'Nothing has yet been settled over my father's debts. How can I consider my future until I know my financial circumstances?'

Richard leaned back in his chair, the gaslight softening the rugged contours of his face as he studied Kara. 'I had meant to keep this from you until after my meeting. Tomorrow I have an appointment with Holman.'

As Richard learned the true extent of Abel Wyse's debts, his anger had mounted. It was obvious that Mrs Holman had purchased many of the bills of credit after Kara's betrothal. Abel Wyse had needed Ernest to invest capital in his company to stop it going under. The haulage company had recently secured two sizeable new contracts which would have put it back on its feet. These had mysteriously been cancelled the day before Mrs Holman had called in her loan. Investigation had proved that a letter from Holman's Bank had declared Wyse Haulage a bad risk.

Richard had spent a morning in Brentwood. His interview with Ernest Holman had been stormy.

'My mother acted to secure the interests of the bank,' Ernest Holman declared haughtily.

'At the expense of destroying your fiancé's father,' Richard countered. 'I see you wasted no time in finding another rich heiress to become engaged to. It was in *The Times* last week that you are to wed Miss Eugenie Carlyse-Smythe. She's worth five thousand a year, isn't she?'

'That's none of your damned business.'

'Isn't it?' Richard eyed him coldly. 'Breach of promise is a serious offence. I have advised Miss Wyse to seek retribution through the courts. I shall draw the judge's attention to the underhand moves made by Mrs Holman to bring an end to your engagement with Miss Wyse.'

Holman blanched. 'Miss Wyse ended the engagement,' he blustered.

'Not according to her statement. And with the evidence I have against your bank, it would not look good to allow the matter to go to court.'

'Are we talking about a settlement then?' Ernest Holman hedged. 'How much will it cost for Miss Wyse to settle out of court?'

'We are talking about a man's ruined reputation. Abel Wyse's debts were the cause of his death. From the accounts it is obvious that if Wyse Haulage had been allowed to continue trading, even without you as a partner – but of course without the loan being called in – the company would have made a profit in the next year. Enough for Mr Wyse to have settled with his creditors. In two years the mortgages on his property would have been cleared. Can your bank afford such adverse publicity?'

'You know damn well we cannot.' Holman got out of his chair and angrily paced the room. 'Damn you, Tennent. You've got me over a barrel and know it. How much will you settle for?'

'Ten thousand pounds. Just two years' worth of your new bride's income. That sum will also clear Abel Wyse's debts.'

'That's extortion!'

'I think it's small payment for ruining the reputation of a respectable citizen and robbing his daughter of her inheritance. Yes, ten thousand really is too small an amount. We will make it fifteen thousand.'

'That's...' Holman froze as he saw the brittle gleam in Richard's eyes. The solicitor was just waiting for a chance to increase the amount. He knew if the case was brought to court it would cost him far more than that in lost custom. A discredited bank was a ruined bank.

'I shall consult my solicitor,' Holman blustered.

'Do that.' Richard rose to leave. 'You have a week to agree to my conditions, or I start court proceedings.'

Kara found it difficult to concentrate on her meetings with shop managers. She had begun to feel that it was all a waste of time. So far Ernest had ignored Richard's ultimatum.

'He has no choice. Holman will pay what I have asked,' Richard advised.

Kara wished she had his faith.

Irene was still in Richmond. Her absence had considerably lightened the atmosphere in the Tennent household. Elizabeth had joined Kara in a few shopping forays, and they had all attended a concert at the church hall.

'I have enjoyed myself immensely these last weeks,' Kara said as she finished playing the piano for Elizabeth and Richard one evening. She blushed at Elizabeth's enthusiastic clapping.

'You play so well,' she said, smiling broadly. 'You give us so much pleasure, Kara.'

Kara remained on the piano stool, aware that Richard was watching her with fixed concentration.

'We must hold a party, Richard,' Elizabeth announced, laughing. 'It will be more fun with Irene away. We will have musicians and dancing. It is so long since I have danced the waltz.'

'Would it not overtax your strength, my dear?' Richard asked.

'I would ensure I rested. Richard, do say yes. Kara will adore it.'

'Would Kara enjoy it?' Richard said, his tone teasing.

Kara clutched her clasped hands to her breast, thrilled by the prospect. 'Yes, but I cannot dance. Papa did not approve.'

'That is soon remedied.' Elizabeth's voice was breathless with excitement. 'Richard is an excellent dancer. We'll hire a pianist and he will teach you to waltz and to polka.'

'I could not impose. Richard is so busy. I already take up so much of his time.'

'It will be my pleasure to teach you.' Richard swept aside her protests. 'We will begin tomorrow.'

Again she felt the heat of his gaze on her and felt a blush rise up her cheeks. She quickly turned away to collect up the music sheets.

The next evening the furniture in the upper salon was pushed to the side of the walls and the carpet rolled up. A short, dark-visaged Italian played the piano for them as Richard showed Kara the dance steps of the waltz.

'It is simple. Just keep the rhythm in your head: one, two, three ... one, two, three...'

He held out his arms for her to partner him. When his hand rested in the centre of her back, she felt it burn through her clothing, and the touch of his fingers curling over hers made her breath catch in her throat. She could smell the musky scent of his cologne and hair oil, and the tang of lemon soap on his skin. They pervaded her mind, destroying her calm.

'Don't look so worried,' he teased. 'It is easy.'

They stood with their bodies poised several inches apart. At least he had not guessed the tumult her emotions were undergoing. The music began and, watched by an excited Elizabeth, Kara groaned when for the second time she stepped on Richard's toes.

'I fear you will be crippled if we continue,' she apologised.

He laughed. 'Nonsense! You have a natural grace. Just follow my lead,' he encouraged. His slow smile sent a thrill of pleasure weaving through her body.

Richard was a superb dancer. Within moments they were moving together with a fluid grace which made Elizabeth applaud.

'That's it, Kara,' she encouraged. 'Richard is such a wonderful dancer. He makes it all seem so easy.'

Kara surrendered her body to the rhythm of the music and dance. With each graceful turn she felt as if she was floating, whilst her senses were besieged all round by the masculine power of Richard's attraction. The awareness of his laughing breath fanning her cheek, the touch of his hand in hers and on the small of her back, wrecked her composure. Her heart was racing. When the music ended she was breathless and laughing.

To cover her confusion, she jested, 'I can understand why Papa considered dancing to be decadent. I have never felt so exhilarated, so alive.'

'You dance as if you were born to it.' Richard's smile was tender. For a long moment his gaze held hers. Kara saw his hazel eyes were now flecked with green. They smouldered with an emotion so profound that it made her breath catch with longing to return to his arms.

She stepped back, the encounter leaving her harrowed with guilt. No married man should look at a woman other than his wife with such admiration. She turned to Elizabeth, who reclined on a day bed by the wall. Her friend's beautiful face was alight with pleasure as she stared devotedly at Richard.

Kara said, 'You must dance with your husband, Elizabeth.'

Elizabeth waved a hand in denial. 'I feel tired just watching you both. You dance so perfectly together. Now you must learn the polka. I have always found it too energetic.'

Her instinct for self-preservation dictated that she should flee the temptation of being held again in Richard's arms. But to do so would look so strange to the unsuspecting Elizabeth that her friend would be bound to question her. At all costs Elizabeth must never guess her guilty secret.

For an hour Kara continued her lessons. She adored the polka, the pulsating beat of the dance throbbing through her veins. The strength of Richard's arms around her added to the magic of her first experience of dancing. As they spun to their final halt, she was breathing heavily, her face aglow with pleasure, her lips parted as she breathed deeply. Behind her she heard Elizabeth dismiss the musician.

'Superb, Kara.' Elizabeth smiled her delight. 'You will be the belle of the ball. Now I will retire. Watching you both use up so much energy has tired me. Goodnight.'

'Goodnight, Elizabeth,' Kara said as her friend left the salon. She went to collect her Indian silk shawl which she had earlier discarded.

Richard put his hand on her arm to halt her. 'Don't go just yet. I have news from Holman.'

She paused, looking up at him, expectant and fearful.

'He agreed to all I asked. He transferred fifteen thousand pounds to your bank account this morning.'

Kara stared at him, stunned. 'But Papa's debts were only ten thousand. And the furnishings were taken in part payment of them.'

'They were sold for less than their value. Why should you lose out? And I asked for a further five thousand to compensate for the humiliation you suffered when Holman ended your engagement.'

He had expected her to be pleased. Instead she looked horrified. 'I want nothing from them after the shame they brought upon Papa. Certainly not their tainted money. Return the five thousand and whatever else is left over.'

'Kara, you need capital to start your business. The sale and auction of your father's property raised less than a thousand pounds. The jewels raised only another five hundred. I thought you wanted security. Why shouldn't the Holmans pay for what they did to your family?'

'I want no reminders of them.' She turned away. 'I don't want to live on their charity.'

'It's not charity.'

'Please, return the money to them.'

'At least keep the full ten thousand. You must have some security behind you if your business is to succeed. You'll need stock, don't forget.'

Kara was breathing heavily, her mind whirling.

'Take the ten thousand at least, Kara,' Richard urged. 'There'll be little enough of that left once the remaining debts are settled. In two years your father would have had the means to clear all his debts. They robbed him of the means to regain his pride.'

'Very well,' she said reluctantly. 'But I don't want their guilt money. My business would be tainted if it was founded upon Holman money.'

He turned her to face him. 'You are proud and very noble. I admire that in you. As I admire many things.'

Her breathing was still fast and, on seeing the passion in his handsome face, her heart thudded so hard she felt it vibrating through her figure. A tingling heat spread over her flesh as he closed the gap between them.

'You must know that I care for you, Kara,' he said huskily.

She was held spellbound. Her body was more alive than it had ever felt before: every nerve, every sense was attuned to his presence. His face filled her vision, the scent of his skin tantalised her awareness of his masculinity. His hands were on her shoulders, his eyes enforcing her to hold his gaze. Their depths darkened entrancingly as his face bent over hers. She knew she should draw back, but a force greater than her will was holding her transfixed. The green-flecked depths of his eyes were compelling her, and something more intense – something beyond her imagination or experience – ignited between them, leaving her lightheaded.

Then Richard's hands were around her, his mouth moving closer. Her gaze was drawn to his full lips – mesmerised, entranced – unable to break free of the spell he was weaving.

There was an unexpected reverence to his kiss, his mouth warm and gentle, moving sensuously and with provocative slowness. A deepening pressure parted her lips and she tasted the sweetness of his breath. A warmth as potent as mulled wine spread through her veins, causing her blood to pound and robbing her legs of the strength to support her. Her fingers curled over the broadness of his shoulders to steady her swaying figure. Through half-closed eyes she saw the passion in Richard's face and knew it must be mirrored in her own. For a moment she gloried in this taste of heaven.

Then her conscience smote her. Appalled at what she was permitting, she pulled back. 'This is wrong.'

He dropped his hands to his sides. 'Kara, you must know how I feel. I can't stop thinking about you.'

'You are married, Richard. Married to a woman I regard as my friend.'

Tension whitened the lines at the side of his mouth, and his gaze was anguished. The pressure in his fingers tightened, drawing her closer. 'It's been a marriage in name only for some years. I never wanted this to happen. Now it has, I can't deny what I feel for you. You feel the same. I can see it in your eyes.'

She swallowed, fighting against his seductive coercion. Her dreams had been filled with imaginings of him kissing her. The reality of the yearning that his touch had evoked harrowed her.

'It is a sin,' she forced out. 'And disloyal to Elizabeth.'

'Do you think I find it easy to betray my wife?'

'No. You care for Elizabeth. And you are an honourable man.'

'But I'm falling in love with you, Kara.'

'It cannot be.'

With a sob rising to her throat she ran to the door, ignoring his harsh call of her name as she fled up the stairs to her bedchamber. Her body was on fire with guilt and yearning. She had fallen in love with Richard, a love that was doomed never to be fulfilled.

She was ill at ease when she met Richard over breakfast the next morning, but his greeting was cool and polite in front of Elizabeth. He sifted through the morning post and frowned over the contents of one of his letters.

'I have to leave for York.' He addressed Elizabeth. 'A client's son has been arrested for murder. He's only fifteen and it looks to be self-defence, but the victim was the son of an alderman. I will be away for some days. We had better postpone the party, my dear, until I know for certain when I will return.'

'I did not realise that you took on criminal cases,' Elizabeth said, her expression pouting that he was leaving.

'You forget, criminal law was my main interest. I took over father's cases out of duty. I intend to take on a partner to deal with the litigation and trust funds. In future I will concentrate on criminal law.'

Elizabeth shot Kara an accusing look before addressing her husband. 'I've heard you and Kara discussing the criminal cases covered in the paper. Has she encouraged you in this?'

'Kara has made me realise that I was wasting my knowledge and talent,' he replied curtly. He gathered his post together and, as he stood up, turned to Kara. 'I regret I won't be able to accompany you to your meeting next week.'

'You've already given so much of your time on my account,' she answered, hiding her disappointment. 'Mary will accompany me. Don't worry if you cannot return in time for my meeting with Mrs Henshawe.'

'I shall be back by then.' He subjected her to a grave stare and bowed to her before kissing his wife's cheek and leaving for the office.'

Elizabeth hung her head and Kara saw her blinking rapidly to hide her tears. 'I wish you had not encouraged him to go back to criminal law. It takes him all over the country. I see so little of him as it is.'

'Isn't that rather a selfish attitude?' Kara lost patience with her friend. 'Richard is a talented lawyer. Hasn't he given up enough out of duty by taking on his father's cases? The expedition to Mexico was important to him. You must have known that when you married him. If you love him, you should encourage him in his interests. Richard isn't a man to be tied to any woman's side. If you try and stop him you will lose his respect and eventually his love.'

She looked horrified. 'Do you think so? He's been so kind about my illness. But I love him so much. I can't bear to think of him so far away. I miss him. I would be so lonely if he went away.'

Her fierce possessiveness irritated Kara. Too often the spoilt little rich girl in her surfaced. She might love Richard, but Kara suspected that she loved her own self more.

Then, as quickly as the sullenness had appeared on Elizabeth's face, it disappeared and she smiled enticingly. 'Such a pity we shall not have our party. I know how you were looking forward to it.'

'It does not matter,' Kara said warmly, her guilt at having fallen in love with Richard making her want to protect her friend from hurt. 'I enjoyed the concerts.'

'And you've learnt how to dance,' Elizabeth said with a laugh. 'You have been such a wonderful friend, Kara. You are right. I must not try and keep Richard at my side.' She dabbed at her eye with the corner of her handkerchief and sniffed theatrically. 'I love him so much. I want him to be happy – but with me. I must be strong for his sake.'

She smiled weakly as she went on. 'It's a long time since Richard has allowed himself to relax and enjoy himself. He takes his responsibilities so seriously. I had not realised he hated his work so much. If it weren't for Irene and myself being such a burden on him, he'd be in a jungle in South America searching for a lost city of the Incas.'

She laughed as though she found the idea preposterous, and Kara was annoyed at how selfish Richard's wife was.

Elizabeth was studying her, and when Kara did not ridicule Richard's ambitions, she hung her head and began to twist the lace points of her deep collar. 'I've been a poor wife. Richard is such a healthy, vigorous man. He cannot abide illness. He was rarely home in the evenings before you came to stay. He tries so hard not to show it, but I know I annoy him with my silly chatter.'

'You must not torture yourself so.' Kara began wondering if perhaps she had misjudged her friend.

'How can I not? Since my miscarriage...' She drew a shaky breath, her eyes haunted as she stared at Kara. 'I haven't been a proper wife to him. Dr Clifton said I may not survive another pregnancy. If I lost Richard's affection I would want to die.'

'Richard adores you,' Kara hastened to assure her, though her heart felt as if steel stakes had been hammered into it.

'He's a wonderful and considerate man,' Elizabeth babbled on. 'I was an only child. Papa was a major in the army. When I was five he was killed at the fall of Khartoum in 1885 when the Mahdi's followers murdered General Gordon. Mama became rather strange after that. She died three years later and I was reared by my grandmother. She died when I was sixteen. I married Richard a year later. He's all I have.' She reached across the table and squeezed Kara's hand. 'Him and you. Your friendship means so much to me.'

Kara felt a lump rise in her throat and guilt gnawed at her breast. For Elizabeth's sake she must leave this house. Constant contact with Richard would eventually lead to the inevitable. The way her body burned at nights for the feel of his touch and lips warned her that she would not be able to resist him for ever. When her shop was opened, she would have to end all contact between Richard and herself.

'You won't ever abandon me, will you, Kara?' Elizabeth said fervently. 'I know I'm a silly creature, with my fainting fits and breathing attacks, but your friendship means so much to me. I love you as a sister.'

Hot tears prickled behind Kara's eyes. Her father had denied her any close friendships. Now she had found one, she had betrayed it by falling in love with the woman's husband. Yet how could she desert Elizabeth when the invalid relied on her? It must be her cross to bear. Elizabeth must never suspect her love for Richard. It would be a double betrayal to end her friendship with Elizabeth. Somehow she must arm herself against her love. Otherwise she had a choking feeling that it would destroy them all.

Chapter Seven

The day of the annual reunion between Nanny Brewster and Kara's mother drew ever nearer; excitement at the prospect at being reunited with her mother helped ease the pain of Kara's illicit love. She barely slept on the night before the meeting. When the day dawned with a cloudburst, her heart ached with frustration. Would Florence keep the rendezvous? She might think that Nanny Brewster would not venture out in such atrocious weather. At breakfast her nerves were so taut she could not eat.

Elizabeth had received a letter from Richard and was so happy she did not notice her friend's disquiet. 'He's returning in two days,' she declared breathlessly. She had already read the letter twice and was again scanning the pages. 'Isn't that wonderful? He hopes your meeting today goes well. Who did you say you were seeing? Is it important? Oh, what a shame, he does not mention the party. That's not like Richard. I shall insist. No, better still, we shall make the party a surprise for him on the day following his return.'

'What if he is delayed?' Kara cautioned, worried by Elizabeth's flushed cheeks. The thought of a party now filled her with dread. How could she refuse to dance with Richard without Elizabeth questioning her? Yet how could she afford to dance with him? One touch would ignite her blood and she would be lost. Every night in her dreams she had relived the ecstasy of his kiss. There was a passionate side to her nature she had never suspected. Ernest's hot, moist kisses had not stirred her senses as Richard's had done.

Elizabeth had been gabbling on and Kara's thoughts were jerked back to the present by her friend's over-excited tone.

'But Richard would not be so cruel as to allow

himself to be delayed. He knows I miss him.' Elizabeth's face was flushed and her breathing began to harshen.

'On such an occasion his first duty is to his client. The boy's life could depend upon it.'

Elizabeth sighed and gave Kara a rueful look, her breathing becoming more agitated. 'I'm being selfish again, aren't I? I do try so hard not to. But I miss Richard so much.'

'Of course he will not be delayed,' Kara assured her, trying to avert the attack.

'Then we shall have the party.' Elizabeth's eyes were over-bright. 'Musicians must be engaged and a guest list drawn up. It will be the grandest affair.' Her breathing was coming in gasps, her voice rising as she began to speak rapidly. 'Forty guests. Food. I must speak with cook.' She put her hand to her chest. Kara was appalled at the wheezing sound in her lungs as she raced on. 'The dance floor must be polished. Is a string quartet enough? Or shall I ... I engage a small orchestra, with pianist? So much to do. So much to remember.'

Elizabeth was gulping for breath now and Kara dashed to fetch the smelling salts which were kept in each room.

'Elizabeth, breathe slowly. You're too excited. Richard will not want to return to find you ill. Forget the party. Think of your health.'

'No... There must be a ... party. You learnt to dance ... for it.'

Elizabeth was close to collapse. Kara rang the handbell to summon a footman.

'I only want you to be well. Rest now, Elizabeth,' Kara urged. 'If the thought of a party has brought on this attack, what will the event itself do? Richard will be cross if you are ill. You must rest. If you are well enough when he returns, we could go to another concert. That's something special to look forward to.'

'Yes. You are right…' All the colour had drained from Elizabeth's face as she struggled for breath, her voice now a fragmented whisper. 'Must be well … for Richard… He hates my illness … I will rest.'

The footman entered and Kara gave him instructions to carry Elizabeth to her room and for the doctor to be called.

'I will send Mary to sit with you,' she said to Elizabeth. 'I wish I did not have to go out, but this meeting really is vital.'

'Go,' Elizabeth gasped. 'So … silly … of me.'

'It's not silly.' Kara took her friend's hand. 'You made yourself ill because you wanted to do something special for your husband. Shall we plan something together later? But I think a party would be too much of a strain for you.'

Elizabeth nodded and closed her eyes. The attack was abating, but it had drained all her energy. 'Who are you meeting? You never said.'

'I will tell you about it when I return,' she evaded. 'Rest now.'

Kara hated leaving Elizabeth when she was so ill, but if she missed the meeting with Florence, she might have to wait a whole year before she could make any contact with her mother.

She took a hansom carriage to Hyde Park, in preference to the cramped omnibus. The ride seemed to take for ever in the press of London traffic. The downpour had become a light drizzle, and the park was almost deserted. She was half an hour early for the meeting, but was too restless to go elsewhere. Kara still wore mourning and an umbrella protected her from the drizzle as she approached the bandstand. A young flower-seller, with pale, pinched cheeks, was huddled under a skimpy piece of sackcloth which was ineffective in sheltering her from the rain.

A woman in a faded burgundy woollen dress, black shawl and black straw hat had taken shelter beneath the canopy of the bandstand. Kara's heart beat faster. Was it Florence, also arrived early? As she neared and studied the woman, she saw her hair was grey. She looked much older than her mother's forty-two years. The hem of the dress had been turned several times where it had frayed, and was now some inches from the ground, revealing the woman's low-heeled black lace-up boots. The style had been fashioned over a decade ago.

Seeing Kara approach, the woman peered short-sightedly at Kara. The woman's face was gaunt, her complexion ashen with ill-health. She hugged her arms across her thin body, drawing her crocheted shawl more tightly around herself as she paced. She began to cough, the harsh hacking one of long illness. Her body shook as she lifted a handkerchief to her mouth.

Kara brought a large bunch of flowers from the flower-seller and, taking pity on the woman whom she presumed to be a beggar, pressed a florin into her hand. The woman looked startled, then accepted it with a shrug. Kara hovered for a few minutes, but feeling conspicuous she walked further down the path by the Serpentine lake and paused to watch the ducks in the water. Ten minutes later she was drawn back to the flower-seller. It had stopped raining, but the older woman remained, pacing the floor of the band-stand, her stare fixed in the direction of the park entrance.

Kara, with time still on her hands, studied the woman more closely. She was moving slowly and, despite the shabbiness of her clothing, there was a refined grace in the way she held herself. She saw now that, though the dress was worn and faded, it had once been of a fine quality, as were her leather boots. No doubt they had been purchased from one of the second-hand clothes shops in Petticoat Lane. The woman frequently glanced in Kara's direction. Each time she frowned, her eyes squinting short-sightedly.

As the minutes passed, other people appeared in the park, but none lingered near the flower-seller. Kara glanced at her watch and saw that it was five minutes after the appointed time. The woman in the bandstand was pacing more agitatedly, her hands in their scuffed leather gloves wringing together.

A pain pierced Kara's heart at belated recognition. Was the woman she had mistaken for a beggar actually Florence Wyse? Stunned, she continued to study her. Surely she was wrong? This woman looked nearer sixty than her mother's age. But Nanny Brewster had said that

Florence had worn the same dress for years at their meetings. A quiver of excitement quickened her pulse. On closer inspection she saw that those short-sighted eyes were the same violet blue as her own.

'Florence Wyse,' she said softly as she climbed the steps of the bandstand. Her palms were moist with nervousness, fearing now that she had been mistaken and that her mother was not coming to the meeting.

The woman started and backed away.

'It is Florence Wyse, isn't it?' Kara persisted.

The woman paused, but did not answer. The nervous twisting of her hands increased. 'Nanny Brewster said you'd be here. She could not come. Her arthritis makes it hard for her to walk now.'

The proud carriage of the woman slumped and she gripped the ironwork railing for support.

'Are you ill?' Kara instinctively reached out to touch the woman.

Again she backed away. 'I am all right.' Her voice was cultured and out of keeping with her shabby appearance. 'Thank you for telling me that Nanny Brewster could not come.' She began to cough, and turned away to hold the railing until the fit passed.

Her words confirmed that this was her mother. The turmoil of emotions raging in Kara stunned her to silence. Her heart swelled with love, but Florence looked destitute and so ill – so unlike the woman she had expected to find.

When Florence turned back and saw Kara watching her intently, her eyes scanned her face, searching. 'Who are you?' she said, unsteadily.

Kara swallowed against the pain which clenched her throat. 'I am Kara Wyse,' she said softly. 'And you are my mother.' A tear rolled down her cheek as she spoke. Self-consciously, she held out the flowers she had purchased. 'Papa told me you were dead.'

A spasm of pain crossed her mother's gaunt face. Closing her eyes, Florence put a hand to her mouth, her throat working against her own shaken emotion.

'Florence Wyse is dead,' she said harshly. 'I wanted nothing of that man's name. I am known as Florence Kempe. My maiden name.' Her eyes opened to study Kara. There was hunger and longing in her gaze, but she made no move to touch her. 'Are you really Kara? My Kara?'

Kara nodded, too overcome to speak, and pressed the flowers into her mother's hand. Her eyes prickled with hot tears of joy. 'Mama.' Her voice was a cracked plea of entreaty.

She longed to hug the woman close, but Florence stood stiffly. After so many years of having her love rejected by her father, Kara checked her impulse to gather her mother into her arms.

Florence held the flowers to her face and inhaled their scent, then said with a tortured groan, 'You must despise me for what I did. Your father would have told you I'm a whore. That I abandoned you.'

Florence lifted a trembling hand towards Kara, but did not touch her. Instead she shaped the contours of her face from a distance, her eyes filling with tears.

Kara took her mother's hand and held it against her cheek. She was appalled at the frailty of her fingers and lack of flesh on her bones.

'Until the day before his death, Papa never permitted your name mentioned,' she said in a choked voice. 'I was told you had died when I was young. I don't despise you. If I did, I would not be here. I know what Papa was like. I was a virtual prisoner in his house. I don't blame you for wanting to escape.'

Tears were streaming down Florence's cheeks. Her eyes were sparkling with joy which made the years slide away from her haggard face. 'I don't deserve such kindness. It broke my heart to leave you, but Abel would not let you go.'

'That was to punish you.' Kara's own cheeks were wet with falling tears, her throat cramping with happiness at this long-awaited reunion. 'Papa never loved me. I was not the son he wanted.' Her restraint broke and she hugged her mother. For a long moment both women were too choked with emotion to speak.

'But I've found you now,' Kara eventually managed to say. 'We won't ever be parted again.'

She felt Florence stiffen. She leaned back, her expression again saddened. 'That is not possible. We have different lives. Look at you: so elegant, so beautiful.' Her adoring gaze took in every detail of Kara's figure and the joy returned to her face. 'This is a proud day for me. Nanny Brewster told me how you were progressing. I never forgot you, Kara. I never stopped loving you. Abel would not let me see you.'

'I know, Mama. I understand.' They clasped

each other tightly again, uncaring of the curious glances directed at them by the people beginning to fill the park. 'Where are you living now?'

'But what are you doing in London?' Florence ignored her daughter's question. 'You must tell me everything about yourself.'

'Papa is dead.' Kara explained the circumstances.

'So, Abel is dead. Shot himself because he could not face the shame of bankruptcy and prison.' Florence nodded, knowing the man she had married so well. Memories of her miserable marriage were pushed aside. She was reunited with her daughter – her first-born. No bitter memories of Abel Wyse would spoil that.

'If Abel died a debtor, how will you manage?' Florence said worriedly.

'Grandmama Wyse bequeathed me her jewels. I've sold them, and will invest the money. Also I plan to start a business. A bookshop.'

'Your own shop!' Florence could not hide her astonishment. 'But I saw in an old paper that you were to be married to Ernest Holman. Though his mother is a snobbish, domineering woman, as I remember.'

'Our betrothal was ended after Papa's death. Besides, I do not see marriage as my salvation; rather as another cage to bind me to man's dominance,' Kara said fiercely. 'Does that shock you, Mama?'

'Nothing could shock me now. I've seen too much in recent years. I was miserable in my marriage. Yet my freedom was bought at a high price. Near starvation and drudgery.'

'If you had to make the same choice again, Mama, what would you do?'

Florence sighed, and stared for a long moment at the distant outline of Marble Arch visible through the trees. At last she said, 'Without love, I would not see marriage as the path to happiness – only to oppression. With the right man, though, it need not always be so.'

Whilst they strolled through the trees, Kara linked her arm through her mother's. She continued to speak of her plans for the future. The sun had broken through the thinning cloud. Young boys had materialised from nowhere and, when they approached a park seat by the lake, one vigorously dried off the seat with a cloth and waited expectantly. Kara tossed him a couple of pennies and they sat down. The ducks from the Serpentine waddled around their feet, hopeful for scraps of bread.

'Shall we take tea at the Adelphi, Mama?' Kara said when she came to the end of the story of how she had come to London.

Florence looked aghast. 'No. I would not be seen in so grand a place with you. My dress has seen better days.'

'You will have new dresses, Mama. All that has changed.'

Florence's heart filled with pride. If only she could speak of her present life; explain why what her daughter offered was not possible? But she could not. She did not want to see Kara's joy in their reunion turn to shame, or regret.

The sun had brought the usual press of people into the park. Genteel ladies in pale-coloured suits with long sweeping trains paraded with their liveried footmen following them. Several pompous-looking men, with huge moustaches and whiskers and high starched collars, were casting appreciative looks in Kara's direction. Florence could not hide her pride. Kara was beautiful, intelligent, and obviously had none of her father's vicious streak to her nature. Unlike her sister.

Perhaps it was not fair to compare Beatrice with Kara. Beatrice had endured poverty and was the product of her environment. She had the same ambition as Kara to better herself. Only the path which Beatrice had chosen was more unsavoury.

It was with less pleasure that Florence noted one similarity with Beatrice. It was in the boldness in her eye and the way her hips swayed as she walked. Both her daughters had inherited her passionate nature. It had led Florence to ruin. And how ill it had served Beatrice. She prayed Kara would avoid being wholly governed by her feelings.

The elegant ladies and gentlemen on their horses, in carriages, or slowly ambling along the paths, were part of Kara's world. A world which had once been hers. That Kara ignored the amorous interest of several handsome men proved how very different she was from her sister.

Florence suppressed a sigh. In the distance, horses were being ridden along Rotten Row. Women in top hats and jackets with a masculine cut paraded on horseback. There to see and be seen. As she looked across the lake, Florence imagined the gentry in their silks and velvets, their flunkeys running at the side of a smartly turned-out curricle. She had ridden there as a young woman. She was the only child of a widowed financier who owned a country mansion in Harold Wood and a house off the Strand.

In those days she had flirted with beaux, discussed the social round of parties, dances or dinners with her friends. And if they were feeling reckless they would drive their carriage down Piccadilly. There Florence would coquettishly glance up at the window of the Turf Club, hoping for a glimpse of a particular swain who had danced with her at a ball the week before. They were giddy, carefree days, and all so long ago. Another life – another world.

'I have a sister, I believe.'

Kara's words jerked Florence abruptly back to the present. 'Yes, Beatrice,' she said cautiously. 'She is three years younger than you. She was born six months after I parted from Abel. I never told him I was expecting her when I left. I feared he would take my baby from me. Then one year she became ill with the typhus and I had no money to buy her medicine. I humbled my pride to write to Abel. He threatened to have me arrested if I approached him again. He refused to accept that Beatrice was his child. Thank God she lived, and no thanks to that evil devil. Though when I think of her life now...'

Outraged anger, which Florence had thought long forgotten, flared into life. When she had married Abel, her substantial dowry had been used to expand his business as he tried to compete with the railways. When he had first met her he had been charming; eager to please her and win her hand. That had changed within weeks of her marriage. He had become domineering and possessive, forbidding her friends, restricting her leaving the house. She had become another of his possessions – less loved than the horses which pulled his precious carts. He did not love her. He had married her for her money. Her duty had been to produce a son. The once weekly fumblings she had endured in their bed had resulted in a daughter. He had seen that as her failing.

From that moment he never lost an opportunity to deride her. The following year she had inherited all her father's fortune. She had thought that would please Abel and make her marriage to him less onerous. He hadn't changed and she had become more and more miserable.

When Abel had turned her out of his house, he had slapped a pouch of ten guineas in her hand and told her to go as far away from Brentwood as the money would take her. The fortune from her father, which was rightfully hers, he kept. Obviously it had been squandered on bad investments.

She began to cough, and held a handkerchief to her mouth. When the fit stopped, she hastily hid the blood-flecked material. She did not want Kara to know that she had consumption, which was slowly killing her.

'I have to go now, Kara.' Florence glanced at the angle of the sun and knew that she would be late. Big Joe would be angry. He didn't like it if his meal was not on the table when he returned from work. Still, it would be worth facing his anger. She had seen her Kara. Her lovely, bonny baby had grown into a beautiful and accomplished woman. She had the world at her feet with her talk of opening a bookshop.

'I'll come with you,' Kara said brightly. 'You've told me nothing of your life – or of my sister. I want to meet her.'

'No.' Fear sharpened Florence's voice. 'Beatrice does not live with me. We will meet again. Here, on your birthday. That's in two months' time.'

'Mama, you can't just walk away now we've found each other.' Kara was staring at her in hurt bewilderment.

It almost broke Florence's heart. She wanted so desperately to make up for every day that they had been apart. But that was not possible. And if Beatrice and Kara met... She mentally shuddered. She had never told Beatrice about her marriage, or Kara. Her younger daughter would have been wild with jealousy that she had been denied such an upbringing. And Beatrice, when jealous, could be vindictive and malicious.

She loved Beatrice. Sadly life had hardened her younger child, in a way which often frightened Florence. It would be better if Beatrice did not learn of Kara's existence yet. Any meeting must be carefully planned. Kara had so generously forgiven her for deserting her as a child. Beatrice would resent the wealth and position she had lost. Florence inwardly flinched. When crossed, Beatrice had a nasty way of making people pay.

'Mama, where do you live? And Beatrice. Tell me, so that I may call on her and surprise her.'

There was a determined look on Kara's face. For an instant she resembled her father. Florence knew how strong-willed Abel could be. A wave of panic threatened to engulf her. She had thought that all her pride had been stripped from her in recent years. But it reared its head now. She could not bear Kara to learn of her present life. She had to get away.

Her gaze quickly scanned the park. It was filled with people. If she could slip away in the press, she would be spared the humiliation of her daughter learning how low she had fallen.

She put a hand to her temple and sat down heavily on the seat she had just vacated. 'I feel rather faint, Kara. There's a barrow-boy selling tea over there. Could you kindly get me a cup?'

'Of course.' Kara gave her hand an affectionate squeeze before she threaded through the crowd towards the barrow.

Florence stared at her daughter's back, her heart wrenching with the agony of how they must part. Then, with a sob, she hurried in the opposite direction. A military band had begun to play in the bandstand and a thick press of people shielded her escape.

Kara held the steaming cup of tea and carefully made her way back to her mother. The cup fell from suddenly lifeless fingers. The seat Florence had occupied was empty.

Lifting her long black skirt, Kara ran through the crowd. She was rudely jostled as she frantically tried to see which way her mother had gone. Two boys playing with a hoop collided with her, their bony shoulders jarring her arm so sharply that her hat and veil were knocked askew. She cried out as she toppled backwards.

'Young louts, watch where you're going.' A deep male voice shouted and strong hands gripped Kara's elbow to stop her falling.

'Thank you, sir,' she said absently, and stood on tiptoe to look over his shoulder, still searching for her mother.

'Are you all right, miss?' the man inquired. 'Have you lost something?'

'My mother.'

'You're a bit old to look so upset at being parted from a parent,' he said with evident amusement.

'But I'd only just been reunited with her after sixteen years,' Kara blurted out. She bowed her head, shaken and hurt that Florence had left her so abruptly. She was so overcome she could not stop a rush of tears. 'I'd waited so long for this day.' In her distress she spoke more to herself than the stranger. 'It was wonderful. But she sent me for a cup of tea. Then left. I don't know where she lives. And she looked so ill. So poor. Why did she leave like that? Was I such a disappointment to her?' She drew a shuddering breath and saw a clean white silk handkerchief thrust into her hand.

'I'm sure you were not a disappointment.' The deep voice was compassionate, piercing the pain at her mother's flight. 'I'm sorry I jested at your expense.'

She looked at the stranger, noticing the debonair handsomeness of his swarthy, Byronic features. He was tall and she found herself tilting her head to look up at him. Thick dark hair waved to just over his high starched collar, and a moustache curved across his upper lip to meet up with his flaring side whiskers. It added to the attractiveness of his high cheekbones and lean cheeks. The only imperfection was a break in his long, slender nose.

'I can feel you trembling,' he added. A curved brow lifted in query, and beneath lashes so scandalously long that a woman would give her soul to possess them, amber eyes smiled admiringly at her. 'Would you like to sit down?'

'I must find my mother. She can't have gone far.' Kara began to twist and turn. 'The gates are over there, aren't they?' As she made to break away, a firm hand on her elbow stopped her.

'There must be a reason why your mother left you in the way that she did. If she did not wish to be followed, she'll soon lose herself in this crowd. With your permission I will help you search for her.' His thin lips stretched into a wide smile.

A swift appraisal had shown Kara that his fawn checked trousers and brown frock coat were of the finest quality, and there was a diamond pin in his dark-brown silk necktie. She was still naturally wary about accepting help from a strange man, even one who appeared to be a gentleman.

His smile did not waver at her scrutiny and he said, 'I noticed you earlier. You were engrossed in conversation with a woman wearing a faded dark-red gown. She headed towards the corner of Oxford Street. Though that's where the congestion of people is thickest.'

'I must find her.' Kara broke away and began to push through the crowd.

'Permit me,' the stranger said, again taking her arm. His superior height and build cut a swathe through the people; Kara was half running as she matched his long stride. 'I think I see her ahead,' he encouraged as they increased their pace.

Kara dismissed her qualms about accepting his help. She was distraught over her mother's flight, and it was comforting to have someone to aid her search. At the gates the traffic blocked the road. An old horse pulling a totter's cart had collapsed and died between his shafts, bringing the traffic to a standstill. Drivers shouted and pedestrians craned their necks to view the sad spectacle. Florence Wyse was nowhere in sight.

'I've lost her,' Kara said forlornly.

'Wait there,' the stranger commanded.

To Kara's astonishment, he leapt on to a stationary omnibus and dashed up the stairs to the open top to look across the closely packed traffic. He was down again in seconds, laughing aside the conductor's demand for a fare.

'I was right. She's in Oxford Street. But we must be quick. If she takes any of the turnings off from there we've lost her.'

He held up a gold-topped walking cane and strode purposefully across the road, guiding Kara between the traffic. Fifteen minutes later they had to abandon their search. No one they asked had seen Florence.

'It's no use, is it?' Kara said, halting in her

tracks. 'But thank you for your help and your time.'

'It is always a pleasure to assist a beautiful woman in need.' He doffed his fawn Homburg in salute to her, and Kara was again struck by his handsome countenance and the devil-may-care glint in his unusual-coloured eyes. 'May I be of further service to you?'

His solicitation was comforting after the upset of failing to find her mother. 'You've been very kind.' Kara managed a tremulous smile, though inwardly she was heartbroken at the way Florence had run away. 'If the congestion has cleared, I'd appreciate you hailing me a hansom cab so that I may return home.'

As he turned to scan the road, a speck of grit blew into Kara's eye, and she groped for the drawstring bag which hung from her wrist to take out a handkerchief. 'My bag has gone! It's been stolen!'

She winced as the grit scratched her eye and it began to stream with water.

'Please, permit me,' the stranger said again, producing a clean handkerchief. 'Open your eye wide. I'll try and remove whatever is in it.'

He stood very close to her, and Kara could smell the spicy cologne he used. Gently, he managed to remove the speck of grit from her eye and, as her vision cleared, she found herself staring into his admiring amber gaze. He was extremely handsome, and she could feel a blush spreading over her cheeks as she stepped away from him. What was the matter with her, reacting to men this way? First Richard, and now a total stranger.

Discomfited, she cleared her throat and said, 'The two boys in the park must have stolen my bag. I never noticed. I was so upset over Mama going. I've no money for the hansom cab. I shall walk to Belgravia.'

'I will not hear of it,' he protested. 'Allow me to take you home. You've already been accosted by one thief. The streets of London are dangerous for a woman alone.'

She smiled apologetically. 'I can't accept your generous offer, sir. We've not been formally introduced.'

The corner of his wide mouth twitched with amusement. 'I am Captain Zachariah Morton, recently of the First Essex regiment. Your servant, ma'am. Whom have I had the pleasure of assisting?'

'You were with the Pompadours? What an amazing coincidence. Their barracks are at Brentwood. That was where I was brought up. I am Miss Kara Wyse. With respect, Captain Morton, it would not be proper for me to share a carriage with you. It is not far for me to walk.'

'Then you must permit me to escort you,' he insisted.

'I would not take you out of your way.'

'You are an independent woman, Miss Wyse.' His voice was teasing and his eyes remained admiring.

She suspected few women refused any offer of help from this charming and handsome man. But she was adamant, and though she found the stranger a delightful companion, her strict upbringing could not so far break with convention. She had no wish for Captain Morton to think her other than a respectable woman. 'I have taken up too much of your time, sir.'

'Will you not let me decide upon that? Your misfortune has been my good fortune, to meet and aid such a beautiful woman. At least permit me to pay your carriage fare.'

Kara shrugged off his compliment. She knew she was not beautiful and disliked flattery, but before she could protest, he had hailed a passing hansom. As it drew to a halt he turned back to her. 'I will not foist my unwanted attention upon you. I see you are in mourning. May I offer my condolences. Was it a close relative?'

'My father.'

'I'm sorry.'

He addressed the driver. 'The lady wishes to go to Belgravia. Here's a half a guinea for your trouble.'

Kara knew when to be gracious and accept a generous gesture for what it was. 'You have been most kind.'

She held out her hand and he raised it to his lips and bowed. There was a sparkle in his eyes which brought a blush to her cheeks. Despite being in love with Richard, she was not immune to Captain Morton's attractive looks, or his obvious charm.

Stepping into the carriage, she gave the driver Richard's address, then turned again to Captain Morton. 'I will not forget your generosity.'

'It was my pleasure, Miss Wyse.'

As he watched the carriage pull away, Zach

Morton grinned to himself. There was a woman who pricked his curiosity, and she was uncommonly attractive into the bargain. He had been surprised at seeing Kara Wyse in conversation with Florence Kempe. He remembered Kara from his last day in Brentwood after resigning his commission. Florence Kempe, as she called herself, he had recognised as Big Joe Donovan's woman. She was the mother of Beatrice Kempe, one of the most exciting and beautiful whores he had ever taken to his bed.

What a small world it was. So Abel Wyse was dead. Was Kara his heir? If so, that made her an extremely wealthy woman. Abel Wyse had owned a large haulage company. From what little he knew of the family, Kara was the only child he acknowledged as his own. Beatrice must be her half-sister.

He was astounded that Kara was also the daughter of Florence Kempe. What had parted them sixteen years ago? She was clearly desperate to learn the whereabouts of her mother. That would make her beholden to him when he gave her the information.

His step held a trace of a swagger as he set off towards Piccadilly and the Turf Club. If Florence was Kara Wyse's mother, there was a mystery here to unravel. One that could prove profitable to him. Florence had the bearing of a gentlewoman, despite the depths to which she had sunk. She had never fitted into the life she had adopted. Unlike Beatrice. Now that young woman was both an opportunist and a survivor.

He stored away Kara's address, determined

that he would meet the wealthy heiress again. This was an opportunity too good to miss. He began to whistle a jaunty tune, his spirits buoyant now that he felt his luck was about to change for the better.

Chapter Eight

Florence was coughing violently by the time she reached her home. The musty smell of damp and mildewed walls was stronger than ever today. Big Joe came into the dark narrow corridor to bar her way.

'Where's me grub, woman? Bin 'ome arf an 'our and I'm starving.' There was a trickle of gravy on his chin where he had dipped a ladle into the stew cauldron simmering over the kitchen fire. He was a second-generation London-born Irishman. 'Ain't no bread to go with the stew.'

'I was held up, Joseph,' Florence said between coughs. 'If there's no bread, it's because those young rascals Stinker and Swipe have been in and eaten it again. The new dough's risen by now. It won't take long to bake.' In an hour a dozen men and boys would file into the kitchen. They all lived here and it was Florence's job to cook for them. She glanced at the rickety table and saw that half of the large wedge of cheese she had purchased that morning had also been eaten. There would not be enough to go round and the others would be surly.

'It ain't good enough.' Big Joe scowled and raised a menacing fist. He was a big man, tall and broad-chested, and knew how to throw his weight around. 'A man needs 'is food. Lazy slut. Yer too weak to work in the match factory, and yer think yerself too good ter soil yer 'ands lifting a purse or two for Slasher Gilbert, same as everyone else in these tenements. Useless bawd. Yer can't even get a meal ready on time.'

'I'm sorry, Joseph.'

He continued to scowl. His large face was sprinkled with freckles and his wiry red hair stuck out around his cloth cap. Removing the cap he scratched the bald dome of his head, then rubbed his hooked nose. Often too ready with his fists in a street brawl, he had never struck Florence. Although the woman drove him close to it at times with her superior airs. But that was what had attracted him to her from the first. Superior, fragile, and in need of protection. How proud he had been when she became his woman.

Nothing angered Joseph Donovan more than to have his meal late, Florence reflected. And that was not the only appetite he liked to be regularly satisfied. Few nights passed when he did not make love to Florence.

At first his passion had delighted her. He was so different from Abel Wyse. But within a few years Florence's health had begun to suffer from deprivation and the damp of the tenements. Sometimes she wished that Joseph was less attentive, his lovemaking draining her energy when she should have been resting. Yet she would never deny him. He was rough and ready, but she loved him as she had never loved her husband.

Another coughing fit tore her lungs apart. She slumped weakly against the wall and several cockroaches scurried away. Panting, she held a handkerchief to her mouth. She had never found it easy to accept the squalor in which they lived. Her meeting with Kara had only emphasised the difference of the two worlds she had inhabited.

Even so, as her gaze fell upon the Irishman, she felt a warm glow encircling her heart. Big Joe had provided for her to the best of his means. He was too fond of his ale and lost half his wages each week gambling. He was like a big kid, and between the sheets at night was still tender and loving. She knew he'd cut out his tongue before he admitted it, but Joseph loved her. Without him, she would have ended her days in the workhouse years before this.

It was he who had come to her rescue when Beatrice was ill with typhus and Abel had turned her away. There had been no lover, as Abel believed when he had thrown her out of their home. She had met a major, whose troop had been temporarily posted to Brentwood's barracks before being shipped out to India from Tilbury. He had recently lost his wife in childbirth, and had been lonely. They had met at a church social. He had flattered her and complimented her in a way Abel had never done. He was tall and handsome and his attentions turned her head. She had been unable to resist seeing him again. They had met on four occasions. All completely innocent, though the major had made no secret of his growing affection for her. At their last meeting he had kissed her. He was to march out of Brentwood the next day with his men.

Florence had been upset that he was leaving, and also fearful of the emotions he had aroused in her. She had felt ashamed. She'd wanted him to make love to her. Yet when he had suggested they take the train to Romford – where no one would recognise her – and spend the afternoon in a hotel room, she had refused. Adultery was a sin, and at the time she had been deeply religious. She could never live with the guilt if she submitted to her desire. She refused even to allow him to write to her when he was abroad.

Upon returning to Abel's house, she found her bags packed and her husband waiting for her. Someone had told him that she had twice been seen with a soldier. When she left the house that morning, Abel had paid someone to follow her. They had witnessed the kiss and reported it to him. Abel did not want to hear that she was innocent. Even to see another man was betrayal enough in his eyes.

She had no one to turn to. She could not seek out the major, whose duty was taking him to India the next day. Alone and frightened, she had fled to London. For a few months she had tried to earn a living by taking in sewing, but she was a poor seamstress. The only work she could do was to sew dishcloths, and the long hours stooped over her needle paid a pittance.

To earn enough to keep herself, she had taken also to selling flowers on the streets. On the second day, Slasher Gilbert had appeared, demanding a percentage of her takings. When she had refused, two of his bullies had trampled her stock. The same happened every day for a week. She could pay up or give up. Both options grated against her pride. When a second man from a rival protection gang thrashed her, as well as destroying her flowers, she paid Slasher Gilbert for his protection. The first lesson she had learned in her poverty was that pride was small recompense for an empty stomach and no place to sleep.

That first winter, pregnant with Beatrice, she had sold flowers in all weathers in Oxford Street. That winter had almost killed her. It was when she had first contracted the consumption which had plagued her life ever since. Her pregnancy was a difficult one. Unable to work she had faced the humiliation of life in the workhouse. The memory of the shame and degradation, of the vacant faces of people without hope, filled her mind. Those had been her darkest days.

'Where yer bin?' Big Joe cut through her thoughts.

At seeing how weak Flo appeared, Joe frowned. He felt no guilt at shouting at a sick woman. All women needed to be kept in line, and his Flo did have some hen-witted notions. It didn't do to let a woman get above herself, although he loved the frail and once beautiful Florence. Providing she did not deny him her bed, he'd never look at another woman. And there were plenty to offer it to him.

Big Joe Donovan wasn't used to much softness in his life. His mother had died in childbirth, his father was unknown. He'd been raised in an orphanage, where love was as lacking as the meals. Half-starved, he'd begun thieving at the age of five. Just food to keep himself alive at first. At eight he'd run away from the orphanage and joined a gang of urchins who thieved for Old Snappett, the hunchbacked Jew whose brother owned a pawnbroker's. Big for his size, Joe had learned to use his fists at an early age. His heavy figure was not built for fast getaways, and he soon stopped thieving when he got work in the docks. Trained as a waterman, he was proud of his work. Any extra money he needed came from keeping troublemakers out of the Gilbert brothers' gambling house.

He frowned at seeing how thin Florence had become. She was the best thing that had ever happened to him. Concern for her health made his voice gruff. 'Get a move on, woman, I'm starving.' In Joe's opinion it didn't do to let a woman see he were soft on her. They'd only take liberties. And wasn't his meal already late?

'Bea were here asking fer yer,' he added as he followed Florence into the kitchen, which was the only warm room in the house. 'She said a rat-catcher saw yer in Oxford Street. What yer doing there? You ain't on the lay, so it weren't for that.'

'I've told you I will not steal. I'd rather starve,' she said, removing her worn hat and gloves and placing them on a shelf out of harm's way.

'Yer ain't the one's who's staving, I am,' Joe grunted in reply.

When she bent to lift the large pan of peeled carrots and potatoes from the floor, he brushed her hand aside and heaved the pan on to the table.

'Yer look done in, ol' girl,' he attempted to tease, knowing as he did so that his manner was awkward. Flo, with her natural grace and soft-spoken, cultured voice, always made him feel at a disadvantage. 'God knows I picked a duff one wiv yer, ol' girl. Yer ain't got the strength of a sparrow.'

She touched his large hand. 'You've been a good man to me, Joseph.'

He grinned self-consciously, showing several gaps in his teeth where they had been knocked out in his continual fights as a waterman, or his evening work as doorman at one of Slasher Gilbert's gambling houses.

'There you are, Ma,' Beatrice flounced into the kitchen. 'Where yer bin? I've rubbed a bleeding blister in me heel searchin' fer yer.'

Florence winced at the affected roughness of her daughter's voice. Beatrice was doing it deliberately to annoy her for, when she chose, she could speak as well as Kara. Suppressing a sigh, Florence studied her younger daughter. Who'd have thought the brazen chit was only seventeen? The tight bodice of her scarlet dress decorated with black lace was cut scandalously low, revealing her full breasts almost in their entirety. Already the hardness of her nature was beginning to mar the prettiness of her heart-shaped face. The image was further spoiled by her naturally curly auburn hair, which was matted and still loose. Beatrice was fast becoming a slut, and her love of gaudy clothes offended Florence's good taste.

Her eyes were sad as they regarded the heavy cosmetics on Beatrice's face. She had tried so hard to protect her from the influences of the people around them, but how miserably she had failed. Beatrice was a night-bird, never abed until dawn. She worked in Slasher Gilbert's club. A hostess, she called herself. Florence didn't want to know what else Beatrice got up to. She'd certainly been Fancy Gilbert's mistress for some years. He was an unpleasant man with a wicked temper – thoroughly no good. Beatrice might hate her protector, but she was proud of her status as his mistress. No one crossed the Gilbert brothers. They ruled like princes in this district – not by justice, but by a reign of terror.

Poor wretch, Florence reflected. Beatrice had never had much of a chance in life. She'd even been born in the workhouse. Joseph had saved her from the horror of being raised there. He had seen Florence when he visited the waterman who had taught him his trade. An accident had severed the older man's arm, and he had ended up in the workhouse. Florence had been shivering in a corridor, her baby huddled close to her chest for warmth. Her frail beauty and story had moved Joseph. The next day he had returned and brought her to live here. His help had saved Beatrice from the typhus; after that Florence had become his mistress.

Florence sighed and lifted the covered bowl containing the half-proven bread dough which was near the fire. She made three batches every day to feed the men who lodged in the tenement. Thank God that Kara at least had been spared this poverty.

A shrill affected laugh from Beatrice brought her attention back to her younger daughter. Two of the male lodgers had entered the kitchen. One was carrying a large bundle of clothes he had stolen from someone's washing line. The continual thieving was another side of life here which Florence found hard to accept.

Beatrice sidled up to the shaggy-haired man with the stolen clothes and fingered the heavy lace on a linen petticoat. 'Nice that. Gonna let me 'ave it, Charlie darling?' She rubbed herself against the man, her fingers spread out across his patchwork waistcoat. 'Give us it, Charlie. I'll put in a good word for yer with Fancy.'

'Piss off.' Charlie shoved her aside. 'If yer wants it, yer can pay fer it.'

Beatrice scowled. 'Would yer 'ave me tell Fancy that you made a pass at me?' Beatrice said slyly, running a broken-nailed finger provocatively along Charlie's stubbled jaw. 'Fancy don't like men making passes at what he considers 'is property. 'E slit the nose of the last bugger who tried to buss me at the club.'

'Yer've tried that on before, Bea.' Charlie's thin face had paled, despite his defiance, and his small ferret's eyes shifted about the room, refusing to hold Beatrice's gaze.

'Leave Charlie alone, Beatrice,' Florence chided. 'He has to give Slasher Gilbert a quarter of what that lot's worth on the second-hand market. If you want it so much, ask Fancy to buy it for you.'

'Fancy wouldn't buy me so paltry a garment.'

Beatrice's mood changed. She sashayed across the kitchen, swinging her hips and flouncing up the hem of her skirts to show her red and black striped stockings beneath. 'Fancy says I should only wear silk against me skin.' She spread her hands over her breasts and down over her hips. 'Do yer think I should wear silk next ter me skin, Charlie?' The thief's eyes were starting from his head as he leered at her.

'Beatrice!' Florence said sharply. 'I will not have you conducting yourself in such a manner in my house.'

'Jus' teasin' the li'l bleeder, Ma.'

'And you can moderate your language when you visit me,' Florence snapped. 'I brought you up to speak like a lady, not a guttersnipe.'

'Well, I don' see no bleedin' ladies 'ere.' Her grey eyes hardened to flint and her scarlet-painted lips pouted. 'What did all me posh airs 'n' graces ever get me as a kid? Nothin' but a lot of bullyin'. Queen Bea they used to call me. Buzz, buzz, buzz, the ragged-arsed urchins would jeer. Queen Bea – bumble bee. They don' dare call me that now. Fancy would 'ave their guts for garters.'

Florence turned away from her daughter, her voice weary. 'Beatrice, if you cannot behave, please leave.' She began to cough, the pain in her chest so severe she had to grip the table for support.

Instantly Beatrice enfolded her in her arms. 'Oh, Ma, I'm sorry I upset you,' she said in a cultured voice, her manner contrite. 'Sit down. I never meant to offend you. But the devil gets into me at times. Shall I make you some tea? You don't look at all well.'

The coughing subsided and Florence took her daughter's face in her hands, her eyes bright with unshed tears of regret. 'You are so beautiful. You don't need all that awful common make-up. You speak so well you could get a good job serving in that nice Harrods store. You could better yourself. Get away from this place.'

Beatrice shook her head, her voice low enough for only her mother to hear. 'You know Fancy would never allow it. He would kill me before he let me leave. If I am no longer Queen Bee, I am at least Madam Bea. People show me respect for being Fancy Gilbert's woman. It isn't such a bad life, Ma. Not now I know how to keep Fancy sweet.'

Florence was not deceived. She saw the dark fear in her daughter's eyes. The rough cockney role she played as her armour against the knocks the world had given her. Beatrice hated her lover, but was sly enough not to show it. Fancy had raped her when she was thirteen. Because she had fought him until her strength had failed her, and even then spat expletives at him until he slapped her into semi-consciousness, he had admired her wild spirit. He had taken Beatrice into his home and locked her in for a month, forcing her to be his whore.

Florence had been distraught. She had begged Joe to save her daughter. But no one dared to cross the Gilbert brothers. They ran numerous criminal rackets, from prostitution to fencing stolen goods in this part of London. For a price, a murder could be arranged. Violence was second nature to them. Those who had tried to get the better of them ended up with their throats slit, floating in the Thames. That was how Slasher Gilbert had earned his name. And in this district it was always spoken in hushed tones.

Many women would have been broken by Fancy Gilbert's treatment. Not Beatrice. Not only had she survived, she had triumphed. For four years she had been his mistress. If Fancy Gilbert, the hardened mobster, had a chink in his armour, it was Beatrice. Thank God he had not put her on the game; though Florence knew he occasionally insisted Beatrice whore for him if the price was high enough.

The knowledge filled Florence with greater fear for her daughter. Recently, Beatrice had become too assured of her power over Fancy. If she ever overstepped the line, it would be her body floating in the Thames.

As the day for Kara's meeting with Mrs Henshawe approached, she became increasingly nervous.

'There's nothing to worry about,' Richard said, laughing as she picked at the fringe of her black shawl as they drove to the shop in Holborn. 'Sophia Henshawe will adore you. How could she not?'

He had returned yesterday from his visit to York; this was the first time they had been alone together. His presence added to her unease. Each jolt of the carriage threw their bodies into contact with each other, and she longed to be taken into his arms. Vainly, she tried to block the wanton path of her thoughts. If she didn't curb her feelings for Richard, she would go mad.

When his hand came down over hers to still her fidgeting, she gasped softly. A thrill of pleasure sped through her body. For a moment their gazes held, and the tenderness and admiration in his eyes made her heart beat frantically. She struggled to overcome the effect his nearness was having upon her emotions.

'I have a lot to be thankful to you for, Richard.' She made her voice sound cool. 'If Mrs Henshawe agrees to our partnership, I will move in with her as soon as I can.'

The gravity of his stare deepened and he smiled, wryly. 'The house will not be the same without you. We will all miss you, even Mama. I'm glad you took no heed of her banishment and continued to work with the unmarried mothers. I had a letter from her whilst in York. She admitted that she had been too hasty in condemning you. You've charmed her and won her over. There has been nothing but praise for your work by the other members of the hostel committee.'

Kara laughed. 'Charmed is not the word I'd use to describe my effect on your mother. She tolerates me because you insist that she does. She's still at Richmond, isn't she? She won't return to Belgravia until I leave your house. Still, her views are unimportant. I sympathised with the unmarried mothers. Not all of them are prostitutes. Some are barely in their teens and have been raped by lodgers, or abused by friends of the family. Some were even sold at the age of eleven to a brothel.' She blushed. 'Have I shocked you by speaking so openly on such a delicate subject?'

'You're not a hypocrite, Kara. That's what I like about you.'

'I wish I could do more for those women. So many of the grand ladies who purport to show them compassion are only on the committee as a matter of duty.' They despise those poor women. The inmates don't want pity. They want help to rebuild their lives. So many think that the only way they can support themselves is as a prostitute. Many hate the life. Perhaps when I'm not so involved in starting my business, I'll be able to do more for them... The conditions in those places are barbaric. The women are treated like dirt because of their condition. I don't agree with that.'

He lifted her hand to his lips and kissed it. A pang of yearning swelled in her breast. It took all her willpower to draw her hand away and lower her gaze.

'You cannot right every wrong in the world on your own, Kara.'

'I know. You must think me very foolish the way I prattle on.'

'I don't think you foolish at all. Rather the opposite in fact.'

At the tenderness in his voice, her pulse raced, almost stifling her. 'Richard, you should not talk that way.'

'I thought you respected frankness between friends?'

'I do.'

'And we are friends, are we not, Kara?'

The taunt held both a barb and a challenge. 'I would like to believe so. But in the way that Elizabeth is my friend.'

The carriage had halted before Henshawe's Stationer's, and with relief Kara alighted.

Sophia Henshawe was surrounded by three of her four daughters as the maid led them into the widow's parlour. 'Take Rose, Violet and Iris to the nursery, Sarah.' Sophia addressed her maid. 'I do not wish to be disturbed until Mr Tennent has left.'

The girls, aged between three and eight, filed demurely from the room. They were entrancing children: cherub-faced, all were dressed alike in a lilac dress with a white frilled pinafore; their blonde hair, adorned with a large purple bow, was curled into ringlets.

'Mrs Henshawe, may I present Miss Kara Wyse?' Richard introduced them. 'I explained her interest in becoming your partner in my letter. I hope today we can come to an amicable agreement which will benefit you both.'

'You have three lovely girls,' Kara said as she held her hand out to the tall, amply proportioned woman who had risen to her feet. Mrs Henshawe's face was plain but kindly, surprising Kara that she had produced such beautiful girls, though they all had her thick blonde hair.

'They are the joy of my life, as is my baby Heather.' She had a light breathless voice and her blue eyes were looking at Kara with approval. Some of Kara's nervousness left her. She felt an instant rapport with the widow, whom she guessed to be in her early thirties. There was a warmth and serenity about her which Kara found appealing.

'I hope we can come to some arrangement, Mrs Henshawe,' she said, her enthusiasm obvious in her wish to convince the woman. 'Your late husband's business is exactly what I need to invest my capital in. I will work hard to make it prosper. I know I can make it work, if you give me the chance.'

Sophia Henshawe became visibly flustered. 'Oh dear, I don't wish to disappoint you. I had decided upon selling it and moving to a smaller house. It's such a worry. Such a responsibility.'

Richard had moved to the fireplace and was studying the two women seated either side of him. 'It is wiser to keep your capital intact, Mrs Henshawe,' he advised. 'I thought you were happy here, where you are close to your friends.'

'It would be a wrench to leave them.' Mrs Henshawe sighed. 'But would it be fair on Miss Wyse to become her partner? I could not have the worry of running a business. Though I would serve in the shop as I did when my dear Basil was alive. You meet so many nice people that way.'

'I would not expect more from you, Mrs Henshawe,' Kara insisted. 'I've learnt a great deal about the business in the meetings Mr Tennent arranged for me with accountants, publishers and shop managers. One retired manager gave up hours of his time to painstakingly explain everything I needed to know. Mr Tennent has kindly offered to advise us whenever we may need it.'

Mrs Henshawe became more distressed. 'I simply do not know what to do. I am torn this way then that. The responsibility seems so great.'

Kara came out of her chair and smiled down at Sophia Henshawe. 'I know it will work. I will not fail you.'

'You are so convinced and so determined,' Sophia said but her eyes remained troubled. 'But you are so young. Shouldn't you be devoting all that passion to marrying and bringing up children?'

'There is time for that later. I want my own business. I want to keep my financial independence if ever I marry. Please, give me the chance to prove myself. You will not regret it, I promise.'

Sophia looked up at Richard.

'I have every faith that Miss Wyse will succeed in this venture,' he answered her unspoken query.

Sophia considered them both and then, with a sigh, said, 'With both of you so determined, how can I say no?'

'I will make it a success, Mrs Henshawe,' Kara said excitedly. 'I have so many plans.'

'And Mr Tennent also suggested that you take the upper rooms of the house,' Sophia added. 'It would be companionship for me in the evenings to have a young woman in the house I can talk with. But won't you find sharing a house with my four noisy children a strain?'

'I was brought up as an only child, and always longed for brothers and sisters. After the long hours in the shop, it will be a comfort to have the friendly atmosphere here to return to.'

'Then it is agreed.' Sophia rang a handbell on the table at her side. 'We will celebrate with a glass of sherry.'

The weeks before the shop opened passed swiftly. Papers were drawn up and signed. Each day Kara visited the shop. She had hired two lads to help her rearrange the shelves for the opening next Saturday, and new stationery stock was ordered. Carpenters were engaged to build bookshelves in one-third of the shop, and an archway was constructed to segregate that part of the business from the stationery. Comfortable leather-upholstered chairs were put in the reading room for the benefit of browsing customers. Having written to all the leading publishers for their book lists, Kara carefully selected her titles of good quality novels and works of non-fiction. When she returned each evening to the Tennents' house, she was tired, but with a feeling of growing excitement and satisfaction as the opening day approached.

On the evening before she was due to take up residence with Mrs Henshawe, it was arranged that Elizabeth, Richard and herself would attend the opera. Elizabeth had not had an attack for some weeks, and it was at her insistence that Richard purchased tickets. Kara, who had never been to the opera, was thrilled at the prospect.

She left the stationery shop in the late afternoon, to ensure she had plenty of time to dress for such a grand occasion. When she arrived at the Tennent house, Mary stopped her in the hall.

'Mrs Tennent is resting on her husband's instructions. She was becoming very excitable, and he feared an attack.'

'Then I will not disturb her,' Kara said. She was concerned that the evening's entertainment would be too much for Elizabeth.

When Kara had signed the contract with Sophia Henshawe, she had planned to move in with her the same evening. Elizabeth had protested. She had been so upset that Kara had delayed leaving Belgravia until the end of the week. It had added to the strain knowing that Richard was so close. He had stayed away from his home in the evenings so that they would not be thrown into each other's company. Yet twice when Kara lay abed, she had heard him return in the early hours of the morning. Kara had lain sleepless, her body burning with desire. She was wracked by guilt that she yearned to be made love to by another's woman's husband.

Tonight she could enjoy Richard's company with the protection of Elizabeth in attendance. It would be a bitter-sweet torture, but one she would not miss for the world. After the opera they were to dine at Rossini's in Soho, a newly opened restaurant which was fast becoming the most popular in London.

When Kara entered her room, she saw that laid out on the bed was another black mourning dress which had been adapted for evening wear. Tonight was special. She did not want to go to the opera in mourning. It was three months since Papa had died. She was going to enjoy herself tonight and wear something cheerful, not depressing.

She pulled the bellrope. When Mary appeared she held out the oyster silk gown she had worn at her betrothal. It was the only suitable gown she had. Even though that also had unhappy memories attached to it, it was better than the black she was beginning to hate. Last week she had considered having a new gown made, then decided against it. Until the shop proved a success, she must be careful how she spent what little was left of her capital.

'Mary, will you please have this pressed for me to wear this evening? I do not intend to wear mourning any longer.'

A light snack had been left in her room, and she smiled at Mary when the maid came to help her dress. Mary left her to assist Elizabeth, and Kara finished arranging her hair so that it was piled high on her head in soft, honey-coloured curls. Several ringlets fell over her bare shoulders. To adorn her hair she had treated herself to two orchids: these she secured on one side above her ear. As she stared at her image in the mirror she was satisfied with the effect. She could never match Elizabeth in beauty, but her excitement had brought a beguiling sparkle to her violet eyes and her hairstyle flattered her high cheekbones. Picking up her cream Indian silk shawl, she left her room just as Mary came out of Elizabeth's bedchamber.

'The mistress would like a word with you, Miss Kara.'

Kara entered Elizabeth's room, and was con-erned to see the gaslight turned down low. Her friend was lying on the bed in her nightclothes.

'Elizabeth, are you not well?'
'So silly of me,' she answered faintly. 'I've the headache. All the excitement of this evening must have brought it on. You must still go.'
'No, I will stay with you. We could not possibly leave you on your own when you are feeling so ill.'
'Please, Kara, go with Richard. He loves the opera. I do not particularly. It is all too loud – too unrestrained. I could not rest knowing I had ruined your evening. I have already told Richard that you must go, and also to dine afterwards. He has agreed.'
Still Kara hesitated.
'Kara, you look beautiful. You've even come out of mourning for tonight. I'll feel wretched if I know I've ruined it for you. You must go. It will be a night you'll always remember.'
It would indeed be a night she would remember, Kara speculated. An evening alone with Richard at the opera, and then an intimate supper in a hotel restaurant would fulfil her wildest yearnings.

Chapter Nine

As Kara descended the stairs, Richard came out of his study. In his black frock coat, slim-fitting trousers and white waistcoat embroidered with silver thread, he cut a handsome figure. The admiration in his eyes as he watched her approach robbed Kara of breath.

'You look enchanting,' he said smiling. 'I'm glad you're no longer wearing mourning. Pale colours suit you.'

'Thank you. I've just seen Elizabeth. I feel guilty about leaving her when she is unwell.'

'She is no lover of the opera. It's better that she rests. Besides, Mary will sit with her.'

There was impatience in his voice, and Kara guessed that a man of Richard's good health and athleticism must be irked by a wife's continual malaise. Kara carried a sapphire velvet cloak over her arm and, as she was about to drape it around her shoulders, he stopped her movement by taking her arm.

'Lovely as you look, there is something missing.' He drew from his pocket the wide pearl choker she had given him to sell. 'I could not allow you to part with all your jewels. Especially as you still have money in the account from the Holman settlement.'

'But the recent expenditure on stock: surely there was little money left once Papa's debts were settled?'

'More than enough. The property got a better price than we had hoped. There's about a thousand pounds left.'

'So much!' Kara was about to throw her arms around Richard with gratitude but managed to check herself. 'I can help Mama now. And the business ... I need not have gone into partnership with Sophia. But of course I would not now consider buying her out: she needs the income from the shop. It will mean I can consider buying another sooner than I anticipated.'

Richard laughed. 'Steady on. One step at a time. I am sure the stationery and bookshop will be a great success. But it is best to wait and see how well it does before considering expanding.'

'I could not have achieved any of it without you.' Her voice dropped. As she held his tender gaze she wished her heart would not somersault so crazily.

He moved behind her and she held her breath as he fastened the clasp of the pearl choker. The warmth of his fingers on her neck caused a thrill of pleasure to pass through her. It took all her will-power not to sway back against him. His fingers lingered for a fraction longer upon the bare skin of her shoulders before he took her cloak from her and placed it about them. He then held out a small leather case.

'Please accept these as they are intended, as a goodwill present to a friend on the start of her new business venture.'

Opening the case, she gasped at seeing a pair of long pearl earrings. 'It is too generous, Richard,' she said, softly. 'It would not be right for me to accept them.'

'I insist. You should always do as your solicitor tells you.'

She hesitated, unwilling to offend him. 'I will wear them tonight, but I cannot keep them.'

His eyes smiled into hers. 'Stubborn and tenacious. You should go far in business, Kara.'

He picked up his top hat and opera cloak lined with white silk. 'Come, we would not wish to be late.'

From the moment their carriage drew to a halt before Her Majesty's Theatre in the Haymarket, Kara fell under the spell of the opera. As they neared the brightly lit frontage, Kara's gaze was drawn to the chestnut- and flower-sellers by the kerb. A man with a drum strapped to his back, and several other instruments fixed to his knees and sides, strutted up and down the pavement, performing a popular music-hall song. When Richard helped her alight on to the pavement, her excitement was momentarily abated at the sight of a skinny woman with a baby clutched to her breast.

'Sixpence, sir. Sixpence to feed meself and the child.'

When Richard made to move past her, Kara whispered, 'Can you not spare a sixpence when you have given me pearls tonight worth fifty guineas.'

'The woman is a professional beggar,' Richard said tersely. 'She hires the child by the week. It's gin she wants for her belly, not milk for the babe. Whilst stopping to throw a coin to her, I'd likely have my fob-watch lifted by a pickpocket. Not the common type, but well-dressed men who specialise in robbing the wealthy of their valuables in such surroundings.'

'And what of the matchgirl over there? Look, her feet are bare and blue with cold and her shawl is in holes. She can't be more than ten.'

Richard flipped a florin into the matchgirl's tray. Few of the other opera-goers even glanced in the girl's direction. They were too busy calling out to acquaintances to care about the unfortunates reduced to beggary on the London streets.

Once inside the theatre, Richard guided Kara through the throng and settled her in a private box. The horseshoe-shaped auditorium buzzed with conversation. The huge chandeliers picked out the sparkle of diamonds laden upon the throats and necks of women. As Kara studied the audience she was surprised that, in many of the private boxes, older men were accompanied by beautiful and elegantly attired women. She averted her eyes, belatedly realising that they were courtesans, the men their paramours.

Several men inclined their heads in greeting to Richard, and Kara saw their stares flick speculatively over herself. A blush rose to her cheeks. Did they think her Richard's mistress? She drew back into the shadows and concentrated on the programme for the evening.

'Is something wrong, Kara?' Richard asked with concern.

She could not tell him of her fears. 'I was wondering how Elizabeth was,' she evaded.

'How like you to be so considerate of others. Most people would be too interested in their own pleasure to care.' The admiration in his voice brought a return of heat to her face. It was an admiration she did not deserve at that moment. Though she had wondered about Elizabeth during the carriage ride, she could not banish from her mind the memory of his kiss. Now the memory was like a burning ember igniting her passions and destroying her self-control.

'Don't attribute to me virtues I do not possess,'

she countered, trying to conquer the spell of his nearness. When he leaned sideways to talk above the noise of the audience, their shoulders touched. She desperately strove to ignore the warmth permeating her body.

The orchestra struck up the overture and the lights gradually dimmed. Kara stared straight ahead, her body stingingly aware of Richard's closeness. She struggled to close her mind to it and concentrate on the tenor who was singing. Within minutes the magic of the opera began to captivate her. Her gaze never left the stage until the curtain came down for the interval. Her heart was beating fast, roused by the passion of the story and by the sheer spectacle of the music and singing. Her eyes were half closed as she savoured the closing aria, the pure notes still thrumming through her mind.

'The lady approves of Mozart's *Marriage of Figaro*,' Richard said with amusement.

'I have never seen, or heard, anything like it. It is breathtaking.'

'Then we shall come to the opera again.'

The tender way Richard was looking at her filled her with forbidden longing. 'I will be happy to accompany you and Elizabeth,' she forced out, fighting to control the yearning to succumb to the temptation he offered. 'I'd not encourage gossip by being seen alone with you again.'

'You are here as a friend of the family. What could be more natural? All my acquaintances know Elizabeth has little love for the opera, whilst I adore it. Why deny yourself such an innocent pleasure?'

'But is it so innocent, Richard?'

Immediately his expression shuttered, a barrier drawing down between them. Its effect was to make Kara feel as if she had been caught in an icy shower of rain. Had she misinterpreted Richard's kindness for a deeper interest? Had his kiss the other evening been spontaneous, and now he regretted it? Was she reading too much into mere sophisticated flirtation? She had lived such a sheltered life, how could she know?

The clamour of voices in the theatre rose as people began to circulate during the interval. There was a knock on the door of their box. A liveried servant appeared carrying an icebox containing a bottle of champagne.

Richard poured her a glass. 'Relax and enjoy the evening, Kara,' he said, but his eyes said so much more as they held her gaze. Desire – love – pain – regret.

She knew that her love for him must be emblazoned in her eyes, and to cover her confusion she sipped at the champagne. Their desire could never be expressed in either words or deeds. As their gaze held, she saw a pulse beat in Richard's jaw, and barely caught his soft groan and broken whisper.

'God, what a mess.'

As she regarded him there was a slight stiffening to his shoulders, and the shutter again drew across his eyes, shielding their expression. There was a wryness to his smile when he lifted his champagne glass. 'What shall we toast? Friendship! Happiness!'

'Success,' she suggested tautly. 'Let us drink to

the pleasure of this evening. A special evening I shall never forget.'

The door to their box opened and several men entered.

'Richard, my dear fellow,' a blond man greeted him effusively. 'I couldn't believe it when Rogers said it was you.'

'Toby.' Richard stood up and clasped his friend's hand. 'I've not seen you in an age. May I present Miss Kara Wyse, a client and a friend of the family who is staying with Elizabeth and myself. I suspect that it's her pretty face, and not my grizzled one, which brings you to our box.' He joked affably as he continued to introduce Kara to the other men. One had stayed in the shadows, and he stepped forward as Richard was completing the introductions. For some moments the two men appraised each other warily.

Toby chuckled. 'I forgot, Richard, you don't know Morton, recently back from India!'

Richard bowed stiffly.

'Captain Zach Morton, at your service, sir.'

At Kara's astonished gasp, Richard regarded her with puzzlement.

She smiled, flustered. 'Richard, Captain Morton is the man who came to my rescue when my bag was stolen in Hyde Park.'

'Then I am obliged to you, Captain Morton.' There was a chilliness to Richard's voice which startled Kara.

A bell sounded, warning that the opera was about to recommence. As the other men filed from the room, Captain Morton bowed to Kara.

'I trust you have recovered from your ordeal, Miss Wyse.'

'Yes. Your kindness was most appreciated.'

There was a merry twinkle in his admiring gaze. 'I've been making inquiries about the woman you met in the park,' he added. 'I've a meeting tomorrow with a man who believes he knows where she lives. He's checking his facts. May I call upon you and give you this information?'

Richard extracted a business card from his waistcoat pocket. 'You may call at my office, Captain Morton. I deal with all Miss Wyse's affairs.'

Kara was stung by Richard's abrupt manner. He appeared to have taken an instant dislike to the officer.

'Captain, I will be at Henshawe & Wyse stationer's all tomorrow. It is in Oxford Street,' she said, to ease the affront to his generous gesture. 'I am a partner in the business and we reopen in two days. Please call on me there when it is convenient to you.'

'It will be my pleasure, Miss Wyse.' He clicked his heels and raised her hand to his lips before departing.

'Kara, I am surprised you encourage that man,' Richard said stiffly. 'I don't altogether trust him. There's something about his manner.'

Over the top of her champagne glass she smiled at Richard. 'Captain Morton was courteous when he came to my assistance in the park. The man you employed to search for my mother has not discovered her address. What harm can it do if Captain Morton wishes to help? I shall be quite safe in the shop with the other assistants present.'

'I am your solicitor, not your guardian.'

She could see he was struggling to control his feelings, and her heart pounded wildly. Clearly Richard resented the captain's attentions towards her.

The lights went down and the pure notes of a soprano halted any further conversation as the opera recommenced. Kara could feel a tension in Richard which lasted until they were in the carriage which was taking them to Rossini's restaurant. Kara had drunk three glasses of champagne during the performance and now she chatted brightly about the opera, hoping to dispel his gloomy mood.

At last she sighed dramatically. 'You haven't heard a word I've said, Richard. It seems pointless going to a restaurant if you are so lost in thought that...'

'Elizabeth will be upset thinking we have returned early because of her illness,' he said tautly. 'She wanted this evening to be special for you. I had not meant to be morose. The opera was delightful, was it not?'

In the dim carriage light, she saw the warmth in his smile and wished her heart would not beat so fast. She did not want the evening to end, but at the same time she was aware of the danger of being in his company.

Richard resumed his usual teasing banter until they reached Rossini's. Kara was surprised at its intimate atmosphere. Ruby velvet curtains shaded secluded alcoves and her feet sank into the thick ruby carpet. They were led past the main dining area to one of several doors leading off from a corridor. The private dining room was almost decadent in its opulence. Sapphire and gold brocade draped the walls. The carpet here was of palest amber. There was even a day bed in one corner of the room.

'I had not realised we were to dine alone,' she said guardedly.

'I booked this room for Elizabeth's benefit. If she was overcome by too much excitement, she could rest here without attracting attention. As you see, the table is set for three. If you wish, I will see if there is a table free in the main dining room, but I doubt it. The restaurant is always booked up days ahead.'

Feeling foolish that she had made such a fuss, Kara shrugged. It had been thoughtfulness for his wife's health which had prompted him to take a private room. 'I have never dined alone with a gentleman before. Will people not talk?'

'The waiters are paid well for their discretion. But if you do not trust me, Kara…'

It was not him she did not trust, but her own wayward feelings. They were making her over-react. He had come to stand close behind her, his hands on her cloak waiting to remove it from her shoulders. She could feel the warmth of his breath on her neck, and briefly closed her eyes to combat its sensual effect. She knew she should insist that they leave, but the opportunity to have this one intimate meal with Richard was too much of a temptation to resist. A meal was innocent enough, was it not?

She smiled and allowed him to remove her cloak, saying, 'I would not spoil your evening. It was generous of you and Elizabeth to take so much trouble on my account.'

He smiled enigmatically. The affection she saw in his eyes was both her joy and her torment. It was wrong to be so attracted to this man. She must never forget that he was Elizabeth's husband.

To cover her confusion she moved to the dining table. He was there before her, holding out her chair. Then he rang the bell and two waiters entered. One wheeled in a trolley containing several silver tureens, and the other carried two bottles of champagne resting in an ice-bucket.

'I took the liberty of ordering beforehand. You said duck was a special favourite of yours. The way they prepare it here with a spicy sauce is sensational. I hope you will enjoy it.'

'I'm sure I shall. That was thoughtful of you, Richard.'

Kara was feeling light-headed from the champagne she had already drunk, and resolved not to drink more than one more glass. The waiter placed before each of them a salmon mousse moulded into the shape of a small fish. When he hovered by the food trolley, Richard waved him away, pressing a guinea in each of the waiters' hands. 'We will serve ourselves and ring if we require anything further.'

The salmon looked delicious, but as Kara raised her fork to her mouth she found her throat was dry and cramped with nervousness. Forcing herself to eat it, she found it impossible to swallow.

'You do not like the mousse?' Richard asked. 'I thought it was also a favourite of yours.'

'It's delicious.' As she met his gaze, her voice froze and she felt like a tongue-tied schoolgirl. For what seemed an eternity they regarded each other without speaking.

Richard raised his champagne glass in a toast. 'To the success of your new venture.'

She was thirsty and had drunk half the glass before she realised it. A troubled shadow remained in the depths of Richard's eyes.

'Are you annoyed with me for agreeing to see Captain Morton?'

An anguished groan was torn from him and he pushed aside his plate. 'What right have I to be annoyed? None whatsoever. I'm a married man. I don't want you to waste your life. But I can't bear to see another man looking at you as Morton did.'

'Then it is as well that I am leaving your house.' She swallowed against the tightness in her throat, her tongue moistening her lips. A gesture unintentionally provocative, and revealing her nervousness.

'I can't stop thinking of you, Kara.'

'Richard, please don't talk that way.' She stood up quickly and the sudden movement made her head swim. She put a hand to her temple to check the swaying of her body. She should not have drunk so much champagne. A covert glance at Richard showed him watching her intently. His face so ruggedly handsome in the gaslight. A lock of wayward brown hair fell over his brow in the way she loved. Her heart twisted with longing.

She would not ruin this special evening together by reflecting on a love which could never be fulfilled. A bright smile animated her face, and her eyes sparkled as she remembered the heady thrill she had felt at the opera. She twirled around, her hands crossed over her heart as she hummed one of the arias.

'Tonight was wonderful,' she said, light-headed from both the wine and the intoxication of Richard's presence. 'I wanted to lose myself in the music. I can hear it still, throbbing through my mind. But why are all the sopranos and tenors who play the leads so huge?'

She giggled, blowing out her cheeks and waddling across the room as the soprano had done during a love song. 'They could barely get their arms around each other their girths were so vast.' She mimicked the two singers, laughing as she held her arms wide and pretended to be the soprano holding the tenor in a passionate embrace.

She knew the champagne had affected her and was making her reckless, but she wanted to lighten the mood and didn't care. Her laughter trilled and, with eyes bright with mischief, she exaggerated another scene, her pulse racing as she heard Richard's deep laughter mix with hers.

'The singing was superb,' she added, 'but the acting. It was so overdone at times, it was almost comical. When the heroine swooned and threw herself on to her bed in a fit of melancholy like this…' She put a hand to her brow and collapsed theatrically on to the day bed, emulating the soprano.

Richard threw back his head, his laughter unrestrained. 'You know I actually saw the bed shudder when she did that,' he cut into her play-acting. 'I thought it was going to collapse.'

Kara sighed happily, savouring the pleasure of their laughter. Richard looked relaxed after the strain on his face from recent weeks. They really did have so much in common – even humour. How different her few weeks in his home had been from her dour existence in Brentwood. She felt reborn, more confident and assured, and she owed it all to him.

She lay her head back on the couch. 'Even so, the opera was magnificent. I can't remember ever enjoying myself so much.'

'Neither can I. It's good to see you shed the inhibitions your father imposed on you.'

She lifted her head to rise and was shocked when her vision swirled and a wave of dizziness made her head flop back. She giggled, pushing herself to her feet and swaying slightly. 'Oh dear, I've had too much champagne. I've been acting childishly.'

He shook his head. 'Why stifle your joy of life, Kara? It's infectious. Don't ever change. But yes, I do think you have had a little too much champagne.'

Richard was at her side, his arms steadying her, smiling tenderly in a way which made her heart tumble crazily. As he gazed into her eyes, Kara's love for him was overwhelming. The strength of his arms around her was destroying her calm. His nearness quickened her pulse, stirring the passion in her blood as it coursed through her veins. She tried to hold on to her reason, to remember that this was her friend's husband. But the warmth of his body, standing so close, and the fragrance of his musky cologne and skin pervaded her senses. Reason deserted her. It was her intention to pull away. Somehow her body was caught in a web of enchantment, held immobile, with no will of its own.

Their gazes locked as they both battled to overcome the inevitable. For a moment their wills triumphed. They were barely touching. Unbidden, their bodies were inexorably drawn together. It acted like a catalyst, and the desire in his eyes was answered in hers, resistance swamped by the floodtide of consuming passion.

'Kara, my darling,' he said hoarsely.

She was trembling like a fawn scenting danger. The magnitude of the desire which consumed him was like a dam bursting. His need to possess her, to make her fully his own, clouded reason. His blood, volcanic in heat, was demanding her submission to his will. His senses were enslaved by her slender, inviting figure. The gaslight turned her hair to molten gold. Eyes of sultry indigo beckoned with seductive promise. The beguiling enticement of her perfumed body, just within his reach, drove him beyond control. He teetered precariously on the edge of a precipice, honour deserting him, toppled by the love which would give him no peace.

Then his lips were on hers, tender, insistent, his tongue tracing the outline of her mouth and parting her lips. His thumb traced a lazy circle upon her throat, easing her head back so that she was looking into his eyes which were heavy-lidded with desire.

'Kara, my love, my love,' he murmured against her hair until her blood beat to the compulsive rhythm of the words. Where her fingers touched his skin they tingled with awareness of his strength and masculinity. His passionate kiss shattered her high intentions as she surrendered to the sweetness of his ardour.

When he drew back, she gasped, feeling bereft.

'I will lock the door,' he said huskily. 'We will not be disturbed.'

Her eyes widened with shock. 'This is a place of assignation!'

'No harm will come to your reputation,' he said as the key turned in the lock and he again gathered her close. 'Rossini's has built its reputation on discretion. Private business meetings also take place within these secluded rooms. In the main dining room many respectable families are dining tonight. Yet here, if we wish it, we will have our privacy.'

His lips were upon her throat, destroying her will to resist. 'Don't deny me, my darling,' he whispered.

Then his lips returned to claim hers. His kiss deepened. His tongue enticed with honeyed seduction, expertly cajoling and inciting, rousing her body to fire, casting her into a maelstrom of desire which banished coherent thought.

With a soft moan, her passionate nature, so long suppressed, blossomed like flowers in the desert after the first rainfall. His mouth continued its sensual caress over her feverish skin, and he eased the narrow shoulder of her low-necked gown down over her arm. Her senses were spiralling, her mind drugged by the magic he was weaving. He had become the centre of her universe. Logic and restraint were overwhelmed by the storm of her enlightened sensuality. It bathed her in its radiance, blinding reason as the emotions that neither could any longer deny consumed them in a building furnace.

Kara surrendered to the ecstasy. Their kisses deepened and were unending, until every shred of restraint had been demolished.

When he released her breasts from their flimsy covering, his fingers teasing the hardening crest, a moan of pleasure sighed deep in her throat. His head bowed, following the path of his hand, and her flesh burned where each kiss laid its fiery imprint.

'Oh, Richard, I love you.'

'I love you, Kara. I want you. Need you so badly,' he sighed as he reverently slid his hands up her satin skin to touch her hair. Deftly he removed the pins, and watched it tumble in a glorious honey-gold mantle about her shoulders and hips.

Under the spell of his seductive lovemaking, Kara closed her eyes. She could feel the heat of his adoring gaze as unfaltering kisses continued to besiege her senses. Her heart was pounding wildly as he lifted her tenderly into his arms and carried her to the day bed.

'Kara, my love.' A muffled groan escaped him as he pressed her deeper in to the cushions.

A liquid heat fanned through her veins. Her

throat ached with the force of her longing. Beneath her petticoats his hand caressed the bare flesh of her thigh. She moaned in building pleasure, her body writhing with the exquisite joy of his caresses. When his mouth again captured her breasts, gently sucking their peaks, she gasped in breathless rapture. A sensuous flame scorched the centre of her being. Her fingers spread in his thick dark hair as she cried out. Then his hands were on her thighs, gently easing them apart. There was an explosion of nerve-tingling sensation as he continued to caress her. The movement of his fingers created a mind-searing sensation that melted the central core of her into a river of fire.

Lost in the throes of passion, Kara moved to the building rhythm. Body and soul writhed in abandon. She whispered his name, wanting him to make her irrevocably his.

He rose above her, bracing himself before penetrating her.

'Don't stop, Richard,' she moaned. 'Please, don't stop now.'

Kara gasped at the sharp jab of pain and froze.

'My darling, the pain is fleeting,' he murmured, withholding his own pleasure until she was ready to succumb completely to his will.

Slowly he began to move. The resistance gave, and Kara felt her body contract with heat as he slid deep inside her. A ravening hunger drove her to match his thrusts. Her body arched up to meet his and he guided her legs up around his waist. Nothing had prepared her for the explosion of sensation, as magical as stardust, cascading through her loins. With a shudder Richard made to withdraw. Kara cried out in dismay. Her legs and arms wound tightly around him, holding him captive as his seed spilled into her.

'I had meant to spare you that,' he said, kissing her tenderly.

'But it was so glorious, I did not want it to end.' Kara's eyes were still misty with passion. She gazed lovingly up at him, her face at the centre of a halo of golden hair spread over her pillow.

He had never felt such euphoric satisfaction, and he hoped that Kara would not pay the price for the innocence of her passion.

'I can't let you go, Kara. I love you too much. I'll make arrangements for us to meet in private,' he said, kissing the damp curl above her ear. 'We cannot deny what was meant to be.'

Kara started at the implication of his words. Richard expected to keep her as his mistress. The spell was shattered by guilty reality. How could she so cold-bloodedly betray Elizabeth? The heat cooled in her blood and her palm pushed against his chest, easing him away. Tears of regret sparkled on her lashes as she swallowed against the pain which was threatening to destroy her.

'It cannot be, Richard. This was a glorious moment, but we cannot allow our passion to rule our heads. It is wrong of us to betray Elizabeth.'

She felt a shudder go through his fingers and he cupped her face in his fingers. 'I'm trapped in marriage to a woman I pity, but cannot love. Darling Kara, why didn't I meet you before I married Elizabeth?'

'I would only have been fifteen, and still an

awkward schoolgirl.' She attempted a weak jest. Sitting up, she pushed her petticoats down over her legs and covered her breasts from his gaze.

'What have we done, Richard? I never meant to fall in love with you. I never meant to betray Elizabeth.'

Richard frowned blackly. 'Neither did I. I never loved her as I love you. She was a beautiful girl, alone and vulnerable after her grandmother's death. I'd known her for years and was drawn to protect her.'

'You are a romantic – an idealist,' Kara said tenderly, her speech crackling from the pain of her heartache. 'She is your wife and she adores you. Once you must have cared for her.'

Kara forced herself to be cruel, to build a barrier between them. It was a barrier of gossamer at the moment, but she was determined to strengthen it until it was as hard as concrete.

Rising to her feet, she turned her back on him and adjusted her clothing, her voice strained with returning guilt. 'Because Elizabeth is an invalid, it does not excuse our love, or the wrong we do her. If she did not love you, then perhaps my conscience would be easier. She worships you, Richard. If she learns that we are lovers, it will devastate her.'

She was fighting to keep back her tears. There was a harsh expulsion of breath as he came to stand behind her.

'Do you know to what you are condemning us, my darling?' he began.

She faced him and put a finger to his lips. It was impossible to keep the pain and yearning from her voice. 'You know what I say is the only course possible. I will never forget this night. A perfect night of love and happiness. But it was built on the foundations of another's misery. And you must think of your career. If ever it became known that you had had an affair with a client, you would be dishonoured and ruined.'

She moved away to look in the mirror, repinning her hair into place. When they again faced each other, his face could have been carved from marble, so effectively had he erased from it any emotion.

'Kara, I do love you. Never doubt that.'

For several moments, in silence, his gaze scanned her face as though memorising each precious detail. 'It is my marriage which is a lie, not what I feel for you. But you are right. Elizabeth deserves better than our betrayal of her trust.'

He held her close and kissed her tenderly, but without passion, then said, 'You are worthy of so much more than being any man's mistress. I love you too much to shame you. You must make new friends. But not Morton,' he insisted. 'I don't trust the fellow.'

She smiled indulgently. 'I don't believe it's possible I will love anyone as I love you, Richard.'

He touched her cheek, his expression tender. 'I wish I could do the honourable thing and marry you. The scandal of divorce would be worth it. But it would kill Elizabeth.'

'I don't regret tonight.' Her eyes sparkled with tears she was too proud to let fall. 'I shall treasure it the more, because it cannot be repeated.'

Chapter Ten

Beatrice lay back on the rumpled bed and regarded her lover drowsily. Fancy Gilbert stood before the oval mirror with its ornate gilt surround, and adjusted the fall of his red cravat. Finally satisfied, he pulled down the points of his gold brocade waistcoat. He then sleeked a hand through his sandy-gold, curly cap of hair. The only attractive feature about Fancy was his hair, and he was inordinately proud of it. His brown eyes narrowed as he turned his face from side to side. He had a long, hooked, broken nose, and thick straight brows which met over its bridge. Two of his front teeth were missing and a scar on his top lip, from a knife fight, gave him a perpetual sneer. Another scar disfigured his cheek. At thirty-one his stocky figure had become so stout that he had taken to wearing a whalebone corset under his elaborate waistcoats. As he leaned forward to flick a thread of white cotton from his fawn and green checked cutaway jacket, Beatrice heard the corset creak.

She did not laugh. No one laughed at Fancy Gilbert's dandified looks. Any flicker of emotion other than respect, or cringing obedience, was met with a violent attack. Fancy was not Slasher's right-hand man – and partner in organising the underworld gang of criminals and second-rate clubs – on the strength of brotherly love. He'd earned that right by being the second cruellest bastard in the district after Slasher.

As he pulled on his gloves to cover his stubby, freckled hands, Fancy bent over Beatrice, his eyes hardening as he gripped her chin and stared down at her.

'Yer were wonderful,' she said dutifully, and feigned a contented sigh. 'Such a vigorous lover. I'm all worn out, me darlin'.'

He laughed, satisfied. 'I want yer ter sing at the club this evenin'. Make sure yer play up ter the toffs and keep 'em sweet and buyin' the best champagne whilst they're gamblin'. But no goin' off wiv any of 'em. Not unless I says so, and then they'll be paying 'igh for the pleasure.'

Beatrice smiled enticingly. 'There ain't no one to compare with yerself, Fancy.'

He paused at the door, his expression brutal. 'Get orf yer arse and get this place cleared up, yer lazy slut. If it ain't done when I get back, yer'll feel the back of me 'and. Yer ain't irreplaceable, Bea. And yer ain't as young as yer were. I like me women young and wild. And yer know what 'appened last time yer forgot yer place.'

Fear drenched her in an icy sweat, and she absently rubbed her arm where, in a drunken rage, Fancy had broken it. When the door closed behind him, her smile turned to a sour scowl. God! How she hated Fancy Gilbert. She might be his woman, but he did not hesitate to make her whore for him if he thought she'd lure some still-wet-behind-the-ears toff deeper into his net. At first she'd thought the toffs would be her means of escape. Plenty of them were taken with her looks, and hinted at setting her up in a place of her own. Always Fancy's reputation scared them off. Their wealth would not protect them, if Fancy wanted them dealt with.

She ached all over where that bastard had hammered into her last night like a battering ram. The man was a stinking pervert. She was sick of being abused by him. She lay back, her gaze discontented as it roamed over the room. Petticoats and brightly coloured stockings were scattered everywhere. Two ostrich boas, one red, one purple, were draped over the top of the wardrobe, the door hanging open on broken hinges to reveal the row of Fancy's checked suits and her second-hand, gaudy gowns. Cheap jewellery, with imitation stones, was thrown amongst the open make-up pots on the dressing table, and disgorging from the open drawers were corsets and garters. The room smelt of cheap perfume and stale beer fumes. Beatrice hated the tawdriness of it all.

She wanted to dress in the finest velvets and silks and wear diamonds and be driven in a carriage, or a grand motor car. It was the life her mother had schooled her for. She hated the poverty and squalor of her surroundings, but she was trapped.

Not that she considered herself a victim of her surroundings. If she saw an opportunity she seized it. As a child she had mercilessly used her good looks and the neat clothes that Florence insisted she wore, and had gone begging.

'A shilling to help my poor, dear Mama, and my four brothers and sisters,' she used to plead.

'Abandoned by our wicked father we were. He left us penniless. And no family to turn to. Mama is sick with the consumption. She's too weak to work. Save us from the poorhouse, dear lady. We're gentlefolk fallen on hard times.' Her cultured voice had won the sympathy of many a kindly matron who would press a half crown into her hand. 'Tell your mother she is a brave woman, but you shouldn't be out on the streets begging.'

Beatrice would look crestfallen. 'It's just until little Johnny and I can get work in the match factory. We'd rather risk phossy jaw than beg.'

'Oh, not the match factory!' The matron would usually groan and part with another half-crown before hurrying on.

If the ruse did not work, she would rub chalk into her face and a light smudge of ashes from last night's fire under her eyes. This gave her an ethereal, gaunt look that few women could resist when she asked apologetically for a shilling to buy medicine for her ailing mother. Once Florence had caught her. It was the only time she could remember her mother giving her a smack.

As she grew older and begging was less effective, she had taken to stealing. To win acceptance amongst the other children in the rookery, she accepted any dare they challenged her to do. With each year she became bolder and more hardened. She shunned her mother's upbringing to climb higher in the hierarchy of the underworld.

When Fancy Gilbert had shown an interest in her, she had seen it as a challenge. She wasn't a virgin. She'd lost her maidenhead when she was twelve to a young Irish pickpocket, with the brightest blue eyes and the most dazzling smile. He'd given her a silver bracelet, then ditched her a few months later when he had moved out of the district. She'd sold the bracelet to buy a red dress, and that was when Fancy had noticed her.

The Irish youth had shown her sex could be fun. It wasn't with Fancy: she'd been terrified of him. She still was.

Two years ago she'd nearly succeeded in escaping Fancy's clutches. She'd found a lover who wasn't afraid to stand up to Fancy. He'd been in the army. If the stupid war with the Boers hadn't broken out, which meant he'd been posted abroad, he would have saved her.

The memory made her groan in frustration. She pulled the covers over her head to shut out the room she shared with Fancy. She yearned to escape. She dreamed of a real man as a lover. Tall, handsome, with a touch of class and refinement. A lover like her dashing soldier.

Her dreamy expression turned to a scowl. Sometimes she feared that Fancy would never let her go. Fancy never usually kept the same woman above six months. She'd endured his sadistic cruelty for four years now. Her position wielded great power in the underworld, but sometimes the price was too high, even for Beatrice's vaulting ambition.

Perhaps now that her soldier was back in England her life would change. Last night, when leaving the club, she had been bored and defiant. The alley had been unusually deserted. Seeing a toff approaching, devilment had spurred her to call out, 'Looking for company, mister?'

It had been more out of mischief than intent. Fancy would beat her senseless if he learned she'd taken someone he'd not chosen to her bed.

The man had appraised her in the light from a tavern window. When he tipped back his top hat and she could see his face clearly, her eyes widened in astonishment and her heart quickened its beat.

'I heard you were back in town.' She dropped all pretence of her rough speech and sauntered around his tall figure. She cast a look over her shoulder to ensure no one was watching in the darkened street. All the taverns were full and the sounds of boisterous singing drifted from the open doors. 'Were you looking for me?' she invited, leaning against his arm so that he could feel the fullness of her breasts. 'You've not forgotten your Beatrice, have you? We were good together.'

'How could I forget such an enchantress,' he said smoothly. He, too, looked over his shoulder, wary that Fancy, or one of his men, might be watching. 'Are you still Gilbert's woman?'

'You never let that hinder you before.' Her smile was all enticement.

Just the touch of his elbow against her breast was enough to torch her blood. She wanted him as she had never wanted any man before. He was so devilishly handsome, even when not in his soldier's uniform. The roguish look she so adored was still bright in his eye. For him she would risk Fancy Gilbert's rage. She'd been besotted with him since they had first made love. It had been an experience never equalled. Memories of his lovemaking had kept her sane at nights. In the years he had been away, it had been the vision of him which she fixed in her mind whilst she suffered Fancy's brutal coupling.

'I'm surprised that with your looks and figure you're still in this hell-pit. I'd have thought some wealthy lord would have rescued you and set you up in style.'

Taking that as a cue, she linked her arm through his and was dismayed when she felt him stiffen. Did he no longer desire her? There had been times in the past when she had wondered whether her attraction to him was partly due to the danger of brushing with Fancy. Often, after they had made love, he had made jokes at Fancy's expense. She was so in love with him that she cherished every second in his company, feeding her dreams that he would take her away with him. Unfortunately his regimental barracks had not been in London, and his visits to the capital had been few and far between. She had been heartbroken when she had learned that his regiment had sailed from Tilbury to fight the Boers. He'd gone without even a goodbye. At that time she'd vowed to make him pay for his callousness. Yet a smile from him last night had dispelled her thoughts of vengeance. All she wanted was to have him back.

'I'd leave Fancy tomorrow if the right man had the guts enough to put the bastard in his place. Such a man would become a name to be reckoned with in these parts. Even so, Fancy will be at the club for hours. Time enough for us to get properly reacquainted.'

He released her hold on his arm, his smile never faltering or his voice losing its smooth charm. 'Much as your offer tempts me, my dear, I've other business this night.'

Masking her disappointment behind a bold wink, Beatrice chuckled throatily. 'Then you be sure to visit me soon. There's a lot of loving for us to catch up on.' She smoothed the fading velvet of her purple gown suggestively over her hips. 'If you still think you're man enough to pleasure me.'

He stopped to kiss her cheek and squeezed her buttocks. 'I'm more than man enough for you, Beatrice sweetheart.' He pushed a guinea into her cleavage and tipped his hat in farewell. 'Don't let Fancy catch you selling yourself on the street like a common strumpet. I wouldn't like to see your pretty face all cut up.'

There was a sarcasm in his voice which she did not like. He'd been away nearly two years. Before he left, he'd never have turned down the invitation she'd just offered. Two years apart had not dimmed her love. It had heightened it. She knew him as a swell-mobster – a fashionably dressed pickpocket specialising in stealing from the gentry. But he had been born a gentleman, the son of a country squire, no less. Her refined speech amongst the rough-voiced slatterns of the underworld he frequented attracted him. It was her abandonment in bed which had kept him returning to her. He had been her dream of escape. Now it was all crumbling about her feet.

'Not thinking of turning respectable, are you, Zach Morton?' she teased. He turned on her. His handsome face hardened and his eyes glittered with deadly intent. It sent through her a bolt of fear more powerful than any Fancy Gilbert could instil.

'Take care that mouth of yours doesn't get you into trouble, Bea. What happened between us was two years ago.'

She forced a sultry smile, determined to fight for the man she loved. 'You can't have forgotten how good we were, Zach?' she wheedled. 'It will be good again.'

She saw the glimmer of interest in his eyes and worked on it ruthlessly. Sidling against him, she pressed her hand against the flat of his stomach and allowed it to press downwards until she held his swelling member in her hand.

'Is your business so important, Zach? Couldn't it wait for just an hour?' Her hand caressed him and she licked her lips seductively as she felt him rise hard and powerful in her hand.

Zach was tempted. He had forgotten what an enticing baggage Beatrice could be. Dim recollections of their impassioned couplings returned. She had certainly been imaginative. He shuddered as his body responded to her skilled fingers. But the cold voice of reason was the stronger.

Gently, he put his hand over hers and stilled the movement. 'No, Bea. I've business with Slasher. I'd rather not arrive smelling of your perfume.'

She laughed with relief. 'There's not another woman then, just illicit business.'

He did not contradict her. 'Give me a kiss for luck.'

She moulded her lips and body suggestively

against his and he groaned as her hand again reached for his groin.

'Minx!' he said as he drew regretfully away. Casually he asked, 'Is your mother still at the same address? I'd like to pay my respects. I never did thank her properly when I hid in her cellar, that time the Peelers were searching for me.'

'Ma still lives in the same tenement. I go there every Wednesday,' she added hopefully.

He had got the information he needed, and did not look back as he walked away. Beatrice was a temptation he must resist – at least for the moment. There was too much else at stake.

Two years in South Africa had slowed his reflexes when it came to the specialised stealing he did from the rich. Lifting wallets and fob-watches was a lucrative way of making a living, but it was risky. If caught he would end his life in jail.

Since leaving the army, he had daily spent an hour using his manservant Dipper Jones to practise on. Dipper had been a London guttersnipe, convicted of robbery with violence. After escaping from his guards whilst being transported to Pentonville he had enlisted in the army under a false name to avoid recapture. Zach had caught him pilfering from his belongings during his first week in South Africa. His challenge in thieves' cant had startled him into dropping his booty. Zach had then suggested that Dipper become his batman.

To finance his gambling whilst abroad, Dipper and Zach had often broken into many wealthy houses whilst billeted in a town. Zach had earned

Dipper's loyalty when he had seen his servant shot down as the army retreated from a Boer ambush. He'd doubled back and thrown the unconscious Dipper over his saddle and ridden hard, bullets whizzing dangerously close to his fleeing figure, but none finding their mark.

Their profitable relationship continued into civilian life. Zach had no intention of working for a living. He was thirty and it was time he found himself a wealthy wife. Unfortunately his wild youth had left him with a reputation as a rakehell and a womaniser, and he was ostracised by many wealthy families.

Lady Luck had smiled on him the day he met Kara Wyse. His interest had been aroused when he had first seen her in Brentwood on the day that he had resigned his commission. Abel Wyse's heir would be a wealthy prize. He'd left Brentwood the next day, and given her no further thought until seeing her in Hyde Park with Florence Kempe. Then he had been struck again by her unconscious sensuality. That she was also rich fuelled his interest. If she was anything to compare with Bea, marriage to her would be a pleasure, not a chore.

Yet Bea could be a problem. Her jealous rages in the past had marred their affair. Bea was not a woman to cross lightly. He'd have to find a way of dealing with her. He would not risk ruining his chances with Kara.

Kara checked her watch. It was three minutes before eight and the shop was due to open at eight. She stood in the hallway which led to a small private parlour behind the shop. Here, stairs led up to a door which opened into the main house.

The door opened and Sophia, dressed in a brown skirt and cream silk blouse, smiled at her. 'Everything ready, my dear? Are you nervous?'

Kara nodded.

'Sarah is with the children until their governess arrives at nine. I will serve with you and introduce you to our established customers.'

'Thank you, Sophia. I appreciate it.'

Sophia patted her blonde hair, which was parted in the centre and pulled back smoothly into curls covered in a fine, pearl-studded net. 'I enjoy an hour or so in the shop from time to time. Friendly service was always my husband's motto. It is so important, don't you think, Kara?'

'Very important.' She looked at her watch again and her palms broke into a nervous sweat. 'Time to open the door. What if there are no customers? What if people disapprove of two women running a shop?' Her fears tumbled from her before she could halt them.

Sophia looked at her sternly. 'Where's the confident woman who persuaded me to go into partnership with her?'

Kara, her hair styled in a neat chignon, took a deep breath and smoothed the skirt of her navy suit. The trumpet-shaped skirt and bolero with its high-necked white blouse beneath was elegant and functional.

'This business is what I want,' she affirmed. 'It will be a success.'

Sophia smiled, but concern remained in her

eyes. 'Forgive me for speaking openly, Kara. We've not known each other long, but in the time since you moved here, I believe we have become friends.'

'I had thought so, Sophia. Is there something on your mind?'

'Perhaps I speak out of turn, but...' She put a hand on Kara's arm. 'I can sense you are unhappy in some way. Is it because of a man? Captain Morton, when he called the other day, was very attentive. I don't wish to pry, my dear. I am just concerned for you.'

Kara felt her guilty secret must be branded across her face, and schooled her expression to neutrality. It would never do to underestimate Sophia's perception. She was a kindly woman, but a keen gossip. Had she noticed anything between Richard and herself? No, that was impossible. The last time Richard had called on Sophia had been before the visit to the opera. Still, she must be careful. Loving Richard so fiercely, she must ensure that her emotions were carefully guarded.

'Captain Morton is an acquaintance.' She deliberately turned the emphasis of the conversation. 'He's a charming man, but I hardly know him. I am a little tired, that is all.'

Sophia smiled. 'I have seen you gazing dreamily into space when you think yourself unobserved. That is the sign of a woman in love. Captain Morton is a handsome man. But there is no need to fear. I've seen the way he looks at you. He is enamoured.'

Kara was about to protest, then decided that if

Sophia suspected that she was in love, it was better for her to believe it was with Captain Morton than Richard Tennent.

'It is time to open the door,' she said, walking through into the shop.

Though she had checked everything was in readiness a dozen times before retiring last night, she paused to run a critical eye over the shop. Everything was in order. At seeing the gold-leaf lettering in an arch across the bay window, HENSHAWE & WYSE, she felt a thrill of pleasure. She had done it. She was a partner in her own business. This was her first step towards achieving the financial independence she craved. Her hand shook as it turned the key in the lock, and she stepped back for James Paskin, the middle-aged shop assistant, to pull back the bolts at the top and bottom of the door.

Four men were waiting outside to enter.

'Good morning, gentlemen,' James greeted them, peering over the top of his horn-rimmed spectacles, his thick white hair frizzing around his red jovial face like a mob-cap. 'How can I help you?'

From that moment until lunchtime, Kara had no time to stop and reflect on whether the shop would be a success. Customers never stopped coming into the store. Her only disappointment was that few women came in to browse at the books. Kara served them personally, recommending the latest novels she thought would interest them.

Sophia dealt efficiently with the stationery customers.

'Changed it all around,' one gruff-voiced man commented with obvious disapproval. 'Hope it doesn't mean you've changed the efficiency of the service. What are you doing selling books, Mrs Henshawe? There's a perfectly good bookshop four hundred yards down the road. I don't expect they will take kindly to you stealing their custom.'

'We never intended to steal anyone's custom, Mr Potts.' Sophia became flustered, unused to dealing with such rudeness.

Kara saw her distress and went to her assistance, her voice pleasant as she answered the man. 'There's always room for competition within the trade, sir. We have a wide selection of both fiction and non-fiction, if you would like to inspect our stock.'

'What would a woman know about non-fiction?' he derided.

Kara bit her lip to control her anger at his prejudice. Her voice remained sweet as she replied, 'We have consulted all the publishers' representatives, Mr Potts. Mrs Henshawe has spoken of your valued custom. If you have a particular interest in any subject, I would be interested to hear your views as to what stock you believe would sell well.'

The pompous light in the man's eyes mellowed. He preened his large grey moustache and began to list several topics.

Kara smiled at him. 'You are a man of discernment, Mr Potts. If you have the time, I would appreciate your opinion of the stock we have on our shelves. However, you may be surprised that we have several eminent works on those subjects.'

He grunted, unconvinced, but Kara had skilfully guided him to the section containing the subjects he had mentioned. 'What is your opinion of this set of volumes?'

She took two of a set of six from the shelf and handed them to him. When Mr Potts eventually came to the counter, he deliberately chose James to serve him. Kara saw that he had chosen the set of six books together with three other works.

'A wise choice, sir. Especially selected by Miss Wyse, they were,' James enthused as he wrapped the purchases. 'It is company policy to ask whether you could suggest other titles which may be of interest to our customers.'

'I could indeed, if I were so inclined.' Mr Potts puffed out his narrow chest.

'And we would value the advice of such a respected authority as yourself, Mr Potts.' Kara flattered him outrageously. The man seemed to grow two inches with pride. When he suggested four titles that Kara should stock, she wrote them down and assured him that they would be on her shelves by the end of the week. As she thanked him, she saw that his antagonism had lessened.

'I noted you have several works on astronomy. I have a friend I will recommend them to. Good day, madam.'

It was not only the men who were reserved when first entering the shop; the women also seemed wary of a female who had taken a man's place as manager and owner. Kara set out to win their confidence and rarely failed. She asked them all their taste in books. Then suggested several titles and showed them to the private area of four chairs set aside for women to browse at their leisure. One or two starch-faced matrons sniffed their disapproval and departed, but most of the women were grateful for the opportunity to talk about their favourite authors. They left with purchases, vowing they would come again and recommend the shop to their friends.

'It looks as though you are all set for a great success,' a male voice commented.

Kara looked up from wrapping a customer's books. Seeing Richard standing in front of her, she was unable to halt a blush rising to her cheeks.

With her heart pounding wildly, she finished serving the customer. In the last few days she had tried to blot thoughts of Richard from her mind. She had concentrated on the shop opening and settling into her rooms with Mrs Henshawe. One glimpse of him had shattered her good resolve. When she turned to Richard, Elizabeth, whom she had not noticed earlier, threw her arms around her and kissed her warmly on both cheeks.

'It's wonderful, Kara. I knew you'd be a success. I insisted Richard brought me today. How could I miss your opening? And so many customers.'

Kara smiled, though her heart was aching at the affection Elizabeth was showing to her. She did not deserve it. In the final day of living in their house, she had managed to avoid any contact with Richard, but it had been difficult when Elizabeth grilled her about the opera and meal. She had been forced to talk brightly whilst hiding her guilt. But nothing had compared to the agony of each night as she lay in bed, her mind and body aching with the loss of a love that could never be.

'And now you are so successful,' Elizabeth went on, 'you won't forget our friendship? You won't spend every moment of your time here, will you? I've told Richard I expect you to dine with us each Friday evening.'

'I cannot promise that,' Kara stated. She could not bear to spend an evening so close to Richard and not feel his arms around her. She knew he would insist on accompanying her home, and the temptation for them to continue as lovers would be too great. 'I will visit you when I can.'

Her eyes were sombre as they gazed over her friend's head to meet Richard's guarded stare.

Elizabeth began to chat excitedly to Sophia Henshawe, and Richard drew Kara out of his wife's hearing. The early rush of customers had dwindled, and James was dealing with those who remained in the shop.

'I wish you well with your venture, Kara.' There was a mask of control over his handsome features. 'If there's any help you need, I'd be hurt if you did not turn to me.' His expression and formal manner was again that of the staid solicitor she had first met. Knowing him so much better now, she knew how the mask hid the frustrations and burdens of family duty. Their forbidden love had added to them.

'I am thinking of taking on a partner. In a few months I intend to take a sabbatical from the firm.'

'You are going to Mexico?' she said, guessing his intent.

He nodded. 'It won't be easy for Elizabeth. To avoid causing her unnecessary distress, I have not yet mentioned it to her. It would only upset her to learn of it too far in advance.'

There was so much strain in his face that Kara longed to reassure him, to kiss away his troubles. Somehow she managed to speak casually. 'You give so much of yourself to others' problems, you should make time to follow a dream which is important to you. While you are away I shall make sure that Elizabeth is not lonely.'

'I could not ask so much of you.' His voice lost its cool veneer and she heard the hidden yearning.

'Oh, Richard,' she said with an anguished sigh. Perilously close to losing control, she took a grip upon herself and forced a shaky smile. 'I value my friendships highly. Perhaps if I did not...'

With his back to the rest of the people in the shop, his expression became tender. 'That is what makes you so exceptional. It will be easier for us both if I'm out of the country for a while.'

She nodded, knowing that no amount of distance could ever ease the ache of loving him. 'I will only visit Elizabeth on an evening you will not be at home,' she said heavily. 'You usually dine at your club on a Tuesday. I shall come then. But you won't leave England without letting me know. It's wrong, but I could not bear...'

'I will keep in touch.'

'What are you two discussing?' Elizabeth said teasingly. 'You both look so serious.'

'I was telling Kara that we will take a fortnight's holiday in Brighton this year.'

Elizabeth slipped her arm through her husband's, gazing up at him with such adoration that Kara felt her stomach twist with white-hot jealousy.

'It will be wonderful,' Elizabeth prattled, missing the tension between them. 'Richard suggested the Italian lakes and travelling on to Florence. But I get so sea-sick and insisted on Brighton.'

'How could you not want to visit Florence? You can go to Brighton any Sunday by train.'

'I like Brighton,' Elizabeth said defensively. 'Besides, travelling tires me. Before we go we must take you to the opera again.'

Kara dared not look at Richard for fear of betraying the rush of memories crowding her mind. 'Perhaps later in the year when things are more settled. I have the shop accounts to write up each night.'

The shop bell rang and she left them with relief. She served two more customers before Elizabeth brought her purchases to be wrapped.

'Richard said you will dine on Tuesday. But that means he will not be there. Can't you make it another day?'

'Not at the moment.'

'Then Richard must change his day for dining at the club.'

'No,' Kara interrupted hastily. 'I will not hear of it. Tuesday is the day he meets the friends he was at university with. I know how much an evening with them means to him. And besides,' Kara smiled, 'it will give us a chance to catch up on female gossip which will only bore Richard.'

'Until Tuesday, then,' Elizabeth said, picking up her purchases and handing them to her husband.

Richard tucked them under one arm and, taking Kara's hand, raised it to his lips. 'Goodbye, Kara,'

She thought she would choke on the emotion knotting her throat. As Richard escorted Elizabeth to the door, Kara tore her stare away from his beloved figure, aware that Sophia was watching her. It was impossible to stop the agony clutching at her heart.

Chapter Eleven

Murmuring a hasty excuse, she went to tidy the books which had been disturbed during the morning. The shop remained busy during the next hour, and she served the customers automatically, her smile never faltering. In her misery she was scarcely aware of what she was saying or doing.

'Kara, it's time you took a break,' Sophia said. 'You're looking pale.'

At that moment the shop bell rang and Captain Morton entered. She had forgotten that he said he would call again today. Her face lit with pleasure, hoping that this time he had news of Florence's address.

He removed his top hat and bowed to her.

'Good afternoon, Miss Wyse. May I extend my good wishes for the success of your venture. Though I am sure they are unnecessary. You do not look short of customers.'

'Let us hope they are not here just out of idle curiosity,' she responded.

He laughed, turning the heads of two of the customers purchasing stationery. 'With two beautiful women to serve them, every man in London will be queuing to buy their notepaper and books here.'

'I would rather they queued for the quality of our goods,' Kara replied, then her restraint broke and she asked, 'Have you any news of my mother?'

'Captain Morton!' Sophia called, hurrying to join them. 'How good of you to come on our opening day.' She smiled knowingly at Kara. 'I will leave Kara to serve you. I am sure she has your best interests at heart.'

'Ah, if only that were true, Mrs Henshawe, I would be a happy man,' Zach returned with a roguish grin.

'How easily you are pleased, Captain,' Kara taunted. She knew she should not encourage him to flirt with her, but she was desperate to avert any suspicions Sophia might have concerning Richard and herself. As Sophia was still hovering within hearing distance, Kara did not wish to broach the subject of her mother. 'Captain Morton, is it stationery you require, or a book of some kind. Are you interested in sport?'

He raised a dark brow, his amber eyes gently mocking. 'The most interesting sports are those where one can be partnered by a woman...' The intensity of his gaze deepened, making it obvious that the sport he had in mind was of the most intimate kind. 'Tennis and the like,' he added, again the seductive smile in his eyes, making nonsense of his words. 'Do you play tennis, Miss Wyse?'

She should be angry at his innuendo, but he had delivered it with such panache that she found it difficult to take offence. 'Sadly, Papa did not approve of young women cavorting so indecorously. But I have always thought it a fascinating game. Since Papa's death, I have been too busy for such pastimes.'

'That must be remedied. A friend of mine is having a garden party next Sunday. There is always tennis and I have no partner. Would you honour me by accepting my invitation, Miss Wyse?'

'I would be a poor partner, Captain Morton, since I cannot play. And it would not be proper for me to accompany you without a chaperon. People will talk.'

'I had already thought of a suitable chaperon.' He turned to Sophia. 'I hope that you will also accept my invitation, Mrs Henshawe, and bring your adorable children. It will be a pleasant outing for them.'

'I would be delighted, Captain Morgan.' Sophia beamed her approval and moved away to serve a customer. A woman was hovering with a book in her hand to purchase. Excusing herself to the captain, Kara dealt with the customer. From the far side of the shop two teenage sisters were staring rapturously at Captain Morton over the top of the novels they had supposedly selected. Their stern-faced mother hissed in their ears and shoved her daughters to another part of the shop. When the two girls still continued to look dreamy-eyed at him, their mother gripped them by their elbows and dragged them protesting from the shop.

Zach was unaware of the discord he had caused. His gaze remained on Kara. Despite the pain of her loving Richard, she found she was not completely immune to his handsome looks and charm. Pride squared her shoulders. She had made her decision not to be Richard's mistress, and she was not going to spend the rest of her life moping about the cruelty of fate.

Another customer claimed her attention, and when she finally returned to Captain Morton, the main reason for his visit was uppermost in her mind.

'What news have you of my mother, Captain?'

If he was annoyed at her abruptness, he concealed it. 'I do have news, though here is not the place to discuss it.'

Kara hesitated. She was burning to know all she could of her mother, but was torn at being unable to leave the shop. To walk out with Captain Morton would horrify Sophia's sense of propriety. 'I have not taken my lunch-break, Captain. Would you join me in the parlour? We can speak in private there.'

She crossed to Sophia, who had earlier lunched with her daughters. 'Captain Morton is to join me in the parlour whilst I take my break.'

Sophia looked momentarily uncomfortable. 'I trust for the sake of propriety that you will keep the door open.' She smiled conspiratorially. 'Who am I to stand in the path of true love?'

Kara nodded, but Sophia's constant reference to love, linked with the captain's name, was increasingly irksome to Kara. She gestured for Zach Morton to follow her to the parlour.

'What have you learnt about my mother?' she asked without preamble.

'I located the district where she lives and met her in the street. She was wary of my approach, but I managed to convince her that I meant her, or you, no harm. She'll not meet you in her home. She's ashamed of her poverty.'

Kara lifted the kettle from the trivet by the fire and poured water into a teapot. 'But I want to change all that.'

Zach nodded compassionately. 'Florence Kempe, as your mother is known, is a proud woman. She loves you too much for you to see her shame.'

Kara hugged her arms close to her chest, wrestling with her disappointment. At last she said, 'I can understand that. But she is my mother. I haven't told you this, but I also have a sister. A sister I have never seen. Why should they live in poverty if I can help them?'

'You have a generous heart.' Zach propped himself on the corner of the table and regarded her with admiration. 'There is a way. Your mother wavered when I suggested that you meet again in a neutral place. There are few places open in the evening which would be suitable. A fair and circus opens this weekend. I said we would meet Florence by the horse carousel on Monday evening. I gave her sufficient money to cover her fare.'

'But the shop. How can I leave the shop? We do not close until nine.'

He smiled and lifted a dark brow in provocation. 'I will meet you at nine. Mrs Kempe will meet us at nine-thirty. You don't sound very pleased. I thought you were impatient to meet your mother.'

'I am. It's just that I haven't told Sophia about my mother. I'm not sure she would understand.'

'Then tell her you have an appointment with a suitor,' he grinned wickedly. 'She seemed pleased that I had called.'

'I fear you are incorrigible, Captain Morton. I will not encourage idle speculation,' she said, returning his smile. How could she give up the opportunity of seeing her mother again? It was only then that she realised how deftly he had manipulated the meeting so that he would accompany her. To regain her composure she poured the tea and took the cover from a plate of cold chicken and salad which she had earlier prepared for herself. 'I had not meant to take up so much of your time. You really have been extraordinarily kind.'

He glanced regretfully at the open door, his eyes sparkling with teasing affection. 'How else was I to get to know you? I hope that we will become much better acquainted.' He rose from the table and studied her significantly before adding, 'I trust that Mrs Tennent has now recovered from the illness which prevented her attending the opera.'

'Yes, she is well. She was in the shop earlier.' Kara felt a twinge of alarm. Had he guessed that she and Richard had been lovers?

His amber stare seemed to penetrate her thoughts, but he smiled as he said, 'Mr Tennent was very protective of you at the opera, even for a family friend.'

Kara bristled at his probing. 'You are impertinent, sir.'

'That was furthest from my intent.' He lifted his hands, about to take hers, then glanced ruefully at the door before dropping them back to his side. 'I think of nothing but you since we met at Hyde Park.'

'I must ask you to leave if you continue in that vein, Captain Morton. I am indebted to Mr Tennent and his wife for the assistance and friendship they have shown me. My father, before his death, had been a client of Mr Tennent's firm for many years. He felt responsible that I was alone in London.'

'You have no other relatives?' He continued to question her.

'Only an aunt and uncle who disapproved of me coming to London to search for my mother. They disowned me.'

His expression was concerned. 'You have borne a lot alone. But you could have remained in Brentwood and employed someone to search for your mother.'

'Mr Tennent had no luck. Besides, I wanted a fresh start. Having a business of my own was important to me. Where better than London to open a shop?'

His gaze was admiring. 'I hope you will allow me to continue to help you. Though I admire you too much to wish that we remain only friends.'

'You are too forward,' Kara rebuked.

His smile was irrepressible. 'I doubt you are a woman to favour faint-hearts. Trust me, Kara. I would reunite you with your mother.' He bowed to her. 'Until Monday. I will call for you at nine.'

'You have not given me my mother's address,' she said as he walked into the corridor leading to the shop.

'Mrs Kempe made it a condition of her coming to the fair that I did not divulge it to you. I could not break my word to her, even for the sake of your trust, Kara.'

He marched from the shop before Kara could gather her wits. He certainly had an authoritative way about him which was difficult to resist.

'Where is Mama,' Kara asked distraught. 'It was arranged that we meet half an hour ago.'

The light was beginning to fail, making it difficult to see one person amongst the crush of people. The fair had drawn hundreds of people, and the noise from a large pipe-organ next to the carousel was deafening. Kara scanned the fairground absently, noting a man on a tightrope high above their heads. Several showmen had set up their booths, their posters announcing such spectacular melodramas as 'The Rescue of Helen of Troy' and 'The Sultan's Tragedy'. Others proclaimed to have on display freaks of nature such as a two-headed pig or a puppy-sized calf.

'I'm afraid it looks as though she could not get away,' Zach said. 'But don't let it spoil your evening. There's much to see here. Would you like to attend one of the theatre tents. We are still in time to catch a play?'

'I could not leave here yet,' Kara insisted. 'She may have been delayed.'

Zach hid his impatience for another fifteen minutes as Kara strained to catch sight of Florence in the crowd.

'You must accept that your mother is not coming.'

Kara hung her head to hide her disappointment.

'I'm sorry.' Zach was forced to raise his voice above the music drifting across from a large marquee which had been turned into a ballroom and the loud chatter of excited voices. 'I wished only to make you happy and now you are sad.'

'It is not your fault that Mama did not come.' Kara managed a weak smile. 'Will you take me home now?'

'It's still early,' Zach said, taking her arm and tucking it through his to assist guiding her through the press of people. 'You've seen little of the wonders that are here for the people's enjoyment. Am I such poor company that you would desert me so soon?'

'It is I who am poor company.'

'You could never be that, Kara.'

She was about to rebuke him for the familiarity of using her first name when he smiled.

'Are you about to insist that I continue with the

formality of addressing you as Miss Wyse?' His smile broadened. 'I mean no disrespect, but I can think of you only as Kara. It's an exotic name for an exceptional woman. It suits you. Whilst Miss Wyse conjures the image of a prim, rather stern spinster, definitely with horn-rimmed spectacles perched on the end of a hooked nose.'

'I have often wondered why Papa, who always disliked anything fancy, chose it. But he wished me named after his grandmother, whom he greatly admired. She was Katharina, a name which apparently his grandmother loathed; she promptly declared that I must be called Kara instead.'

'A Wyse woman indeed. Kara is delightful.'

Despite her disappointment at her mother's absence, she found herself smiling in return. The rebuke was forgotten.

'That's better. A smile is just the beginning. I want to hear you laughing before this evening is out.' He leaned closer and his breath stroked her cheek, his eyes adoring as they held her gaze. 'There are sad shadows in your eyes. I would chase them away so they never return.'

There was only one man who could do that, and Richard was for ever denied her. Yet Zach Morton was a handsome and charming companion, and with each meeting she enjoyed his company more. She was too much of a woman to want to shut herself away from masculine company. If she returned to her rooms now, she would only dwell on the lost chance of seeing her mother.

'There is a circus here and a marionette show,'

Zach suggested. 'Would you enjoy those?'

'You choose. I saw some circus folk preparing for a parade when I first came to London, but I have never seen them perform. Papa did not approve. He did not approve of many entertainments. He would be appalled that a daughter of his had frequented a fairground. Yet it does not seem a sinful place, for that was how he viewed them.'

'Forgive me for speaking so ill of the dead, but your Papa sounds a pompous–'

'Please do not insult him,' Kara interrupted. 'He is dead and he acted as he believed right. If he had not had such strong moral principles, he would be alive now.'

'How did he die?'

Kara shuddered, remembering the bloodstains on the wall of his bedroom where he had blasted out his brains. Her body began to tremble. 'I really would rather not speak of it. It was very sudden and unexpected.' She did not want to lie to him, and since the authorities had accepted his death as an accident, that was how she preferred to think of it. 'It was an accident.'

'How callous of me to remind you of such a painful event. Forgive me.' Both her hands were clasped between his as he swung round to stare down into her face. 'I meant no disrespect. You are loyal to his memory, as is right. I admire that. There is much that I admire about you, Kara.'

'You are too forward, Captain Morton.' Kara felt herself sliding out of her depth with this accomplished man. She suspected women were easily attracted to his Byronic good looks, which had a devilish air about them. She was already finding it difficult to resist his charm.

'Did we not agree upon informality? It is Zach. You have led a very sheltered life, Kara. You also take the responsibilities of your business seriously. There is a time for work and a time for play.' He gave a carefree laugh and drew her towards the circus tent. 'Tonight put your mourning and disappointment aside. I want you to enjoy yourself.'

Kara watched the performing bears, dogs and horses with delight, and then stared spellbound at the trapeze artists hurtling through the air high above them. The antics of the clowns brought tears of laughter to her eyes, and when the lion-tamer put his head in a lion's mouth, she gasped, and turned her face into Zach's shoulder, terrified the man would be eaten alive. Zach chuckled and put his arm around her shoulder. She drew back, smiling shyly at his intimacy.

When the performance ended, he led her towards a tent which held exotic birds in cages, and she marvelled at their colours and birdsong. Afterwards they rode the horse carousel and the boat-shaped swings that swung high over the crowds at the pull of a tasselled rope. Kara's cheeks were flushed with excitement and she felt more carefree than she had in years.

They paused for refreshment in a secluded trellised area, fenced off from the rougher element of fairgoers who were seated at wooden tables and benches. Throughout, Zach entertained her with witty anecdotes of some of the most famous people of the day, until she found herself holding her sides and laughing. No longer was she scanning the crowds lest Florence should unexpectedly appear.

'I have enjoyed this evening very much,' she said as they finished a light meal.

'It is not yet over.' They resumed their walking and the music from the dance tent was growing louder. 'There may be fireworks later. But first...' He took her hand and drew her into the dance tent, tossing the entrance fee to the man at the opening. Over thirty couples were already on the dance-floor. 'You would not refuse me a waltz, would you, Kara?'

How could she refuse? He was manipulating her, but she did not care. The touch of his hand in hers did not affect her in the ungovernable way that Richard's had done, but it made her aware of his strength. She was also aware that several women's heads turned to watch him as they whirled by. By the end of the second waltz, Kara had begun to notice an auburn-haired woman who kept moving as though to keep Captain Morton in her sight. There was a look of such venom on the woman's beautiful face that Kara felt a chill pass through her.

When the woman again moved to continue her study of Zach, Kara appraised her more closely. She wore a dress of scarlet edged with black lace which was too showy for good taste. The low-cut bodice revealing the woman's heavy breasts, told Kara that this was the type of low woman she had heard spoken of in hushed whispers, but had never seen so openly flaunting her profession. Surely such a woman was not acquainted with Zach.

The dance ended, and when she saw the red-haired woman begin to walk determinedly towards them, she felt Zach stiffen. He had paled beneath his habitual tan and his eyes were glacial.

'Come, my dear,' he said, guiding Kara away from the advancing woman.

They wove an intricate path through the now thinning crowd, and Kara had to quicken her pace to keep up with Zach. The sky was now black and the oil-lamps from the booths illuminated the grass.

'Do you know that woman?' Kara asked.

'What woman, my dear?' He sounded ruffled.

'The one in the red dress.'

'I noticed no such woman. You're the only woman I've eyes for tonight.'

'She seemed to know you.'

'Do you doubt my word, Kara?' Zach pulled her behind a wide oak tree and pressed her up against its trunk. His expression revealed in the feeble light from an oil lantern was tight-lipped. 'I dislike my honour questioned.'

His hold was gentle, but Kara was aware of the menace in his stance. His amber eyes glittered as he stared down at her, like a lion assessing its prey. She felt a shudder go through his powerful body, and he removed the hand which restrained her. 'Forgive me.' He sounded appalled. 'I have acted like a brutish boor.'

She relaxed. He had done so much to help her that it would be churlish to have accused him without just cause. 'I should ask your forgiveness for questioning you in that way. The strain of the past weeks are making me suspicious of people's intentions. I was wrong to doubt you, Zach. But that woman had been watching you for some time.'

A slow grin spread across his lips. 'As many men watched you as we danced. I am sure we made a striking couple.'

His lack of modesty made her laugh. He was incorrigible, and there was something roguish about him which she knew she should beware of. Yet perversely it was that aura of danger which attracted her.

Beatrice stood in the shadows, glowering across at the couple under the oak tree. The woman's figure was obscured by the trunk. Briefly Zach glared across at her, his look filled with such lethal warning that she had thought better of challenging him. His companion was elegantly dressed in a cream suit trimmed with brown braid and lapels. Everything about the woman proclaimed her genteel upbringing and wealth, from her elegantly coiffured hair, long pearl earrings, wide matching cream hat tipped at a jaunty angle, to her fine leather shoes, glimpsed as her gown swirled outwards in the dance, which also revealed silk and lace petticoats Beatrice could kill to possess. As the couple waltzed past her she had smelt the expensive perfume the woman used, and her hatred had been instant.

Beatrice's temper flared. Zach had been so enamoured of the woman in his arms, he had not noticed her on the edge of the dance-floor. She'd come here tonight to filch what she could from the pockets of the wealthy. The contents from three wallets were already hidden in the secret pocket beneath her skirts. It had been a profitable evening's work, and she had been content until her glance had fallen on Zach. Then jealousy had consumed her.

Her fury exploded as she watched Zach lift a hand to touch the woman's face, his expression tender. Damn him! Beatrice's eyes narrowed. Zach was her man. No simpering ninny was going to take him from her, just because she had wealth and Beatrice did not.

Beatrice stayed hidden until the couple moved on. Then she followed them. Once, in the crush of the crowd, she saw Zach knock shoulders with a well-dressed gentleman. He paused to apologise and brush the man's coat down. She grinned to herself despite her anger at him. Even with his wealthy lady-love on his arm, Zach was still at work lifting fob-watches from the unsuspecting.

She trailed Zach until he and his companion left the fairground. When he hailed a hansom cab, she strained her ears to catch the address he called to the cabbie. Henshawe & Wyse Stationer's, Oxford Street. She made a mental note of the address.

Jealousy raged through her. Zach was the one man she could not bear to share. Nor would she. Woe betide that haughty bitch if Zach was interested in her. He was her man. Hers alone. Any woman who came between them would suffer the consequences.

As the hansom cab drew away from Henshawe & Wyse, Zach sat back in the seat and grinned to himself. The evening had been a success. Kara had begun to trust him and had accepted his invitation to the garden party next Sunday. He'd wager the fifty guineas he'd get for the fob-watches he'd lifted this evening that she would marry him. Tonight, to woo her, he had restrained himself and played the perfect gentleman. Soon he must arrange a definite meeting between her and Florence. That would bind her more closely to him. There had been no such arrangement this evening. It had been a ruse to get Kara to meet him. When he had visited Florence he had found her too ill to rise from her bed. He'd given her the money for medicine and had promised to arrange a meeting with her daughter when she was recovered.

Thoughts of Kara filled him with satisfaction. She would make an acceptable bride even to his father. Although his eldest brother Jonathan would inherit the country manor and estate, Zach had always been his grandfather's favourite. On his death, the old man had left him a thousand a year once he married a woman approved of by his father. Kara must be worth at least another few thousand a year from her father's estate. They would live comfortably on that.

Zach patted the inside pocket of his frock coat and drew out the three gold fob-watches he had skilfully lifted when he had bumped into men at the fairground. Kara had been the ideal companion. There was innocence written all over her lovely face, and her impeccable dress averted any suspicion falling upon himself if the theft had been noticed too soon.

The only blight in the evening had been the unhappy chance of Beatrice discovering him with Kara. Beatrice was proving a problem. She had tracked him down at his lodgings last night, and it had been difficult to evade her company. He had been embarrassed when she'd declared that she loved him. A hastily remembered meeting was the excuse to evade her. He was not about to ruin his chance of marrying Kara by taking Beatrice as his mistress again.

He had seen the fury on Beatrice's face at the fairground. It was imperative that she and Kara did not meet until after their wedding. He would have to placate Beatrice in some way. She could ruin his plans.

Sunday dawned bright and sunny. Kara rose early. She wanted to spend the morning working on the reams of paperwork involved in running the shop. It was a task she did with relish. In its first month of opening the shop had been a great success, especially the book department. She had spent several hours with publishers' representatives to improve her stock. Every evening she had sat over the accounts as she entered the figures, her heart racing in excitement that the improvements she had made in the stationery displays had increased sales by a quarter. Next week she would devote more of her energies to that side of the trade. From the meetings Richard had arranged for her before the opening, with accountants and retired shop managers, and from her forays into rival stores to study competition, Kara had devised a plan aimed at gradual expansion. From the outset she discovered she had a natural flair for business and figures. Even Richard had been surprised at her acumen. His encouragement, and his faith that she would eventually realise her dream of having a chain of shops, strengthened her resolve to succeed.

She suppressed a sigh as the image of Richard filled her mind. She had not seen him for a month, and her heart ached with yearning. The figures on the page blurred. Angrily she brushed a wayward tear from her lashes. She must think of the future, not the past.

Her visits to Elizabeth every Tuesday were a strain. When Elizabeth learned that Captain Morton had escorted her to several functions, she wanted to know all the details. She wanted to hear everything about Kara's growing romance. It was so far from the reality of where her true affection lay that Kara often made an excuse that she was tired, so that she could leave early. It was hard to visit Richard's home and not see him, but the alternative – of Elizabeth guessing what had happened between them – would have been even worse.

At the garden party that Zach had taken her to after the fair, he had charmed Sophia: she approved of him calling upon her business partner. Zach behaved impeccably. He always ensured that a suitable chaperon accompanied them on the outings he arranged. They had visited the Zoological Gardens and the Egyptian Hall in Piccadilly, whose acts included animals, conjurers, and occasionally freak shows. Rarely a day passed when he did not call at the shop to present her with a bouquet of flowers or chocolates as a mark of his affection. He had now begun to teach her how to play tennis on her half-afternoon off from the shop, and at seven each morning he arrived at the shop on horseback, leading a mare for Kara to accompany him on a ride.

To try to forget Richard, Kara saw more of Zach. She was grateful for the entertainments he took her to, which drew her thoughts momentarily away from the impossibility of her love for Richard. She even began to look forward to his company, and was becoming very fond of him.

Now that the shop was proving successful, her main aim was to rescue her mother from the poverty in which she lived. Zach had told her something of Florence's circumstances, though Kara sometimes worried that he was keeping a lot from her. He would not be pressed, insisting that he had given Florence his word not to break her confidence. At least Zach was in contact with Florence and, through him, Kara sent food parcels, medicine and presents to her mother. He was now convinced that Florence would accompany him to the shop at closing time one day next week to dine with her.

At each meeting with Zach, she found she enjoyed his company more. Today she had packed a picnic and was looking forward to taking a boat along the river to the botanical gardens at Kew. Sophia and the children were to accompany them. From outside in the garden she could hear Sophia's daughters playing. She smiled and went to the window to gaze down at the neatly kept flowerbeds and lawn at the rear of the shop. Rose and Violet were playing with their dolls on the grass in the morning sunlight. The two sisters laughed and Rose, always loving and impetuous, hugged Violet. Kara smiled. This was how she always thought two sisters should behave. Would Beatrice and herself become close like that? It was what she dreamed of.

Chapter Twelve

A family of swans glided in stately procession, along the riverbank and past the picnic party, their feathers ruffled by the cooling summer breeze. The Henshawe girls were playing with a ball, their laughter mixing with the sound of a skylark high in the cloudless, azure sky. Kara stretched, breathing deeply of the jasmine- and meadowsweet-scented air. She tilted back her head to allow the sun's rays to caress her face and neck.

'Kara, you will give yourself freckles,' Sophia murmured drowsily. 'Where's your parasol?'

Sophia was sitting on the tartan rug with her back to a tree trunk, her eyes closed as she held her parasol to protect her face from the sun. Too restless to sit, Kara joined Zach, who stood by the water's edge watching the swirling current, his expression thoughtful.

'It's been another lovely day, Zach. Sophia and the children have enjoyed it enormously. The gardens at Kew were delightful.'

'Did you enjoy yourself, Kara?' He smiled at her indulgently.

'Very much.' Her violet eyes sparkled with pleasure. 'I've been to more places in the last month than I had in my life before.' She tilted back her white parasol, which matched her muslin dress, and lowered her voice as she grew serious. 'Have you seen my mother recently?'

A frown drew his arched brows together. 'Is that why you agree to see me, Kara? Because I bring you news of Florence?'

'You are my only means of contact with her, it is true,' she answered softly, 'but I would not be here if I did not enjoy your company.'

His expression brightened, and his amber eyes were admiring in a way which no woman could fail to be moved by. Zach was very handsome; in his company, Kara could not help but feel the pull of his easy charm and masculine attraction. He held out his arm for her to take. As they sauntered further along the riverbank, Kara felt the tension building in the muscles beneath her fingers.

Finally he said, 'Florence has agreed to come to the shop next Thursday after you have closed for the evening.'

Kara swung round to face him, her face glowing with pleasure. 'Thank you, Zach. You've been a good friend.' Impulsively she stood on tiptoe and kissed his cheek.

His finely etched features were grave as he placed a hand over hers as it rested on his arm. 'Surely you know that I would be more than a friend, Kara. Have I a chance of winning your affection?'

'You have that already.'

They were passing a thickly branched willow and he drew her under its shielding canopy. Sophia was still in sight, but from the way her head had drooped on to her chest, it was obvious she had fallen into a doze. The children were playing on the far side of the tree and were unable to see them.

Kara's arms were taken by Zach as his voice deepened with insistence. 'May I hope for more than affection, dearest Kara? You must know how I feel about you.'

'Please, Zach.' Kara shook her head, her eyes scanning his face. 'It is too soon to speak of such things.'

'I knew what was in my heart from the first moment I saw you.' He drew her closer. 'I love you, Kara. I want you to be my wife.'

Kara felt a moment's panic. She did not want to lose his friendship, but marriage… How could she contemplate that when she still loved Richard?

Zach saw the hesitation in her eyes and acted swiftly. Drawing her further behind the concealing veil of the overhanging willow branches, his arms slid around her and his lips took hers in a tender kiss. When he felt her stiffen, he used all his skill to overcome her resistance. With a restraint he did not know he possessed, his lips moved with greater demand over hers, reverently but insistently, with a mastery no woman had ever opposed.

Kara was taken by surprise at his kiss. She had seen him on several occasions, and never had he attempted to kiss her. She had even begun to wonder, with typical female perversity, whether he did not find her attractive in that way. As his mouth took hers, she expected to feel nothing but a pleasant warmth, in the way Ernest's kisses had affected her. She certainly did not expect to experience the cataclysmic sensation which Richard's kisses had aroused. Neither had she expected this sudden heady swirling of her senses, this wild leaping of her heart, or the frisson of wayward response. Her lips parted, soft and yielding beneath his accomplished persuasion. The soft hair of his moustache made her upper lip tingle, the sensation was sensually abrasive. The parasol was gripped tightly in one hand, whilst the other of its own volition slid to the back of his neck.

With a shocked gasp she drew back from him. She was appalled that her body could respond so wickedly to a man she did not love. Her hand was shaking as she lifted it to her swollen lips. To regain her composure she swept aside the curtain of willow branches and walked quickly towards Sophia.

Swiftly her arm was taken, and she was gently pulled round to meet his amused stare. 'Kara, forgive me. I've wanted to kiss you since the first moment we met. You are too sensible to take the kiss of a man who adores you as an insult.' His lips quirked in a beguiling smile. 'Besides, you enjoyed it.'

'You are forward, Captain Morton.'

'Honest, I'd call it.' The dancing gleam in his eyes was unrepentant. 'Will you marry me, Kara?'

She knew she should rebuke him, but he was smiling disarmingly in a way she found irresistible. The sun had turned his swarthy complexion to an unfashionable golden tan. With his dark hair and his proud soldierly bearing, he looked as shameless as a brigand. To Kara, who hated the frigid formality of most Edwardian men, his roguish looks were favourably impressive. If only she had met him before she had fallen in love with Richard, she suspected that he could have stolen her heart. Though she did not return his smile, her eyes were not condemning of his conduct. 'I am honoured at your proposal, Zach, but I…'

'I'm rushing you.' He cut across her protest, so that she did not actually refuse him. 'I should not have asked you so soon.'

'My mind is upon helping my mother, meeting my sister, and running a new business. How can I think of marriage yet?'

The admiration in his eyes warmed her, despite her misgivings that their relationship was developing faster than she wished.

'For you, I will be patient, although it is torture. I will wait until you are ready before I ask again. But you will be my wife. I have known that from the first moment we met.'

Kara did not immediately answer. The heat was

making her queasy for the third afternoon in a row this week. Finally she answered him. 'When things are resolved with Florence, I will find it easier to think of my own future.'

Zach would never get used to the foul odours which permeated the alleyways of London's infamous rookeries. Tall, slate-roofed houses, many with gaping holes and with high brick chimneys, which belched out choking smoke both summer and winter, leaned crookedly towards each other. The labyrinth of fetid backstreets stretched behind New Oxford Street. Situated so close to the West End theatres and restaurants, it provided the cut-purses, pickpockets and beggars with an easy access to their victims. Even at midday the alleys were dark, the gutters little better than open sewers, alive with scavenging vermin and flies. Dispirited bawds lounged against worm-eaten doorposts seeking customers. Above his head, wooden bridges linked the houses at first floor level, and provided escape routes for thieves fleeing any constable intrepid enough to risk his life in pursuit.

A glimpse through a cracked, grimy window showed men surreptitiously handing over their pickings to a fence. Any gold or silver was later melted down. Promiscuity was in evidence everywhere. Youths of both sexes shared the same cramped beds of a night. The young girls often became pregnant, and the boys were seduced by seasoned sodomites.

In one kitchen Zach saw a line of freshly washed handkerchiefs stolen earlier that day. In another, six children were walking past a stoop-backed crone, their nimble fingers darting into pockets or brushing against her to relieve her of purse, watch or jewellery. Her instruction was rigorous: when she felt a clumsy touch, she clipped the child hard on the ear. Such schools of thieves abounded. The young children in the district either thieved or starved. Then there were the beggars, the lowest order in the criminal underworld. A glimpse into their domains showed exposed limbs being rubbed with ratsbain to induce weeping ulcers, young children's bones deliberately broken to provoke sympathy from charitable citizens.

The years of familiarity, even the bloodied battles he had fought in, had not lessened Zach's disgust at his fellow man's mutilation and degradation. The sight of a young child, legs bowed with rickets, and all too frequently its mouth covered with sores from the syphilis it had been born with, made him despair at mankind's plight.

Zach leapt over a puddle of urine and turned into a small dingy courtyard. Several men, their flesh showing through the holes in their dirty shirts, were lounging against a soot-blackened wall. Their shoulders were slumped in dejection, their hands pushed deep into the pockets of ragged trousers. They studied his fine attire with narrow-eyed cunning. One, on recognising Zach, muttered to his companions, and they returned to their desultory murmurings. Zach hated the need which drove him to fence his goods here.

For years he had lived beyond his army pay and

had turned to crime to support his extravagant lifestyle. His gambling debts had run up in Slasher Gilbert's gaming house. He had been twenty when Slasher had warned him, with a knife at his throat, to pay up, and he had seen his death in the gangleader's eyes. But Slasher had been intent only upon scaring him. He had other plans for Zach. To pay back his debt to the Gilbert brothers, he began to bring his wealthy associates to the gaming houses.

That was how it had started. But with each year he had become more embroiled in the underworld fraternity. On his return from South Africa he had received a visit from Slasher Gilbert. In no uncertain terms, the gangleader expected him to continue as before. He was of the élite class of swell-mobster who stole only from the gentry. When attending a soirée, or dining at a house with friends, he would ensure a window was left open to enable a sneak-thief to climb inside. It was a life where few lived to make ancient bones. When his regiment was posted to fight the Boers, it had given him a reprieve from Slasher Gilbert's clutches. And now he despised the life he had once led. He wanted out. He had not escaped the army to spend his days running from the law. Kara was his chance to regain his respectability. But it would not be easy to break away from the Gilbert brothers. He had no intention of getting his throat cut. There was only one way to get the better of the Gilberts, and that was to beat them at their own game.

Florence stared around the dingily lit kitchen as

she sat back on her heels. She had been scrubbing the cracked, flagstone floor, and in an hour it would be dirty again when the men returned from their drinking at the pub. Already four of the 'mudlarks', as they called the young boys who scoured the river mud for anything of value, were sitting in the courtyard where she had banished them. They were hunched around a pile of foul-smelling filth, which they had emptied from their baskets as they searched for bits of coal, bone, tin, or any salvageable scrap reaped from the riverbed, or the mouths of sewers.

Florence fought a daily battle against the encroaching dirt, vainly trying to keep the cockroaches, mildew and fleas at bay. Her gaze fell upon the recently scrubbed table, and her stomach knotted in disgust at seeing a small army of cockroaches already marching across the wood where she had placed her half-drunk cup of tea. With a scream of frustration, she swept them all on to the floor with her wet brush and stamped them into the ground. No matter how many she killed there was always another regiment of the horrid creatures to follow them.

At the sound of a footfall in the yard, she glanced up from sweeping up the dead cockroaches to see the tall figure of Captain Morton pass the window. Two glass panes were missing from the frame, and had been replaced by old newspapers to keep out the weather.

She brushed the creases from her patched brown cotton gown and removed the large white apron which had been splashed by water. She allowed no one to see her in a dirty apron. Her clothes might be worn and often patched, with their hems frequently turned, but she was always immaculately clean. She sighed as she saw that her gown hung loosely on her emaciated figure. Only a month ago she had taken in the sides of this bodice so that it fitted. The consumption was wasting her flesh, and even in summer she was never free from coughing.

Zach strode into the kitchen and smiled at Florence. 'Good day, Mrs Kempe.' He held out a bunch of roses, his other hand behind his back.

'You spoil me, Captain Morton,' Florence said, taking the flowers and inhaling their heady scent. 'I do so love the smell of roses. They are one of the things I miss most.'

'There is a person who would change all that,' he said gently.

Florence hung her head. 'Don't try and persuade me against my better judgement, Captain Morton. It's too late for that. Besides, it would be a gross ingratitude to Joseph after all his generosity.'

'You call this generous?' Zach frowned at the gloomy room. One of the walls was constantly covered in black mildew from the damp. Apart from the missing window glass, there was a crack above the doorpost, stuffed with straw and rags, which a man could lay his arm along. Outside was a single privy which was shared by fifty or more people, and the nearest water-pump was at the end of the street.

'He took me in when I was destitute and he saved Beatrice's life,' Florence said with quiet dignity. 'Joseph is a good man. My life is here. I am satisfied that at least Kara is safe and well. She does not want to see her mother living like this.'

'She loves you,' Zach persisted. 'She was heartbroken when you ran away. She has no one. I've told her you will visit her one evening next week after the shop has closed. If you had seen the delight on her face you would not refuse.'

Florence shook her head. 'Tell her I love her, but I will not be a burden. She has just started a new life. She does not want the shame I would bring her.'

'Then you must convince her of that. You owe her that much.' He drew his hand from behind his back and held out a parcel tied with a yellow satin bow. 'Kara has sent you this.'

Florence stared at the gift for several moments not daring to move. She could feel tears prickling beneath her lids. Her daughter's generosity always moved her. She did not deserve such kindness. She would never forgive herself for abandoning Kara. Lovingly, she touched the bow, which in itself was an extravagant item amongst the poverty of her surroundings. She would use the ribbon to decorate her old straw bonnet. Her thin hand slowly peeled back the wrapping. A high-necked maroon bodice with a deep lace collar and cuffs and a row of jet and diamanté buttons met her eyes. She gasped at the elegant beauty.

'I don't deserve this,' she said, emotion choking her throat. Lifting out the bodice, she saw beneath it a skirt of the same material, its hem trimmed with scalloped braid. Accompanying it was a black lace shawl, and a wide, circular, black straw hat decorated with maroon silk ribbons.

'You deserve this and so much more,' Zach encouraged. 'Why deny yourself and Kara the happiness you can bring each other?'

'You're a persuasive rogue, Captain Morton.'

The threatening tears spilled on to her cheeks. Her last dress had been bought five years ago, and that had only been second-hand. Her throat cramped and she had to swallow several times before she could speak.

'It is a beautiful dress, but how can I accept it? It will only be stolen.' Reverently she touched the fine material. 'And how do I explain to Joseph where it has come from? He knows nothing of Kara.'

'You cannot keep your daughter a secret. Be proud of her, as she is proud of you. Joseph will understand.'

Florence sighed, torn by diverse loyalties. 'And Beatrice? Will she understand? Joseph is a good man, but he is proud. He would be hurt if I accepted Kara's generosity.'

'Then tell Joseph that I bought you the dress second-hand. You did hide me from the peelers. I said then I would not forget your kindness.'

'Joseph will not believe that.'

Zach grinned. 'Then he may believe that I have my eye on you, Florence Wyse. And if he does not make a respectable woman of you, now that you are a widow, he may find I've beaten him to it.'

She laughed and then winced at the pain biting into her chest. 'You're a wicked man, Captain Morton.' Her gaze rested on the dress and she could not stop herself holding it against her body.

'You'll look the real lady you were born to be when next you meet Kara,' Zach said, bowing to her. 'I shall tell her you will come on Thursday.'

'Ma, where did you get that dress?' Beatrice was across the room, snatching the bodice and skirt from her mother's hands.

Florence had not heard her enter, and hoped that she had not heard their conversation. She studied her younger daughter closely, but all she saw in her beautiful face was greed.

Beatrice was twisting from side to side to allow the dim light to fall on the gown. 'It is a little dull in colour, but must have cost a fortune.' She pressed it against her curvaceous figure and scowled at seeing that it would not fit. 'You'll never wear it, Ma. But I could have a couple of panels inserted in the bodice. If I took all that prim lace off and had the neck lowered...'

'The dress is your mother's,' Zach cut in sharply. 'I bought it for her to thank her for hiding me from the constables two years ago. I would be most displeased to learn that it had been taken from her by anyone.'

Beatrice rounded on him, her lovely face screwed into a spiteful snarl. Zach saw his error. At all times he must tread warily with Beatrice until he had wed Kara.

'Besides, my dear,' he added as he allowed his gaze to travel admiringly over her plump curves. 'That colour is not for you. I chose it especially for your mother. You should be dressed in emerald green and golds to show off your magnificent Titian-red hair.'

Beatrice sauntered across the room, her hips swinging provocatively. She put a hand on Zach's chest and he smelt the reek of her cheap perfume and staleness of her body. Kara always smelt of jasmine and soap. She reminded him of the freshness and promise of a spring day, whilst Beatrice had the blowsy sultriness of a hot summer's night.

She smiled seductively and rubbed her hip against his thigh. 'And what would I have to do, for you to buy me a dress of emerald silk, Captain?'

'Beatrice!' Florence grabbed her daughter's hand and jerked her away from Zach. 'How dare you behave in that way to a guest in my house?'

Beatrice shrugged, her gaze bold as it continued to appraise him. His body had responded to her touch, and it was with difficulty that he remembered the danger involved in again taking Beatrice as his mistress. If Kara ever learned of it, she would never marry him.

He drew out his fob-watch and looked suitably annoyed at discovering it was so late. 'I am due at Lord Kilgavin's at four. He values my opinion on horseflesh and wants me to inspect his new racehorses. He's convinced he has just bought the next Derby winner.' Zach turned to Florence and, when he bowed over her hand, whispered, 'I will be waiting in a hansom at the top of the alleyway on Thursday evening at nine. Kara will be expecting you. Please do not disappoint her.'

With Beatrice present, Florence would not protest. Turning to the younger woman, he thought it wise to placate her before leaving. With an enigmatic smile, he put an arm around her waist and led her outside. He halted in a darkened alley where the shadows afforded them some privacy.

'I was displeased to see you following me at the fairground,' he said coldly. 'We had something special, Bea. We could have that again.'

'Who was the woman you were with?' she challenged.

'It is the woman I intend to marry. It's the only way I shall get my legacy from my grandfather.'

'Marriage! You?' She mocked to hide the pain tearing at her heart. 'You ain't the marrying kind. What decent family would accept a black sheep like you?'

Her chin was gripped in steely fingers. 'This marriage is important to me. Remember that.' His amber eyes glittered with warning, chilling her blood. 'Don't cross me in this, Bea.' He raised a dark brow, his voice deepening to seductive coercion. 'But afterwards…'

His promise was completed as he pulled her hard against him and kissed her with savage passion. For a second there was resistance to his dominance. Then, as his tongue tantalised the inner softness of her mouth, Beatrice moaned. Her arms went around him and her body moved enticingly against his thigh.

He felt his blood take fire and, when his hands caressed her heavy breasts, the ache in his loins to possess her almost broke his control. A shudder went through him as he mastered his desire and drew back. 'Bea, you are a beautiful and tempting woman; but, even for you, I will not risk destroying my plans for the future. Be patient, my darling. Did I not promise that one day I would help you to escape from Fancy Gilbert? My marriage will be the means of your escape, I promise.'

'You mean that, Zach?'

He smiled and ran a finger along her cheek. 'Trust me, Bea.'

At seeing the questions forming in her eyes, he kissed her with a thoroughness which made her sway against him. He left her abruptly, his backward glance seeing her reach out to touch the wall until the strength returned to her limbs. He grinned. She was a passionate baggage that needed taming. Women like Bea had always fascinated him. There was an element of danger surrounding Fancy Gilbert's mistress which heightened Zach's attraction. And she was dangerous in her own right. He would keep her guessing at his intentions, her hopes expectant of a future for them together. Her disillusion could come later when he had achieved his ends.

Would the last customers in the shop ever make up their minds as to which book they wanted? Kara fretted with impatience. Florence could arrive at any minute, and this woman and her friend were dithering from one shelf of books to another. They did not even look the type who would be educated enough to read. Their clothing was too brightly coloured for good taste and, even from across the floor, Kara could smell a sickly sweet cheap rose perfume.

'Was there any particular book you were

looking for, ladies?' Kara asked.

The auburn-haired woman in the pink and black striped skirt and pink velvet bodice watched her approach with open animosity. Often Kara met with censure from women customers, who did not approve that she managed the shop on her own. Prejudice was still engrained: trade was a male domain, unless a woman was a dressmaker or milliner.

'Actually, I was looking for something for a birthday present for a gentleman friend. Possibly a book on thoroughbred horses. Being an ex-army officer, he's something of an authority.'

Kara took from the shelf a cheap edition of a work on famous racehorses. She felt a growing dislike for the woman's insolent manner.

'Don't you have one bound in leather? The quality of this looks rather inferior.'

'Of course, madam.' Kara swallowed her anger at the woman's derisive tone. She handed her a leather volume embossed with gold leaf.

'You'll not make a profit if you select the cheapest as first choice,' the woman said nastily. 'Or didn't you think I could afford such a fine edition? Appearances are deceptive, are they not?'

Somehow Kara got the impression that the woman was not talking about the novel. There was something disturbingly familiar about her, which she could not place. As she watched the customer flick absently through the pages, she belatedly recognised her. It was the woman who had been staring at her so venomously at the fairground when she had been dancing with

Zach. And Zach had been an officer in the army. Was this woman an acquaintance of his? Unaccountably, she felt discountenanced. She had thought better of Zach than that he could mix with such low women.

'Does madam wish to purchase the book?' she inquired smoothly, refusing to show that the recognition had ruffled her.

The woman's painted lips curled back disdainfully. 'No, I don't think so. I've seen what I came to see and I'm not impressed. You think yourself something special don't you, Miss Wyse? A business of your own; a handsome beau to escort you about town. A business like this…' The expensive book dropped from her hands to the floor, the corner damaged. 'A woman should not take on more than she can handle.' Another gold-embossed book was taken from the shelf and tossed into a corner.

'What do you think you're doing?' Kara grabbed the woman's wrist as she reached for a third book. 'Leave my shop at once.'

The shop bell jangled and Kara turned with relief, expecting to find Zach and Florence at the door. Instead, two thickset men with the hard faces of bullies had entered. Alarm prickled her scalp as one of them pulled down the blind over the door and the other turned down the gas jets so that the shop was only dimly lit. Their clothing proclaimed them villains, although one wore a good quality suit which looked slovenly on his menacing figure. They planted their feet apart and regarded her with open hostility. With a laugh the two women left.

Kara's heart pumped frantically with mounting fear. The woman was these men's accomplice. She had delayed Kara closing the shop until they could arrive. Kara had dismissed James a quarter of an hour ago, so that he would ask no awkward questions when Florence arrived. She did not like keeping her mother's identity a secret from Sophia, but she was still unsure as to the best way to introduce the two women. It would be better once Florence had agreed to come and live with her.

'We are closed, gentlemen,' Kara said, gripping her hands together so they would not see that she was shaking.

One of the men stepped forward. He was of medium height, stockily built with wide shoulders and heavy arms. An untidy mop of sandy, grizzled hair fell over his narrow brow, adding to the brutish appearance of his blunt, ugly features. A thick rambling moustache covered his upper lip and cheeks. His small eyes were cruel and his stare was calculating as it took in the stock and furnishings of the shop. He nodded to his companion, who withdrew a small cudgel out of his jacket.

'First we'll relieve you of the trouble of counting up the day's takings,' the stocky man grunted. 'Give us the money from the till.'

Kara's knees quaked. She was alone and at their mercy. 'There is only small change.' She defied them, though her throat was dry with terror. 'My assistant took the money to the bank's night safe when he left this evening.' She prayed they knew nothing of the safe at the back of the shop where she had actually placed the day's takings.'

'Now that disappoints me,' the man who was clearly the leader declared. He brought up a hand the size of a ham and banged it down on the counter, sending an arrangement of embroidered greetings cards, which they had just begun to stock, spilling on to the ground. 'And it don' do to disappoint me,' he growled. 'I gets angry. When I gets angry, I gets nasty. And when I gets nasty, people gets 'urt.'

He again nodded to his companion, who was a gruesome scurrying beetle of a man, dressed in rusty black and with an eye-patch further disfiguring a face covered in yellow-headed boils. The cudgel came down on to the glass-topped counter, smashing it. He reached inside and scooped out the gold pens in their cases.

Kara screamed. 'Stop it! Thieves! Thieves!' She knew the constables patrolled the road. Please God let them be close by!

'Shut yer caterwauling!' The leader slapped her across the face with such force that she reeled back against the damaged counter. She tasted the iron tang of blood from the cut at the side of her mouth. As her hand came down on the broken glass, it tore into her flesh. The pain was agonising but, as her fingers closed around a shard of glass, she yanked it out of the wooden frame and brandished it before her like a dagger.

'Get out of my shop.' She swiped it across the stout man's body. With a cruel laugh he leapt back and drew a vicious-looking knife from inside his jacket.

'A woman wiv spirit. I likes that. But not when it goes against me orders. And such a pretty neck. 'Twould be a pity to slice it from ear to ear. Don't mess with Slasher Gilbert, lady. Yer can't win.'

There was the sound of books crashing to the floor, and another glass display cabinet was smashed. A hasty glance behind her showed Kara that the other man was systematically wrecking the shop.

'I've told you, I've got no money here.' She continued to make jabbing movements with the dagger of glass which kept the stout man cautiously at bay, but his grin remained evil.

He dodged behind the counter and opened the silver-coloured till. When he scraped out several banknotes and silver coins, Kara screamed.

'Thieves! Help me! Thieves!'

At any moment Zach was due here. Dear God, let him not be late.

There was the sound of running feet outside.

'Run fer it, Slasher,' the accomplice shrilled. 'Could be the peelers.'

Kara's eyes were large with fear as she stared at Slasher Gilbert. He lunged at her with a speed surprising for such a bulky man. She screamed again as the edge of his knife was laid against her cheek.

'This ain't the last you'll see of us,' he threatened, brandishing the stolen money in her face. 'We'll be back next week and every week. If'n yer don' want ter see yer pretty face all torn up, or this fancy shop go up in flames, yer'll give us fifty pounds each visit.'

He ran out of the shop, and Kara heard the

shrill-voiced thief cry out in pain as someone attacked him. There was the sound of several punches meeting a solid body. Then a curse, and the sound of fleeing boots on the cobbles, followed by a threatening shout.

To her relief Kara recognised Zach's voice. She staggered to the door as he entered the shop. There was a cut on his cheek and his expression was murderous. 'Kara, my darling, are you safe? I tried to stop the robbers, but they overpowered me and ran off.'

Kara ran sobbing into his arms. She had never been so grateful to see anyone before in her life. 'Those awful men. The things they did. They stole… They stole…'

'Hush, my darling. They got away, but I'll recognise them again. They'll not escape justice.'

Kara clung to Zach, her body shaking from the reaction of the attack. 'But they said I had to pay money… Every week… Or they'd cut my face and burn down the shop…'

'Empty threats, my darling, to scare you into paying,' Zach assured her. 'You were so brave. So wonderfully brave, I'm proud of you. Thank God you're safe.'

He looked over her head to see Florence standing white-faced in the doorway. Like him she had recognised Slasher Gilbert. Zach had attacked Chalky White, Slasher's accomplice. He had also hissed a warning in Slasher's ear that, if he wanted him to continue to bring toffs to his clubs, he'd better lay off troubling Miss Wyse for protection money.

Slasher had answered him with a knife slash to

his ribs. A soldier's quick reflexes had saved him from being wounded. Slasher did not take kindly to warnings. He would have to find some way to make his peace with the underworld gangleader, or his throat might be the next slashed for interfering in the Gilbert brothers' rule.

From out of the shadows across the road, Beatrice stared at the dimly lit shop and smiled. Slasher would teach that uppity bitch a lesson. She grinned as she saw the woman threaten Slasher with something and he backed off. To her surprise the woman screamed as the shop was wrecked and refused to cower at Slasher's brutality. She had guts, she'd give her that. Then Slasher had lost patience and she'd seen the glint of his knife as it was laid against her throat. Serve her right if Slasher ruined her face. Perhaps then Zach would not be so keen to marry her.

Beatrice had been tempted to go for the woman herself and leave her disfigured, but if Zach found out, he'd leave her. She couldn't risk that. She loved him too much. In recent weeks, deprived of his company whilst he courted that haughty bitch, her love had become an obsession.

It had been a shock to see Zach appear on the scene, and she had ducked back into the shadows to avoid him recognising her. He'd never guess that she'd tipped off Slasher that the woman was an easy target. Most of the smaller shops in this area paid protection money to Slasher. Even so, she felt uneasy.

It had turned quickly to astonishment when she saw who had accompanied her lover. What was Florence doing here – and wearing her new dress?

When the shopkeeper ran into Zach's arms, her fury exploded. He was holding her so tenderly, as though she was precious to him. Beatrice could not bear to watch further. When Florence returned she would force her mother to tell her what her business was with Miss Kara Wyse.

Chapter Thirteen

'What has happened?' Sophia demanded as she entered the shop parlour and stared in horror at Kara's hand. It was dripping blood and was being bathed and bandaged by Florence. 'What was all that noise and crashing about?'

Kara shot Zach and her mother a warning glance before answering. 'Some youths were being boisterous. I broke a glass and cut my hand.'

'Does your hand need stitches?' Sophia said with such concern that it made Kara feel guilty about having lied to her. She did not want Sophia upset at learning about Slasher Gilbert's threat.

Kara shook her head. 'No, the cut isn't deep.'

'And this woman, is she a customer?' Sophia turned her concern upon Florence. 'Did the youth annoy you too?'

'This is my mother, Sophia,' Kara said simply.

'I thought you were an orphan.' Sophia sounded hurt.

'It is a long story, Sophia, and not one for tonight.'

Sophia's normal curiosity was dampened by her fear for the shop. 'Did the youths cause any damage to the premises? We are vulnerable as women alone. Wasn't James here?'

'There is little damage,' Kara reassured her. 'I will tidy it up. I had sent James home early.'

'How much damage did they cause?' Sophia made to enter the shop, but Zach waylaid her.

'They did little damage,' he said. 'Just knocked some books on the floor. Don't upset yourself, Sophia. It's Kara's job to see to the running of the shop.' As he spoke he guided her back to the stairs which led into the house. 'Isn't that little Heather I hear crying? Go see to her. You are not to worry. I warned the lads off. They'll not trouble you again. You have my word on it.'

Sophia still looked worried, but Zach had won her confidence from their first meeting and she was prepared to trust his advice. 'It's Kara I worry about. It is she who works in the shop at night. It's not right for a woman alone. She needs a husband to protect her.'

Zach smiled and whispered, 'I'm working on that, Sophia.'

The widow's face lit with joy. 'Nothing would give me more pleasure than to see the two of you wed. Kara is an independent woman who is too stubborn to admit she needs a man. Be patient, Captain Morton.'

Kara saw Zach reassuring Sophia and was grateful that he was allaying her partner's fears. Later she would have to explain to her partner about her mother. All that mattered for the present was to get the mess in the shop cleared up. They must open for business as normal tomorrow morning. But how was she going to replace the two smashed display cases? If Sophia learned the true extent of the damage and of the threats made, she would be too frightened to continue the partnership. Although Kara had the money to buy her out, what would her friend do to support herself? And Kara wanted to open a second shop as soon as possible. She could not do that if she purchased Sophia's share of the business.

A wave of nausea made her clutch her hand to her mouth and she swayed in the seat.

'The shock has been too much for you,' Florence said as she finished bandaging her daughter's hand.

With a gasp Kara stood up, unable to hold back her nausea. She fled to the sink in the narrow kitchen behind the parlour. As she straightened, her mother's arm was around her shoulders. When she turned to face Florence, her mother was studying her with concern.

'I think you should marry Captain Morton without delay. For more than the sake of his protection. You are carrying his child, are you not?'

Kara stared at her mother in astonishment. A glance over her shoulder showed her that thankfully Zach had not overheard. Having quietened Sophia's fears, he had returned to the shop; she could hear him collecting up the broken glass.

'I must get the shop put straight,' Kara began, refusing to understand the implication of her mother's statement.

'Kara, you do realise that you are expecting a child?' Florence took her shoulders and forced her to meet her worried gaze. 'I doubt you were told anything about how babies come into the world. But I know a pregnant woman when I see one. It's something about their eyes which tells me, before sometimes the mother knows her condition herself.'

Kara was still shocked from Slasher Gilbert's attack. The realisation that the queasiness she had been experiencing in the last days' – and the lateness of her monthly course – could mean she was pregnant, stunned her.

'You must marry Captain Morton as soon as possible. Otherwise your reputation will be ruined, and with it your business,' Florence urged. 'It's clear you need a man to protect you from the Gilbert brothers. I recognised the man who was threatening you. He's dangerous and does not make idle threats. The captain can handle him. You must marry him, Kara.'

'It's not his child,' Kara whispered. 'And I cannot wed the father. He's married already.' She bowed her head, expecting her mother's wrath to descend upon her.

Instead Florence took her into her arms. 'You were such an innocent to be cast into the world after Abel's death. How many weeks since your last course?'

'Six.'

'Captain Morton clearly adores you. Marry him without delay and you'll convince him that the child is his.'

'That would be dishonest.'

'It will save a lot of heartache. Trust me. I know men. What right has the real father to know you carry his child, if he is wed to another? How will it affect his life?'

Kara knew she could never tell Richard. But to deceive Zach, after he had been so kind to her, seemed equally wrong.

'Marry Zach Morton,' Florence urged, though she hid her misgivings that the charming rogue was not the ideal husband for her daughter. She knew little about him. She suspected that he was a swell-mobster. It concerned her that Beatrice appeared to have taken a fancy to the officer. But Beatrice was flighty in her affections. She did not think that her younger daughter was foolish enough to take another lover whilst she was Fancy Gilbert's mistress. Fancy would kill her if he suspected. At least Zach Morton had been born a gentleman. He would protect Kara. Perhaps marriage would end his life of crime, and he would settle down to a respectable life. She hoped so. Kara must wed soon. If she did not, once it was obvious that she was pregnant, she would be branded a fallen woman. No respectable citizen would then enter her shop.

'Kara, you must safeguard not only the child, but your business,' she continued. 'Let him believe the child is his. His pride would demand that much from you.'

'But I know so little about him, and I don't love him.'

'Few marriages are founded on true love. From what I know of Captain Morton he will look after you. Though you may be wise to ensure that he cannot get his hands on your money too easily.' At Kara's angry frown, Florence hastily added, 'It would be prudent to protect your financial independence with some legal document. Had I been so foresighted, I would not have ended up destitute when Abel threw me out. He kept the money I had brought to our marriage. Now, let's get the shop tidied up.'

Florence swept up the last of the broken glass and Kara put the books back in order on the shelves.

'Fortunately only seven of the expensively bound volumes were damaged. I'll sell them at cost price. But what about the display cabinets?'

'I'll see to that,' Zach announced. 'I'll be back in half an hour with a glazier.'

True to his word, he was. The glazier and his apprentice were carrying several large pieces of glass to repair the cabinets. It was four in the morning before all the work was finished and the shop neat and tidy. To Kara's surprise, Zach had worked as hard as the two women to ensure the shop would open tomorrow as usual. Kara was swaying on her feet with exhaustion. She embraced her mother, who had not stopped working all night.

'This was not much of a reunion – and you've got your lovely gown all dusty,' she said with a sigh.

'I'm delighted to have been of help. Though I could have wished that the circumstances were not so harrowing.' Florence held Kara at arm's length and her voice dropped to a whisper. 'Remember my words. Marry Captain Morton.'

Kara pressed her fingers to her temple. Her cut hand was throbbing painfully, but she had scarcely noticed it until now. With a shudder she remembered the destruction in the shop and Slasher Gilbert's threats. At recalling Sophia's frightened face, she knew that she could not stand up to brutes like Slasher Gilbert alone. Also her baby would need a father.

Her mind whirled in confusion and she looked across at Zach. He had removed his frock coat and had worked in his waistcoat and shirt sleeves. Few men would have spent six hours sweeping, dusting and rearranging the stock. A rush of affection warmed her chilled body. He was handsome and charming enough for any woman to be proud to call him husband. Despite Richard's warnings that he was not to be trusted, Zach had shown her nothing but kindness and consideration. And his kiss at the weekend had proved that she was not unsusceptible to him as a man.

The baby had changed everything. She had so fiercely wanted to be independent in her success, but she would be condemned as morally corrupt if she bore a child out of marriage. If she did not marry she would lose her reputation and her business. Since it was impossible to marry Richard, why not Zach?

'That's everything done, I believe,' Zach called out. 'Is it to your satisfaction, Kara?'

'I could not have managed without you.'

He grinned. Although Florence had sat down to rest on a chair and was watching them speculatively, he stared tenderly at Kara.

'I have longed for the day when you would say

that. Surely you must see now how dangerous it is for you to be without a man's protection. I love you, Kara. No one would harm your business if I was your husband. Marry me. Say yes, and I'll get a special licence. We could be married in a week. The sooner the better to stop these thugs attacking you again. When I think what might have happened if I had not come along when I did...'

The anguish in his voice made up Kara's mind. Zach was so eager to wed her he would never question the haste of their wedding. If only she did not have to deceive him about the child. Yet instinctively she knew that Florence was right. Zach might claim to love her, but he was a proud man. If they married quickly, he would never suspect that the child was not his. Wasn't it better that way? The child would grow up with a loving father, rather than with one riddled with suspicion.

'Marriage is a big step, Zach. I would not want to give up the shop,' she still prevaricated.

'I know you too well to ask that of you. But don't expect me to become a shopkeeper myself. I have my own affairs to run.'

Kara was reassured that he did not want to take over her business. That would have been unacceptable to her. She realised that she knew so little of Zach and now felt it prudent to ask. 'Since you left the army, you have taken no employment that you have spoken of. I assume you are a gentleman of independent means.'

There was a flicker of annoyance on his face as she questioned his means of income, but she dismissed it as pride. The frown was gone almost as soon as it appeared, and he laughed. 'Does that mean you are considering my proposal? When I marry I inherit a legacy from my father's estate. It was his way of ensuring that I settled to a respectable life. Until now, I shied away from such a commitment. But as soon as I met you, my darling, I knew that marriage and respectability do not form an onerous yoke. As to my financial circumstances, I have contacts at Tattersalls: I buy and sell horses on a commission. That and other ventures, details of which I will not bore you with tonight.'

He clasped her hands, taking care not to hurt her wounded fingers, and sank down on to one knee. 'Will you honour me by becoming my wife, Kara?'

For a long moment she looked down into his handsome face. The tenderness in his eyes moved her. In her heart she knew he was something of a rogue, but was she any better? She was carrying a married man's child. Zach had shown her only kindness and consideration, precious values so lacking in her childhood. If she was capable of caring for any man other than Richard, it would be Zach.

Behind her she could feel Florence holding her breath.

'Yes, Zach. I would be honoured to be your wife.'

The marriage was set for two weeks later. Bearing in mind her mother's advice about her money, Kara visited Richard at his office. She needed to ensure that her capital could not be touched if she needed it for expansion.

'You are to wed Morton!' He could not have reacted more violently if she had pulled a pistol on him. 'Why? You can't love him.'

'I don't want to spend my life alone, Richard. And I was frightened by a visit from the leader of a criminal gang. He wants me to pay protection money to prevent having my shop wrecked, or burnt to the ground. Zach has said he can stop the Gilbert brothers carrying out their threats.'

'No doubt, since he is probably embroiled in some of their nefarious schemes. He's a rogue and a scoundrel, Kara.'

'Have you proof of that?' she blazed back at him. They stood on either side of his desk, both bristling like bantam cocks, each battling to hide their pain. 'Or are you jealous? You can't marry me, Richard, and you don't want anyone else to.'

Richard rounded the desk and lifted his arms as though to embrace her, then let them fall to his side. 'I want only what is best for you. Morton will not make you happy. He has a reputation as a ladies' man and a gambler. If you're not careful, he'll squander your money and leave you destitute.'

'Then to safeguard my business I want a document drawn up which stops him drawing any money from my account. Does the Married Women's Property Act provide for that? Will such a document hold up in a court of law?'

'Are you truly set upon this marriage, Kara?'

'Yes.'

'Do you love Morton?'

'You know the answer to that. But I believe I can find contentment in my marriage. It is enough.'

Richard sighed and ran a hand through his dark hair. 'I suppose at least he will protect you from the Gilbert brothers. He may even help your mother. I suspect that I was unable to trace her because she lived in one of the poorest quarters. It is a way of life there to protect another's anonymity. As to your money... The best way to protect it is to invest it immediately in a second shop. Your business bank account will be solely in your name. But what would Sophia think of expansion?'

'She's against it. I intend to buy other premises and open them under the name of Wyse Books, but I shall keep my partnership with Sophia until she wishes to end it. That is only fair to her. As soon as possible I shall open a shop in the suburbs where they are building all those new houses for the middle-classes. Can you arrange for me to see some property at the end of the week?'

'If that is what you want.'

'It is.'

'Might I also suggest that you have a solicitor on the Board of Directors and pay him a retainer. My new partner is a man of impeccable character.'

'You do not suggest yourself,' she said sorrowfully.

'I am leaving for South America in three months. I intend to be away for at least a year,' he announced gruffly, his manner stiff and formal.

Kara rode the blow, her emotions shielded, though her heart felt that it was breaking. She blinked rapidly to dispel the tears which pricked her eyelids. They were acting as coldly and remotely as strangers, yet she was carrying his child. She longed to throw herself into his arms to beg him to make a life for the three of them together. It was an impossible dream.

'If you feel you must marry to protect your business,' Richard said in a heavy voice, 'must it be Morton?'

'What have you against him?' she demanded fiercely, hurt by the coldness of his tone.

'I don't trust him.'

'He has given me no reason to doubt his integrity. He discovered the whereabouts of my mother. Sophia and her children adore him. He has shown me nothing but kindness. He has always been there when I needed him.'

'As I was not.' The pain in his voice pierced her composure.

'As you could not be,' she corrected truthfully. 'I don't blame you, Richard. Our love was ill fated. Do not begrudge me a chance to find contentment, if not true happiness. Life is a compromise. If our marriages are not formed on love, then we both have other passions. Yours is South America. Mine is to own a chain of shops.'

He closed the space between them and Kara's heartbeat quickened. Silently, she stared into his beloved face, committing every feature to memory. Memories would be all she would have in the future.

She could feel her pulse begin to race and, to

control the need to feel his loving arms around her, she asked, 'Have you told Elizabeth that you are going to South America?'

'I intend to do so whilst we are holidaying in Brighton next week. It may soften the blow.'

'I shall be married when you return. Elizabeth will be upset that she missed the wedding, but it is best if I wed whilst you are out of London. I doubt I could go through with it if you were there.'

'Neither could I witness you being wed to another.' His expression was grave and his eyes dark with tortured longing. 'Or is it that you feel you have to marry Morton? Were there consequences from our night together?'

'I do not have to marry him,' Kara needed all her willpower to force the deception out. 'I was frightened by Slasher Gilbert's visit and Zach has been kind to me. I believe he loves me.'

'Not as I love you,' he said softly. 'I will never stop loving you.'

'Nor I you.'

Without conscious thought they were in each other's arms, their lips forged in a passionate kiss. Kara briefly surrendered to this glorious moment of forbidden passion, then with a strangled sob wrenched away.

'Don't make it harder for me than it is,' she said raggedly. 'Know that I will always love you. That if our love is meant to be, it is not at this moment in time.'

He smiled wanly. 'You will no more divorce Morton than I will Elizabeth. Marriage is until death do you part.'

The hairs on Kara's neck prickled with foreboding. Spoken like that, the words seemed an ill omen.

With Florence's consent, Kara explained to Sophia that her mother had just returned from a sanatorium abroad. Florence's obvious ill-health gave credence to their story. It also meant Florence could still evade questions as to where she resided.

'Does your mother live close by?' Sophia persisted, her love of gossip making her probe more deeply.

Much as Kara liked her partner, her curiosity could be annoying, especially when she did not want to be open about a subject. She was also aware that, although kind-hearted, like all gossips, Sophia could not be trusted to keep a confidence.

'She frequently visits the spa towns, and when in London stays at either the Ritz, or with friends,' Kara improvised.

Sophia accepted Kara's story, though Kara disliked the deception. She could hardly tell her friend that her mother refused to tell Kara where she lived.

The day following the visit from Slasher Gilbert, Zach arrived at the shop and presented Kara with an engagement ring of five diamonds in a half-hoop. It had obviously cost a small fortune, proving to her that Zach was not marrying her because he believed that she was wealthy.

Indeed, they never spoke of finances. Although

he knew the truth behind Florence leaving her father and, from being billeted in Brentwood, knew that her father owned Wyse Haulage Company, she had never told him that he had committed suicide because he was bankrupt. Nor did she mention the breach-of-contract settlement she had received from Ernest Holman. There would be little of that left once she opened the second shop as Richard had suggested. They would in future live off the income from the two shops, though she was still determined to save most of the profits towards the next shop she would open.

Zach had been equally evasive about his finances. She suspected that there were some aspects of his life which he deliberately kept from her. To be able to say that he could stop Slasher Gilbert carrying out his threats must mean he had some hold over the man. He refused to be drawn on the matter. Usually he turned the subject so skilfully, it was not until much later that Kara realised he had not answered some of her questions.

Word had spread of the quality of the books and new stationery lines in the shop; the business rapidly increased. New premises were found in Walthamstow; Kara planned to open any further shops in Essex and London to re-establish the name of Wyse in the county of her birth. She was kept busy with the orders and fittings for the new shop, and with interviewing staff. Also she was investigating further ways of improving existing stock.

To her surprise, Zach was pleased when she

told him that she intended to purchase a second shop. It never dawned on her that he would see it as proof of her unlimited wealth.

At Sophia's insistence, Kara left the wedding arrangements to her and Florence to decide upon. All she insisted upon was that the affair was to be simple and the wedding breakfast was to be in the house and garden. Sophia was in her element, hiring extra staff, organising the menu, caterers, the flowers and the dresses for the three eldest of her daughters who were to be bridesmaids. Zach had invited his father and his brother's family to the wedding, but only his father had accepted.

At Zach's suggestion they were to spend their honeymoon in Paris. Kara had protested, saying she could take no time off from the shops, especially as the new one was due to open in a few weeks.

'Then delay the opening,' Zach firmly insisted. 'You only get one honeymoon. I want my wife to myself for a few weeks. Is that so unreasonable?'

She reluctantly conceded. She intended to make her marriage work, and that must of course start on the honeymoon itself. 'I'll open the Walthamstow shop in September. Does that satisfy you?'

His prolonged kiss had been his response. 'You work too hard, Kara. Life is for playing as well as working. And talking of playing, you mentioned a wish to see Henry Irving playing *Dante* in Dury Lane. There're rumours he's shortly off to America. I've got two tickets to see him tonight.'

'Zach, you spoil me.' She threw her arms

around him. She had planned to work on the accounts tonight, but the thought of seeing the great Irving perform excited her. With Zach there would always be more play than work, she suspected.

The days sped by and the wedding loomed closer. Kara still had so many arrangements to make to ensure the shop in Oxford Street was fully stocked and the interior of the new one in Walthamstow was fitted with shelves to her specification. Another saleswoman was also needed in Oxford Street as Kara had no intention of overloading Sophia with work whilst she was on honeymoon.

Until now Florence had refused to take any money from her. In her evening visits to the house she had become friends with Sophia as they planned Kara's wedding. Avoiding Sophia's questions about her life had not been easy, but she had managed by turning the questions back upon Sophia, who loved to talk about her late husband and her children.

From the redness of her mother's hands, it was obvious that she worked at some menial task. Kara offered her employment in the shop and was touched by the eagerness with which she accepted. To keep up the ruse which Florence had adopted of affluent respectability, Kara paid her mother's salary out of her own income. As far as Sophia was concerned, Florence was helping out as the shop had become so busy.

'It will give me an opportunity to wear the lovely maroon dress you gave me,' Florence said with obvious pleasure. Then with a frown she looked down at her reddened hands and sighed. 'But just look at these. When Sophia notices them, she will know we've lied to her.'

'I saw some pretty lace gloves the other day when I was in Harrods looking at material for my wedding gown. Wear them. You can always say you've a skin condition if anyone asks. But what will make Sophia suspicious will be you wearing the same dress every day. This afternoon we will visit Harrods. I'll buy material for three gowns for you which will be suitable for work in the shop. You must have a special outfit for my wedding as well.'

'Kara, I will not allow you to spend so much money on me.'

'Nonsense. Sophia is a sweet person, but a fearful snob. You refuse to tell me of your present life. But nothing you do, or where you live, would make me ashamed of you. I know it could not have been easy. But I can afford to buy you new dresses, and I want to do so. That money is as much yours as mine, but you won't accept it.'

'The Holmans treated you abominably. You deserve the money they paid for breaking off the engagement. And you need it to build your business. I will not be a burden to you, Kara.'

'You could never be that.'

Reluctantly Florence agreed. The material was purchased and she was fitted by the dressmaker who came to the house the next day. After great persuasion, Florence also accepted a matching silk hat and parasol to accompany the lilac silk she would be wearing for the wedding.

After the dressmaker left, Kara turned to

Florence, her expression serious. 'Mama, I want Beatrice to be at my wedding. Why do you still refuse to allow us to meet?'

Immediately Florence's manner became guarded. 'I wanted you to be settled first. Please, Kara, wait until after the wedding. Beatrice needs to be handled carefully. Her life has been so different from yours. She will resent your wealth when she has suffered so much poverty. When she learned that I was in your shop after it was wrecked, she was very abusive, insisting that I tell her who you were. I've never seen her like that before. She frightened me, Kara. I told her that I was there because I had applied for the job of shop assistant. That fitted, since I have now started work in the shop.'

'If she would resent my wealth, let me give her a present,' Kara urged, determined to end this prevarication. 'Surely as my sister she is entitled to half of Grandmama's legacy?'

'No, Kara. That is your money. You will use it wisely to build your dream of a chain of shops. Beatrice would squander it. Her portion would be gone in a year. Besides, the money was left to you, not to Beatrice.'

'Only because her existence was not known to Grandmama Wyse.'

'Kara, you are too generous and trusting for your own good.' Florence's eyes shone with affection. 'You must not give of yourself so readily. I want you and Beatrice to be friends, but you are so different in temperament and personality. Be patient.'

Kara could not accept that. 'At least let me

have a gown made for her to attend the wedding. And I have one you can take to her tonight when you tell her who I am.' Kara ran into her bedroom. She came out with the oyster silk gown she had worn for her engagement to Ernest, and on the night at the opera with Richard. The memories of Richard would stop her ever wearing the gown again. If her marriage to Zach was to stand any chance of happiness, she must have no reminders of Richard in the house.

'The dress is beautiful and too expensive,' Florence protested.

Kara shook her head. 'Nothing is too expensive for you, or my sister.'

Florence sighed, unable to withstand Kara's stronger will. 'I will give Beatrice the dress, but I wish you would wait until after your wedding to meet her.'

'There is something more, Mama.' Kara hedged, not sure how to say the next words without hurting her mother. 'I believe that you do not live alone, but with a man. It explains your refusal to move in here with me. Your loyalty does you credit. I would like to meet him also. Isn't it time for the deception to end? And isn't my wedding the best chance to end it?'

To her dismay, Florence burst into tears. Kara took her into her arms. 'Mama, it doesn't matter to me who you live with, or where you live. I just want us to be together as a family.'

'You will have a husband, and soon there will be the child,' Florence replied as she controlled her tears. 'They are your family. Zach would not want us living with you. You have done enough,

Kara. I've lived with Joseph Donovan for several years. He's a waterman. He's a rough man, but has a large heart. I would never have survived without him.'

'I would like to meet him,' Kara insisted.

'I will tell Joseph the truth tonight. I never mentioned that you were my daughter. He was surly when I told him I was to work for you, but he admitted that my wages were better than the pittance I earned cooking for the men in the tenement. He is a rough-spoken man. He would feel embarrassed and out of place at your wedding.'

Kara nodded. Florence's words were enough to tell her of the hardships which her mother had endured to survive. She also recognised the pride which wanted to keep that part of her life private. Kara did not persist. At least by offering work in the shop, Kara could help Florence more easily; she had deliberately made the wages high.

'I would still like to meet Joseph,' she went on. 'Would he come here to dine with me one evening?'

'I'll ask him.' Florence hid her misgivings. Joseph could be unpredictable, especially if he had more than a quart or two of ale inside him. He was a proud man. He believed that the man was the provider. If he knew that Kara was paying her twice as much as he earned, he would resent it. Florence owed Joseph Donovan too much ever to want to hurt his feelings or wound his pride.

When Beatrice heard that Zach was indeed to

marry Kara Wyse she was furious. Jealousy knifed her, and her hatred for Zach's chosen bride filled her with a murderous rage. It burned through her body and soul, yet her expression remained a mask of unconcern. She was seated on Fancy Gilbert's lap in his brother's office in the largest of their gaming houses. Her unfocused stare fastened on one of the framed photographs of boxers on the Gilberts' circuit. Beneath her skirts, Fancy was stroking her bare buttocks. What she hated most about Fancy was the way he openly treated her as a whore. Tonight his coarse fondling went unheeded as she listened to Slasher's and Fancy's conversation.

'Well, wot d'ye say, Slasher? Do we leave the Wyse shop alone like Morton asks?'

'He's getting above hisself,' Slasher said, tapping his dagger blade against his palm. 'But at the moment we needs 'im. He brings in too many toffs ter do away wiv 'im as yet.'

His close-set brown eyes glinted evilly in the dim gaslight. Setting the dagger aside, he took out a gold snuff box and tipped some on to the back of his hand. With a loud sniff he inhaled it, specks of brown snuff dusting his monstrous sandy moustache. Wiping his nose with a large red-spotted kerchief, he leaned forward over the gilded French desk, which was incongruous in this seedy room. His necktie was hanging loosely and the front of his shirt was splashed with gravy from his last meal.

Beatrice hid her disgust at his slovenly appearance. Slasher thrust his head forward; his body was braced like a bull-terrier about to attack. His expensive suits, perfectly fitted and sewn by a Jewish tailor in lieu of protection money, always looked ill kempt on his stout, slouching frame.

Just being in the same room with them made her feel sick. Their brutal faces were smirking as they considered Zach's use to them. In their thirties, they had ruled the underworld in this part of London for seven years, after blowing up a warehouse where their predecessor was having a meeting. Nine villains had been murdered that day. And it had begun the Gilberts' reign of terror.

They had been born in these streets and orphaned when their father killed their mother and her lover after discovering them making love in a back alley. In a night of drunken rage, he'd assaulted several other men and had knifed a peeler who had tried to arrest him. He had been hanged two months later.

The orphaned boys had lived wild on the streets. From the age of ten, Slasher was fond of using his knife and bullying other youths into joining his gang. It was rumoured he'd killed his first man at twelve, sitting his throat before he robbed him. At fourteen he was already pimping for six whores. Twice he'd been in prison for robbery, the peelers unable to convict him on any murder charge.

Fancy's life had echoed his brother's. Only he preferred his fists to the knife. Slighter of build than Slasher, he'd taken the eye of Abraham Jacobs, a Jewish fence. He was his lover for a year before he had tied Jacobs up and beaten him to death. He'd then cleared his house of all valuables and set fire to it and the body. That money had bought the Gilberts their first club. Then they had begun to challenge rival gangs for supremacy in the underworld.

'I still think Morton should be taught a lesson,' Fancy grunted.

At that moment, Beatrice wished Zach Morton beaten to a pulp. He'd been so charming when last they met, so full of lying promises. A pox on the bastard. Who did he think he was, stringing her along?

With grim reflection her gaze roamed over the assortment of ancient instruments of torture which hung on the walls. Slasher had a love of any macabre and gruesome means of inflicting pain. Beatrice had seen them many times, but they still made her blood run cold. There were thumbscrews, the cat o' nine tails, evil tongs to gouge out eyes, a boot for crushing feet, and various iron devices to cramp a body in restricted and unnatural positions in order to extract a confession. Slasher kept his collection in working order, and did not hesitate to use them if given an excuse. The deep cellar below this club prevented any tortured screams being heard in the street. Not that Slasher needed such instruments to inflict his cruelty on any who crossed him. He prided himself on his skill with the dagger. Once he had skinned a rival pimp alive.

Fancy was painfully kneading Beatrice's buttock as his agitation grew. 'Morton needs teachin' a lesson. Now 'e's getting wed 'e wants ter turn respectable. He refused to open a window in Lord Kilgavin's house for the sneak-thief last week. ’E says his debts are long since paid to us. Reckons we can go to ’ell.’

A particularly painful pinch made Beatrice leap to her feet and strike Fancy on the shoulder as she rubbed her bruised flesh. Her blood froze as she caught the cruel glitter in his eyes. His hand shot out to grab her wrist, and he twisted her arm up behind her back, forcing her down on his lap. ‘I didn’t tell yer ter get up, slut.’

Beatrice kept her stare defiant. It was her only defence. Had he suspected that Zach had been in her bed? You could never tell with Fancy. He did not always retaliate at once. He was like a spider waiting in its web. He would enjoy seeing victims squirm as they became entrapped, delaying until the last moment the death blow to release them from their agony. God help her if he had suspected Zach had been her lover.

‘Leave the whore alone, Fancy,’ Slasher said irritably. ‘Wot she doin’ ’ere anyways? Get ’er out.’

Beatrice was pushed on to the floor.

‘’Op it,’ Fancy snarled, showing his missing teeth.

God, how she hated the pervert Fancy. She couldn’t take much more of his sadistic mauling. Zach had been her hope of escaping. He was betraying her by marrying that rich bitch. Rising to her feet, she moved to the door, relieved to get away from Fancy. As the door closed behind her, Slasher’s voice made her press her ear to the panelling.

‘Morton ain’t gettin’ off the ’ook that easy. ’Is marriage will make him respectable. ’Im and ’is missus are bound ter be invited ter the houses of swells. He had damn well better make sure there's a window left open for the boys to get in through. Just to make sure, I'll 'ave a couple of men pay a call on 'im. Just so 'e knows to stay in line after 'is marriage.'

So Zach was going to get done over, Beatrice mused. Serve the arrogant bleeder right. He had it coming. Even so, her rage was directed at Kara Wyse, not her faithless lover. Zach was not a one-woman man. She'd give him a month at the most of married life before his eyes began to wander. And she would ensure that she was in his viewing line when they did.

Later, as she strolled through the press of gamblers in the club, her thoughts were all filled with vengeance against Kara Wyse. There was a fight on in the basement tonight, and the club was filled with dandies. The room was thick with tobacco smoke and excited shouts rose from gamblers at the dice table. Several whores, wearing open robes over their corsets and stockings, hung on punters' arms, encouraging them to gamble more recklessly. In a curtained alcove, the groans of a couple rutting like rats in a midden could be heard; they were being egged on by three ragged urchins peering through a rent in the curtain. The atmosphere sickened Beatrice. She'd had enough of the pale-faced, drunken, foul-mouthed whores. She didn't want to end up like them, with eyes devoid of animation from the nightly degradation they endured to survive. She was getting out whilst she was still young. As soon as the first opportunity presented itself.

Several toffs called out for her to give them a song. She was about to tell them to sod off, when she caught sight of Fancy watching her. He nodded for her to sing.

She painted a smile on her lips and sauntered over to the gents. 'I can't be singing with a dry throat, now can I?' The only money she earned in the club was on the number of bottles of wine she could encourage the punters to drink.

'Champagne for the lady,' one called. 'Champagne for us all.'

Beatrice sipped from her glass and nodded for the bald-headed pianist to play her introduction. As the music started, there was a lull in the conversation and two tables were pushed together to provide a makeshift stage. The toffs milled around her, vying with each other to assist her on to the table.

She accepted their drunken praise of her beauty and figure, and kissed the cheek of one who tried to make an assignation with her.

'Yer'll 'ave yer song, gents, but I'm spoken for, yer know that.'

'But, Bea, I die for love of you.' His words slurred into a hiccough.

She laughed brittlely. 'Yer'll probably die all right if me boyfriend catches yer with yer 'and up me skirt.' She removed the prying fingers, at the same time assessing the value of the diamond pin in his cravat.

Impressed, she pushed to the back of her mind her fury at Zach's forthcoming marriage. The toff was still attractive, though he was in his late forties. He looked like he could handle himself. It might be worth the risk of seducing him. And she'd give him a night unequalled to any he had spent before. If she pleased him well enough, he might make Fancy an offer generous enough to allow her to escape from this life. It was only with such optimism that she could get through the dreary repetition of each squalid night in the club.

She smiled enticingly at the toff. A hasty scan of the room had shown her that Fancy had again disappeared.

Emboldened she whispered, 'Now if you was to show me a little generosity, I might be persuaded to take a meal with you one evening. But it would 'ave to be our secret.'

She rubbed her hip against his thigh, her breasts brushing the hand holding his glass. 'Just remember,' she added. 'I can't abide clutchfists. I like a man who knows how to value my worth.'

With a broad wink she left him and, hoisting her scarlet skirt high above her calves, climbed on to a chair and then on to the table. Keeping one side of her skirt raised to her knee to display a shapely stockinged leg, she paraded up and down as she began to sing.

Silence fell on the audience. Beatrice's voice was not exceptional, but her song was suggestive. She emphasised each bawdy innuendo with a provocative tilt of her hips, or stooped forward with a finger pointed at a toff's flushed face, so that their gazes could feast on her generously exposed breasts. Beatrice sashayed and pouted invitingly, her smile enticing to any who looked as though they could lavish jewels on her. From the first time Fancy had told her to lie with certain of the wealthier customers, she had decided that, if she had to be a whore, she'd make damn sure she was an expensive one. They might leave her bed grossly poorer, but they never left disappointed.

The only man besides Fancy to whom she gave herself for free was Zach Morton. And the faithless sod had thrown her generosity back in her face. Well, Zach Morton could pay for it in future. And he'd pay dearly with his rich wife's money. That would make her triumph over them both the greater.

Chapter Fourteen

'So you've taken a job with that bitch!' Beatrice screamed on hearing Florence's news. 'What do you want to work in a bookshop for?'

'Because I'm sick of being the skivvy to a score of uncouth men.' Florence struggled to keep her temper at her daughter's surly manners. 'And I don't include Joseph in that crowd. He's a good man and I'm grateful to all he's done for me. But just for a few hours each day I want to mix with my own kind.'

'So she's bought you, like she bought Zach,' Beatrice fumed.

'It isn't like that.' Florence was desperate to placate Beatrice. 'Kara Wyse is a kind and generous woman. When I told her I had a daughter she even gave me a dress for you.'

'Do you think I want that haughty cow's cast-off?'

Choosing to ignore the venom in Beatrice's tone, Florence crossed the room to where a brown-paper parcel lay on the table. 'Perhaps you should look at what you call a cast-off,' she said, unwrapping the paper. 'It is the finest gown you will ever possess.'

Beatrice scowled at the oyster silk and sneered. 'A mealy colour for a mealy woman.'

As Florence shook out the gown and held it against her figure, Beatrice's scowl changed to one of sly cunning. 'I suppose it's not too bad. A few scarlet bows would brighten it up.'

She snatched it from her mother's hand and pressed it to her body. The cool silk was like a balm to her roughened hands, and she could smell the scent of jasmine in its folds. It was worth more than she earned in a year.

'So you're going to work for this woman.' Beatrice continued to scowl.

'Why do you dislike her?' Florence said heavily. 'Hasn't she just given you a beautiful gown.'

'I hate all her kind,' Beatrice pouted, but the dress remained clutched possessively against her.

'Has it anything to do with Captain Morton? You were familiar with him the last time he was here.'

Beatrice fidgeted with a gold bracelet given to her by an admirer last night. She'd have to hide it from Fancy, as she had several other items of jewellery, or he'd sell it. Even to her mother she would not confide that she loved Zach. She shrugged. 'He's a handsome cove. I've always had an eye for handsome men. It's nothing more than that.'

'I'm glad to hear it.'

'But he could do better than that haughty bitch.'

'I won't have you speaking that way about her.' Florence finally lost her temper at Beatrice's stubborn and sullen manner.

Hands on hips, Beatrice screeched, 'She's won you over with her grand airs. I suppose you wish I were more like her. She can marry Zach with my blessing. But will she keep him? A crook of my finger and a rogue like him will be eating out of my hand.'

'You stay away from Captain Morton. I shall never forgive you if you take him as a lover.'

Beatrice glared at her mother. For days she had been holding back her anger and hurt over Zach's marriage, and now all her bitterness flowed from her. Grabbing Florence's shoulders, she began to shake her.

'Go on, take that sodding bitch's side.' Her face was screwed up with hatred. 'She can't buy me with a dress. She's bought you, though. And she thinks she's bought Zach. If I want him, I'll have him. And you won't stop me.'

'I forbid it.' Florence began to cough. Tears streamed down her cheeks at witnessing the hatred Beatrice felt for Kara. It was worse than she had feared. She suspected that she had made matters worse by not telling Beatrice that Kara was her sister from the start.

Beatrice thrust her face close to her mother's,

her grey eyes like chips of flint. 'Take her side. I don't care. I never could do anything right in your eyes. I hate you. And I hate that scheming bitch. I'd kill her if I could.'

'Beatrice, that's enough.' Joseph Donovan entered the kitchen, appalled at seeing Florence being attacked. Hauling Beatrice off the sobbing and shaken Florence, he slapped her across the face. 'Yer an ungrateful sod. After all yer mother's done fer yer, yer treat 'er like that.'

'Wot's she done fer me 'cept ensure I was born in the gutter and stayed there?' She roughened her speech to emphasise her loathing for their poverty.

'You always 'ad more lip than sense,' Big Joe rapped out as she glowered at him. 'That's wot attracted Fancy Gilbert to yer in the first place. Only yer didn't reckon on the consequences of attracting scum like 'im. Yer thought it was a joke ter cheek 'im back, and 'ave one of the biggest villains in the district panting after yer. Well, he showed yer 'e weren't a man ter pant fer long. Goin' round at thirteen, showin' off yer tits like any whore, yer 'ad it comin'. Yer mother brought yer up to act like a lady, not a tart. Yer could 'ave made something of yerself. Got a decent job.'

Joe led Florence to a seat after one of the longest speeches of his life. Normally he was a man of few words, but he couldn't bear to see Florence upset. That Beatrice, she had all she got coming to her. She was trouble.

'Ma don't care about me. She never did,' Beatrice snivelled. 'She thinks I'm trash. But I'm what life made me. And what good did her airs and graces do her? She's lived in this dung-heap for years, same as me.'

'Stop it, Beatrice,' Florence pleaded.

'Yer started it, Ma,' Beatrice blazed. 'I was treated like a freak the way you made me speak and dress. I always had ter talk proper and act like a lady. I hated being called Queen Bee. I 'ad no friends.'

'Yer stupid slut, yer 'ad yer self-respect,' Big Joe raged.

'Please, Joseph,' Florence interceded, her voice crackling with her misery. 'All that is over and done with. It does no good to rake over the past.'

'She owes you, Flo.' His craggy face softened with tenderness as he regarded her. 'Yer did everything yer could to give 'er a chance to better 'erself. Stupid bitch couldn't see it. Thought she knew better.'

'I don't need yer charity, Ma,' Beatrice shouted. She was still clutching the silk gown against her breast, and showed no sign of giving up that prize. 'Fancy is an evil bastard. Yer don't know the 'alf of what I 'ave ter put up wiv. He's a perverted sod. But I can 'andle 'im.'

Tears ran down her rouged cheeks and her lips were trembling, but she maintained her defiant hauteur. She was angry with the world and that was her defence against it.

'One day I'm goin' ter show Fancy and yer all that I can get out of this stinkin' hell-pit. I'll 'old me 'ead up amongst toffs and their ladies.' Her breath was coming in jagged sobs. 'Keep yer new friend in that posh bookshop. But Kara Wyse had better look to her back. Who d'ye think put

Slasher Gilbert on ter 'er as an easy target? Me! I was the one who stayed in the shop till all the customers left and her assistant had gone home. I made sure she was alone. Slasher would have done me a favour if he'd sliced her up good and proper then.'

Florence sank down on to a stool, staring at her daughter as though she was demented. When her outpourings had first started, she had felt a wave of sympathy for Beatrice. Her life was worse than she had imagined. But this poison streaming from her lips appalled her.

'You are an unnatural child,' she said brokenly. 'Don't you know what you've done? You set the Gilbert brothers against your own sister!'

'Sister!' Beatrice squawked. 'Sister!' She jerked her mother to her feet and shook her. 'Sister, you say? What sodding lie is this?'

Big Joe grabbed Beatrice's auburn hair and pulled her off her mother. The young woman was hysterical and he slapped her twice across the face. Then, going to Florence, he held her sobbing figure against his broad chest.

'There, me darlin'. It's all right. You know Bea would take on like that. She's got the devil's own temper. Hush, me darling.'

Florence shuddered and pulled her shaken nerves together to regard her younger daughter. 'I should have told you before. But I knew you'd take it badly. Now I've made things worse.'

She drew a shaky breath and held Joseph's arm for support. 'Kara Wyse is your sister. My married name is Florence Wyse. I took my maiden name when I left my husband. Kara was three and he forbade me to see her. I was three months' pregnant with you when I left Abel. Later, when you were ill, he refused to acknowledge you as his child. Kara is your sister.'

'But she's rolling in money.'

Florence hung her head. 'Abel Wyse was a wealthy man, though he died bankrupt. Kara was left a legacy from Abel's mother. She used that to go into partnership with Sophia Henshawe. And there was some money from a threatened lawsuit after her fiancé broke off her engagement when Abel died. Kara has not had it easy these last months. She's fighting against prejudice to make a success of her shop.'

'Me 'eart bleeds fer 'er. I've lived in poverty all me life,' Beatrice screeched. 'She lived in a fine house and wore pretty clothes. Everything I wore had been worn by several others before they grew out of it.' With a sob she cast the silk gown she was still holding on to the floor. 'Even this was worn by her. I wasn't even worth a new dress – just an old cast-off.'

Beatrice was tearing at her hair. She whirled on her mother, her eyes cold and calculating. 'Does she know she's got a sister?'

'Yes. It was I who stopped her seeing you. I knew you would take it badly. Kara wants to be your friend. That is why she sent the dress. She wants you at her wedding. She'd like you to be her bridesmaid.'

'I'd rather be the devil's slave.' Beatrice raised her fist to her mouth, biting on it as she turned away. Raging thoughts scalded her mind. That rich bitch was her sister. She had been brought up in a posh house with servants, whilst she… At the memories of her own sordid life, bile rose to her throat. She swallowed it, her hatred scouring her.

What did that spoilt cow of a sister know of poverty? Or of the degradation of selling your body in the hope of escaping from a life you despise. She'd swear Kara Wyse had never been cold or gone hungry in her life. Beatrice had lost count of the times she'd cried herself to sleep as a child, her bones aching with cold in the winter, her belly gnawing and growling with hunger. Why had Kara had everything, and herself nothing? It wasn't *fair*. It wasn't bloody *fair!*

Beatrice's eyes slitted as she dwelt upon her grievances. Knowing Kara Wyse was her sister did not change her hatred towards her. Rather it increased it. Why had her sister had so much in life and she so little? The haughty bitch had even stolen the man she loved.

Beatrice burned to right the injustice. She wanted to make Kara Wyse suffer as she had suffered. She would succeed. The score would be settled between them. She had as much right to the money Kara Wyse had inherited as her sister did. One day, she vowed, the tables would be turned. She would be the one with everything and Kara Wyse would have nothing.

For days after learning that Kara was her sister, Beatrice fumed at the twist of fate which had condemned her to a life of deprivation. Her hatred for Kara grew, her resentment fuelled by the comparison of their lives. She wanted what

Kara had. Wasn't she equally entitled to it?

She now regretted her involvement which led to Slasher wrecking the bookshop. Kara was bound to recognise her as the accomplice involved. Beatrice shrugged, her eyes narrowed with cunning. Already a plan was forming. She'd not survived on her wits for so many years without being able to tell a story to get herself out of any trouble. By all accounts Kara was open-hearted and trusting. That was to Beatrice's advantage. She would weep and throw herself upon her sister's mercy.

With every passing day, Beatrice schemed to find a way to win her sister's favour. She did not want to wait until the wedding. On that day, she would be so possessed by jealousy that she doubted she could be civil to Kara. It had to be before that. But the timing must be right: the timing of any confidence trickster to achieve their goal was all-important. Kara might be generous with her money, but she wasn't a fool.

Impatiently, Beatrice bided her time. She had begun to study her sister, watching her from across the street at Henshawe & Wyse. Through the shop window she saw how Kara dressed and acted towards the customers. She even spied on the shop when she suspected that Zach was to pay a call in the evening. Twice she had seen Kara leaving with him to dine in a restaurant or visit the theatre. Zach did not take her to the coarser musical halls that Beatrice knew he frequented. When she'd first known him he'd often come to one of Slasher's clubs with a gaiety girl on his arm.

On the occasions Kara was escorted by Zach, she had changed from her prim navy or grey work dresses to elegant evening gowns in pale silks with modest necklines.

Beatrice looked down at her scarlet skirt and the plunging neckline of her red and black bodice. It displayed the full curves of her heavy breasts and left little to a man's imagination. No wonder men treated her like a whore, she dressed so blatantly as one.

With deliberate calculation, Beatrice began to make adjustments to her clothes. When not working at the club, she discarded the bright garish colours and revealing necklines. She pawned a gold bracelet which had escaped Fancy's clutches to purchase two second-hand dresses of good quality material, their bodices buttoned high to the neck. She also left off her make-up, except the carmine she put on her lips, and this she used sparingly.

Each evening, before changing for work at the club, she visited Florence.

'You look so much better, Ma,' she said sweetly, handing Florence a bunch of flowers which she had stolen from a flower-seller. 'The work in Kara's shop agrees with you.'

Florence eyed the flowers with suspicion. Obviously she had not forgotten Beatrice's flare of temper when she had told her about her sister. Beatrice knew she had to convince her mother that she bore no grudge against Kara.

'Do you like the work, Ma?'

'How could I not? The shop is a great success. Kara has a natural eye for the trade and what people want.' Her voice warmed with enthusiasm. 'Word is spreading of the quality of the products, and new customers frequently come to us who have been recommended by others.'

Beatrice swallowed her anger at her mother's fond smile. Florence was thinking of Kara. Why did she never smile like that for her? Then, as though Florence had sensed her resentment, she pressed the flowers to her nose and inhaled their scent.

'These are lovely, Beatrice. And you are looking very pretty today. You have such a lovely face, you don't need that awful common make-up.' Florence's expression lightened as she regarded Beatrice's high-necked blue dress. 'That is a fetching gown and in very good taste.'

'I know I've been such a disappointment to you, Ma.' Beatrice knelt at her mother's side and clasped her frail hands. 'I want you to be proud of me. As you are of my sister. I went to the shop today. I did not go inside. I stood across the street, watching Kara at work. She has grace and dignity. I felt so ashamed.' She hung her head.

Florence gathered her in her arms. 'But you could be like Kara. I know you adopted rough speech and manners to be accepted here. But it's not the way. Have pride in who you are. You're a survivor. You are so much more worthy than this life you have settled for.'

'I can't break away from Fancy,' Beatrice groaned. 'He'd kill me first.'

'Not if you paid him enough to let you go. I'm saving the money I earn at the shop. If you are really resolved to leave this life behind you, then

I am sure Kara will help you.'

'I don't want her charity.' Beatrice assumed a demure expression.

'That's a change of heart, Beatrice. When you learned about Kara you said you hated her.'

'It was the shock. Of course I resented that she had lived in comfort whilst I...' She broke off theatrically. 'You know how I've been forced to live. But the more I thought about it, the more I realised I was wrong. You did everything you could to bring me up as a gentlewoman. But without money I was just another street urchin. It isn't you, or Kara, I hate. My father is to blame for the poverty I've suffered. No one else. I'm glad he's dead.'

Florence was still wary of Beatrice's change of heart, but she was pleased with her appearance. At least she was trying. Yet deep in her heart Florence still did not trust her. But how could she throw Beatrice's good intentions back in her face? It would only make her more resentful.

'If you are truly repentant of your way of life, then I will introduce you to Kara.'

Beatrice was satisfied. 'Shall I meet you from work tomorrow? We could meet then.'

Florence hesitated, but knew she could not keep the sisters apart. Was it possible for Beatrice to change so drastically? But hadn't she prayed for years that Beatrice would dress and act like a true gentlewoman?

The next day Beatrice was in such a good mood that she got up early and put on her new clothes. Throughout the afternoon she strolled in Hyde Park. To her delight she found that, dressed demurely and without her make-up, men showed her a greater deference. It took all her restraint not to openly encourage them. Speaking with the perfect enunciation which Florence had taught her, she conversed with several respectable matrons, praising their children. In her old attire such women had shunned her. Now they accepted her as their own kind.

Her confidence and spirits were high when she returned to the rooms she shared with Fancy. This afternoon had proved she would be accepted amongst the middle-classes. It was just a matter of time before she could put her present life behind her.

'Yer ill, woman.' Fancy eyed her with disapproval when he returned before she'd had a chance to change. 'Yer look like death. Don' like that dress. Yer look like a school ma'am. Get it off. Customers at the club buy more drinks fer a woman when they can see 'er tits.'

'I'm not wearing it to the club,' Beatrice snapped. 'Yer can't pick pockets in Hyde Park looking like a tart. To mix with the gentry you have to look and act like them.'

'So what did yer make today?'

Beatrice grudgingly opened the drawstrings of her velvet bag and lifted out three purses and a gold brooch. The purses were heavy and Fancy nodded with satisfaction. 'Yer did well. Jus' take care yer 'and over all yer filtch. Yer know the rules.'

He counted the contents in each purse and gave her a quarter of their value. Then he added another crown for the brooch which Beatrice knew would fetch him ten times that amount. She took the risks and the Gilberts got fat on the profits.

'I wouldn't cross you, Fancy.' Beatrice hid her hatred behind a coercing smile. She had already taken several coins from each purse and hidden them in the bottom of the wardrobe.

'Take care you don't, me girl.' He twisted her arm behind her back. As she cried out in pain, he ground his mouth down on hers with such savagery that her teeth cut into her lip, drawing blood. He pulled back with a grin. 'Yer me woman, Bea. Remember that. Be a pity to have Slasher do fer yer pretty face. Now, where's the rest of what yer stole today?'

Fear iced her spine. Was he testing her, or did he know there was more money? The man was a devil.

'There ain't no more money.' She forced her stare to hold his.

'Lying bitch!' He slapped her hard, sending her reeling across the room. Lunging after her, his hands circled her throat. His thumbs dug into her windpipe as he pressed her down on to the floor.

'I ain't 'olding nothin' back from yer, Fancy. 'Onest I ain't,' she croaked before her breath was cut off.

His fingers tightened. Seeing her death written in his face, she clawed at his hands, her eyes bulging from their sockets as he increased the pressure. Then she saw the light in his eyes change. Her terror was arousing him. Suddenly he released her throat.

'Yer gettin' airs above yerself, slut. Duds like this are for gentry – not whores.'

Crazed by lust, he ripped the material of her new gown until it was in shreds. 'Slut, yer were seen 'anging around that tart's bookshop. The one Morton warned us off from. Wot's yer interest in the shop? Is it Morton?'

'No, Fancy. I'd never look at another man.' She massaged her bruised throat, her voice hoarse and painful. 'Only if yer say I must. I was curious that was all, wot wiv Ma getting a job in the shop.'

'Bitch! If yer lying…' He slapped her hard and rolled her on to her stomach, taking her violently as a man would his catamite. It was his usual way of punishing her.

Fancy hated all women, believing them whores like his mother. In his eyes his mother was to blame for his father being hanged, and for all the misery he had suffered as a child on the streets. But if he hated women, he hated men more. The Jew had abused him, and now he made his catamites pay the price for his corrupted youth. There were many young men who shared Fancy's bed, as well as women. Yet it was Beatrice he kept as his favourite. And that was the greatest punishment of all.

She ached all over. Her throat was so bruised it was painful to swallow. Fancy stood over her, fastening his breeches. 'I want yer in the club this evening.'

'I won't be able to sing,' she croaked.

'I want yer there anyways. Jus' so I knows yer ain't up ter no good.'

An hour later she dragged her sore body into the club. Around her neck was a purple feather boa to conceal the livid bruises on her throat.

She moved despondently around the gaming tables. The gaslamps hanging low over the green baize hurt her cut eye, the blue fug of tobacco and cigar smoke cloyed her nostrils. The whores' voices were shrill and the men's crude suggestions jarred on her nerves. Beer and whisky fumes mingled with the stench of sweat and cheap perfume, and Beatrice was sickened by it all. Many of the toffs gambling at the tables were drunk. When one groped her breasts and whispered an obscenity in her ear, she slapped his hand away.

'That's not like you, Bea,' the customer whined, swaying drunkenly. 'Let me buy you a drink.'

It was an ageing roué who was already deep in debt to Slasher. She would have liked to tip his champagne over his leering face, but that would have earned her another beating from Fancy for upsetting a customer. She accepted the champagne that she insisted he order, but she did not drink it, and soon found an excuse to move away. She'd been at the club an hour and Fancy was nowhere in sight. Discontented, and finding the noise and press of bodies stifling, she sauntered out into the back yard for some fresh air.

Leaning against the rough wall, she sighed and stared up at the tiny patch of black sky visible above the tall chimneys. The stars winked mockingly back at her. The breeze carried the stench of the privy at the end of the courtyard. Two ragged men were wheeling away the midden cart after digging out the privy's contents.

She put a hand to her swollen cheek. A salty tear, escaping through her lashes, stung as it rolled across an open cut. She'd had such hopes and plans this afternoon and now that vicious sod Fancy, had put paid to them. How could she meet her sister looking like she did?

She was supposed to meet her mother outside Kara's shop in an hour. Even by the wedding the bruises on her neck would still be visible. God, how she hated Fancy. She'd kill him if she ever got the chance. It wasn't capture by the law she feared, it was retribution from the Gilbert gang.

It was years since she'd given way to self-pity, and she was not about to indulge now. Dabbing the tear from her cheek, she resigned herself to returning to the gaming room. A whispering voice drifted to her from the door she had left ajar. When she heard Zach's name mentioned, she drew back further into the shadows, scarcely daring to breathe for fear of discovery.

'Morton's jus' gone up to the gaming room.' Slasher Gilbert's voice carried to her as she strained to listen. ''E's 'ad it comin' for months. Giv 'im a good goin' over, Chalky. Enough to spoil 'is 'oneymoon, but no marks on 'is face, mind. The marriage 'as ter go ahead. We want 'im dancing to our tune when 'e visits 'is gentry friends.'

'Yer can count on me, Slasher,' Chalky White sniggered. 'That bastard broke me bleedin' nose when he clobbered me the night we did the bookshop.'

'Jus' giv 'im a warning,' Slasher cautioned. 'No

one gets out of paying their due to us. They're either wiv us or agin us. If they're agin us…' He sniggered and Beatrice could just imagine Slasher drawing his finger across his neck in a significant gesture.

She began to shiver in the warm evening air. The Gilbert brothers would never let her escape their clutches, no matter how much she tried to bribe them. She knew too much. Wherever she ran, they would track her down and her throat would be slit.

And now Zach was about to be done over. She knew Chalky White. He was a vicious bastard. Once he started to get the boot in, the sadistic sod often went too far.

She didn't want Zach crippled for life. He had promised to help her escape from Fancy. She didn't regard Kara as a barrier to her continuing her affair with Zach. He'd been hers first. And, as her sister's husband, he'd not be able to forget his promise to her, or she'd tell Kara of their affair. Blackmail was a weapon to be used, and she would use it without compunction.

Beatrice was set upon vengeance. Zach owed her. If he thought he could squander her sister's wealth – wealth she had convinced herself was rightly hers – and leave her to rot in this stinking rookery, he would discover that she made a dangerous enemy.

For days she had been planning to get even with Zach for asking Kara to marry him. He must have known that she was her sister. He'd done it for the money, of course, and the need to get his hands on his own inheritance. He did not love Kara. Beatrice was convinced of that. It was the only way she could accept the wedding.

A rush of love for Zach overwhelmed her. She did not want his beautiful body battered by Chalky White. Her plans for revenge were wiped aside in her need to protect him. She'd warn him, and that would make Zach deeper in her debt.

Returning to the upper rooms, she found Zach at the dice table. A quick survey showed her that neither Slasher or Fancy were present. Aware that several of the women working in the club resented her superiority over them, and would jump at the chance to make trouble between her and Fancy, Beatrice was careful not to make her approach to Zach too obvious. When she eventually reached his side, she was annoyed that, after a curt nod in terse greeting, he proceeded to ignore her.

'A word, Zach,' she whispered. 'It's important.'

To her fury he did not reply, and moved further down the table. Taking up the dice he began to shake them. His handsome face was tense as he concentrated on the rolling dice. Four times they rattled against the side of the table and a cheer went up as he won. Each time he let his winnings ride, and each time they doubled. By the fifth throw, if he won, Slasher would be out of pocket by three hundred guineas.

From the brightness in his eye he had been drinking heavily. In such a mood he was reckless. A cheer filled the room as the fifth roll again won. Zach left the stake to double again. An expectant hush fell over the crowd which had gathered around the table. Tensions crackled in the air. Six hundred guineas would be at stake if he won. And Slasher did not pay out such winnings with good grace.

The reckless fool. If he won, the beating he received would be doubly vicious. And he'd not see a single guinea of his winnings once Chalky started into him. He'd be robbed and left half-dead in the gutter. Like as not they'd also take the diamond pin in his necktie and his gold watch and chain. Not satisfied with that, they'd strip him of his fine clothes as a further humiliation.

Zach was shaking the dice and lifted his clenched fist to his mouth to blow on it for luck.

'Come on, my lovelies. Don't let me down now,' he said as he flicked his wrist and the dice clattered down on to the table.

Beatrice prayed he'd lose and held her breath. The ivory cubes rolled to a halt. Double six. He'd won. Her heart clenched with fear. Raising her stare, she saw the white-lipped fury on Slasher's ugly face. He nodded to Chalky to do his worst, and the bully's brutish face smirked with satisfaction. Zach would be lucky if he escaped the beating alive. He had to listen to her.

Several toffs were clapping Zach on the back. Two of the women eager to have some of the winnings spent on them were hanging on each of Zach's arms. He was laughing, his amber eyes triumphant as he ordered champagne for everyone. Beatrice was about to push her way through the people to ensure he listened to her warning, when she saw Fancy watching her. It was impossible to approach Zach now.

For half an hour she was on tenterhooks, watching him drink glass after glass of champagne. He always held his liquor well. But tonight there was a noticeable stagger to his step. Becoming desperate, she knew that the only way to speak with Zach was to waylay him when he left the club.

Fancy was signalling her to join him. Beatrice shuddered. Every night at midnight in the club's cellar, wagers were made around the rat-pit. It was a popular sport which Beatrice found disgusting. How people could watch a terrier kill dozens of rats in a given amount of time, and wager on the number killed, was beyond her. She hated vermin, but the nightly sight of the decapitated bodies and their shrieks of pain turned her stomach. One of Slasher's proudest boasts was that he provided seven hundred rats a week in his pits.

Already several men, one or two toffs included, had disappeared into the cellar carrying yapping terriers. The larger dogs, sensing the sport was about to start, barked and strained at their leads. Several cocked their legs up against the bench or table legs. An occasional shout of anger from a customer was followed by a yelp when a less discriminating animal chose a trouser leg instead. One particularly snub-faced, bandy-legged, white bull-terrier with a black eye-patch over one eye, snarled and snapped at any passing leg within its vicious range.

'Lay off, Titch,' its pock-marked owner grunted. 'Save yer strength. I'm wagerin' yer can kill two hundred rats in record time.'

Beatrice hid her disgust. She took Fancy's arm and pressed her body against his stocky figure. 'I'm feelin' real queasy, Fancy. Do I 'ave to watch the ratting tonight? Me 'ead's splittin'. Couldn't I go 'ome early? I feel I could throw up at any minute.'

'Yer ain't breedin' are yer?' Fancy eyed her sullenly. 'If'n yer are, it's down to Mother Baggart ter get rid of it. I ain't 'aving no snivelling brats round me.'

'I ain't breedin', Fancy.' Every month was a waking nightmare that she had conceived. Fancy was too selfish in his lust to bother with taking precautions.

Twice she'd faced the excruciating agony of Mother Baggart's vicious needle. The last time the tiny babe had taken several hours before it finally aborted into the slops' pail. The brief glimpse she'd seen of its distorted form had resembled nothing human. The vision had haunted her for months. She had haemorrhaged so badly that she'd thought she'd die. Florence had nursed her back to health, but she'd been too weak to stand for six weeks and, since then, she had miscarried on three occasions.

Beatrice suspected her insides were so mutilated by Mother Baggart's butchery that she would never have a child of her own. She certainly did not want to bear a monster spawned by Fancy. And a child was just another responsibility, another drain on her time and energy.

'No, I ain't breeding.' She rubbed her side, which stabbed every time she drew a breath. 'Yer done me bleeding ribs in. I got ter lay down,

Fancy. I feel real queer. 'Onest I do.'

He regarded her sullenly. There was no compassion in his expression as he stared at her bruised face. 'I laid inter yer 'arder than I intended. Didn't mean ter make yer face such a sight. The toffs shy away from yer in that state. There was a young lord who'd taken a fancy to you: would've given me five guineas to 'ave 'ad yer tonight. Lost it now. Sight of yer frightened him off. Yer costing me money when yer can't whore. Yer becomin' a liability, ol' girl,' he said nastily. He turned to smile at young Bessie Brown, a thirteen-year-old strumpet with brassy blonde hair and a figure still slender as a boy's.

Beatrice saw the young girl's face blench as Fancy's regard fell on her. So he'd had her already. Dirty sod. Beatrice knew that look of fear. And Fancy liked them young.

'Go 'ome, Bea,' Fancy snarled and, pulling Bessie to him, rubbed his hand over her buttocks.

The girl winced as he pinched her through her thin yellow gown. 'Bessie is a good gal. She don't give me no lip, or no grief.'

She wouldn't, would she? Beatrice thought as she watched Fancy drag the girl down the stairs to the cellar. The poor cow's terrified out of her wits.

She was relieved to see that Zach was still carousing with his friends. As she watched, he began to make his way to the door. Alarm speared her forward.

'Not leaving already, Morton?' one of his companions called after him. 'It's still early.'

'Things to do.' He waved his arm airily.

'Like a night with a gaiety girl,' another sniggered. 'Make the most of your last nights of freedom, Morton.'

Beatrice hurried outside and hid in the narrow alley leading to the club. Her heart was hammering. She suspected that Chalky White would not be far away. She dared not be seen warning Zach, or she would meet the same fate.

Chapter Fifteen

Beatrice recognised Zach's jaunty whistle before his tall silhouette was outlined in the moonlight.

'Psst, Zach. You've got to listen to me,' she called softly.

He paused to tilt his head in the direction of her voice.

'You're in danger from Slasher. Over here.' On hearing his harsh expulsion of breath, she knew he was irritated by the encounter. But she was too concerned at regaining his affection and saving him to pay heed to his displeasure. 'For God's sake, man!' she snapped. 'Get out of the moonlight and listen to me. Slasher's got you marked.'

The silhouette vanished into the shadows, and she smelt the cologne he favoured as he peered down at her. His breath was heavy with wine fumes.

'Why did you have to drink so much champagne tonight?' she groaned in exasperation.

'Slasher has put Chalky on to you. He said you had to be taught a lesson.'

'I've bested Chalky before in a fight. He's a runt.'

'He's an evil bastard. D'ye think he'd take you on alone?' The effort of so much talking made her rub her bruised throat.

The hoarseness of her voice belatedly penetrated the alcohol blurring Zach's brain.

'You all right, Bea? You sound odd.' He pulled her hand away from her throat and, seeing the bruises, swore profanely. 'Who did that? Was it Fancy? It's time that bastard got a dose of his own medicine.'

She made light of her injury, too worried about him to dwell upon it. 'I've survived worse. Zach, I'm frightened for you. Slasher is bent on revenge. Don't go back to your lodgings tonight.'

'I have to.' His voice was impatient. 'My father arrives early tomorrow. He's promised me a generous settlement on my marriage – if I've reformed. Don't want him thinking I've been out on the tiles all night.'

The mention of his marriage sparked Beatrice's anger. 'That's what your marriage is all about, isn't it – money? From the start you had your eye on Kara Wyse as an easy target. You must have recognised Florence when you saw them together in Hyde Park. She told me all about that meeting. You're a bastard. You knew Kara was my sister. Why didn't you tell me? I could have done well for myself there. Now I've got to grovel because I worked with Slasher when he was after protection money.'

'You always were too spiteful for your own good, Bea.' He mocked her, the drink making him incautious.

'And my sister's not a fool, Zach. She just won't hand her money over. She wants it to expand her business.'

'And when her business expands, so do her profits,' Zach declared haughtily. 'Play your cards right, Bea. I'm sure your long-lost sister will be generous with the inheritance from your father's haulage company. I won't begrudge you a cut. Just don't be too greedy.'

He did not bother to deny that he had deliberately set out to win Kara, and it was obvious that he believed her sister to be wealthier than she was. He did not know that Abel Wyse had died bankrupt. She bit back the impulse to fling the knowledge in his face. Serve him right. His sneering hostility rankled. She knew Zach would never marry her, and felt a perverse satisfaction that the marriage would not be all he desired. Least that way he would be inclined to look more favourably upon herself for comfort.

'I won't be greedy. Why should I?' Beatrice put her arms around him. 'We were good together. Your marriage needn't end that. It's not as though you love Kara.'

She felt him stiffen and gave a harsh laugh. 'Perhaps I should insist that Kara has you living with us. It may be interesting to have two women so readily available under one roof. A regular seraglio.'

'If that's a posh name for a knocking-shop, you can go screw yourself.' She hated him when he was mocking and sarcastic. 'You owe me, Zach. Haven't I risked the Gilberts' wrath by warning you tonight?'

'And I won't see you go without, Bea. I promised to get you away from the Gilbert brothers. I will keep my word. I don't want any scandal attached to my wife's name. It would ruin trade and affect her profits.'

'Bastard!' She slapped his grinning face. 'You never think of anyone but yourself. I've a good mind to tell Kara what a slimy worm you are.'

Her hand was caught between iron fingers. 'That would be foolish, Bea. We both know too much about each other. Don't threaten me. Kara is eager to meet her sister, and she will be generous to you. She can afford to be. I don't begrudge you a chance to better yourself. If I were to spill the beans on your life, Kara would turn from you in horror. She's going to be suspicious enough when she recognises you as the woman who was Slasher's accomplice that night.'

She wrenched her hand away from him, her body shaking with fury. 'I hate you. I hope Chalky does do you over proper. If your handsome face is carved up and you're half crippled, Kara won't want you, and she'll be more generous with me.'

Zach was not so drunk he could not recognise the spite which now contorted Bea's face. He became uneasy. He'd gone too far. Bea could cause trouble. A scorned woman was a dangerous enemy, and Bea was more dangerous than most.

He chuckled softly and slid an arm around her

waist. 'Do you really think I'd neglect you, my dear?' He kissed her lingeringly until he felt her resistance melt. But Beatrice had never been a passive lover. Her hands could drive a man to the brink of madness with desire, and she was using all that expertise now. His intoxication roused his passion, the ferocity of his need to possess her overriding common sense or caution. Her breathing was fast. Her hands and the sensual pressure of her swaying hips against his were driving him crazy, his need now at fever pitch.

'Take me back to your lodgings, Zach.'

'I can't, not tonight,' he forced out through his own laboured breath, his mouth seeking the breasts he had freed from her bodice.

With a provocative laugh, Beatrice slid to her knees, taking his swollen member into her mouth and driving him beyond reason. With a smothered groan, he raised her up and pressed her against the wall. Bunching her skirts to her waist, he thrust into her. She gasped and curled one leg around his waist, her moans of pleasure muffled by the depths of his kisses. As he drove into her, her body matched his frenzied rhythm, then with a shudder she collapsed against him, clinging with trembling limbs as her body convulsed with the pulsing heat of her climax. His hands kneaded her breasts as he achieved his own satisfaction. For a moment they stood entwined, their breathing subsiding to normality.

He adjusted his clothing. 'You're one hell of a lay, Bea.'

Beatrice leaned heavily against the wall, her eyes closed. Desire had triumphed over the pain in her body. Now it felt bathed in a glorious sense of well-being. In all her years as a whore she had met no lover who excited her like Zach. Her legs were still shaking as she steadied herself. With annoyance she saw that he had already left her, his footsteps fading towards his lodgings.

Her love for him lulled her anger. Tonight had proved that he could not resist her. But had he heeded her warning? He had appeared to discount it earlier and had been in a jubilant mood from his success at the dice table. Fear for his safety doused her sensual euphoria. She must make sure he understood the danger.

Lifting her skirts above her ankles so as not to hamper her pace, she hurried after him. By the time she reached the end of the street, her ribs felt as if they had been run over by a steam roller. Pressing her hand to them, she rounded the corner into a poorly lit alleyway. Her heart stopped. Five men were bending over Zach, who had been knocked to his knees. In the moonlight she could just make out the men lashing in to him with their fists and booted feet. Zach was still trying to fight them off, but he was overpowered by the most brutal bullies in the Gilbert gang. She could do nothing physically against so many.

Disguising her voice, she yelled as loud as her painful throat permitted. 'Away, lad. I can see the bleeding peelers coming this way. Six of the bastards.'

With a last vicious kick, the bullies ran off, and Beatrice hurried forward. Mindless of the filth in the cobblestoned central gutter, she fell to her knees and cradled his head in her lap.

'Oh my darling, my darling. Why didn't you listen to me?'

The muted groan of agony wrenched at her heart. He was unconscious. There was a stickiness seeping over her fingers from a gaping wound below the hairline on his neck. One arm hung at a distorted angle where it had been broken. Anxiously she ran her hands over his ribs and surmised that, from the kicking he had received, at least one of them was cracked. None appeared to be broken. Her own bruised ribs from Fancy's beating ached as she peered at his face. Apart from a graze on his cheek it was unmarked. She had got here in time to stop Chalky killing him, but it was impossible to tell how seriously he was wounded. She had no money for a physician. Searching his pockets, she swore profanely at discovering his winnings had been stolen.

There was only one person she could rely on for help. Thankfully, Kara lived only a few streets away. Somehow she had to get Zach there. A part of her mind reasoned that, by delivering her injured betrothed to her, she would win her sister's trust. But how to get Zach to the shop?

She froze at hearing the heavy tread of workmen's boots on the cobbles. Was it the bullies returned to finish working Zach over? Then the squeak on an unoiled wheel told her it was probably a coster returning from his pitch. As the approaching figure passed under the corner gaslamp, the pale yellow light shone on a man pushing a barrow.

'Hey, you there,' she called, deliberately choosing her most cultured voice to instil authority. 'Could you help this man? It will be worth a guinea or two. This gentleman has been beaten and robbed. He lives nearby. If you help me to get him home, you'll be paid well for your trouble.'

The costermonger sniffed as he stared down at Zach's prone figure. 'I knows 'im. Seen 'im about Covent Garden liftin' a watch or two.' He scowled and stared at Beatrice's upturned face. 'I know yer, don' I? Yer Gilbert's woman. Wot yer doin' 'ere with the likes of this swell mobster? And why yer talkin' all posh? Wot's yer game?'

Beatrice curbed her impatience. 'I were jus' passin' and saw 'im lying in the gutter. Thought I'd lift his wallet. Only it'd already bin took. Didn't know who yer were, did I, when I called out? Yer might 'ave bin a flash cove and he'd hardly trust the likes of me. But Morton's badly beaten. It's 'is fiancée who lives nearby. He told me that much 'fore he passed out. She's a rich woman. Owns a shop. She'd be mighty grateful 'e was helped. Left 'ere 'e could die.'

'So what's that to me?' the coster grunted. 'Likes of 'im don't do me no favours.'

'There ain't no profit in letting 'im die. Could be five guineas in it, if we take 'im to 'is fiancée. Worth ten minutes of our trouble, ain't it?'

'Five guineas, yer say.' The coster sounded more agreeable.

'I reckon.'

Zach groaned as he was lifted on top of the coster's limp cabbages, and they set off towards the stationer's. The shop was in darkness, as was the house. Beatrice knew from her mother's chatter that Kara had rooms on the second floor at the back of the house. Since the stationer's was on a corner, there was a side gate to the garden. To her dismay it was locked.

'Give us a leg up,' Beatrice ordered. 'I'll climb over and throw some pebbles up at a window to rouse the woman.'

Beatrice's ribs felt on fire as she strained to climb over the wall and drop to the far side. She gasped and held her side as she staggered to the house. 'You owe me for this, Zach,' she said, wincing. 'Cheat me after this, and God help me I'll swing for you. Truly I will.'

Raking her fingers blindly over the flowerbed, she found several small pebbles and began to throw these up to the second-floor window. Even that movement stabbed through her body. Tears of pain stung her eyes.

'Sod it,' she swore softly as the first six pebbles brought no response. 'Wake up, Miss Wyse.' Raising her voice a fraction, not wanting to awaken the other old biddy who lived there. She looked a right nosy-parker who was bound to summon the police. That was the last thing Zach would want.

Three more pebbles found their mark. 'Miss Wyse!'

The heavy lace curtain was drawn aside and a pale face appeared at the open sash window.

'Miss Wyse. Captain Morton has been hurt,' Beatrice explained.

Her sister's head came out of the window. 'Who's there?'

'It's Beatrice. Beatrice Kempe. I couldn't get

away earlier as I planned. On my way home I found Captain Morton lying injured in the street. He must have been robbed and attacked.' She had worked out the story she intended to spin on the walk here. 'I didn't know what to do. I hired a costermonger to put him on to his barrow and bring him here. The captain is hurt real bad. He needs a doctor. I had to promise the coster five guineas.'

'Beatrice? My sister Beatrice?' Kara sounded confused and sleepy. 'Are you saying that Zach is hurt?'

'Yes, I'm your sister. Captain Morton is hurt real bad. He's on a barrow in the alley by the side gate. I climbed over the wall.'

'Oh, sweet heavens.' Kara finally found her wits. She could see nothing in the garden below as the disembodied voice spoke to her.

'I'll be down directly.' She grabbed her night-wrap, tying it securely as she hurried from her room and down the stairs to the kitchen door. Her mind was still dazed from sleep. When Beatrice had not arrived for their meeting she had been bitterly disappointed. Florence had mumbled something vague about it sometimes being difficult for Beatrice to get away.

Could it really be that she was going to meet Beatrice at last? But Zach… How badly was he hurt? Her thoughts whirled chaotically as she snatched the key to the side gate from its hook. Her hands were shaking when she unlocked the kitchen door and withdrew the bolts.

'Hurry,' the woman's voice in the garden urged.

Kara made out a pale shadowy form by the

gate. As it was opened, the coster's face loomed close to hers.

He grunted sourly. 'Five guineas the wench said you'd pay if I brought the man here.'

'Yes, of course. Can you bring him into the house? If you will also go for the doctor, there will be another two guineas for you.'

Kara watched appalled as the costermonger was about to sling Zach over his shoulder.

'Mind his arm,' Beatrice warned. 'He's broken it.' She snatched off the Indian shawl she wore over her gown and fashioned it into a crude sling to support the arm.'

'Wait,' Kara commanded as the coster heaved at Zach's figure. 'Carry him gently. If his ribs are broken you could damage his lungs.'

'Don't think they're broken,' Beatrice stated. 'Just bruised.'

'It's best not to take any risks,' Kara continued. 'You, man, take his shoulders. Beatrice, take one leg. I'll take the other. There's a chaise-longue in the parlour behind the shop. We'll put him there until the doctor has seen his injuries.'

Kara was too concerned at Zach's unconscious figure to pay much heed to the presence of her sister. The woman worked silently at her side. Once Zach was placed on the chaise and the coster had gone to fetch the doctor, Kara hunted for the box of matches. When she turned up the flame in the gaslamp, her first concern remained with Zach.

'Dear God,' she cried as she saw the blood drying on his shirt and coat from the cut on his neck. 'Who could have done this?'

'Ma said he's warned Slasher Gilbert to lay off demanding protection money from you.' Beatrice spoke from the far side of the room. 'He wouldn't have taken kindly to that.'

'Then it's because of me he's been hurt.' Kara knelt at Zach's side, feeling helpless in being unable to deal with his injuries. She knew it was best to wait for the doctor. She rose to go to the sink and fill a basin with cold water. Dampening a cloth, she laid it across Zach's hot brow.

At a movement from the shadows, she swung round. 'Beatrice, I'm so sorry. How appallingly rude of me. I've waited so long for this moment.' She peered into the shadows, seeing the outline of her sister in a yellow evening gown with a low neck. To Kara's surprise she was also wearing a rather cheap feather boa.

'Once Zach has been tended to,' Kara added, 'I am so looking forward to getting to know you.'

'I think you will despise me.' Beatrice forced humiliation and contrition into her voice. 'My life has been very different to yours.'

'But I want to make up for all that. Papa was unjust in the way he treated Mama. He was wicked to keep us apart. Come forward into the light so that I may see you.'

'When you see me, you will hate me,' Beatrice continued. 'There is so much I'm ashamed of. I didn't know this was your shop until a few days ago. You have to believe me.'

Kara was puzzled by her sister's manner. But her mind was still too absorbed by the magnitude of Zach's injuries for her to pay full attention to what Beatrice was saying.

'The past is behind you, Beatrice. Our future starts from today.' She held out her arms. 'I'm sure learning you had a sister has been as much of a shock for you as it was for me. I want so much for us to be friends.'

'That may not be possible when you realise who I am.'

Kara smiled. 'I am beholden to you already, Beatrice.' But as a thought struck her, she frowned. 'How is it you know Captain Morton? He is such a modest man, he refused to say how he came to track Florence down.'

'I'd seen him before. A handsome man like him gets noticed,' she said lightly. 'Ma said he was your fiancé.'

Slowly Beatrice stepped out of the shadows, her head bowed and presented in profile.

Kara saw that it was not an evening dress she was wearing, but a low-necked gown, which immodestly revealed a great deal of her breasts. When Beatrice lifted her head, Kara was at first shocked by the thick make-up on her sister's face. Then a more forceful blow hit her.

'You are the woman who was Slasher Gilbert's accomplice on the night my shop was robbed. That's where you saw Zach.'

Beatrice's head came up higher. Unwittingly, Kara had saved her the trouble of making up an elaborate lie over knowing Zach. 'I had no choice that night. I didn't know who you were. Where I live, you do whatever the Gilbert brothers ask you. That's if you want to stay alive. Try and cross them and that's what happens.' She nodded at Zach.

Kara was shocked at her sister's confession. This wasn't the joyous reunion she had envisaged. She fought to come to terms with the knowledge that Beatrice was involved with criminals. From the way she dressed, she looked like a whore.

'I'll leave Captain Morton in your loving care,' Beatrice said tersely. 'I was ordered to work tonight. I'd never have come to you looking like this.'

Kara felt a stab of guilt. What right had she to condemn her sister by her appearance? Beatrice had begun to move purposely towards the door. As she did so the boa slid from around her neck. When the gaslight fell across her throat, Kara was appalled to see livid bruises circling it like a necklace of jet. There was a stoop to her figure as though she too had been beaten.

'You also have been hurt,' Kara said, aghast.

'It's nothing I haven't had before. You don't cross the Gilbert brothers with impunity.'

'I won't let you go back to that awful place,' Kara declared. 'I don't blame you for that night. You must stay here and let the doctor tend your injuries.'

'It's nothing. Just a few bruises. I daren't stay. If I don't go back they'll take it out on Ma. You can't save us all, sister.'

'Is she also involved with these villains?'

'Ma would never do anything dishonest. But the Gilbert brothers rule the rookery where we live like medieval barons. They rule by brutality and terror.'

'I want to take you and Mama away from that

life. Why won't she let me?'

'Big Joe is proud. He'd see your help as charity. Don't worry, I'll get him to see sense. Ma's health won't take another winter in that place. I've got to go now. You might as well know the worst of me. I live with Fancy Gilbert. Not out of choice. Out of fear. He'd kill me if he knew I were here. It were his men who attacked Captain Morton.'

Her head came up, her stance defiant. 'I don't want your pity.'

Kara reached out to take her sister's hand. 'I still want us to be friends. Please say you will come again. We mustn't let the past come between us.'

'Try and keep me away,' Beatrice answered flippantly, relieved that Kara had fallen for her act.

'Will you come to my wedding? I want you to be my chief bridesmaid. I took the chance of giving the dressmaker the rough measurements Florence gave me for you. She's made up a gown in pale green silk. Can you be here for a fitting tomorrow evening?'

'Never had no brand-new silk dress. Be a fool to refuse, wouldn't I?' Beatrice replied off-handedly.

There was a loud rapping on the door.

'That must be the doctor,' Kara said, hurrying to answer it.

Beatrice paused to gaze lovingly at Zach's white face. His eyelids were beginning to flutter and his groans were getting louder. She wanted to be gone before he regained his wits. Kara was bound to tell him that she had brought him here. This was one debt he would never be allowed to forget.

As the doctor swept past her to bend over the patient, Beatrice gently drew Kara aside. 'It's best if I leave now, I will come tomorrow.'

Tears of happiness sparkled in Kara's eyes, and Beatrice mentally labelled her a gullible fool. She momentarily stiffened when Kara lightly embraced her. The fresh perfume of her sister's skin made her ashamed of her own grimy flesh. Bathing was unheard of in the rookery.

'If I came early, could I have a bath before the seamstress sees me?' she asked sheepishly.

Kara was relieved that her sister had made the suggestion. She was fastidious in her own bathing habits, but had not liked to remark upon so personal a matter on their first meeting.

'Of course.' Kara hugged her again, her lips brushing her cheek in an affectionate kiss.

To Beatrice's surprise, she felt a reluctant spread of warmth around her heart. She immediately quashed it. Watch it, girl, she remonstrated with herself. Don't go getting soft on her just 'cause she's your sister. You're gonna milk her for all she's worth.

Zach stirred. Immediately pain shot through his body and arm. When he forced his eyes open, the light stabbed into his brain.

'My dear, you must lie still.'

He heard Kara's voice nearby. Forcing his eyes to focus, he saw her seated on the chair next to him. As his wits cleared he saw that he was in a bed in a strange room.

'You were set upon and robbed last night.' She leaned over him, speaking softly. 'The doctor said you'd had a lucky escape. Your arm was broken and you've sustained severe bruising, but fortunately no ribs were broken. Neither did you sustain any internal injuries. He put three stitches in a cut on your neck. That's what made you lose consciousness again.'

'How did I get here?'

The scent of jasmine enfolded him as Kara leaned forward and smiled. She was dressed in a cream muslin gown, her lovely face drawn with concern. 'Beatrice found you lying in the street. She had the sense to get a coster to bring you here on his barrow. She told me you were beaten because you warned the Gilbert brothers to leave my shop alone. Is that true?'

Zach wished his head did not feel so full of muzzy wool. Any answers concerning the Gilbert brothers, or Beatrice, needed his wits to be at their sharpest. He hedged. 'The Gilbert brothers objected to me warning them off.' He put a hand to his head and winced. 'So you've met Beatrice?'

'Are you in pain?' Kara ignored his comment. 'The doctor left a remedy to ease the discomfort and to help you sleep.'

He smiled. 'You are the only remedy I need. To awake and find you watching over me is like a beautiful dream. Tell me how you and Beatrice got on.'

He needed to know what was happening. Beatrice was an adept liar and would have her own interests at heart. The solicitude Kara was showing him was all he desired. Even so, he had to be sure that he made no mistakes that might jeopardise their wedding.

Kara took his hand and squeezed it gently, but he noticed the frown shadowing her brow. 'Beatrice did not stay. I think she was embarrassed. She was the woman involved with Slasher Gilbert on the night they robbed me. She was so upset. She said they forced her to work with them that night. That was how she recognised you. And she had been beaten like you. I dread to think what her life has been like. Of course Florence had mentioned to her that we are soon to be married.'

She fidgeted with the lace trimming on the sheet, smoothing its crumpled edge. Clearly she was nervous. Why?

'Listen to me babbling on,' she said with a shaky laugh. 'I've been so worried about you. You were unconscious for so long. It's my fault you were attacked. I should have paid those villains their money. Then you would not have been harmed.'

He took her hand and raised it to his lips. 'Isn't it a man's duty to protect the interests of the woman he loves?' he answered, pleased at her concern. There were moments in the last few days when she had been restrained in his company. Although she had accepted his proposal, she had never said that she loved him. That made him uneasy. What if she was having second thoughts?

She pulled her hand away from him, her manner again distracted. 'Beatrice has agreed to be my bridesmaid and is coming for a fitting for her dress this evening.' She swallowed, and the frown again appeared, adding to his fears. 'Beatrice is not as I expected,' she said with a sigh.

He relaxed. It was Beatrice she was worried about, not their wedding.

'My love, from what little I have learned from Florence of your sister, she has had a difficult life. Don't let yourself be taken in by her.' He did not want to say too much, just enough to ensure that Kara did not believe any tales Beatrice would tell her about himself.

To regain her sympathy, he pressed a hand to the back of his neck. Touching the line of stitches, he winced. 'I'll look a sight for our wedding. Father won't be pleased. He thinks our engagement meant I had reformed. I'm afraid I was not above street brawling in my early army days.' He gave his most disarming grin. 'I fear you are about to marry the black sheep of the family. I never thought I'd settle down. That was until I met you. You've captivated me and stolen my heart. You're a fighter, I admire that. You proved that in the way you were not intimidated by Slasher Gilbert. You have transformed the business you took over. You are remarkable and beautiful. My life would be nothing without you beside me, my darling Kara.'

He was satisfied at the softening light in her eyes. 'Don't make virtues of my stubbornness and determination to succeed. We are alike, Zach. We both know what we want in life. And we make sure we get it.'

He laughed and bit off the sound with another wince as pain shot through his skull. He was in too much discomfort to heed the warning behind her words. Absently he rubbed his hand across the stubble on his jaw. 'What time is it? I must meet my father at St Pancras at eleven-thirty.'

'It's only nine o'clock. If you wish I can send James to have him paged at the station.'

Zach cautiously tested his limbs. He was wearing a large white nightshirt. At his frown, Kara laughed. 'That belonged to Sophia's husband. The doctor said you are covered in bruises and will find it painful to walk. There's only a slight graze on your cheek.'

He stared at his broken arm in its splints and sling, his dark brows drawn together. 'Seven years in the army and barely a scratch. I walk home through the London streets and this happens.'

Kara tenderly smoothed back a lock of dark hair from his brow and he caught her hand. She glanced at the open door, aware of the improprieties of being in a man's bedchamber, even if she was to be wed to him in two days' time.

'Could you send for my manservant Jones to bring me clean clothes?'

'I've already sent James to your rooms. Your suit was ruined beyond repair.' She touched his jaw with a rush of genuine affection. Because of her he had been beaten. He was handsome, brave and, from his words, obviously in love with her. She did not love him, but her heart was moved at seeing him vulnerable for the first time. She enjoyed his company, and knew that if she could banish Richard from her mind, if not her heart, then their marriage would stand a chance of happiness.

Smiling into his amber eyes, she said fervently, 'Thank God Beatrice found you. When I think what those ruffians did to you…'

With his uninjured arm, he reached for her, drawing her close. 'My darling, your concern is the best remedy for my recovery. In two days we shall be wed.' His eyes darkened with passion and he smiled wickedly. 'Those two days will seem like two years, I long so much to make you truly mine.'

'You are incorrigible. You're supposed to be injured,' she teased, wishing that her heart would beat more wildly at the thought of him making love to her. All she could think of was the soul-stealing rapture of Richard's kisses. To cover her guilty confusion, she stood up. 'I will leave you to rest until your manservant arrives.'

Zach was grinning. 'So pure – so innocent, my darling. But I did not shock you, did I? You feel as I do?'

Kara could not look at him. The longing he had seen in her eyes had been all for Richard. To her relief she heard voices on the stairs. 'That must be James and your servant. I'll leave you to dress.'

His expression sobered. 'I'd rather my father did not know about the robbery. He'd bound to take it amiss. I'll say I was thrown from my horse whilst hunting to account for the broken arm. And besides, the truth would only alert Sophia to the danger you faced from the robbery. You don't want to frighten her, do you?'

Kara felt a twinge of disquiet that he was prepared to lie so readily to his father. Though he had told her he was a difficult man, she supposed that Zach knew how to handle him best. And he was right about Sophia.

'Are you sure you're strong enough to get up? The doctor advised rest.'

'If you were to stay by my side, I would be tempted indeed to play the invalid.' He grinned roguishly. 'Though not to the extent of being completely incapacitated.'

At her blush, he laughed. 'That's what I like most about you, Kara. You are so innocent.'

Her blush deepened, not from embarrassment, but from shame at how she was deceiving him. For a moment she was tempted to tell him the truth. Then Florence's warning stopped her. She was only eight weeks gone with child. Seven-month babies were not unknown. She must convince Zach that the child was his.

'I don't feel very innocent,' she said shyly. 'Not after the worry I had last night.' It was not all an act. She was very fond of Zach and was determined to make her marriage work.

He chuckled. He looked so handsome, his Byronic features with the graze on his angular cheek wrenched at her heart. She bent forward and kissed him lightly on the lips. He responded instantly, his kiss demanding, its intensity slowly drawing an answering response from her. Her face was flushed as she drew back. At seeing the passion darkening his eyes, her heart fluttered. It would not be a hardship to be married to Zach. She would be a good and loyal wife to him always.

'I'll leave you and send up your servant.' She left the room quickly.

Watching her, Zach reflected on his good luck. Since he had to marry for money, he was fortunate to have found a beautiful and passionate bride.

Chapter Sixteen

Kara was trembling when she returned to the wedding guests in the garden at the rear of the stationery shop. She had just changed out of her champagne silk wedding gown and veil and into a travelling dress of turquoise crêpe de Chine. The late afternoon sun was still bright, and the dozen guests were flushed with wine and good cheer as they conversed. On Kara's insistence the wedding was a small affair, for which Sophia had happily thrown open her house. Her cook had prepared a magnificent wedding breakfast for the couple. As Kara entered the garden, she saw Zach standing beside his father. His dark frock coat emphasised his military bearing and the white silk sling over his broken arm aroused a wave of tenderness for her handsome husband.

Since living with Sophia, Kara had attended the Sunday service at the Georgian church of All Saints in Langham Place. It was in this elegant spired church with its semi-circle entrance of Greek columns that she had been married two hours earlier.

Yesterday Zach's father, with his tall, broad figure, red face and large, waxed moustache, had been stiff and pompous on their first greeting. He had mellowed as the champagne flowed. Knowing how important it was to Zach, Kara had set out to charm Harold Morton, and gradually his stiff manner had melted. When she realised that he was as ill at ease as herself, she relaxed. Shortly after that, the squire took her aside from the other guests and handed her a jewel case.

'A wedding present, my dear. And all my blessings on this match. You will be good for Zach.'

Kara opened the jewel case and saw a sapphire and gold necklace with matching bracelet and earrings.

'They belonged to my mother. She was very fond of Zach,' he explained. 'She wanted Zach's wife to have them. And I could not imagine a more beautiful neck for them to grace.' After several glasses of champagne, there was a twinkle in his eye as his gaze swept over her trim figure. Kara blushed. She had already seen the squire flirting with Beatrice, who seemed to encourage his attentions. When his gaze searched the crowd and rested on Kara's sister, he frowned at seeing Beatrice talking with Zach.

Her husband's back was to her, but there was something about the way Beatrice was unable to stop her hand touching his arm as they spoke which disquietened Kara.

'Hard to imagine that saucy minx is your sister,' Harold Morton said, his frown deepening.

Zach was now walking swiftly away from Beatrice, his expression bleak. What had her sister said to annoy him? She had hoped that Zach and Beatrice could be friends.

'Beatrice is high-spirited,' Kara explained. Apart from her flirtatious behaviour, which had remained within the bounds of acceptability, Beatrice had been on her best behaviour all day. Though Kara was aware that Florence attempted to stay close to her younger daughter's side.

Kara dismissed her unease. Beatrice looked pale and had hardly spoken to her all day. Even her congratulations had been stilted.

Zach had earlier laughed aside Kara's concern at Beatrice's behaviour, saying, 'You've only just been united and now you're off on honeymoon for a month. That's all that's wrong. Aren't you about to see the sights of Paris and Vienna, whilst your sister remains in a squalid quarter of London? She's jealous.'

'I feel so guilty when I think of how different our childhoods must have been.' Kara shuddered at remembering what she had learned of Beatrice's past.

'Don't be. I'm sure Beatrice would not be feeling guilty if your roles had been reversed. She's a tough woman, that one.'

'Hasn't she had to be to survive?'

Zach smiled wryly. 'Don't endow her with your qualities. You're a survivor, my dear. But I think whatever hardship you faced, you would never lose your integrity or sense of honour. Beatrice isn't like that. She's an opportunist. She doesn't care whose feelings, or lives, get trampled on, just as long as she gets what she wants.'

'Clearly you don't approve of her life,' Kara returned. 'Are you ashamed to own her as your sister-in-law? Beatrice has assured me that she wants to escape that life. Isn't it our duty to help her?'

His thick lashes had canopied his eyes, and with a shrug he looked away. 'Don't let your heart rule your head where she is concerned, that's all, my dear.'

Kara was absently nodding agreement as Harold Morton complained about the number of beggars who had accosted him since his arrival in London. When Zach rejoined them, his father spoke more affably to his son than he had all day.

'Fine woman you've wed, my boy. Done yourself proud. Better than you deserve, I suspect. So you're off to Paris and Vienna for your honeymoon?'

Zach raised Kara's hand to his lips, smiling tenderly. 'I know when to count my blessings, and they're all in the shape of this ravishing woman.'

Embarrassed, Kara answered with a laugh. 'Zach insists we honeymoon for a month on the continent. I have always wanted to visit Paris and other cities of ancient culture.'

'It won't be the ancient monuments Zachariah takes you to enjoy.' The squire favoured his son with a grim look. 'With him play is always more important than exploring the cultural sights. But you're a sensible woman, as well as a beautiful one. You'll ensure he does not stray back into his wilder ways.'

Noting the warning, Kara felt her unease

return. There was much she did not know about Zach's past. He had clearly caused his father concern.

Zach was scowling. To disperse the tension, she smiled at him. 'I would not change my husband's ways. We suit each other well. Am I not unconventional in my ways, sir? Does it shock you that your son's wife owns and manages her own business? Within a few years I intend to have shops in several of the leading towns in England.'

'Ay, you've ambition, which is no bad thing.' He turned to his son. 'So, Zachariah, you've settled for trade then as your future. It could have been worse.'

Kara was about to interrupt that the shops would be all her concern, for she had no intention of Zach taking over her business.

'No, Father.' Zach spoke first. 'My wife can amuse herself with her shops as she wishes. I'll not interfere. I intend to invest Grandpa's legacy.'

'You mean you will gamble and fritter it away,' the squire said darkly.

'No, sir, I said it would be invested.' There was an edge to Zach's voice which made Kara's blood chill. Clearly there was little love lost between father and son.

'It is almost time for us to leave, my dear.' She put her hand on Zach's arm, hoping to defuse the growing antagonism. 'Mama is beckoning to me. I would say a proper farewell to her and Beatrice before we leave.'

As Kara left them, Squire Morton's eyes narrowed. 'You've a good lass there. Better than you deserve. Don't bring her to ruin by returning to your old ways.'

As Kara kissed her mother's flushed cheek, she saw her eyes were misty with tears of pride. 'You made such a lovely bride, but you must take care. Your marriage is built upon fragile foundations. Zach is enamoured. But he's no one's fool. Ensure he has drunk plenty of champagne before you retire this evening. If he suspects you are not a virgin...'

Kara stiffened, her heart thudding wildly. She had grown very pale.

'My dear you can handle Zach,' Florence reassured her. 'If his head is muzzy with drink, he will not suspect.'

Beatrice sauntered towards them. 'What are you two conspiring over?'

'Motherly advice,' Florence said baldly.

'Perhaps I should give Kara a few tips on how to keep a man happy,' Beatrice offered. 'Especially a man like Zach. You wouldn't want his eye roving whilst you're in Paris, would you, sister?'

'Beatrice, that's enough!' Florence said sharply. 'There's no need for such common talk.'

'I was only funning.' Beatrice lowered her lashes over her eyes to conceal the jealousy which burned in her gut. 'Weddings are a time for bawdry. Kara knows I wish her every happiness. Though it's not easy to be parted from her so soon. We've hardly had time to get to know one another.'

Beatrice's words so echoed Kara's own mood that she hugged her close. 'When I return we will make up for all the lost time.' She held her sister's face in her hands. Without her heavy make-up and in her bridesmaid's gown of pale green watered silk, her auburn hair swept up and held in place by sprays of tiny rosebuds and gypsophila, Beatrice looked every inch a gentlewoman. Her gaze dropped to the band of green silk around Beatrice's throat which concealed the fading bruises.

'Must you go back to your old life?' Kara said, distraught. 'You are welcome to stay here.'

'And have Fancy come and drag me back? No thanks. When I leave him it will be on my terms. Then I'll go far away so he can't get his filthy hands on me again. But he owes me…'

'Beatrice, don't think like that,' Florence beseeched. 'You can't get even with a man like Fancy Gilbert. It will be enough if he just lets you go.'

'It ain't right what he did to me, Ma. He should pay.'

'Then go to the law,' Kara suggested. 'Surely what you know about the Gilbert brothers could put them in prison for years, if not actually get them hanged.'

Beatrice gave her a look of contempt. 'If I squealed, I'd not live to see the week out. Others would see I was murdered for informing.'

'Then we must find a way for you to leave, Beatrice. If it's just a question of money, I'll pay whatever it takes.'

Beatrice kept her eyes lowered lest Kara see the gleam of satisfaction in their depths. 'It's Ma I'm worried about. First I'll have to persuade her to move out of the Gilberts' district.'

'I've told Mama I'll pay their rent, but she's

stubbornly refused.'

'That because she doesn't want to offend Big Joe,' Beatrice declared. 'He'd be insulted. He'd think your offer meant he hadn't taken proper care of Florence. He did his best. Without him Ma would have died years ago. Joe won't take your charity.'

Kara sighed. 'I can't let matters stay as they are. When I return we must find a way. Zach will know what to do for the best.'

Zach appeared at her side, his laughter jubilant as he slipped an arm around her waist. 'Come now, you all look so serious. Is this not a joyous occasion? Have some champagne.' He held up a large bottle and refilled all their glasses. 'I want everyone to toast the health of my lovely bride. Then I regret that we must leave, or we will not reach Dover before our ship sails.'

Zach's manservant Dipper Jones was already seated as the postilion of the carriage. He leaned down to give a hand to Anne, the new plump maid recently engaged by Kara. Both servants were to accompany them.

As Kara and Zach ran amidst a shower of rice and rose petals to the waiting carriage, Florence came level with Kara to whisper, 'There's a hamper of food and champagne in the carriage. Remember what I said. God bless you. And may you find happiness in this marriage.'

They spent their wedding night at sea. It was a disaster. From the moment the ship left Dover harbour, Kara began to feel ill. By the time they were half an hour out to sea, she thought she was going to die. Zach, who was tipsy from all the champagne he had drunk, was at first annoyed with her malaise which stopped him making love to her. Then, seeing that she was indeed suffering, he was sympathetic. Holding her close, he whispered words of comfort. She felt so wretched that she did not want him to see her so weak and ill.

'Leave me, Zach. Join the other passengers in the dining room. I'm better left alone.'

'I would be a poor husband to abandon you so soon after our marriage,' he teased, placing a cool, damp cloth on her brow.

Another wave of nausea made her groan feebly, and she waved him away. 'I can't bear for you to see me looking so wretched. Please, Zach, Anne will care for me. If the nausea passes I'll join you later.'

He went reluctantly. Several times during the evening he returned to see if there was anything she needed. She grunted in her misery and waved him away. She wanted to be alone. It wasn't just her seasickness which was making her so wretched. All at once the enormity of what she had done overwhelmed her. She was married to a man she did not love, and Richard was further than ever from her reach.

Yet Zach's concern touched her. When they docked she was still shaky from the crossing. He was tender and considerate of her needs, and by the time they reached their Paris hotel she had regained her composure. There was a nervous fluttering in her stomach as she contemplated the night ahead. She was not averse to Zach's kisses, and she knew he was capable of stirring her desire, if not her love.

A meal was ordered in their suite, and tactfully Zach left her to bathe and refresh herself after their journey. When he returned to their room it was early evening. She was resting on the bed, not expecting Zach to return just yet, and was wearing only a white silk peignoir. She had dismissed Anne some minutes earlier. Hearing the outer door to their suite open, Kara rose from the bed and moved to the doorway dividing the bedchamber from the lounge. Her honey-blonde hair, tousled from her nap, hung thick and straight to her hips. She stood in an amber ray of sunlight from the setting sun, her creamy skin glowing with a pearly sheen.

Zach caught his breath as he saw his wife. He'd been irritated at her illness and it had taken all his restraint and willpower to play the role of tender husband. He'd waited months to possess her. Longer than he had waited for any woman. To be robbed of his wedding night had sorely tried his patience. Now as she stood in the doorway, bathed in the golden aureole of light from the setting sun, she was entrancing; as seductive as a siren. The weeks of waiting had proved a potent aphrodisiac. It had brought him to a fever of impatience and yearning, rousing emotions within him, both sexual and protective, he had never considered he could fall prey to.

'How are you feeling, my darling?' he said huskily.

She smiled, enticingly, though she was inwardly quaking – not with fear, but with anticipation.

Remembering Florence's warning, she felt a chill of dread. Zach appeared sober. Her seasickness on their wedding night had prevented them making love. If he was sober, surely he would realise that she was not a virgin. She moved to where two bottles of champagne stood in an ice-bucket on the table.

'I am quite recovered,' she said, overcome with shyness. To cover her confusion, she filled two glasses.

He crossed the room and circled her slim body with his uninjured arm, his kiss hard and passionate. She tasted the brandy on his breath and felt easier in her mind. Even so, she knew she had to be careful. When his hand squeezed her breast she stiffened and pulled away. She caught a glitter in his eyes which clenched her stomach with alarm.

'I've ordered champagne.' Her voice shook with nerves. 'Will you not take a glass with me first?'

Zach stared at his wife and stifled his impatience. He could feel the perspiration on his skin, his body already aching to possess her. He forced himself to remember that she was a virgin. His first. He preferred his women experienced. Now the thought of being the only man to possess her tantalised him. He alone would be this incomparable woman's teacher and, from the rapid beating of her pulse at the base of her neck, she would be an avid pupil. But he must not rush her. He was too used to courtesans. He must not forget that this was a gently reared woman, who had no knowledge of what was expected of her.

He drank down two glasses of champagne in quick succession as she moved away to stand by the window. The sunlight behind her made her peignoir almost transparent. Her lithe, shapely silhouette was outlined seductively beneath the loose folds of the silk. He refilled both their glasses, knowing that the wine would relax her and hopefully dispel any inhibitions.

Kara closed her eyes, accepting that she must allow Zach to make love to her. She had thought his broken arm might stop him. Clearly it would not. He came to stand behind her and she could feel his presence like a pervading warmth. He lifted the heavy tresses of her hair and pressed a kiss against the hollow of her neck. He felt her tremble and looked at her with tender concern.

'My darling, I will not hurt you.'

He took her chin in his hand, compelling her to look up at him. His voice thickened with desire and his fingers lazily traced the line of her jaw. Without haste, gently, tenderly, and infinitely seductively, he began to kiss her brow, her lids, her cheeks. The warm touch of his mouth skimmed the surface of her skin, until her lips parted in breathless expectancy.

'It is natural that you are nervous,' he coaxed, his mouth nuzzling her ear. 'There is nothing to fear.'

'I fear only that I will not please you,' she answered softly. She spread her hands over the firm muscles of his chest, and felt the rapid pounding of his heartbeat.

His mouth slanted down over hers, tender and sweetly caressing. He clasped her body against him, the pressure of his chest and thighs burning through the flimsy silk of her robe. Her lips parted beneath the insistence of his kiss and, as it deepened, demanding and coercing, her body responded. With slow assurance, Zach continued to press kisses along her shoulders, easing the peignoir down her arms. When his mouth touched the hollow of her throat, a flame of longing unfurled through her veins. She gasped, her head rolling languorously back.

Zach was delighted at the fervour of her response. Murmuring endearments, he ran his hand over the perfumed curves of her breasts and hips, gently stroking her through the thin silk. Hearing her breathing quicken, he slid the peignoir from her shoulders to her waist. The sight of her pale, perfect breasts, rising proudly against his fingers, almost destroyed his control. He swallowed, checking his own need.

She drew back, her eyes dreamy with stirring passion and, with a shy smile, raised her glass to her lips. Sipping from it, she offered it to him. He drank the contents and tossed the glass on to a chair. His fingers, eager on the sash of her robe, untied it, then slid inside and over the warm heat of her soft skin. When he would have pushed the robe from her arms to strip the last of the covering from her body, he felt her body stiffen.

'Don't hide your beauty, my darling,' he encouraged hoarsely. 'You are so lovely.'

This time it was he who filled their glasses. 'Drink. It will help you to relax.' He quickly downed his own and refilled it, with his free hand he began to unfasten his necktie.

On trembling legs, Kara walked slowly into the bedchamber. Before she reached the bed, Zach was behind her. With a wicked chuckle he caught her in his good arm and swung her round to kiss her with increasing passion. He had removed his jacket and his shirt was open to the waist. Pressing her on to the mattress, he trailed kisses over her breasts and waist, while her hands moved over the smooth contours of his body. She was tense and willed herself to relax.

Gradually his kisses stirred her blood, the masterly onslaught of his touch kindling her passion. Whilst caressing her, he whispered words of love, inciting her to welcome his more demanding attentions. Thrills of pleasure spun like heated whirlpools through her veins. The last of her reserve thawed as his skilled fingers played over her flesh, coaxing her to passion.

She gasped as his tongue circled the tip of her breast, his lips pulling gently, sucking until a soft moan was drawn from deep in her throat. Her body moved against him, her inhibitions dispelled by the pleasure he was evoking. Her senses were spinning as his ardour grew, his lips and touch making her move in a sinuous rhythm against him. When he drew back, hampered by his splint in removing the last of his clothing, she pushed his hand aside. Shyly, she helped him to disrobe.

Then his lips were again insistent upon hers, his naked body hard and commanding upon her own. The tenderness of his kisses became less restrained, a savagery entering into them as his tongue sought the depths of her mouth. His breathing was laboured, his fingers prising her thighs apart as he positioned himself over her. He entered her with a force which made her gasp at the flaring pain. She wasn't ready for him. When he thrust into her time and again, she bit her lip against her cry of discomfort. Then it was over. Sweat peppered his face and, with a groan of pain, he cradled his broken arm and rolled away from her.

Moments later, from his deep, even breathing, she knew he had fallen into a light doze.

Kara lay stunned by the abruptness of his climax. She had felt nothing, her own needs had been unfulfilled. She closed her eyes, hiding her frustration. It wasn't Zach's fault, it was hers. Ultimately her body could not fully respond to a man she did not love.

She swung her feet to the floor to get up. Zach stirred, his arm encircling her waist to pull her back down beside him. Propping himself on to his elbow, he grinned down at her.

'You were wonderful, my darling. Did I hurt you? I'm sorry, it is always that way the first time.'

She closed her eyes, fearful lest he see her elation that she had duped him. Had the wine dulled his senses enough for him not to question that she was not a virgin? He began to kiss her again, and she tried to relax, though every sinew in her body rebelled against his continued caresses. Then subtly his caresses changed, as though he had sensed her withdrawal from him.

'I will make you want me as I want you, my darling,' he murmured. He stared at the sheet crumpled around her thighs, and, following his gaze, she realised that he was expecting to find them spotted with her virginal blood. There was only a faint pink watery smear.

'What's wrong, Zach?' she bluffed.

He frowned and shrugged. 'Shouldn't you have bled more?' She forced her eyes wide in feigned innocence. 'Should I? I know nothing of such matters. Zach, you don't think...' She broke off.

His weight shifted on the bed beside her and his uninjured arm slid around her shoulders. 'Your father kept you a virtual prisoner and you've not seen anyone else since you came to London. Unless it was Tennent. You were alone at the opera with him.'

Kara went pale. 'How can you suggest that anything improper took place between us? He was my lawyer. His wife is my friend.'

He put his hand to his head and rubbed his fingers across his brow. 'Well, what do I know of virgins? I've always avoided them in the past. Forgive me, my dear.'

'I wouldn't want you to think I was–' she began, but her words were smothered by a hard, demanding kiss. When finally he broke away she was breathless. His assumption that she was a virgin won her gratitude. It gave her confidence. This time, as he stroked her body, she responded with greater abandon, a familiar ache of longing building deep in her stomach. She gave herself unashamedly, wanting to feel more of him, wanting desperately to find fulfilment in her husband's arms.

This time her cries of pleasure matched his as

they made love repeatedly throughout the night. Kara was delighted with his prowess as a lover. Her affection for him turned to tenderness that, despite the pain of his broken arm, his passion for her was unrestrained. When finally she dozed, her body was satiated; but she knew she would never quite recapture the heavenly rapture she had experienced with Richard. You only ever found one soulmate in a lifetime.

Whenever Beatrice could get away from her work – or Fancy – she visited her mother in the shop during Florence's lunch-break. Florence had been ill at ease at first, clearly suspicious of her motives. Beatrice dressed demurely for those visits, and wore no make-up. Gradually her mother began to accept that she had changed. She even laughed at the constant bombardment of questions from Beatrice about her sister.

'I know little of Kara's life since I left Brentwood, Beatrice. She rarely speaks of it. Abel was a tyrant. It was obvious she was unhappy.'

Unhappy, but well fed and clothed, given every luxury of a wealthy merchant's daughter, Beatrice inwardly fumed. 'So how did she start out in business? What made her come to London?'

'She had a legacy left her from Abel's mother. Some jewels. They were in the safe-keeping of Richard Tennent, the family lawyer. Mr Tennent took her into his home for some weeks when she arrived. She was also engaged to be married to a banker. He broke off the engagement after Abel's death. Mr Tennent threatened to sue him for breach of contract. I think there was something illegal about a loan from the man's bank and Abel. Anyway, to hush up any scandal, he settled out of court. The money enabled Kara to purchase the shop she will open in Walthamstow next month. Whilst staying with the solicitor's family, she became friends with his invalid wife.'

'And what was Kara to this solicitor?' Beatrice said maliciously.

'Mr Tennent is a gentleman. He welcomed her as a guest in his house out of responsibility towards Abel Wyse, who had been a valued client of his law firm for years.'

'Old, dodderery and past it, was he then? A wrinkled, staid old lawyer, who took pity on a pretty face?' Beatrice's tone was scathing.

'Mr Tennent can't be older than his mid-twenties. His wife was only a few years older than Kara.'

Beatrice's interest was pricked. 'How long did Kara live with them?'

'Several weeks, until she moved in with Mrs Henshawe after she became a partner in this business. After her years as a virtual prisoner in Abel's house, she must have felt exhilarated by the freedom of her life with the Tennents. They took her to the opera. I believe it was during her stay with them that she was taught to dance the waltz and polka. They were good friends.'

'Kara has a knack of landing on her feet,' Beatrice said with false jocularity. 'I bet he had a grand house to take her to.'

'Belgravia, I think it was,' Florence answered.

Beatrice digested this information, unable to believe that, if Richard Tennent's wife was an invalid, the relationship had been so innocent. Didn't she know the true lechery of men? She did not believe any man capable of not expecting repayment for his so-called generosity. She would find out more about Richard Tennent.

The next day she walked to Belgravia, and spent an hour asking the street-traders if they knew the address of Richard Tennent, the solicitor. Finally, a stout milkman in a straw boater who had been ladling out milk from his churns into his customers' jugs, climbed up on to his horse and cart and pointed to a house further down the street.

'If your message is as urgent as you say, miss, you'll not catch him there at this time of day. You'd better try his offices in Chancery Lane.'

The next morning Beatrice visited the offices of Tennent, Tennent & Son, asking for an appointment with Mr Richard Tennent about a fictitious legal dispute. She was told that Mr Richard Tennent was not taking on new clients, but that his associate, Mr Finnemore, would see her. She made an appointment under an assumed name for the following week, which she had no intention of keeping. Frustrated at not being able to meet Richard Tennent, she paused on the pavement outside.

Along the street was a ragged lemonade-seller with his battered, high-crowned hat low over his long greasy hair. His calf-length tattered green coat was patched with brown serge, and his long legs, thin as rowing paddles, showed through the slit seams of his trousers.

Beatrice approached him and inquired, 'This

your regular patch?'

'And wot if it is?' He eyed her belligerently out of a single rheumy eye; the other was covered with a scuffed leather patch. Heavy folds of skin speckled with blackheads lined his large beaked nose.

'D'ye know Richard Tennent from the offices down the road?'

He hawked and spat on the cobbles. 'And if I do?' he challenged.

'Point him out to me and there's half a crown in it fer yer.'

He squinted at her, appraising the quality of her clothing. She had dressed in her second-best dress to visit the lawyers.

'A crown if the infermation is so important to yer.'

'A crown,' Beatrice answered, 'but you'd better not lie.' She held up two half-crowns and whispered a password known only to those in the underworld. He was taken aback, clearly confused by her fine clothes.

'Jus' don't gull me, friend,' she warned. 'I'll wait over here. Jus' give me a nod when Tennent comes out. He's bound to eat in one of the chop-houses at lunchtime.'

An hour later, with her temper fraying and her feet aching in her high-heeled laced-up boots, Beatrice saw two men emerge from the solicitor's doorway. Neither had entered whilst she had been watching. The lemonade-seller nodded to her. As she sauntered past his cart, she dropped the two half-crowns into his grimy hand. 'The dark-haired one,' he muttered.

Both men wore top hats and were striding briskly away from her. The dark-haired man was shorter than his blond companion by two inches, but he had broad shoulders and a slim figure beneath the tailored cut of his frock coat. As yet she had been unable to see his face. She hurried forward through the press of people on the pavement. When she drew level with him, she deliberately stumbled and, with a cry, clutched hold of his arm as she pitched forward.

His hand on her elbow saved her from falling.

'So kind of you, sir,' she said, flustered. 'Some oaf just barged into me, knocking me off my feet.'

'Are you all right, madam?' he asked in a deep, attractive voice. From beneath the brim of her fashionable hat, she looked up into his face. Her blood quickened with interest. He was handsome, and not at all staid and pompous as she had imagined. There was a sensual fullness to his lips, and she noticed the brief flaring of interest in his gaze as it took in her pretty face and figure. He enjoyed the company of women, although his gentlemanly manner hid it well.

'I am unhurt, thanks to your quick intervention.' She knew she should not be staring, but the man's rugged good looks had set her pulse leaping. A frown appeared in his hazel eyes, and she quickly recollected herself. He appeared impatient to be gone. He studied her absently, as though his mind was on weightier matters, whilst he politely waited for her to assure him that she was unhurt.

'Thank you again, I will not detain you,' she said, stepping back.

He raised his top hat to her, the sun highlighting reddish glints in his brown hair which curled over his high collar. He walked away with a long, relaxed stride; she was reminded of a lion she had seen caged at the zoological gardens.

She smiled grimly to herself. She knew men, and that was a man in contest against his own passionate nature. If Kara had spent several weeks in his house and she had not succumbed to him, then the same blood did not run in their veins. If she had learnt anything about her sister on the few occasions that they had been together, it was to recognise the passionate woman beneath the demure façade.

And Richard Tennent didn't look the type of man to remain celibate because his wife was an invalid.

Very likely, her dear sister Kara was not the sweet innocent creature she pretended to be.

Chapter Seventeen

They spent a fortnight in Paris, then travelled through Switzerland and Austria by rail to spend a glorious week in Vienna. Then on to Venice. Zach had extended their honeymoon from four weeks to seven. Kara was enthralled by every new sight and experience, although she fretted at being away so long from her business.

'Why do you worry so?' Zach teased her as they were conveyed in a gondola under the Rialto bridge. 'Relax and enjoy yourself, my darling. You ordered enough stock to keep the shop supplied for three months. It is in the capable hands of Florence and Sophia, and did not Beatrice say she would also help?'

'But Beatrice and Mama know nothing about ordering the latest publications from the publishers, and Sophia hates that side of the business. We must return, Zach.'

He frowned, his eyes golden slits in the bright sunlight. 'I thought to spend a week in Florence and then travel on to Rome before returning home. Think of the sights you will miss. It's not as though you *have* to work.'

'Of course I have to work, Zach,' she said with a laugh. 'We cannot keep spending the money your father settled on you at our marriage at the rate we are. I thought you wanted to invest that.'

He flexed the fingers of his arm, injured before their wedding. It had healed well and the splints had been removed last week. His expression darkened and her own mood became sombre. The last weeks had been happy ones. Zach gave her pleasure as a lover, and his company was amusing. Though at times there was a recklessness about his manner which gave her cause for concern. She put her arm though his and leaned her head on his shoulder. 'We have been away for much longer than I intended. It's important for me to do well in my business, I thought you understood that?'

When he kept silent, staring at the rows of red and white poles dotted along the landing stages, her disquiet increased. 'Of course, for all I know you are independently wealthy without your grandfather's legacy. You know I have no idea how you supported yourself before our marriage?'

'I have various interests in the horse world from my army connections, as I told you. I keep my ears and eyes open for opportunities to invest in commodities which turn a fast profit.'

'Isn't there a risk involved in that kind of speculation?'

He laughed. 'Everything that is exciting in this life involves some risk.' He put his arm around Kara's shoulders and, lowering her parasol over their faces so that the gondolier was hidden from them, he kissed her lips. 'I have a new business venture in mind. There's a suitable property vacant in Westminster.'

'What business is this, Zach?' she asked, interested.

He smoothed the sleek line of his moustache before replying. 'At the moment it's just an idea.' He raised her fingers to his lips, his voice soft and enticing. 'If you really want to return to England we shall, my dear. But do not the sights and wonders of Florence and Rome tempt you?'

She smiled fondly, her mind diverted from the question of his new venture. 'We've been away over seven weeks...'

'That's fifty odd nights, and on every one of them I've made love to you, my darling. As I want to make love to you again now.'

'Yes, fifty nights, Zach. Does that not tell you something?' She kept her smile fixed in place.

He looked at her bemused for several

moments, then her meaning dawned on him and his eyes lit with pleasure. 'I've been so enamoured of the pleasure you gave me, I had not realised that you had not been indisposed during our honeymoon. Are you telling me you are with child, Kara?'

'I was feeling queasy several times last week, and I visited a physician. He said I was with child. Are you pleased, Zach? We have been married such a short time.'

'My darling, I am delighted.' He kissed her resoundingly, heedless of a grinning gondolier on a passing boat, and of the shocked gasps from its two matronly occupants.

'Then of course we must return to England at once.'

When they arrived at their hotel, Kara noticed a large-girthed countess and her equally stout husband complaining in rapid Italian to the manager. The woman was distraught and the man incensed, both of them waving their arms wildly.

As they crossed the reception hall to the stairs, the manager who had quietened the irate guests hurried to their side. 'Signor and Signora Morton. I trust there no has been valuables taken from your room.'

'No, none,' Zach replied haughtily.

'A mercy. The contessa. Her emerald necklace was stolen.' The manager wrung his hands, his pitted olive cheeks almost entirely covered by wide greying side-whiskers. His dark eyes beneath heavy lids rolled heavenwards in vexation. 'No good for business such thefts.'

Kara was appalled. 'Did the countess lose that magnificent emerald necklace she was wearing last night when they dined?'

'*Si.* A family heirloom. Much fine. Much valuable. The countess she is much sad. Much angry. Three people they tell me they have jewellery stolen this week. No good for my hotel.'

Zach stood stiffly at Kara's side. 'Our valuables are in the hotel safe, as should your other guests' have been. In our travels across Europe, several such incidents have occurred. One cannot be too careful.'

The manager nodded and hurried away to tend to another guest's requirements, and Kara turned to Zach. 'There have been thefts at every hotel we have stayed in. I had not realised that crime was so rife abroad.'

He shrugged and adjusted the line of his gold and ruby cufflinks. Their single large stones glinted in the sunlight from a nearby window. 'There are thieves everywhere, my dear. The first thing you learn in the army is never to trust the natives. That's why I insisted that your jewel case was kept in the hotel safe.'

'What does Morton think 'e's about?' Slasher Gilbert grunted the moment his brother joined him in the office at the gaming club. 'Seven weeks he's bin away. Jus' cos' 'is ol' man gave 'im a handsome settlement which enabled 'im to clear 'is debts wiv us, don't mean 'e's off the 'ook.'

''e's trickier than some ter deal wiv.' Fancy rubbed his finger along his scarred cheek. ''E ain't scared of our bullies. From wot I hear spread around, 'e's bin lining the pockets of certain peelers. 'E ain't doin' that without cause.'

Fancy paced the room and paused before a fly-spotted mirror to adjust the line of his yellow cravat. 'Morton could be trouble. 'E were seen takin' an interest in an large old boarded-up house over Westminster way. Rumour 'as it 'e's after starting up 'is own gaming house. Toffs only.'

'That ain't gonna be profitable for us,' Slasher growled, his finger running along the sharp edge of his dagger. ''E needs keeping an eye on. And 'e ain't the only one by all accounts. That tart of yours, Bea. Givin' 'erself airs lately, ain't she? She were in pretty thick with Morton's new wife. 'er Ma's even workin' in 'er shop.'

Fancy eyed his brother belligerently. He resented any implication he wasn't keeping his own house in order. Bea was becoming a problem. He'd begun to suspect she wasn't handing over all the goods she stole, but he'd been unable to prove anything. She was a sly one. Her Ma had ensured she'd been educated properly. That quick brain of hers would get her into trouble one day. She'd certainly changed recently, less respectful and eager to do his bidding. Not that she'd ever been easy to tame. That had always been her attraction. But since young Bessie Brown had caught his eye, Bea's familiar charms no longer captivated him as once they had. Fancy scowled. Trouble was Bea knew too much about him. And he also suspected that her eye had once wandered too often upon Zach Morton.

‘So yer think Morton is about to set ’imself up as a gaming-house owner?’ Fancy declared. ‘We’re gonna need someone on the inside to ensure our interests ain’t forgotten. Someone Morton could trust. Someone who ’as ’er own interests at ’eart. Someone who wouldn’t be so foolish as to forget ’er debt to old friends. Bea will be our spy.’

‘Can you trust ’er?’

Fancy smirked. ‘I’ll ensure ’er loyalty, don’t yer fear.’

It was raining when Kara and Zach’s ship docked at Dover three weeks later. Again Kara had been taken ill on the voyage, and they had been further delayed by a storm. She was feeling queasy, and before disembarking she searched in her travelling case for her smelling salts. Zach had already gone on deck with his servant, and Anne, her maid, was in the adjoining cabin packing the last of Kara’s clothes.

The nausea and faintness increased. Frantic to find the smelling salts, she wrenched open two more valises without success. Could Zach have picked up the bottle and inadvertently thrown it into one of his valises? She opened the smallest one and ran her hands along the side under his folded shirts. Her hand closed over a cold hard object, and her heart clutched in dread. Then all at once the nausea rushed to her throat and she made a dive for the handbasin by their bed. As the spasm passed and she straightened, she heard the door open behind her.

‘My dear, have you been taken ill again?’ Zach

said. The concern died from his voice to be replaced by an oath muttered beneath his breath. Kara turned to face him, her cheeks ashen, her eyes bleak and accusing. With contempt she flung the emerald and diamond necklace she had last seen around the neck of the Italian contessa at his chest. He snatched it to him, his lips beneath his moustache thin and unrepentant.

'So now you know,' he said crisply. 'That is how I earn my living. Stealing from the rich and privileged.' His full lip curled back. 'How else was I to keep myself in the style I intended to live when Father refused to pay my gambling debts?'

'I married a thief,' she said, shocked.

'Only from people who won't miss what I take. It's not as though I'm stealing the bread from a starving child's mouth. That fat contessa had a dozen more to match this.'

'That is no excuse. And the other robberies. Were they done by you?'

He grinned by way of an answer. 'With the help of Dipper, or Jones as you call my servant. They more than paid for our honeymoon, my dear. You've been pretty close with your own money since we wed.'

She sank down on to the bed and closed her eyes, her hand automatically resting over her stomach. What had she done? Just as she had begun to believe that their marriage could be happy, she learned this. 'I thought you an honourable man, Zach. My husband a thief…' She faltered and laid her head in her hands.

'But what if you are caught?' she said at last.

'The trick is never to get caught.' His flippancy

appalled her.

'Promise me you will stop.'

His amber eyes narrowed. 'What, and get an honest job! Like a clerk, my dear? Can you honestly see me as a clerk?'

'I thought you advised men on buying horses at Tattersall's. Couldn't you use your grandfather's legacy to start up a stud or something? We could buy stables close to London and...'

'I'd rather bet on the horses than work with them any day.' He smiled broadly, his manner conciliatory. 'But then, my dear, I never intended that you would learn of my true profession. What were you doing prying into my valise?'

'I was not prying. I felt faint and nauseous. I was searching for my smelling salts.'

'Now you know the worst of me, do I disgust you? You've led such a prim life. What would you know about what it is like to be without money: you, the pampered heiress.' As he spoke he came towards her, his expression grave, but his eyes compelling her to forgive him. 'I hoped you would never find out. I am as I am, Kara. I'm not ashamed of it. I harm no one – just relieve a rich, spoilt aristocrat of a bauble or two.'

His arms were around her. 'Don't look at me like that, my darling. I have no intention of getting caught.'

'And no intention of giving up such a life either,' she said hollowly. 'It's wrong, Zach. I don't want to live with the constant fear of you being arrested.'

His smile was his most disarming as he stooped to kiss her brow. 'Truth to tell, my dear, most of

Papa's money went on overdue gambling debts. Slasher Gilbert is not a man to wait on his creditors. But what are a few paltry thousands to a woman of your wealth? If my thieving upsets you, then I suppose I could open a gambling house of my own for the élite only.'

This time her shocked expression silenced him. 'Such places are little better than bordellos. You would not shame me in such a way.'

A muscle throbbed along his jaw and the expression in his eyes was hidden as he regarded her beneath lowered lashes. 'I've no intention of running a bordello. My club will be a respectable establishment for gentlemen. Fortunately, what is yours is now mine, now that we are married. Of course I won't touch the legacy from those jewels which you used to set up your business with. I'd not be that unreasonable. But your father's money – your inheritance from the sale of the haulage yard … I shall call on the bank tomorrow. I need at least five thousand pounds to refurbish the premises.'

Kara stiffened and craned back in his arms, her eyes wide with disillusion. So that was why Zach had been so quick to wed her. He believed her an heiress? Her temper flared. How dare he use her so! How dare he trick her with his false words of love! Then, as suddenly as her temper rose, it subsided. And hadn't she tricked him? When he had spoken of her father's business, she had not mentioned that Abel was a bankrupt. That would have led to her speaking of the manner of his death, and she had kept that shame to herself. Was she any better than him? Her pride had led her to withhold the truth from him. And worse, had she not tricked him into believing that he was the father of her child?

She began to laugh. Then found she could not stop.

Zach grabbed her shoulders, his puzzled frown making her hysteria mount. 'Kara, stop it. Stop it! You will make yourself ill.'

But she couldn't stop laughing. A flaring pain in her cheek snapped back her head. Then she was clasped tight in Zach's embrace.

'My darling, I had to do that. I had to stop you laughing. You were becoming hysterical. It cannot be good for the child.'

She gasped and held her fiery cheek, her eyes grave as she raised her head to look up at him. 'I'm not an heiress, Zach. There was no money from the sale of the haulage company. Papa shot himself because he could not face the shame of being a bankrupt. I haven't any money left. Everything has gone into the two shops.'

She was released so abruptly that she stumbled, and she clutched hold of the bedpost for support. Her head came up in proud defiance. 'I never told you I was an heiress. I thought you married me because you loved me. Your suit was pressing enough.'

He had grown pale, his eyes glittering. A muscle pumped along his jaw. His hand clenched and unclenched. For a moment she thought he was about to strike her.

'Only a fool weds for love,' he finally ground out.

He controlled himself with an effort, and his

lips tilted into a mocking smile. He lifted the emerald necklace and stared at her. 'Then I had better take this and the other stolen prizes from our honeymoon to my fence.'

His gaze roamed over her tense figure, starting at her hemline and finishing at her breasts which, in her agitation, were rising and falling against the material of her bodice. His look drifted again to her waist.

'What's done is done, Kara. Looks like I've been hoist by my own petard. Still I've no complaints. I've had worse and less imaginative mistresses. Marriage spares me from being plagued by eager matrons avid to have their insipid daughters wed. Perhaps Father will be so delighted with his new grandchild that we can winkle some more cash out of him.'

With that he turned on his heel and strode to the door. 'I'll send Dipper down to carry our luggage ashore.'

Kara stared at his retreating back and, pressing her hand to her brow, sank down on to the bed. Her throat clamped with the agony of Zach's callous acceptance of their marriage. She didn't love him, but she had at least thought they had a mutual respect for each other. He had killed her respect for him. The loss of the vast fortune he had expected had certainly dampened the regard in which he held her. The hollow shell of her marriage mocked her. Yet she had never wanted Zach's love. There would be only one man who could hold a place in her heart, and that was Richard Tennent. By her marriage she had saved her reputation, and her child would not be born a bastard and ostracised by society. For that she would always be grateful.

Now to her surprise she discovered that her pride would not permit her marriage to fall apart. If there was any chance of saving it, and salvaging what happiness they could with each other, she would strive to do so.

'How could you do this to me, Kara? I thought I was your friend. How could you go behind my back?'

Elizabeth Tennent lay propped on a snowy mound of pillows, her hand placed against her brow as she struggled for breath. In the lowered gaslight, with the curtains drawn against the setting sun, Elizabeth looked pale.

There had been no greeting, no preamble, just this accusing outburst which had left Richard's wife weak and gasping for breath.

Kara halted in horror in the middle of the bedroom floor. The words rang in her head. Her guilt gave them only one interpretation. Elizabeth had discovered that Richard had made love to her.

Appalled, she remained silent. Her face was haggard as she stared at the prostrate woman fighting for breath.

'Your silence betrays your guilt.' Elizabeth gasped her denunciation. 'I'm hurt. Terribly hurt. I thought you were my friend. How could you do this to me?' A sob escaped her, her eyes reddened from her weeping. 'Kara, how could you get married and not tell me? I was upset to learn of the marriage from an announcement in the paper. Then you disappear on honeymoon for two months.'

Kara hoped her relieved rush of breath was not too obvious. She forced a smile. 'It was all rather sudden. Captain Morton quite swept me off my feet.' She smiled and held out both her hands in supplication. 'I did write to you from Paris.'

Kara suppressed a rush of pain as she recalled how difficult that letter had been to write. She knew that Elizabeth would read it to Richard, and she had not wanted to cause him pain. 'Will you forgive me?'

Elizabeth pouted. 'Richard was also upset. He's your solicitor, and I had thought also your friend. Though you know men. He would not talk about it. He defended your actions. But I scarcely saw him for weeks.' Her mouth was pursed and she placed a hand over her eyes in theatrical distress. 'Every evening he shut himself away in his study, declaring that he had important papers that had to be dealt with without delay.'

'I'm back now, and when you meet Zach you will be charmed by him. Everyone is. And he will adore you.'

Elizabeth sniffed and daubed at her eyes, the sullenness leaving her beautiful face. 'So silly of me to act like this. I would have loved to have been at your wedding.'

'I know. I am sorry, Elizabeth.' Kara held out a package. 'This is for you. It's the finest French perfume. You see, I did think of you during my honeymoon.'

Elizabeth's eyes sparkled with pleasure. 'A present for me? And French perfume. How wonderful.' Tearing open the wrapping, she removed the stopper from the bottle and inhaled deeply. 'It's divine.' She patted the edge of the mattress. 'Come, tell me about your husband and your travels.'

'I would not tire you. Clearly you've been ill again, or you would not be in your bed.'

'I shall be better now you have returned. So silly of me these attacks. Tell me everything.'

Kara glossed over the details of the past two months when answering Elizabeth's questions. Her friend wanted to know everything about her whirlwind romance. There was no sign now of the difficulty in breathing and, not for the first time, Kara suspected that Elizabeth sometimes used her illness as a weapon to get her own way. Yesterday, Kara had sent a message stating her intention to visit this evening. She had done so in order that Richard would be warned and could absent himself if he wished. Any meeting between them was bound to be strained, and she did not want it witnessed by Elizabeth.

'And your business?' Elizabeth continued to question her. 'You'd not long built up your customers for the Oxford Street shop, and you were planning to open a second. Where was it – Walthamstow? I was surprised you could spare so long away. Didn't trade suffer?'

'The shop is doing well and the new one opens in two weeks' time. I've got a wonderful woman to manage it, an ex-governess.'

She did not mentioned that she hoped Florence would manage the new shop. Her mother had refused and would not give a reason. She suspected it was because of Joe.

'Your mother was another secret you kept from me,' Elizabeth pouted. 'When I visited the shop, Sophia told me all about Florence. Also that you had a sister. I thought you were alone in London. That was why Richard asked you to live with us.'

Kara took Elizabeth's hand, ashamed of the deceit which had followed her arrival at this house. 'I was alone at the time. Richard knew the truth of my circumstances. I did not know Mama's whereabouts. We had not seen each other for several years.'

'Richard explained that Florence had suffered ill-health for years and was forced to take the waters aboard. Though I find it odd you had no address for her.'

Kara silently thanked Richard for keeping Florence's secret. 'Mama will not talk about her marriage. It was not a happy one. Papa could be a tyrant.'

She hated to continue the deception. Elizabeth was a gossip. She would confide in her mother-in-law, and Irene was such a snob, as Elizabeth also had a tendency to be. There'd be gossip enough when her child was born only seven months after her marriage.'

Kara kept that news to herself for the moment. She wished to spare Elizabeth the pain of knowing she had conceived whilst she was condemned to remain barren. Also she did not want Richard learning of her condition before he left for South America. If he should believe the child was his... That was a complication she was not prepared to deal with. Things were better for everyone as they were.

'Mama is looking much better,' Kara said brightly, diverting Elizabeth's questions. 'Working in the shop seems to agree with her. Beatrice has also taken an interest in the business, which surprised me. I've spent the last week replenishing our stock and supervising the work at Walthamstow. The greetings cards have proved a success, and I want to introduce more new lines.'

'Surely your husband will run the businesses now?'

'Most certainly not! The business is my pride – my joy. It was agreed before we married that it was to be solely my concern.'

'And what does your husband do? You mentioned he was a captain, but that he had resigned his commission.'

Zach's profession was also something Kara had no intention of discussing. 'He is of independent means.'

Elizabeth raised a blonde eyebrow, clearly impressed. 'You must bring him to dine with us one evening.'

Kara shifted uncomfortably. That was impossible. It would be cruel to force Richard to meet Zach in his own house. But how could she tell Elizabeth that? From Elizabeth's speech and restored spirits, Kara guessed that she did not yet know Richard was to leave England shortly. By Kara's reckoning he was due to go in about a month.

'How is Richard?' her voice fractured and she cleared her throat.

'He works too hard. He sends his apologies that business takes him away from home this evening.' Suddenly her lips trembled and her eyes filled with tears. 'Kara, I've missed you so much. I've had no one to talk to. No one to confide in. I'm so miserable. Richard is rarely home. I don't believe it can all be work. I think he has a mistress.'

A sharp pain of pure jealousy stabbed through Kara's heart. She struggled to find her voice, but only a croak rose from her lips. Clearing her throat a second time to overcome her emotion, she forced out, 'Richard is devoted to you. What makes you think he has a mistress?'

Tears were streaming down Elizabeth's cheeks. 'I told you that my health is too delicate to risk childbirth. Richard has been so considerate over … over my health. He is a passionate man. The more I think about it, I suspect that he must from time to time visit one of those women who … a courtesan…'

'It would never alter how he feels about you,' Kara soothed.

Elizabeth sniffed and dabbed at her tear-filled eyes. 'I tried not to think about it, but he is away from the house so much. It became so that I could think of nothing else. When I broached the subject with Irene, she told me I was a fool. That I must turn a blind eye to such peccadilloes. It was hard. Yet he always was so kind to me. Until recently.'

She gasped for breath.

'Don't speak of it since it upsets you.'

'I must. You will understand. I have to tell someone. Richard's changed. It began about three months ago. He's hardly ever here. He's always courteous to me, but … he's different. More reserved.'

Elizabeth burst into sobs, her speech erratic. 'A courtesan I could accept … but not … not a mistress… Not a woman he cared for, perhaps loved…'

Her sobs intensified and, assailed by guilt, Kara took her into her arms. 'Don't upset yourself this way. Richard is devoted to you. He did mention to me some months ago that he had several complicated cases. That is why he employed Mr Finnemore.'

'But he is being secretive.'

'That doesn't sound like Richard. He's probably trying to stop you worrying unnecessarily over some matter. He puts your health first.'

Elizabeth's expression cleared. 'How foolish I am. Richard would never betray me.' She laughed nervously. 'He did mention some idea he had of going to South America. So unlike him. I didn't take it seriously. I told him that I could not cope. He said he would engage a companion for me. What nonsense. I told him so. How can he go? What about his responsibility to his clients? The thought of it made me ill. I was so upset I haven't left my bed for a fortnight. He has not mentioned leaving England again.'

This time it was anger Kara was forced to hide. Elizabeth had played on her illness, to try and blackmail Richard into giving up his expedition.

Elizabeth continued to babble on. 'How foolish I am. I've missed you, Kara. So silly of me to doubt my Richard. Of course he adores me. He brought me this diamond bracelet as an anniversary present last week.' She waved her arm in the air to display it. 'Doesn't that prove he loves me? That he would never leave me?'

'Richard will never leave you, Elizabeth,' Kara answered, referring to his marriage and not his planned trip to South America. She did not think she could ever forgive Elizabeth if Richard abandoned a project which meant so much to him.

Kara took her leave soon after that. Her own nerves were strained to breaking point with her guilt. The visit to Elizabeth had become a penance, and one that – if Richard went to South America – must continue.

Siddons, the Tennents' butler, stepped on to the pavement and hailed a hansom which was parked on the corner. As the carriage drew level, Kara absently bade him goodnight and prepared to step inside. She started at seeing the cab was already occupied. About to murmur an apology, her arm was taken and she recognised Richard sitting in the darkened interior.

A wave of longing swept over her. Caught off-guard, desire for him snatched her breath and her body trembled.

He swallowed, his love for her shimmering in his eyes. Then, with an effort, he masked his expression. 'Get in and don't make a fuss, or Siddons will see me,' he ordered. 'We have to talk.'

Chapter Eighteen

Kara had no intention of objecting, she was too delighted at seeing him. Though as she settled in the seat at his side and the cab set off, she had a moment's misgivings.

'We agreed not to meet. This only makes it harder.'

'I had to speak with you.' His voice was gruff. 'I could not bear the cold formality of the office. Not to say goodbye.'

Kara's heart beat wildly. 'Then you are leaving for South America. Elizabeth made it sound…'

'Elizabeth has been difficult,' he interrupted, 'I've lost you because of her. My marriage is a sham. Elizabeth loves me in her way, but it is not how a woman should love a man. I am her security, her provider. This expedition to study the Inca and Mayan people means too much for me to lose that as well.'

'And you must pursue that dream. You've done your duty by your family and father's clients. It's not wrong to want a year to yourself.'

'I may be away for longer than a year. From Mexico I intend to travel to sites in Guatemala and then on to Peru.' The control in his voice cracked. 'I need to know you are happy, Kara. That something at least has been salvaged from this mess.'

She could never tell Richard that she now

viewed her marriage as a disaster. Zach had not stopped his thieving. In fact he had boasted that he was away attending a race meeting at Newmarket this week, where the pickings would be high.

Her pause told Richard more than words. He ached to take her in his arms, to kiss her into submission. He couldn't get her out of his mind. He loved her with a passion which defied reason. Their night together constantly haunted him in bitter-sweet torment, knowing it could never be repeated. He wanted to pour out his love for her, cast aside convention. The smell of her body's perfume pervaded his senses; his need for her undermining his honourable intentions. How could he bear life without her? She was part of him, indelibly merged with his soul. The thought of her sensual body responding to another man's touch pitched him to near insanity. He wanted to kill Morton. That scoundrel did not deserve Kara.

It took all his willpower to remain at her side without holding her close. How could he speak of his feelings? He had seen by the flaring of desire in her eyes as she recognised him that she felt the same. To give voice to that love would ignite a flame which would eventually ruin them both in society's eyes. Such a scandal would destroy both their careers and their lives. He could not bear Kara to be labelled a whore, an adulteress; all the cruel names a hypocritical society heaped upon a 'fallen' woman.

Instead of declaring his love, he schooled his voice to coolness. 'Did you marry Morton because you needed the respectability of a husband to make your shop a success, or because I had failed you? I ruined you.'

'Oh, Richard, you did not fail me.' Her voice was a silken caress, sibilant with desire. 'Neither did you ruin me, as you so quaintly phrase it. I love you. I tried to fight it. It was impossible. Even a look from you would set my body burning for your touch. A few minutes of your company at breakfast, when we did little more than exchange a few convivial words, set my heart aglow all day. I knew it wrong, but each day I became more enamoured, until I was lost. My heart will always be yours, my love. I don't regret what happened between us. It is my most treasured memory.' She faltered.

Their gazes fused, love, adoration and desire naked in their depths. She swallowed, a tear too proud to fall sparkling on her lashes. 'Glorious, unforgettable and incomparable as our union was,' she added softly, 'we both know it cannot be repeated. Zach married me in good faith. And if the scandal ever broke it would kill Elizabeth.'

'Elizabeth is stronger than you think. She gets what she wants by playing the invalid.'

It was the only time he had spoken disparagingly about his wife. And it was what Kara had already guessed. 'It is a tragedy that Elizabeth mustn't risk another pregnancy. It would make your relationship easier.'

A muscle pumped along his angular jaw. She could feel his tension and anger. 'Is that what she told you? There is no risk in Elizabeth conceiving. She is terrified of the pain of childbirth.

Terrified to the extent that, if I were to lay a hand on her, she would start to scream in abject horror of the consequences.'

'But she loves you.'

He looked away, the tension in his handsome face intensified. Kara knew that Elizabeth's cloying affection must be stifling to Richard. Over the top of the half doors at the front of the cab, she stared fixedly at the dark silhouette of the horse's nodding head as it trotted along.

'Does Morton love you?' he asked, still averting his gaze.

'I don't want his love. I will never love him.'

A harsh groan was torn from him, and he put a hand to his mouth as he stared bleakly out of the window. Softly he said,

'Oh, lift me as a wave, a leaf, a cloud!
I fall upon the thorns of life!
I bleed!'

The quote from Shelley so poignantly echoed Kara's own torment that she answered in tremulous voice with a verse from John Donne,

'All other things, to their destruction draw,
Only our love hath no decay;
This, no tomorrow hath, nor yesterday,
Running it never runs from us away,
But truly keeps his first, last, everlasting day.'

Hearing her words, Richard knew himself in purgatory. She was all he wanted in a woman. Intelligent, graceful, beautiful, courageous, sensual, her passion unfeigned. She was without peer; a woman of honour. And how their honour mocked them!

He had waited an hour in the hansom for her to leave his house. To condone his actions, he had convinced himself that he needed merely to know that she was well. In her presence his resistance was melting like snow before a fire. When she had stepped into the cab her lovely face had been framed by the house lights, and he had noted every detail about her. Beneath her tilted hat, one honey-gold curl had escaped the elegant coiffure, the tendril resting on the slender hollow of her neck. He hungered to kiss it aside.

He swallowed as the memory of the joy her body had given him returned to haunt him. Her complexion – unfashionably tinted to pale amber from the sun – gave her the wild, untamed look of a gypsy. He clenched his hands together, fighting to control the need to take her into his arms and bury his head in the perfumed softness of her hair, to make love to her with a ferocity which defied honour and reason.

'You have South America, Richard.' Her husky voice was tender. 'That is worth so much more than anything you could have had with me. Discover the secrets of the Incas.' Her eyes were misty as she fought against her own longing, and her lips were tremulous, her mouth so inviting, that Richard inwardly groaned at the forbidden temptation she presented.

He raised a dark brow and, as they passed beneath a street gaslight, Kara saw that his expression was adoring. 'Your marriage puts you further from my reach. We will not meet again before I leave. Morton came to the office inquiring about your finances. I dealt with him, but he was not pleased to have it confirmed that you were not the heiress he believed.'

'Zach has put a brave face on his disappointment.'

He did not press her further and she did not enlighten him.

In a heavy voice, Richard finally said, 'If ever you have need of me, I will never fail you again, Kara. Promise me that, if I am in England, I will be the first person you turn to if you have need.'

Her throat worked and she fought to stop throwing herself into his arms. Her eyes widened with longing as she studied him. Their gazes held, assessing, memorising every precious detail of the changes wrought by two months of absence. Kara's heart jolted. Tumultuous emotions warred within her, and she sensed the same conflict tormenting Richard. His face was leaner than she remembered, yet infinitely more beloved. Without conscious thought, her hand lifted to place her palm against his clean-shaven cheek. It was like tinder to kindling. They were in a darkened part of the deserted street. Suddenly she was locked in his arms, her own fast about his neck, her lips open and hungry upon his.

Richard sighed against her ear. 'Kara, my love.'

He was lost to reality. One touch from her could destroy his control. He had meant to take her shoulders and push her away, but traitorously his grip had turned to a caress as he felt her soft, yielding warmth through the thinness of her gown. His hand slid to the back of her neck, drawing her head back so that her mouth was lifted to his, already parted in a soft sigh of yearning. He kissed her feverishly, his tongue delving to taste the unique sweetness so vividly remembered. It fanned the heat of his mounting passion.

He had spent two months trying to forget her. Yet every curve, every subtle scent of her was branded in his memory so vividly that there were times when he would awake in the night and believe she was on the bed beside him. On waking and discovering it was only the power of his memories, he knew that, if he paid for it until the day he died, he could not leave England without once more feeling her in his arms.

His kisses continued down her throat to the curve of her neck and he felt her trembling with the force of her passion. His hands caused sensations in her which drew a murmur of pleasure from deep in her throat. An aching need throbbed through him, obliterating reason. With a strangled moan he caressed her breast, his desire raging. All the good intentions, his concept of honour, were shredded. Kara Wyse had cast a spell upon him, had roused a sensual side in him no other woman could satiate.

This could be the last time he would hold her, and he wanted to carry the memory of her yielding body with him to South America. His hand moved to her cheek and encountered a trail of fiery tears. Instantly he sobered. They were again passing streetlamps and could be seen by people in oncoming vehicles. With a ragged sigh he drew back.

'I wronged you once, I will not do so again. I want all you have to give, Kara, or nothing at all.'

He rapped on the roof of the cab and shouted, 'Stop, driver. I'll alight here. Take the lady on to Oxford Street. Henshawe & Wyse stationer's.'

He paused briefly before opening the door. 'Be happy, Kara. I shall never forget you.'

'Nor I you, Richard.'

He nodded, his face taut with emotion. 'I'd write but…'

'It's better if you don't. Zach may see your letters. How could I explain them? Know that my thoughts will be with you at every sunset. It will be our only link. I shall hear of you through Elizabeth. I will visit her whilst you are away.'

Then he was gone and Kara slumped back on to the seat, her eyes blinded by the onrush of scalding tears.

Richard watched the hansom drive away, taking Kara out of his life. It needed all his willpower to control the urge to run after her, to beg her to throw convention to the wind and live with him. Iron will triumphed over his desire. Such action would destroy them both. She did not love Zach Morton any more than he loved Elizabeth. His love for Kara was the more tempestuous because he had never felt more than fondness for Elizabeth, or any other woman.

He quickened his pace, reflecting back on his marriage. Elizabeth's fragile beauty had attracted him, had roused his chivalry to protect her when she was orphaned at fifteen. She had been a shy, but at first pleasing, companion and bedfellow. But soon her cloying adoration had become an irritant. Beneath her pretty, fragile exterior was a woman obsessively concerned with her own selfish whims. Any discord was followed by her using her illness as a means to get her own way. Her father had idolised her and denied her nothing. His death had affected her deeply. Now, at twenty-four, she still behaved like an adolescent, constantly demanding attention and treats. After her miscarriage and the pain she had endured, any intimate touch from him caused such quaking fear in her that his desire for her had been doused. Her childish whims were easily mollified. He indulged them, providing they were reasonable and not in conflict with his wishes. Accordingly, their marriage had survived with less acrimony than most.

Richard's thoughts deflected to the other woman in his life. In the last two years he had kept a mistress, Dolly, in a house in Kensington. Dolly was five years older than him, and had been a governess before her previous employer had thrown her out after getting her pregnant. For two years before he met her she had been a high-class courtesan. Her intellect attracted him as much as her beautiful body. Though he supported her, there were no emotional ties other than affection and the pleasure they gave each other in the bedchamber. In Dolly's arms he had tried to forget Kara, but even Dolly's consummate skill could bring only fleeting relief from the torment of loving a woman he revered too much to bring to ruin.

Beatrice quaked as she recognised Fancy's footsteps in the corridor outside their rooms. He had not slept in their bed for ten nights. Although the rest from his attentions was a relief, it boded ill for her future.

Quickly, she scanned her reflection in the mirror. She wished now she had changed out of the high-necked blouse and navy skirt she wore when picking the pockets of women as they sat crushed together inside an omnibus. At least the room was tidy. Fancy could find no fault in that.

So as to appear unconcerned, she picked up a pink feather fan and idly cooled herself against the late September heat. There was no air in the narrow alleyways of the rookery, and the foul stench from the gutters and overcrowded middens was too overpowering to open a window. As the door opened and Fancy stepped inside, she forced a bright smile.

There was no welcome in his expression. His lips curled back into a sneer as he regarded her dark skirt and lace blouse. The only make-up she wore was light rouge on her cheeks and lips, her auburn hair swept up into a smooth style.

'You look like shit,' Fancy spat out. 'I want yer at the club ternight. Couple of gents bin askin' fer yer. I want 'em kept sweet. They offered a guinea for an hour of your time.'

'I ain't whoring for a guinea.'

He slapped her face. 'Yer'd do it for a florin if I told yer ter. I'm sick of yer fine airs.'

'But I can earn more dressed like this and moving amongst the women shoppers. Look, I've lifted five purses this week. They're in that drawer.'

Fancy didn't even glance in their direction. 'You're getting above yerself, Bea.'

'No, Fancy. I thought you'd be pleased. There's twenty quid in them.'

His small eyes glittered with menace. 'Yer take too much on yerself, Bea. Yer think yerself better than the other sluts. Too clever by 'alf. All that schooling yer Ma insisted yer 'ave. The Ragged Schools weren't good enough fer yer. Yer had ter be taught proper. D'ye think cos I never 'ad no schoolin', I ain't got the brains to know wot yer bin up ter?'

Beatrice swallowed against the sudden dryness in her mouth. Fancy was a sadistic bully. Although devious, he was not bright. She usually kept one step ahead of him with her sharper wits. Now she had to exercise them to the full to escape the punishment she suspected he had planned for her.

'I ain't bin up ter nothin', Fancy. I missed yer. I thought yer'd be pleased I'd lifted so many purses.'

'Sod the purses.' He grabbed her arm and wrenched it high behind her back.

She strangled a scream of pain, but was unable to stop her eyes watering from the agony he was inflicting. 'Word on the street is that yer've 'ad yer eye on leaving us, Bea.'

'No never, Fancy. Not unless yer've tired of me. Yer know I luv yer. It'd break me heart if yer left me for Bessie.'

'Lying bitch!'

He jerked her arm so hard she screamed. There was the click and wrenching of bone as her shoulder dislocated. Scarlet spirals of pain shot through her skull and she fell in a faint at his feet. The cold contents from the unemptied chamber-pot thrown over her face brought her spluttering back to her senses. Through a haze of pain she spat out the acid-tasting urine which had trickled into her mouth. A boot ramming into her gut doubled her over.

'Yer've got in thick with Morton's wife,' he declared, swiping her across the face as she struggled to sit up. 'The likes of us no longer good enough fer yer now?'

'No, Fancy. Yer know it ain't like that.'

Two more slaps blackened her eye and cut her mouth. The pain in her dislocated shoulder was excruciating, making it difficult to think. She had to fight back. Fancy was capable of killing her. Any movement was such torture that it left her gasping in agony, and she knew that she could not physically fend him off. Only her wits could save her.

'Kara Morton is me sister. The bastard Ma was married ter threw her out when 'e thought she were carrying on wiv a soldier. Kara were brought up in riches whilst I… Well, you know me story, Fancy. I hate her. I want ter get even with her. That's why I hang round 'er.'

'That the truth?'

'I ain't gonna lie 'bout a thing like that.'

His lips thinned cruelly. 'S'pose not. But what about Morton? Yer were seen at the club talking ter 'im the night 'e got done over. Alf Levins says yer paid 'im to take Morton to the Wyse woman's house. How come yer knew where 'e was that night?'

'I heard Chalky talking about doing 'im over. I knew Morton was ter wed me sister, but I hadn't met her then. I'd learned who she was after Slasher had me detain 'er in the shop, so he could wreck the place and demand protection money. I'd hardly made a good impression that night. How else was I ter get her sympathy and trust, than by saving her fiancé after Chalky had done 'im over? I followed Morton when he left the club.'

'And yer lied ter me that night ter get away.' Fancy kicked her in the back, his temper soaring. 'Bitch! It's time yer learnt who yer master is.'

Several more kicks and blows turned her already tortured body into a furnace of pain. 'No more, Fancy,' she begged, weakly. 'I was gonna tell yer...' she gasped out through her bloodied mouth, her breathing laboured with pain. 'But I've hardly seen yer ... these last weeks. Yer bin with Bessie Brown ... I wanted to get a plan properly worked out ... before I ... told yer about it. I had ter wait until ... until the Mortons returned from their honeymoon. Meanwhile ... I tried to win their trust ... by playing the reformed sister. Ma was taken in. I think Kara is...'

'So yer'd turn agin yer own flesh and blood?' Fancy shouted. 'Yer scum, Bea. Scum. But yer've got yer uses.'

He yanked the coil of dark hair which had come loose from its pins during her beating. When he jerked her head upwards, her eyes screwed up with pain.

He thrust his face close to hers. 'Yer listen to me. And yer listen good, if yer wants ter live. Morton, like yerself, is getting too big fer 'is breeches. 'E's beholden ter yer fer helping 'im after 'is beating. Slasher's 'eard 'e's thinking of setting up a club in Westminster. Only the property 'e were interested in burned down last week.' Fancy sniggered, remembering his pleasure at observing the flames he had started destroy the building. 'I want Morton watched. Who better ter do that than yerself?'

Beatrice dimly registered his words. The pain was dulling her senses, making it difficult to think clearly. But this sounded too good to be true. She wanted nothing more than to win Zach's confidence. Knowing him for the rogue and gambler he was, she had even considered offering that they work together. A club like that needed a hostess, and Kara was hardly likely to volunteer. She knew Kara hated Zach's thieving. What better way to avenge herself on her sister than by further corrupting her husband? Once she was his partner, it would be a short step to get Zach back in her bed.

'Can't do that from here,' she forced out through her swollen lips. 'Got to appear to live decently.'

He snarled. 'So yer *were* planning to scarper.'

'No, 'onest I…'

Another punch to her stomach doubled her up. Her lip was bitten through from trying to stop her screams. They only goaded the sadistic sod to further cruelties.

'Yer ain't goin' nowhere. Unless…' He paused, breathing heavily. 'Jus' maybe, Morton would be less suspicious if yer 'ad to pay two 'undred quid before I let yer go. Can yer get that money?'

'I reckon so,' Beatrice wheezed through her swollen lips. She was in too much agony to feel any elation at finally escaping from him. 'Kara owes me that much at least.'

His boot ground down on her flattened hand. 'Jus' make sure yer don' fergit who yer master is. One slip, fergit old loyalties, and Slasher will be visiting yer.' He pinched her battered face painfully in his stubby hands. 'Slasher won't kill yer. That would be ter quick an end. He'd rather see yer suffer. No woman as vain of 'er looks as yer are suffers more than seeing 'er face carved up. This beating is just a warning. And it's not only yerself. So don't think to flee and escape our justice. Be a pity if yer sweet Ma got 'urt.'

'No, not Ma,' Beatrice pleaded. 'She has nothing to do with this.'

He pushed her away from him with such violence that her head cracked on the floor. Blackness swamped her.

Elizabeth paced her bedchamber. Richard's firm footsteps had walked unhesitatingly past her door. He hadn't stopped to bid her good-night.

'Damn you, Richard,' she sobbed and flung herself on to her bed. 'You can't leave me. You can't. I shall die. I know I shall die.'

She hadn't left her room for a week after Richard told her he was sailing for Mexico in eight days' time. She had refused all the food sent on a tray to her, sustaining herself only by the hoard of chocolates and biscuits she had earlier accumulated. Her stomach gnawed with hunger, but it was nothing compared with the ache in her heart.

How could Richard abandon her so callously? He'd be away for at least a year, if not eighteen months. Tears had not availed her. Screaming at him that he was heartless had left him unmoved. A breathing attack had caused her to faint, and had resulted in sedation by the family physician. Shutting herself away and refusing food had gained her nothing. Richard's only comment was that she was acting like a spoilt child.

Clenching her fist, she snarled low in her throat. 'It's not fair! It's just not fair!'

She sniffed and raised her head to regard her reclining figure in the mirror. She would not be treated like this. How could she live so long apart from Richard. Who would take her to the concerts she loved? Tell her how pretty she looked? Bring her amusing gifts when she was ill? Only Richard could do that. Irene would ignore her. Kara was so busy with her silly shops, she'd not care if she was ailing or upset. Richard just could not go. He couldn't. She needed his tender concern. He used to be so kind, so considerate a lover. That was before...

She burst into fresh weeping at recalling the horror of her miscarriage. Hadn't she suffered because of his loving? The thought of childbirth terrified her. If a three-month foetus could cause so much pain, what must she endure giving birth to a full-term child? Her sobs increased. She was obsessed with the idea of keeping Richard at her side. Yet everything she had tried had failed. Was he doing this to get back at her for denying him her bed?

Selfishly, she forgot that he had given up his ambition to study the ancient civilisations before they married. She dismissed his loyalty to his father's clients which had kept him bound and tied in London to a life he despised. She chose to ignore that his brilliant intellect and athletic body made him admirably suited to a life of adventure. He was her husband, and his place was at her side.

Her grievances were centred on her loss. Without Richard she would go out of her mind with boredom. Yet once Richard had been so caring and tender. If only those days could return...

She chewed her nail. They would. She must be brave. She must conquer her fear of childbirth. She would prove to Richard that she still loved him. He would not leave England then.

When Beatrice regained consciousness she felt as if her body had been ground between two millstones. Fancy had gone. So great was her agony – and with her dislocated arm useless to her – it took her an hour to fully rouse herself. She had to get help. She could not deal with her dislocated shoulder on her own. With every movement it felt as if red-hot pincers were gouging her back and arm. Fancy had taken the stolen purses from the drawer. When she found the strength to stagger to the hiding place where she had stashed the other stolen prizes, she found the room ransacked. Every last coin and piece of jewellery had been taken.

She was sobbing with pain and frustration when the door burst open a second time. Her eyes widened with fear. She remained crouched over the table, cradling her arm.

Slasher leered at her evilly. 'Good. I see Fancy 'as given you a talking to.'

'My arm,' she said, weakly attempting to stand. The pain was so severe she collapsed, missed the chair, and fell to the floor. She screamed as her arm jarred, her eyes unfocused in the agony spearing her body.

Slasher bent over her. His foul breath, reeking of rotting teeth, stale beer and onions, hit her full in the face. He sniggered. 'Yer stink. Piss on you, did Fancy? Good fer 'im. Yer always did parade about as if there were a bad smell under yer nose. Now there is.'

Beatrice strained to focus her stare. Slasher's hazy face cleared.

His eyes were slits of pure malice. Fear kneaded her stomach with icy fingers. He smiled sadistically as he reached for her shoulder. Then with a shout of evil laughter he gripped it, brutally ramming the joint back into its socket.

Again Beatrice fainted. This time she was slapped back to consciousness. Groaning, she forced herself to peer through swollen, blackened eyelids. What she saw made her gag with nausea. Slasher was standing over her with his trousers round his knees, his swollen cock, red and purple-veined, bearing down towards her mouth.

'Fancy reckoned yer were the best at this,' he grunted. 'Yer ain't got his protection now. He's 'ad enough of yer hoity-toity airs. But he thinks we can trust yer. I rule by fear, not trust.' He cackled malevolently. 'So you'd better please me.' He grabbed her hair at the back of her neck and pushed her face down on to him.

Beatrice closed her eyes. She was too miserable and wretched to care what further degradation he subjected her to. Still dazed from her beating, she concentrated her mind on the drone of a large bluebottle angrily buzzing at the dirty window-pane. It didn't obliterate the horror Slasher was subjecting her to, but, at least she didn't have to feign pleasure as she did with Fancy. Slasher wanted her subjugation, not approbation. He wanted her cowed, degraded. He wanted to prove that no one escaped his tyranny.

When Slasher finally left her, Beatrice was not the broken-spirited woman he had intended, though she allowed him to think that she was. She had slipped in and out of consciousness as he had sweated over her bruised body, his deviant's mind more perverted than Fancy's had ever been. Left alone, Beatrice curled into a foetal ball, too numbed with pain to cry.

Only one thought branded her soul. Revenge. Revenge upon everybody who had brought her to this.

Chapter Nineteen

Single-mindedly, Elizabeth prepared to visit Richard's bedchamber. She had bathed earlier and now sprayed herself in expensive French perfume. Not the one Kara had bought for her, but one she had purchased herself recently. The same perfume Kara always wore. She had once heard Richard remark how singularly memorable it was. Kara had such poise. Such courage. She admired her tremendously, and often wished she could be as strong-willed as her friend. Kara would not lock herself in her room and let her husband run off to the other side of the world. Kara would use all her powers of persuasion to get him to stay.

'I was a fool to sulk in my room,' Elizabeth fumed to herself. 'I should have done this earlier.' The heady, musky scent of Kara's favourite perfume wafted around her and inhaling it gave her the courage to follow through her resolve.

Elizabeth stood before the cheval mirror and studied her reflection. With a toss of her head, she released the ribbon from the single plait which bound her long, silvery-blonde hair. She brushed it a hundred times until it shone and spread over her shoulders to her waist like a glistening cape as fine as moonbeams. From the hallway the grandfather clock struck midnight. The witching hour. The bewitching hour, she amended, smiling at her reflection.

She unbuttoned her high-necked nightgown. She hesitated as it parted to reveal her small breasts. Smiling slyly, she allowed it to fall to her feet. She was still smiling as she opened her bedroom door and walked naked along the corridor to her husband's room. Her heart pounded. The servants were long abed and Irene had retired at ten. She was feeling reckless. Richard had always urged her to shed her coyness, had told her so often that her body was beautiful. Tonight she must use all her wiles to enslave him. Then he would stay in England.

She slipped silently into his bedchamber and paused by the doorway. The room was dark except for a ray of moonlight playing across the bed. Richard lay on his stomach, the sheet low across his waist. His naked torso was dark against the moon-silvered linen. One arm was flung around a pillow and his dark hair curled low on the nape of his neck. From the shallowness of his breathing, he was asleep.

Crossing the room, Elizabeth slid beneath the sheet. The heat of his naked body burned her cool flesh. He murmured and stirred, but did not wake. She boldly pressed herself against him. In the early days of their marriage, that had always been enough to arouse his desire.

Richard had fallen exhausted into his bed. Since his meeting with Kara he had pushed himself hard, sparing himself nothing in his work, or his arrangements for his expedition. Only an exhausted sleep could sometimes chase away the dreams of Kara's body which haunted him. Work could banish his heartache by day, but night was a constant torment. Kara would appear to him in his dreams, laughing and teasing, tantalising him with the memories of her loving body. The smell of her was enticing him now, cocooning him in the warmth of her perfume. Then the vividness of his dream became reality, the touch of flesh against his thigh causing his body to ache with longing. He sighed. Drowsy with sleep, he rolled over and felt her hands on him, her lips light upon his shoulder.

'My love,' he murmured, caressing her.

Strangely, he felt the thinness of a ribcage where he remembered soft flesh. He kissed the hollow of her neck. Her perfume was the same, yet different, the answering kisses less fervent than he recalled. Yet his body was responding to the silken touch of a woman's form. There had been no recent visits to Dolly. On his last visit he had noticed a wariness about her manner. Eventually he had drawn from her that she had met another man who thought her a respectable widow. He had offered to marry her. Generously Richard had wished her well, and agreed to pay the rent on the house until she married in the autumn. They had parted amicably and in friendship, with no regrets and many fond memories.

He reached for full luscious breasts and encountered small globes which did not fill his hands. Passion faltered. He shook himself awake and opened his eyes. He was shocked to find not Kara, but Elizabeth, in his bed.

She smiled up at him, her pale hair spread

across the pillow, her eyes luminous in the moonlight. 'Love me, Richard. I've been such a fool. I'm so sorry.'

Before he could recover from his astonishment, she reared up and began to kiss him ardently, her hands drawing him down, holding him close. 'Love me, Richard. My darling, love me.'

Elizabeth felt his tension, his reluctance, his suspicion. She became frenzied in her need to make him want her. When he would have drawn back she clung to him, her mouth seeking his, her body moving moulding herself against the length of his figure. 'You must love me, Richard,' she repeated softly. 'Love me as a wife should be loved.'

A wild desperation drove her to writhe and move beneath him, her hands caressing in a way a man would have to be made of steel to resist.

'Why now?' he said darkly. 'After all this time.'

That he had not immediately responded to her seduction alarmed her. She kissed him frantically, murmuring between each kiss. 'I was wrong to deny you my bed. I've been wretched this last week. I've acted like a fool. I love you so much, my darling. I want to be a proper wife to you again. I want to make you happy.'

The insistent writhing of her body and kisses worked. With a smothered groan, he responded. She bit her lips as his touch became more intimate, and forced herself to blot from her mind the terror and remembered pain of her miscarriage. She tried so hard to please him. At the moment he entered her, she was frigid with fear. She screwed her eyes shut and willed her body to respond, to give him pleasure.

Afterwards, when he had rolled away from her to lie on his back, staring up at the ceiling, she asked tentatively, 'You do still love me, don't you, Richard?'

'Of course.' He sat up, leaning against the carved wooden headboard, his arms folded across his chest as he stared down at her. His expression was inscrutable.

'And I do still please you – I can give you pleasure?'

He frowned and rose from the bed. Pulling on his navy silk robe, he wrapped it around himself and lit a cigar before replying. As the match flared in front of his face, Elizabeth saw the tension and suspicion.

'Elizabeth, you have chosen an ill time for a reconciliation,' he replied with an edge of impatience. 'Of course you gave me pleasure. But I've had less than eight hours' sleep in three days. I leave for Tilbury in four hours.'

'You can't still mean to leave!' She sat up, her hair tumbling over her shoulders, her eyes wide and pleading.

'So that was what this demonstration of wifely affection was all about?' He regarded her coldly. 'I thought it was to heal the breach between us for when I returned. It was another ruse to get me to stay.'

She couldn't believe he still meant to leave. She screwed up her face and screamed, beating her knees with her fists in pure fury. She didn't hear the dressing-room door click shut, and continued with her tantrum until, growing weary, she looked through her hair to discover Richard had gone.

'Richard!' she cried, scrambling from the bed.

He emerged from the dressing room fully clothed for travelling. He held his top hat in his hand as she stood naked before him. 'You can't go. You can't.'

'I would have preferred to have taken with me the memory of a loving wife, sad at our parting, but understanding of the need which drives me. Since I will be given no peace in my own home this night, I shall embark earlier and sleep in my cabin. My luggage has already been sent ahead. Farewell, Elizabeth.'

'Richard!' she sobbed as he turned to walk away. She ran to him and, grabbing his arm, threw himself at his feet to stop him leaving. 'You can't go, I love you.'

'If you loved me, you would understand why I have to make this journey.' Gently but firmly, he prised her hand from his sleeve. 'Don't make this harder for me than it is.'

Kara had decided that it was time to end at least one deception. She told Sophia Henshawe the truth about her mother, though not that she lived with Joe Donovan. Neither did she think it necessary to tell her too much about Beatrice's former life.

'I'm shocked, Kara. Deeply shocked,' Sophia said, her face white and strained. The embroidery she had been working on slipped to the floor as she sat in her parlour. 'Not only by the facts of your mother leaving your father. You misled me about her life. Deceit is not something I can easily accept from my partner.'

'I did not deceive you out of dishonesty,' Kara answered, her eyes pleading with her friend to understand. 'Surely now that I've told you everything about my life and my family, you can understand how I wanted to protect Mama? I hardly knew her when I came to live here. She's not a bad woman. You know her well enough to have judged that. It is to her credit that, now her circumstances have improved, she wishes to return to her proper station in life. I have been trying to persuade her to take up the post of manageress when I open the next shop.'

'Those shops are yours to do with as you please. I made it clear that, as long as my interests are safeguarded in these premises, that would be enough for me. It was your money, not mine, which opened Wyse Books in Walthamstow. Though why you should want to give yourself all that extra work and worry is beyond me.'

Sophia lowered her gaze from Kara's challenging stare. 'That is a separate issue. I'm offended you did not trust me to tell me the truth about your family.'

Kara could hardly tell Sophia that she thought her a born gossip, despite her kind and generous nature. She paced the room in her agitation. 'I had my own life to rebuild. Have I ever failed you? Does this shop not prosper more than even my wildest dreams? Out of respect for you and our friendship, I am trusting you with the truth now. If the knowledge got out it could destroy all I have worked for. Mama would be too shamed to work in the shop again.'

'I'm not sure that I wish her to, now that I know the kind of woman she is. No decent woman would leave her husband.'

Kara clenched her hands to combat the angry defence of her mother's name. She took a deep breath, and said reasonably, 'You would have had to meet Abel Wyse to know what a cruel tyrant he was. He threw Mama out without a penny. It was her dowry which had enabled him to expand his haulage company. What defence have women got against men like that?'

Sophia gasped, and Kara ruthlessly pressed on to win her partner's sympathy. 'You know how difficult it is for a woman alone. Your own shop manager robbed you blind when you were first widowed. If Richard Tennent had not sacked him, you could have lost everything. You said yourself that, whilst at Bath, several male fortune-hunters pursued you. Your grief for your husband saved you from falling into the trap of a lonely widow.'

'I need to think about what you have told me, Kara.'

Kara forced a false assurance into her voice. 'I know you will come to the right decision. Mama counts you her friend, as I do. Don't destroy her. Don't shame her by refusing to allow her to work in the shop. It has given her back her self-respect. And, please, don't throw away all we have worked for, because you think that, in protecting my mother's reputation, I have deceived you. Look at the account books. Look at how Henshawe & Wyse is now revered as one of the most prestigious stationers' and bookshops in London.'

Sophia sat with her hands clasped, her prim mouth showing her censure. Kara sighed and tried another line. 'I accepted that you did not want to extend our partnership to include any other shops I may open. But I want to ensure your investment in this one is secure. In another year I could buy you out if you wish, but that was not what Richard Tennent advised. Zach and I will be moving to a house of our own soon. Once my child is born we will need our own home.'

It took Sophia two days to come to her decision. Two days in which Kara was tense with apprehension.

Finally Sophia called her into her parlour. The older woman's face was grave. 'I've decided not to end our partnership for the time being. Though I do not countenance the falsehoods you wove about your family, I understand why you acted as you did.'

There was a primness about her manner which had been absent in all their other conversations. Sophia was a snob. Even friendship did not bridge the barrier she had erected between the respectability of her life, and the censure she had put on Kara and her family's.

'Florence may continue to work here if she wishes. I myself will be spending less time in the shop.' She did not once look at Kara. 'I am sure you and Captain Morton will be very happy in a new home.'

'We are not leaving you because we are unhappy here.' She realised how the over-sensitive woman had misinterpreted her news. 'We have been very happy here. I shall miss you, Sophia, and the children.'

'Will you?' The brightness in her eyes was unnatural. 'I thought my use to you was at an end.'

'Sophia, how can you think that?' Kara held out her arms to clasp her close. 'Your friendship means a great deal to me. Without you, I could never have got started in this business which I love.'

Her smile was warm with affection as she kissed her cheek. 'It is time you had your home back to yourself.'

She nodded. 'Then it is agreed. This business is a good investment, and will provide for the future of my daughters. But I do worry you have taken on too much, Kara.'

'I enjoy the challenge. Every week I see new opportunities for stock and expansion. I met a man who rebinds old books in exquisite tooled leather. Then there're antique books. First editions are always increasing in value.'

Sophia held up her hand. 'Stop. You go too fast for my poor head to keep up. My dear late husband used to say, "Never run before you can walk".'

Kara did not press the matter. She had spent hours working on plans for the future, projecting future income and how long it would take her to buy the third shop. She had set herself a goal that, within eight years, she would have a dozen shops.

Kara was six months' pregnant and no longer

able to disguise her condition. She had hoped to hide it until she was further advanced, but she had been startled at how large she had become, especially as she wanted to pass the child off as a seven-month pregnancy. On Florence's advice she had visited a midwife who could be relied upon to be discreet. Her extortionate fee ensured that. The woman had laughed aside her concern after an examination.

'Twins, my dear,' she'd announced. 'You'll have your work cut out with them. From the size of them they seem set to arrive in March.'

Kara was delighted and so was Zach. She was surprised at how proud he was at becoming a father. He never mentioned the disappointment of discovering her father had died bankrupt. He was often from home, attending sports meetings, where Kara knew he mingled with the gentry and relieved them of their valuables. Yet strangely their marriage had settled into a comfortable routine. Though on occasion a clash of wills over his thieving would erupt into a stormy quarrel, peace would eventually be regained when Zach made love to her. Passion always obliterated their differences of opinion – until the next time.

The announcement of the twins explained her large size. By early December she knew she would soon have to give up working in the shop. It was indelicate for a woman so noticeably pregnant to appear in public.

Not everything in the past months had progressed smoothly. Her visits to Elizabeth had found her friend pale and dejected. She'd been angry when Elizabeth told her the means she had used to stop Richard leaving.

'It all went horribly wrong,' Elizabeth wailed early in November. 'Richard left despising me, I know it. I've heard nothing from him.'

'Letters in such circumstances take time,' Kara reassured.

'But that's not the worst of it.' Elizabeth broke into a fresh bout of weeping and Kara curbed her impatience at the woman's weakness. 'I'm with child, Kara.'

'That's wonderful news,' Kara forced out, though her body burned with a jealousy she had no right to feel. The news eased her guilt that she had not told Richard of the twins, and that by not doing so she had denied him the right to acknowledge the only children he might sire. 'Our children will be born close together.'

Elizabeth was still looking far from pleased. 'It will reinforce our friendship that our children are also friends. And you will help me through my travail, won't you, Kara? I'm so frightened.'

Kara felt a shiver of unease. Would it be wise for the children to grow up together? Her conscience argued that they had a right, a half-brothers, or -sisters, to be acquainted. Though how could they ever be told of the relationship? It was a complication she had not considered, and it troubled her. Hadn't she been angry at discovering that her sister's existence had been kept from her.

She would cross that bridge when she came to it, she decided. 'I shall visit you as often as I can. I still have all the paperwork to do for the two shops.'

Elizabeth looked stricken. 'I need your strength, Kara. I could not face the birth if you were not there beside me.'

'Of course I will be there, if you really want me to be.'

Kara had more problems than Zach and Elizabeth to fret over. Beatrice worried her. She had tried so hard to make friends with her sister, but always sensed a barrier between them. Though Beatrice frequently visited, Kara was aware of a guardedness beneath her sister's smile. It made her increase her own efforts at friendliness. Knowing how determined Beatrice was to better herself, she had offered her a position as manageress in one of the future new shops.

'I've got my eye on a different life,' Beatrice had declared scornfully. 'There're easier pickings than wearing yourself out running to a customer's beck and call all day. But Ma would be the ideal person. I know you asked her to take on the Walthamstow shop and she refused.' Beatrice clutched Kara's hand, her expression fearful. 'We've got to persuade her. She's got to get out of London.'

'Why is it suddenly so urgent?'

Beatrice shifted uneasily. 'It just is. Fancy weren't too pleased when I told him I wanted out. I know you paid him off, giving him two hundred pounds to let me leave, but...' She hesitated, chewing her lip and wringing her hands, clearly reluctant to go on.

'Do you think he may make trouble for Mama?' Kara asked.

Beatrice nodded. 'He's a mean bastard. I don't

trust him. Besides, living in that filthy place is killing Ma. But she won't leave Joe. And Joe is a proud man. He could never accept that his woman earned more than he did.'

Kara knew Beatrice was not telling her everything. There had been that strange disappearance of hers for five weeks when no one had seen her. She had refused to speak about it. She had just turned up one evening on Kara's doorstep, looking paler and thinner, and asked for two hundred pounds to get away from Fancy. Kara gave it to her immediately.

If Beatrice was afraid for their mother, it meant that Florence was in danger. She had not yet planned to open a third shop, but if it meant getting Florence out of the rookery, she would do so.

'Mama won't accept what she regards as charity from me. I thought her being manageress of one of my shops was the answer, but she doesn't want to live too far away from either of us.'

'It's you she won't leave,' Beatrice accused, her tone bitter. 'She's found her precious long-lost daughter. She'll not be parted from you again. You'll be the death of her.'

Kara reeled under the venom of her sister's tone. It was rare that Beatrice allowed her resentment of the past to show. Masking her pain, Kara paced the parlour of the house they had rented in Pimlico.

'We have to consider Joe's pride to get Mama to move. I could raise a bank loan for a small shop to be opened in, say Ilford. It's only a short train journey from Liverpool Street station for us to visit her. The railway also links with Brentwood, and Mama has been fretting about Nanny Brewster. I know she'd like to help her. We visited her last month and Nanny was very frail. Both Mama and I love her dearly. If it hadn't been for Nanny keeping in touch with Mama over the years, I doubt we would ever have been reunited. Perhaps Nanny Brewster could be persuaded to live in Ilford with Mama.'

The idea expanded as Kara became more enthusiastic. 'I could convert a house for the shop. And Joe…' She looked worriedly at Beatrice. 'Do you think he would accept work from me as a delivery man? He's very interested in automobiles, and did say that he would like to learn to drive one. I'd buy a van for him. He could work between all three shops. We could get larger stationery orders from companies if we delivered. Do you think he'd take the job?'

'With both of us and Mama also trying to persuade him, I think he might. Joe will think he's the cat's whiskers with a van of his own to drive. I can't see him refusing.'

'I'll ask them to lunch on Sunday and broach the subject then. Joe is always ill at ease with me. I do try to make him feel welcome. I respect him for what he did for Mama. He's a good man. You'll be there as well to back me up, won't you?'

Beatrice smiled. 'I'd do anything to get Ma in a decent house.'

'And what of your future, Beatrice?' Kara changed the subject. 'How will you earn your living?'

'Use what you know to succeed in life, that's what I say,' Beatrice said with a chuckle. 'You had an interest in books and opened the shops. Fancy was a bastard, but he taught me how to survive in a man's world. I've persuaded Zach to let me be his hostess at the gaming house he proposes to open.'

'I had hoped Zach had put that notion behind him when the premises at Westminster burned down. Must you encourage him, Beatrice?'

'I thought you wanted Zach and me to get on well together. To make such a club respectable it needs a proper hostess. Why not me?'

Kara sighed. She had given up trying to dissuade Zach from the venture. 'Don't meddle in my business affairs, Kara,' he had snapped angrily during their last argument on the subject, 'and I'll not interfere in yours.'

At first she had been pleased when he and Beatrice appeared to get on so well. Now she was shocked to learn that her sister planned to be his hostess. Yet how could she stand in judgement on her sister? She had been willing to pay Fancy Gilbert off to allow Beatrice to escape from the Gilbert brothers' clutches. Her sister never spoke of her life with Fancy. There was a cruel set to Beatrice's mouth whenever her past life was mentioned. Kara was too sensitive of the deprivation her sister had suffered to pursue the subject.

On Sunday she broached the subject of the Ilford shop and the delivery job with Florence and Joe. Joe was instantly wary. Throughout the afternoon, together with Beatrice and Zach, they tried to persuade him to take the position.

'I'll give it some thought,' he muttered on leaving. 'I'll let you know my decision on Christmas Day.'

Kara had to be content with that. Throughout November, her mother's health had worried her. She had grown thinner and, at Kara's insistence, now only worked three hours a day. The London smog which hung over the city most days was not helping her condition. Kara had tried to persuade her to move into the country. She had even taken Florence to Ilford so they could view several properties together.

The one Kara favoured was close to the station and the crossroads with Ilford High Road, and only a few minutes' walk from Cranbrook Park.

'The air is so much cleaner here,' Kara said. 'Wouldn't you like to live here and manage the shop? I'll hire two shopgirls so your work will be light until you are feeling stronger. And a maid, of course. She will look after Nanny Brewster. Didn't you think those two back rooms would be perfect for her?'

'Kara, I know what you are trying to do and I appreciate it,' Florence began. 'But the decision must be Joseph's. Especially now.' She blushed and smiled. 'He's asked me to marry him.'

Christmas, Kara decided, was going to be a family affair. In Brentwood her father's stern presence had robbed it of any pleasure. She wanted it to be a time of peace – a time to end the problems. It provided a double celebration. Zach had found the ideal premises for his club, and Joe announced that he would accept Kara's offer.

The conversion of the Ilford house to a shop took longer than Kara had envisaged and, because of her advanced pregnancy, it was decided to delay the opening until the twins had been born. Florence and Joe were married on Easter Saturday, refusing to allow Kara to make the arrangements. It was a small affair. Kara had wanted to treat them to a meal at Frascati's restaurant, but Joe had declined; though he had allowed her to reserve seats at one of the better Soho restaurants.

All day, Kara had been feeling uncomfortable, and by the time they left the restaurant her back was aching. Zach was about to hail a hansom, when they saw Beatrice, who had walked ahead, arguing with Fancy Gilbert at the corner of the alleyway opposite.

'What's that bastard doing here?' Zach said, stepping forward. 'Gilbert! This isn't your district. You were paid two hundred pounds to stay out of Beatrice's life.'

Fancy Gilbert scowled at Zach. 'That were just a payment ter ensure my goodwill,' he returned, pushing open his checked jacket and thrusting his thumbs into his gold brocade waistcoat pockets. ''Appen I think it weren't enough.'

Zach leapt forward, his hand grabbing Fancy's necktie and forcing the stout bully up on to his toes. He pushed him in to the shadows of the deserted alley. 'If I see you near Bea again, you're dead meat, Gilbert. She's put up with enough from you. Your gang of bullies don't frighten me. Leave Bea alone.'

'No one threatens me, Morton,' Fancy blustered. 'Yer'll pay fer this.'

Kara watched in terror. Her heavy pregnancy made her vulnerable, and she could see murder written on Fancy Gilbert's ugly scarred face. 'He's got a knife, Zach,' she screamed, seeing the villain pull the blade.

Zach moved with the speed and skill of a trained soldier. He grabbed the wrist holding the dagger, and brought his knee up hard in Gilbert's groin. Gilbert doubled over. 'I owed you that for setting Chalky White on me and stealing my winnings. Chalky's taken care to stay out of my way, knowing I'd get even.'

Fancy knelt on the cobbles, clutching his groin and groaning. His face was screwed up in agony as he gritted out, 'I'll get yer all fer this. See if I don't.'

Zach hauled Gilbert to his feet by his collar and threw him up against the alley wall. 'Don't you make threats to me, Gilbert. Your days are numbered. I've got my own men behind me now.' He slammed his fist into Gilbert's guts. 'It was you who burned down that property I wanted in Westminster. Heed this. My men are all trained soldiers. Men I served with in the Boer War. They're desperate men, fallen on hard times now the army has no more need of them. These men don't work for me out of fear, but out of loyalty and comradeship. They'll whip your thugs any day.'

Kara was shocked at Zach's threats as much as at Gilbert's. But what concerned her most was the underworld leader's warning. Thank God that Florence and Joe were not returning to the rookery this evening, but would take up residence in Ilford.

A vicious pain suddenly stabbed through her back and side and she stooped over. 'Zach, leave him. The babies. My pains…' She gasped as the contraction receded. 'I must get home. Mama was to attend me, but this is her wedding day.'

Zach dropped Fancy Gilbert like a piece of unwanted flotsam and ran to Kara's side. 'The babies … but it's too soon. Of course Florence will stay with you. I'll send Beatrice for the midwife. We must get you home.'

Ten hours later, Kara lay back exhausted, her eyes filled with tears of joy as she held her twin sons in her arms.

'Boys, Kara,' Zach said with humble reverence. 'I'm so proud of you. So proud of them. Such tiny scraps. Five pounds, and five pounds two ounces. They'd have been giants if they'd gone full term.'

Kara smiled, but there was something in the possessive way Zach regarded the boys which made her uneasy. She pushed it aside. She was tired after the birth. Zach loved the boys, and believed they were his. She should be grateful for that.

'What shall we call them?' she asked.

'Harold, after my father. That should ensure the old boy's sweetened up to part with some cash. And Timothy after an uncle who died in the fighting on the North-west Frontier.'

'Harry and Tim,' she said softly. 'They are fine names.'

Three months later, Kara attended Elizabeth's confinement. Through two days and nights she sweated in the room with her friend as Elizabeth screamed and threw her distorted body from side to side.

'You will harm yourself and the child if you continue like this,' Kara reasoned, appalled at the difficulty Elizabeth was having in giving birth. Her own back and arms ached from bending over her.

Holding her friend's hand, she placed cool cloths on her burning brow, her voice low and encouraging. 'It will soon be over. Be brave, Elizabeth. Try not to scream and writhe, you're tiring yourself and the baby.'

'I can't bear it. I can't be brave. It's tearing me apart,' Elizabeth sobbed. 'Even the chloroform doesn't help any more.'

Kara looked at the doctor, who had been called when the midwife despaired of bringing the baby into the world. 'She can't survive much more of this.'

He nodded and, taking Kara's arm, drew her away from the bedside. 'I'll have to operate. Do a Caesarean to try and save the child.'

'Isn't that dangerous for the mother?' Kara said, frightened.

'It's a delicate operation. Strong mothers survive.'

'But Elizabeth isn't strong.'

'We can't risk losing them both. A Caesarean is the only chance.'

'Then do it,' Irene Tennent, looking haggard,

said wearily. 'The woman's made it worse for herself. Screaming and tiring herself out. I will not risk losing my grandson.'

Kara glared at her. The woman could be remarkably callous at times. 'But it is Elizabeth we must think of. There will be other babies.'

'I doubt that,' the doctor declared. 'Pelvis is too small. She's such a tiny thing. This child is never going to be born on its own.'

Kara hung her head and went to Elizabeth's side. She knew there was no choice. Elizabeth was wild-eyed with fear and pain, and close to madness with the agony she had endured.

'The baby needs help to be born. The doctor is going to operate on you. There's nothing to fear. I shall stay with you.'

'I'll be cut. Disfigured. No!' Another pain twisted her swollen body, and her screams chilled Kara's blood. Mercifully, Elizabeth passed out.

The doctor had already rolled up his shirt sleeves and laid out the instruments he needed. His nurse stood behind him ready to assist.

'You had better leave the room, Mrs Tennent and Mrs Morton.'

Irene left. Kara stayed.

'I promised her I would stay with her. I will not desert her now.'

It was to Kara that the nurse handed the weak and fragile baby. She kissed it lovingly, cherishing it as Richard's child, the half-sister to Harry and Tim.

An hour later it was Kara who closed the lids over Elizabeth's sightless eyes. Baby Louise Tennent was motherless.

PART TWO

In tragic life, God wot,
No villain need be! Passions spin the plot:
We are betrayed by what is false within.

GEORGE MEREDITH

Chapter Twenty

1908

Kara completed her inventory check on the last of her seven shops and sat back in her office chair with a sigh of satisfaction. Hard work and foresight had paid incredible dividends. She had opened shops in the larger towns of Essex and surrounding London. Her gamble and belief that industry and businesses were expanding in this golden new century had paid off.

Assiduous planning and constant re-evaluation of stock had kept them ahead of their competitors. A list of the antique books purchased at auctions was sent every three months to over three hundred collectors nationwide. Books were then despatched by post to the customers. Kara was often approached by customers asking for her to look out for specific titles at the auctions, and these she purchased on a commission basis.

At first she had encountered ridicule and even hostility from male buyers: some even tried to trick her into making rash purchases. They failed. Others, when they saw she was interested in a particular work, pushed the price up extortionately high. She backed out, leaving them out of pocket.

She had ploughed every available spare penny back into the business. Last year she had also purchased a large warehouse to store the stationery in bulk. Hard bargaining had given her large discounts from her suppliers, and shrewdly she had passed these on to her customers. Without skimping on the high quality of the products, she had gradually been able to undercut many of her competitors.

A telephone call on the newly installed apparatus at the London shop in Cheapside, which had become her headquarters, took Kara immediately to Oxford Street, where Sophia still lived above the shop. She was worried that something was seriously wrong. Sophia had sounded flustered. She had refused to speak on the infernal squawking device, as she called the instruments, which Kara had insisted on having installed at all her shops and at her home.

Kara was shown into the parlour by Sophia's maid. Her partner was listening to her eldest daughter, Rose, a pretty girl of thirteen, practising on the piano. Violet, Iris, and even the youngest, Heather, who was six, sat with their heads bent over their embroidery frames. All were dressed in identical pale blue dresses and white frilled pinafores edged with lace.

'Aunt Kara,' they chorused in pleasure at her entrance, and clustered around her as she presented each with a specially selected book.

'You spoil the girls, Kara,' Sophia gently admonished. 'Leave us, children. Aunt Kara and I wish to talk.'

Each girl dropped a dutiful curtsey to Kara as they filed past, their eyes gleaming with pleasure as they hugged their books close to their chests.

Once out of the door, they ran giggling and laughing up the stairs to their rooms.

'What's wrong, Sophia, you look worried. Has something happened in the shop?'

'No. It's nothing like that.' She twisted her hands and patted her hair nervously. 'I've been meaning to speak with you for some weeks, but I see so little of you nowadays. You work so hard.'

'It doesn't seem like work. I enjoy it.'

'At the expense of spending time with your family.'

Kara's head shot up. 'My children are not neglected. The house in Richmond is wonderful for them. It's near the river, and they have a large garden to play in. There's the governess for the twins, and a nanny for baby Amy. I get home most evenings before they are abed to read to them.'

Sophia frowned as she regarded Kara's figure swollen with her third pregnancy. 'You will make yourself ill. The baby is due in a few weeks: early May, isn't it? People gossip that you show yourself so much in public.'

'I am a mother and a business woman.'

'It's about business that I asked you to come here today,' Sophia blurted out as Kara settled herself in a chair.

The heavy curtains were drawn against the evening and in the pale gaslight Kara looked pale and drawn. She took on too much. She had a husband who had become immensely wealthy after opening his club, The Gentleman's Retreat, in the West End. Not that Sophia approved of such places. Gambling was immoral, and led people to further depravity in her eyes. It was also illegal. But Zach Morton could do no wrong in her opinion. She was sure his establishment was eminently respectable. Didn't the highest nobles in the land visit it? On his rare visits when Zach accompanied Kara, he never failed to present her with a large bouquet of flowers, his praises for her children melting any censure she may have harboured. Sophia pulled her thoughts up. She had carefully rehearsed her speech to Kara and did not wish to be side-tracked.

'It's our partnership,' she faltered, feeling she was about to betray Kara and not knowing how to proceed.

'Are you not happy with your share of the profits?' Kara asked, frowning.

'They have made me a rich woman. Though I do nothing now to merit such riches.'

'That was what you wished, wasn't it?'

'I have no complaints. I never wanted the responsibility of management. But Mr Cowper has expressed a wish... Oh dear, I am making such a mess of this...'

Kara's eyes widened. Mr Cowper's name had figured strongly in any recent conversation with Sophia.

'Are you seeing a lot of Mr Cowper?' Kara interrupted.

Sophia blushed. 'Actually, we have come to an arrangement. That is why I wished to speak to you. Mr Cowper has asked me to marry him and I have accepted.'

'That's wonderful news. I'm delighted for you, Sophia.'

'But I have to let you down. I know how much our partnership in the Oxford Street shop meant to you. It's just a small part of your growing business empire, but it was the first. I know how you have expanded. I fear you may have over-stretched yourself and now this...'

Kara knew her partner too well to allow her to continue to torture herself. 'Do you wish to sell your share in the Oxford Street shop?'

'Mr Cowper feels... Yes, I do. I know it's a bad time. What with the new baby. You did have a hefty loan to buy the last shop. I'm not sure you could have recovered your expenditure. But Mr Cowper is a haberdasher. He has a shop on Stratford Broadway, and the premises next door have become vacant. He's seen how you've expanded the bookshops, and sees that as the only way to increase trade.'

'And he needs the money from your share of Henshawe & Wyse to provide the capital for this?'

'Yes. I am sorry, Kara. I feel I am deserting you.'

'Of course you're not.' Secretly Kara was pleased. She had wanted to buy Sophia out for some time, but had never liked to suggest it as she knew how much her partner depended on the income from the shop. 'Is it what you want? I mean, to put all your income into Mr Cowper's venture?'

'As his wife, I feel I must.'

'Then I will have Mr Finnemore draw up the papers of sale and we will agree a price.'

'Mr Cowper has suggested I use his solicitor.'

'Why not Mr Finnemore? Surely he has a better

understanding of your business affairs? And you must know I would give you the market price for your share in the business.'

Sophia shifted uncomfortably. 'If Richard Tennent had returned to England I would not have hesitated to consult him,' Sophia said primly. 'But Finnemore, although capable, does not inspire me with the same confidence. As my future husband, I must trust Mr Cowper's judgement.'

Mention of Richard had thrown Kara into momentary confusion. She was his daughter's godmother, and was now also her guardian, since Irene Tennent had died last year. As such she received occasional letters from him. They were often stilted and formal. Each carefully worded, so that she could read them without guilt to Zach, if she had so wished. He wrote briefly of his travels, first to Mexico, then Guatemala. For the last two years he had been in the jungles of Peru. There he had actually discovered a lost Inca temple and ruined village.

Rarely a day went by when she did not think of him, did not yearn to hear the sound of his voice. She missed his company, the interests they had in common. At night she could still wake trembling in remembrance of the thrill of his lovemaking. It was what drove her to work so hard, to cover her guilt that mentally, if not physically, she was betraying Zach.

Each evening, like a young romantic dreamer, she never failed to leave her work, her guests, or any social function she was attending, and go to a window to watch the sunset. Seeing the crimson sky and the sun sliding behind rooftops, trees or the horizon, she closed her eyes and thought of Richard.

Zach often commented on the oddity of her insistence on watching the sunset. 'It's a special time of day for me,' she answered him. 'So peaceful – almost cleansing.'

'Kara Morton, if I did not know you better I'd say you were a pagan at heart,' Zach joked.

Perhaps she was, Kara reflected. But the sunset was her link with Richard. She could not abandon the ritual. If she did, she felt that something terrible would happen to him and he might never return to England.

Beatrice was triumphant, her body glowing with fulfilment and satisfaction. She had spent the entire afternoon making love. She rolled on her side and smiled at her lover. He had been insatiable; her power over him was growing. Today his desire had been frenzied. It had taken all her ingenuity to gratify his hunger. There was little tenderness in their couplings; their passion was volcanic. Sometimes she yearned to lie warm and cocooned beside him, savouring the masculine scent of him and the hard lines of his powerful body.

She did not care that Zach was too impatient for such softness. His demanding hands and mouth brought her to gasping ecstasy, to the voluptuous pleasure only he could satisfy. Often, long after he had left, she lay in a dazed languor, bathed in a glorious lassitude.

He winked at her and sat up. 'Sorry, sweetheart, I've got to go. I promised Kara I'd be back in time for the twins' birthday party. They're five today.'

Hiding her chagrin, Beatrice watched him dress. 'You never speak of love, Zach. But here in this room I am the one who governs your heart. Is Kara so exciting – so experienced? Does she know how to please you as I do? I wonder what that prim madam would say if she ever found out about us. About how you make your living outside the club.'

The rapidity in which his manner changed alarmed her. He sprang at the bed, gripped her throat and rolled her on to her back. His face was demonic, his eyes glacial with menace.

'Breathe one word. Drop one hint about us, or my business, and I'll kill you. Kara is to know nothing. Do you understand?'

Half choked, she nodded, her eyes wide with fear as she encountered his fierce expression. Zach would kill her if she spilled the beans to his precious wife. The knowledge intensified her hatred for her sister. Precious, pampered Kara had to be protected.

The sound of soft sobbing filled the darkened room. It was mid-winter, and a fire roared in the hearth to combat the freezing temperature of the snowstorm outside. The air in the room was oppressive, laden with foreboding.

Kara knelt at her mother's bedside, holding Florence's hand and willing her to live. The grating rasp of her mother's laboured breath filled her ears as she gently put a moistened cloth to her lips to quench her thirst.

The wasted figure, her grey hair in two thick plaits, barely raised the coverlet. 'Don't cry, Kara,' Florence forced out. 'I've ended my days content because of you.'

'Don't speak that way, Mama.' Kara would not accept the truth that Florence was dying of consumption. 'You've recovered your strength before.'

'Expensive medicine … the trips to Switzerland you so generously paid for … cannot save me now.' Florence laboured to speak, her breathing coming in harsh gasps. 'These last five years with you … with my grandchildren … the twins, little Amy, and baby Florence … have been happy. Look after Beatrice and Joseph. He's drinking too much since I've been ill. Don't let him ruin his life.'

'Mama, rest.' Beatrice leaned across Kara and said tearfully, 'The doctor said you must rest.'

'I'll be resting soon enough … for all eternity. The medicine gives me strength … for a while.' She lay for a moment with her eyes closed, then added, 'I want to speak to you both alone. Kara first.'

Kara could feel her sister's resentment that she had been mentioned first. Nothing she had done for Beatrice in the last five years had erased her jealousy.

Florence waited until Beatrice had left the room before saying, 'I'm proud of all you've achieved. The shops. Seven is it now? Four lovely children … and another expected soon. Yet you're not really happy, are you? You must forget

Richard Tennent. Zach has been a good husband in his way.'

The struggle for her mother to speak was painful to witness, and Kara's throat was tight with the tears she was trying to hold back. 'I'm not unhappy, Mama. You must not worry about me.'

Beneath her fingers, her mother squeezed her hand. 'Zach is a rogue – a bit of a scoundrel. He will never reform. But he cares for you and adores the children. Put Richard out of your mind.'

'I am the guardian of Richard's child, that is all. He is still in Peru, and may not return to England for years. Though for Louise's sake I hope he does.' She raised a dark blonde brow. 'Besides, isn't my fast-filling nursery proof that I love Zach?'

'One day Richard Tennent will come back. The twins are the image of him. Fortunately Zach also has dark hair, and their violet-blue eyes are your colouring.'

Kara sighed. 'I hope the child I'm carrying is a boy. Although Zach makes a fuss of Amy and baby Florence, it's the twins he dotes on most. If he ever learned the truth...' She shuddered, not wanting to upset her mother. Over the years, Zach had hardened. There was a ruthless side of his nature which frightened her. Not that it was ever shown to her, but she had heard rumours about the life he led, and they alarmed her.

'Be careful, my dear,' Florence said. 'Do you know how Zach has amassed his vast fortune in recent years?'

It was something Kara had tried to dismiss from her mind. It filled her with fear for his safety.

Florence added, 'He's a dangerous man to cross, from what Beatrice says.'

Kara nodded.

Her mother reached for her hand. 'Beatrice has told me he's involved with the underworld. Did you know that, Kara?'

Realising that Florence knew a great deal about Zach and was trying to warn her, Kara wanted to put her mind at rest. 'He speaks little of how he has gained his wealth. I suppose he wishes to protect me from the sordidness of it. I know he never forgave the Gilbert brothers for their attack on him. Or how they treated Beatrice. He vowed vengeance on them. Gradually I came to realise that, to be so powerful, and to have escaped the retribution of the Gilbert brothers, he had to have become an underworld leader himself. He surrounds himself with hardened criminals and army misfits – like Dipper Jones, his manservant. His club is hugely successful, but only a man more powerful than the Gilberts could escape paying the extortionate protection money they would demand.'

She did not mention that it had been from one of Beatrice's spiteful outbursts that she had learned the truth about Zach's double life.

'Zach adores you and the children. That's what is important.'

Kara looked away.

Florence detected her inner pain. 'Oh, my poor dear, so you've learned of his peccadilloes. It doesn't mean that Zach does not love you. Was it Beatrice who told you?'

'She did not have to. I caught Zach kissing one of the chambermaids a month after the twins were born. All too often I can smell another woman's perfume on him. But it wounds my pride more than my heart. I've done my duty by Zach, and he by me. I never wanted his love.'

'Then your life is a lie, Kara. It will destroy you one day.'

Kara shook her head. 'I love my children. Long ago I accepted Zach for what he is. But that's not important. What does matter is that I feel Beatrice and I are not as close as we should be.'

'That's not your fault.' Florence interrupted her flow of words. 'You've done everything you can. She's a hard woman. She's had to be to survive.'

'Sometimes I catch her looking at me as though she hates me,' Kara said, heavily. 'Is it because she loves Zach? I've seen the way she acts with him. She has three protectors now, and has no need to keep working at the club; but she won't give it up.'

Florence did not answer, but her eyes were sad.

'Mama, why is it that, when we try so hard to do what is right, we dig a pit so deep we bury ourselves?'

'Beatrice loves only herself,' she said softly. 'And if Zach loves anyone, it is you.'

With each sentence, Florence could feel herself growing weaker, but she had to speak. It was what was giving her the stamina to overcome the pain. She had to try and heal the rift between her two daughters. 'After what Fancy did to Beatrice, she wants power over men.'

'I know the torture of loving a man who is out of reach. I could never divorce Zach. The scandal would bring shame on our children. I've made a mess of my life. I'd hate to think that, if Beatrice loved Zach, I'd also ruined her chance of happiness. They do get on well together. They have so much in common.'

'Yes, Zach and Beatrice are two of a kind. Ruthless and ambitious. Don't blame yourself. Zach pursued you. You had no other choice.' Florence closed her eyes, overcome with weakness. 'My medicine. Must speak with Beatrice now.'

Kara held the remedy to her mother's lips, and they smiled into each other's eyes.

Florence said, 'Before you go, promise me you'll watch over Beatrice. She's wild. I wish she'd live a better life than as a courtesan. If only she'd settle down and marry.'

'Don't worry about her. I will always be there for her.'

Florence closed her eyes as Kara left the room. Kara was too innocent. She would never believe that her sister and husband were betraying her. Though she was close to the truth in suspecting that Beatrice was in love with Zach. God spare Kara from ever learning that, for the past three years, Beatrice had been Zach's mistress.

Not that Beatrice was faithful to him, Florence reflected, unable to understand the wanton streak which drove her daughter. Long ago she had stopped trying to preach to her the merits of respectability. Beatrice had set herself up in

Mayfair, and had an arrangement with three wealthy men who visited her at set times. The oldest was a viscount, another the owner of a large emporium, and the third an eminent member of the king's cabinet. She lived like a countess, bedecked in the finest clothes and jewels from her admirers. Even the house was her own, signed over to her by the viscount before she agreed to be his mistress. It astounded Florence that none of the men resented sharing Beatrice.

If asked, Beatrice always gave a throaty chuckle and a wink. 'I know how to keep them happy. They've no cause for complaint. They're all married to shrivelled-up women who regard sex as a messy and unpleasant duty. They appreciate me, and don't mind paying heavily for the privilege.'

'Ma.' Beatrice's voice cut short her reverie. Florence opened her eyes to regard her younger daughter. She had changed so much since Kara had come into her life. Unconsciously she copied her sister's poise, and never wore the bright colours she had once favoured. Now, her hair was arranged high on her head, and she was a picture of loveliness in pale pink silk. Beatrice could pass as a noblewoman any day. Providing she did not get angry. Then all the foul language of a guttersnipe would erupt from those lightly carmined lips.

'You've done well for yourself, Beatrice. Isn't it time to put the past behind you? Don't bear a grudge that Kara had such a different childhood to your own.'

'I don't blame you, Ma,' Beatrice hastily assured her.

'Then forgive Kara for what she could not help. She loves you. This jealousy and resentment you have will destroy you both. End your affair with Zach. It will break Kara's heart if she found out.'

'I won't give him up. She doesn't love him as I love him. I loved him before she even met him.'

'But does Zach love you? He will never leave Kara. He adores the children. You're a sensuous and provocative woman who few men can resist. Zach is an obsession with you – because he's the one man out of your reach. Through him, you want to hurt Kara.'

'She has everything – even Zach. I survived a childhood in the rookery because I learned to fight for what I want.'

Florence saw the hatred glittering in Beatrice's eyes, and battled against her failing strength. 'Promise me you will stop blaming Kara for the past. You hate her … yet she never consciously did you harm. She's done everything she could to help you. She loves you.'

Beatrice looked away. 'I can't help it, Ma. I've tried, but when I think of Fancy and all I suffered… Perhaps if she had not wed Zach…'

'She had no idea you cared for him. He certainly kept his association with you quiet.'

'He married her believing her rich. He didn't love her.' Beatrice spat out her venom.

'He has a deep regard for her.'

Beatrice scowled. 'I'm not his only mistress. If Zach really cared for Kara he wouldn't carry on so with other women.'

'Wouldn't he? Infidelity comes as naturally to men like Zach as breathing. But you are Kara's sister. She deserves better from you.' Florence's voice was weakening and she clasped her daughter's hand, her eyes beseeching. 'Direct your resentment for the past at me. Promise me that, when I die, your hatred dies with me. I'm the one to blame for your life, not Kara.'

'Even now you defend her,' Beatrice sobbed. 'Ever since she found you, you've praised her. You love her more than me. Well, she's not so sweet and innocent. The twins were no seven-month babies. And I know Zach never touched her before he wed her. They're Tennent's brats.'

Fear washed over Florence that Beatrice had guessed the truth. It was a weapon she would not hesitate to use to her advantage when it suited her.

'That's wicked to even think. Of course the twins are Zach's. He adores them. And I don't love Kara more than you. I missed her terribly when we were parted. But you were my reason for living when I was miserable and lonely. Everything I did in those early years was for you.'

Florence's voice was fading, the room becoming hazy. She was so tired, so weary. The pain was eating into her chest. She wanted to sleep, but she had to convince Beatrice. She could not rest until she had ended the rift between her daughters. Willpower rallied her strength to continue.

'I'm the one who failed you. I couldn't save you from Fancy. Though you brought that on yourself. I warned you to guard your saucy tongue.

What we shared, Beatrice – what we struggled through to survive – binds me closer to you ... than ever I could be to Kara. And look at you now. You've risen above the gutter. You're one of the most fêted beauties in London. End this hatred you have for Kara. Promise me...'

Beatrice remained silent.

'Promise me, Beatrice,' Florence forced out, knowing that her strength was near its end. 'I will die in peace if you and Kara will be close, as sisters should be.'

'I won't give up Zach,' Beatrice said mutinously.

'Then you are no daughter of mine.' Her voice tapered weakly. 'I will go to my grave despising you.'

Beatrice broke into sobs.

'Give up Zach.' Florence's voice was a whisper, her eyes pleading in a way which twisted Beatrice's emotions. 'Let me die happy, knowing that my children are reconciled.'

'You ask too much,' Beatrice wailed.

Florence turned her head away. Tears ran down her sunken cheeks. 'Then I've failed you both miserably.'

The frail voice tore at Beatrice's heart. She didn't blame Florence for the squalid life she had led. Always her mother had tried to better their circumstances. She knew how difficult it was to survive in a rookery, even if you were born to it. For a woman as gentle as Florence, it had been due to her stamina and courage that they survived. She admired her mother for that. She could not let Florence die believing she had failed.

'I promise, Ma,' she said softly. 'I will try to be a proper sister to Kara. I will tell Zach it's over between us. Don't be sad, Ma. I love you. I love you so much.'

Florence turned back to Beatrice and it took all her strength to lift her hand to touch her daughter's cheek. She smiled. 'You have so much to give each other.' The words became softer until Beatrice had to lean forward to hear. 'As you love me, forgive Kara. Promise me.'

'I promise.'

Beatrice stared down at the only person whose welfare she had ever put before her own. Such love shone from Florence's eyes that her heart filled with pride. Florence did love her more than she loved Kara. As Beatrice wiped away her tears, her mother's eyes closed. The peaceful and tender smile on her lips slowly faded and her laboured breathing filled the room.

She never spoke again, and died clasping the hands of both her daughters.

Richard Tennent gripped the ship's rail and stared at the flat marsh landscape distorted by mist as they sailed passed the old redbrick fort at Tilbury towards the docks. It was April 1909, and he had been out of England for six years. He lifted his face to the light drizzle and shivered beneath his thick topcoat. Used to the tropical jungle heat, the chill, damp autumn cut through him like a knife.

He had received little news from England in his years away. The news of Elizabeth's death and birth of his daughter had filled him with guilt. He should have been with her at the birth. He knew how terrified she was at the prospect. Although he had been delighted at the news of her pregnancy, the circumstances of the baby's conception still rankled. Elizabeth had used her body to trap him into staying with her.

Dispirited, he had been on the point of giving up his work in Mexico when a letter from Kara reached him. She had encouraged him to continue his expedition, telling him that, before she died, Elizabeth had made Kara promise to be Louise's godmother. A young baby did not need him, and life without Kara in England was an arid prospect.

Driven by a need to forget Kara and assuage his guilt over his wife's death, he extended his exploration. Sometimes he had lived with remote tribes, the descendants of the Incas, part of their culture handed down through them and surviving in their working life and beliefs. He had filled scores of notebooks on their legends, and made sketches of the carvings on the temples. He had fulfilled his ambition to locate one of the lost temples. His research had thrown new light on how the Incas and Mayans lived and worshipped, and he had become an acclaimed authority on the Inca civilisation. Yet still he felt restless.

His daughter was five and he did not want her to grow up estranged from him. His feelings for Kara had not changed. He had not heard from her since she wrote to him a year ago to stay that Florence had died. Being half-way across the world had not eased the pain of parting from her. At least in England they trod the same soil and watched the same sunset.

Besides, Arnold Finnemore had carried his business for too long. The expedition to Peru had taken most of his fortune. It was time he began earning a living again. Finnemore would continue working on the trust funds for the clients who liked and respected him. Richard had decided to return to criminal law. That was where his real interest lay. The dead could look after themselves: from now on he was drawn to help the living. He wanted to ensure that the guilty paid the price for their crimes and the innocent were not convicted through any miscarriage of justice.

Throughout his travels he had witnessed the contrasts of vast wealth and supreme poverty. It had driven home to him that in England there existed the same disparities. His travels had been an indulgence. Worthy, but he had been too engrossed in the past. He wanted to provide the foundations of a better future. On returning to Belgravia he would dust off his old law books and brush up on his study of criminal law.

It was two in the morning and The Gentleman's Retreat was crowded. Zach stood at the head of the stair balustrade and looked down at the array of noblemen and gentry parading in their evening finery, beautiful and vivacious women milling amongst them. Many were courtesans who partnered the men who attended here. Zach had refused to lower the standard of his establishment to that of a common bordello. No prostitutes were in his employ, although discreet rooms could be hired out and meals provided for a gentleman and his lady companion for the evening.

Zach drew on his cigar. The sight of the great crystal chandeliers burning brightly, and the subdued tones of the silk wallpaper with the large gilded French mirrors on the walls, filled him with pride. Kara's only contribution to his club had been to design its interior, which she had done with her own impeccable good taste. She had advised that it should have all the comforts and elegance of a gentleman's residence, tastefully decorated, its services discreet and respectable.

From the day it had opened it had been a success. It was popular with the wealthy sons of aristocrats and merchants, who spent and lost freely at the gaming tables. Not that these tables were in evidence in the general part of the club. Gambling might be illegal, but it still flourished. There was no common rat-baiting or cockfighting at The Gentleman's Retreat. Occasionally Zach would arrange for the top names on the boxing circuit to fight in the ring set up in the cellar. Admission was by ticket only and the stakes were always high.

To protect his interest, Zach paid heavy bribes to the police which ensured no unexpected raids took place. If one should occur, a warning bell was rung by the doorman. By the time the peelers burst into the second-floor room, they would discover nothing untoward. The specially made gaming tables would be converted by sliding panels into ordinary-looking tables, and the gentlemen would be found lounging and drinking in the comfortable chairs which filled the main room of any gentleman's club.

Further entertainments also acted as a shield to the gaming rooms. A French cook had been installed in the kitchen so that the supper room provided some of the most exquisite meals to be had in London. Adjoining the supper room with its discreet alcoves, subdued and intimately lit tables, and magnificently adorned with thick carpets and velvet drapes, was a small ballroom where musicians constantly played.

Though men did not bring their wives, it became a place of refined assignation. The women were high-class courtesans or gaiety girls, singers or actresses from the many West End productions nearby. Beatrice had proved an invaluable asset in overseeing the conduct of the women. It was not unknown for an actress or music-hall star to become inebriated and loud-mouthed. Beatrice dealt with them deftly, affording their paramours and the other members the least embarrassment.

Though Kara had helped with its décor, Zach had kept her ignorant of many of the functions of the club. She would never have approved that it had been furnished from the proceeds of countless housebreakings and robberies. Kara would never tolerate that side of his life. And Zach protected her from it.

If his marriage had not provided him with the instant wealth he desired, he found Kara a perfect wife in all other respects. She was beautiful, accomplished and although eminently respectable, she was an exciting and fascinating woman with the passionate soul of a courtesan. Everything about her appealed to his masculine pride. She never complained at the odd hours he kept. She never denied him her bed, no matter how late he came to her. Out of respect for her he kept his lapses of infidelity discreet. Her achievements in business had won his admiration. Her respectability rebounded on his own reputation to its credit. He had even sworn Beatrice to secrecy. It never once dawned on him that he loved Kara, for love had never been part of his ideal in marriage.

Beatrice was another matter. He knew exactly his feelings for her. Lust. Pure and unbridled. And a deep distrust. There was a possessiveness about her manner which made him uneasy. Not that he refused her advances. She was too exciting and innovative a mistress for that. But he wished she was not Kara's sister. If Kara found out, it would cause an unbreachable barrier in their marriage. That was something he wished to avoid. He had never considered himself paternal, but the birth of the twins had changed him. Twin boys was something to be proud of. The lads were exceptionally bright and quick-witted, anyone could see that. They would go far in this world, given the right opportunity. Zach was determined that his sons would want for nothing.

From the balustrade he watched Beatrice flirting with a young earl. The woman was incorrigible. He felt no jealousy at the number of lovers she took and discarded. Yet all the softness left his face as he regarded her; the expression in his eyes was bleak, wary and dangerous. He and Beatrice were irrevocably bound together, held by passion and dark secrets. It was the danger she presented that Zach found so difficult to resist. Life was only exciting to him when he lived on the knife-edge. It was the ultimate gamble.

Zach drew deeply on his cigar and exhaled a ring of blue smoke. Idly, he watched it expand as it floated towards the ornate plasterwork covering the ceiling. Employing Beatrice had been one of his many triumphs over the Gilberts: those short-sighted fools had never seen her true potential as an attraction. She had a good singing voice and the figure of a houri. Young bucks flocked to the club on the four nights a week she sang. Dressed in low-necked ballgowns, she would move amongst the men with the sensuous grace of a siren, flirting with them all, her eyes boldly inviting and promising them heaven. Only the richest entered her bed.

Occasionally, Zach wondered why he was amongst the select few of her lovers. He never paid her for her favours. Too often he had glimpsed the hatred in her eyes when Kara was mentioned. There were times when it unnerved him. Countless times he had sworn to end their affair. Yet the darker, reckless side of his nature was drawn to her. They were twin souls, merciless and unrepentant in achieving their goals.

And Zach's goals were high. Fed by success, though first built on the need for revenge. When he had recovered from the beating ordered by the Gilbert brothers, he had vowed to get even with them.

An underworld empire was not something to be built overnight. He had started with recruits from his army days. Men down on their luck and jobless after the army had deserted them. Trained soldiers outmatched any street bully, and Zach had gradually taken over the protection racket in several districts. Many of the soldiers had been born into poverty and in their youth had become accomplished thieves. The appalling slums of the rookeries were slowly disappearing as philanthropists pulled down the old tenements. But the grinding poverty remained, and nimble-fingered recruits to his growing gang of thieves were easy to find. Smaller gangleaders were eliminated, their districts enmeshed in Zach's growing territory. The old, sly régime of underworld bullies was no match for his army veterans, or his agile wits.

There wasn't a crooked dodge he didn't know about, or had failed to master. He specialised in fencing stolen goods of high quality, and had set up a network, either to sell the goods on to a buyer abroad, or to have the gold and silver melted down into bars and resold.

Though the Gilbert brothers were figures still to be feared by many in the underworld, Zach did not fear them. He had not forgotten his vow. He had been patient, biding his time. Gradually he had moved in on the Gilberts' territory. He waited his chance before he made his final assault on them. The time was now right. There was only one outcome. The Gilbert brothers' lives or his own.

Chapter Twenty-one

The dissolute young lord had been a disappointing lover. Beatrice rolled away from his naked figure sprawled across her satin sheets. His handsome face was sulky in repose, the pale blond hair was tousled, and darker side-whiskers and a narrow moustache gave him an imperious air. The smooth skin on his arms showed no definition of muscle, the white slender hands were soft as a babe's and beautifully manicured. A man who had never worked or known want, his inability to satisfy her sexual cravings was bound in with his arrogant need for self-gratification. His philosophy was to hell with the rest of the world. She despised such men.

Rising naked from the bed, she stood before her mirror, lifting her hand to admire the diamond bracelet on her wrist. She turned from side to side surveying it. The spoilt Lord Frederick Mountgibbons had paid dearly for his pleasure.

The bedsprings creaked and she turned to discover Freddie peering blearily at her. 'Come back to bed, my dove,' he drawled. 'Come play your wicked tricks on me. There's not a whore to match you, sweetheart. Come pleasure me, there's a good lass.'

Beatrice laughed, its sound without humour. She threw back her head, her auburn hair tumbling across her shoulders and down her back. She ran her tongue salaciously across her full lips. 'Isn't it for you to pleasure me? Naughty boy. You can't have all your own way.' She brought down her hand to slap his naked buttock.

She saw the leap of expectation in his blue eyes, and correctly guessed the means to rule him.

'Anything, my sweet. I am yours to command.'

He rolled on to his back, his pale thin body, his narrow chest devoid of body hair less appetising than the jewels she would insist he lavish upon her. She wanted a necklace to match the bracelet.

'Then, naughty boy, remember I give the orders and you obey.'

He licked his lips, his eyes glittering with excitement. He sprawled with arms and legs wide. 'Wicked, wanton Beatrice. I'm your devoted slave. Do with me as you will.'

She knew his type: the weakling fag at an expensive public school; a pretty boy to amuse the bullying seniors. He would become another besotted conquest – as all her lovers must be since Fancy and Slasher had brutalised her.

The only exception was Zach. He was too much his own man to be subservient to any woman. Her body burned to be with him now. Her promise to her dying mother weakened with every day that she denied herself the pleasure only he could give her. In the months since Florence's death she had struggled to keep her promise. Not once had she turned her wiles on Zach. And he, curse him, acted as though it was of no consequence whether he was in her bed or not. It was always she who would make the advances, never him.

Her frustration at Zach's aloofness grew with each day. She had thought that, when he again became her lover, she would win his love. Sometimes she wondered if she even had his affection. Too often for her peace of mind, he would leave the club before it closed to return to his wife. Their growing family was testimony to the intimacy of their marriage. Yet would Kara be so willing to have him in her bed if she knew but half the truth behind Zach's new life? Often the temptation to throw her knowledge in her sister's face was almost more than she could bear. Only Zach's threats halted her.

An impatient groan from Freddie jerked her thoughts back to the present. She was straddled over him, holding a feather fan in her hand which she ran across his ribs. Already he was hard and eager to penetrate her.

'Not so fast,' she chided when he tried to roll her on to her back. 'Not until I say. Here I give the orders. Isn't that what we agreed?'

She continued to play the feathers over his body until he was moaning with pleasure and frustration. 'Now, Bea. Now.'

She smiled and, kneeling at his feet, began to press light kisses over his ankles, calves and thighs, until he began to writhe and gasp with pleasure. She deliberately skirted the jutting tumescence to increase his torment. Teasing his flesh with her tongue and giving him small nips, she played with him.

'Beatrice, you're a witch,' he moaned. 'Stop.

No, don't stop! Oh, the pain. The joy. Bitch, I can't stand it! Please, Bea. Now. Now. Now!'

'The impatience of youth,' she said with a chuckle. She hovered over him, refusing him the release he begged for. 'Hasn't anyone taught you that there is pleasure in restraint? Perhaps it is time for a few lessons, my lord.'

Enjoying the power of having a man at her mercy, for Freddie was not the type to exert force, she tantalised his erection, her full breasts rubbing against the swollen flesh. Her own desire mounted.

'Please, Bea. I beg you.'

'You'll get your release, Freddie love, but what about me? If you want to be my lover, you have to learn that I have needs. First, you will learn how to give a woman pleasure.'

She took his hand, sucking each finger before placing it between her thighs. 'There is a skill even in this,' she said throatily as she manipulated his fingers to caress her in a way which brought her to writhing climax.

When finally she impaled herself on him, she moved with hard thrusts of her hips, continuing to seek her own satisfaction long after he had cried out in the throes of his orgasm. She reared back, her long nails clawing red scratches over his panting chest until finally, with a shudder, she slumped gasping over him.

'Was that good for you, Bea?'

It was a question many of her lovers asked, expecting praise for their own prowess. Freddie's tone was different. Surprisingly, he now seemed to want her to have the same pleasure she gave him. It made her feel special, and she studied him with less calculating eyes.

'It was good, Freddie.'

'Teach me to make it better for you.'

A glow of unexpected warmth spread over her heart. She suddenly realised how devoid her life was of affection. Her young lord was not as arrogant and selfish as she had thought him.

Throughout the night she instigated new rituals for them, until at dawn she permitted him to sleep. His legs could still barely support him when he eventually staggered from her house at noon; she felt a deeper contentment afterwards than she had with any man except for Zach.

The next evening he was at the club, the diamond necklace dangling between his trembling fingers. 'I want to see you again, Bea. On a permanent arrangement. I don't want to share you.'

She laughed and, slipping her arm through his, kissed his cheek. 'I don't give exclusive rights, my lord, even for a diamond necklace. You could tire of me in a few months. Then where would a poor working woman like me be?'

'I'll never tire of you, Bea. You'll never want for anything.'

The adoration in his eyes soothed her pain at Zach's lack of recent interest. Beatrice allowed him to fasten the diamonds around her neck. 'You may visit me every Tuesday evening and Friday afternoon.'

Kara attended the offices of Tennent & Finnemore, as it was now known, a bank draft in her bag. She was about to purchase a large, double-fronted shop in Brentwood. None of her property was leasehold. It was all freehold, to give further security in the future. Since buying out Sophia, she wanted Wyse bookshops to outshine any rivals. Increasing the number of her shops was a necessary gamble to achieve that success.

The Brentwood shop was especially important to her. She had left Brentwood under the shame of her father's bankruptcy. This was her way of re-establishing the Wyse name as a company to be revered.

As usual Kara was impatient to have the papers signed and return home. Her latest pregnancy, following so quickly after the last, had drained her more than usual of energy. Any visit to her solicitor's office brought back painful memories of Richard, memories she had tried so hard to put behind her. She kept her visits to a minimum.

Her mind deliberately focused upon the transaction ahead, she followed the clerk into Mr Finnemore's office.

'Good morning, Finnemore.' Her head was bowed as she drew the papers from her bag. She had removed her gloves, but her figure remained wrapped in a beige fur coat against a bitingly cold April wind.

'Mrs Morton, as always you are prompt.'

Kara's bag and papers fell from lifeless fingers as the familiar and beloved voice greeted her.

'Richard!' All colour drained from her cheeks, and for a moment the room spun crazily around her. He rose from his desk, his back to the window, his figure in silhouette as it had been on her first visit. She had no idea he was back in England. Or was it a vision recalled from the past?

'I did not mean to startle you.' He was at her side, alarmed at her pallor. Picking up her papers, he took her arm and led her to a chair.

Richard had thought himself composed; able to meet Kara without his feelings getting the better of him. At seeing the joy in her eyes, he had been unnerved. He crushed the need to hold her close and kiss her on her trembling, parted lips. He stepped back three paces when she was seated. The scent of her was making him lightheaded. In six years he had sought to forget her. How miserably he had failed. His love for her was fiercer than ever.

Kara put a shaking hand to her temple and lifted the net veil which hung from the wide brim of her tilted hat down to her chin. It distorted her vision and she wanted nothing to stop her seeing Richard clearly. For an instant her eyes blazed with love, then a hard kick from the baby in her womb rudely reminded her of their circumstances. Unconsciously, her hand went to her stomach. The child would be born in a few weeks, and even the thick fur could not disguise her condition from Richard's stare. Had she known he had returned to England she would never have come here. Vanity made her want him to see her when she was again slim and attractive, not bloated with Zach's child.

She saw Richard's gaze follow her hand, and a shutter came down over his expression.

'When did you return?' she asked. 'You will be wanting to see Louise.'

He turned away so that his handsome face was in profile. She could feel his tension. She longed to reach out and take him into her arms. Her pregnancy made a mockery of any tender gesture, and she contained the flood of love which blazed through her. One glance into his eyes had shown her that Richard still loved her. Richard was free, but she was not.

'I docked at Tilbury two days ago,' Richard said with a warmness which surprised her. He turned to regard her gravely. 'I stayed at a hotel last night. The house is not yet opened. I'm handing over to Finnemore all my old cases. In future I shall deal only with criminal law. When I heard you were to visit this morning…'

He shrugged and smiled wryly. 'I wanted a chance to see you on neutral ground. Six years, Kara…' He broke off, his voice gruff, and he took a moment to compose himself.

'I read every report in the newspapers about your expedition.' She gazed ardently at his tanned, leaner face, the frantic racing of her heartbeat making her breathless. 'The discovery of the lost temple made the headlines in two of them. You are famous. Will you be giving talks, or lecturing about your experiences?'

'No. My work is chronicled and will be presented before the relevant authorities. In my spare time I may write of my experiences, but I have returned to England to resume my law practice.' He regarded her for a long time before continuing. 'Success and motherhood becomes you. You look radiant. More beautiful than I remember.'

Kara blushed. 'You've spent too long in the Peruvian jungle.'

'There was nothing for me to come back to,' he said softly.

'There is Louise.'

'How is she?'

'She is well. Louise is a happy, adorable child. She promises to have her mother's beauty, but there is nothing fragile about her health. She has your inquisitive mind and is always into scrapes.'

'I am indebted to you for caring for her. There was no one else I would have wanted to bring up my daughter.'

'It was my pleasure. I shall miss her. So will the other children.'

The strain of appearing cool and unaffected by his presence brought on a rush of faintness. Her senses beginning to slip from her, she asked, 'Could I have a glass of water, please?'

Her eyes closed, and when she opened them, Richard was crouched at her side, his eyes filled with such tenderness that a sob was wrenched from her.

Unable to stop herself, she reached out and took his hand. 'I'm sorry. I should leave. Six years has changed nothing.' She tore her gaze away from the love in his eyes. 'Except that I have a husband now and four children. And I'm fat and pregnant. I wish you had not seen me like this.'

The feminine response to her condition and the rare display of vanity was so unlike her that Richard chuckled softly.

Kara drew a sharp breath, aware that tears were sparkling in her eyes, but she did not care. 'You should have told me you were returning. I would have been prepared. Now I've embarrassed you. I'm sorry.'

'You could never embarrass me.' His voice caressed her. 'Especially when you show that you still care. You're right. Six years has not changed my feelings for you, though God knows I've tried to forget you.'

Richard stood up quickly. If he continued to gaze into her lovely eyes, shining so blatantly with her love for him, his resolve would weaken. He had thought he had come to terms with his feelings for Kara. He had forgotten how charismatic a woman she was, and the years had heightened her sensuality. The success of her business had given her an air of confidence and assurance which affected him profoundly.

'My feelings haven't changed, Kara. The moment you walked through that door I wanted to ask you to divorce Morton.' His expression was pained as he regarded her swollen figure. 'That would be selfish. On going through your file, I've seen how successful your business has become. The scandal of divorce would ruin all that. Neither could I ask you to give up your children. I hear Morton dotes on them, especially the twins. Divorce would make you notorious. Unless Morton has given you grounds for it...'

'Zach has not been faithful, but a divorce would also rebound upon my children. They would bear the shame of it. I would not subject them to that whilst they are so young.'

Richard nodded, controlling the black rage which threatened to overtake him. Kara did not love Zach Morton, that was obvious. Now it was duty which held her fast, as it had bound him to Elizabeth six years ago.

Nothing of the pain he was experiencing showed in his face. 'I should not have mentioned it. Especially in your condition.'

'Do you despise me, Richard?' Her voice was quiet, uncertain.

It destroyed his resolve. 'I could never despise you. You are the honourable one, whilst I … I betrayed your trust and Elizabeth's when I fell in love with you.'

Kara's heart was so full she touched his beloved face and quoted, '"O, what a tangled web we weave, when first we practice to deceive!"'

He turned his face into her palm and kissed it. 'If you quote Sir Walter Scott at me I must answer likewise.

'"O Woman! in our hours of ease,
Uncertain, coy, and hard to please,
And variable as the shade
By the light quivering aspen made;
When pain and anguish wring the brow,
A ministering angel thou!"'

His voice dropped to an intimate caress. 'I never deceived you. You are the only woman I have truly loved. I'll not ruin your life with a scandal.'

Her mind screamed that she had deceived him. Oh, how she had deceived him! The twins were his. Boys he would be so proud of. Had she a right to deny him the truth of their birth? Yet how could she tell him? Zach had accepted them so unequivocally as his own. She had made her bed and must lie on it.

'Then you are stronger than I, Richard. My head tells me to run from here. My body heralds so clearly that I belong to another. Yet my heart, my treacherous heart, belongs to you. You must be strong for both of us. We must not meet alone. In two weeks my child will be born. Now you intend to settle in England you must make your arrangements for Louise. She should have her father's love.'

As she spoke they had moved inexorably closer, until their breaths fanned each other's cheeks. Her shimmering gaze took in every change in his features. The darker bronze to his skin, the fine lines around eyes accustomed to squinting against bright sunlight, the face devoid of side-whiskers, the dark hair – now receding slightly – which curled over his collar. Treacherously, her gaze lingered upon his firm lips. Her longing to feel their touch was so fierce that she gasped and abruptly sat back.

'Where are the papers I must sign?' she asked in a voice shaky from her emotions, which remained in turmoil.

Richard placed a document in neat copperplate handwriting in front of her. 'I will call my clerk to witness your signature, then another Wyse Bookshop will be yours. You've done well for yourself, Kara. From the file, I saw that you had paid Sophia a generous settlement when you bought her out last year. How is she?'

She kept her head bowed as he rang a handbell. 'She is well and happily married and now living in Stratford.'

When the clerk appeared, she signed the document with a flourish. As the clerk added his signature, she stood up, preparing to depart, her tone formal. 'Thank you, Mr Tennent. My success is due to your faith in me.'

Richard nodded for the clerk to leave. 'About the arrangements for Louise. I have several business matters to attend in the next few weeks which will take me out of London. It would be difficult for her to stay in Belgravia until I engage a nanny; but until I do, I would like to visit her whenever I can. It will be easier for her that way. I've no wish to upset her by suddenly whisking her away from the only home she has known, and the family she loves.'

'She is prepared for that. I read your letters to her and the newspaper reports. She's very proud that her father is an explorer. When shall I tell her you will call?'

'May I visit her tomorrow afternoon at three o'clock? I realise it will be strange for her to suddenly uproot herself and live with me. With your permission I would like to get to know her better before she leaves your house. I think that would be less unsettling for her.'

Kara nodded her assent. 'Louise must not be upset. You are welcome to visit her whenever you wish, until she is comfortable about leaving us.' She hesitated. 'I will inform Nanny you will be calling.'

'You will not be there.'

'It would be better if I were not.'

Her words denied him, but the torment and love in her eyes betrayed her.

Chapter Twenty-two

Derby day was an event all London was eager to attend. Kara, Zach and the twins, Tim and Harry, arrived in the Morton Daimler at noon. Beatrice, with Freddie Mountgibbons and two other young noblemen in attendance, accompanied them in a Lanchester. In the warm sunshine they picnicked on the Epsom downs together, champagne corks popping, laughter merry. They had left early, the stream of vehicles and pedestrians all heading towards one of the year's most celebrated events. Every inn and tavern on the road was crowded with travellers. Closer to the racecourse, the congestion was thicker. Constantly the motor cars were brought to a halt as racegoers spilled out of a tavern. Potboys carrying fistfuls of foaming tankards shouted, 'Make way', as they pushed towards the omnibuses. Men leaned down from the open roofs, and giggling ladies thrust hands through the open windows, eager to slake their thirst on the hot, dusty road.

Beatrice twirled her parasol as she sat back in Freddie's motor car. She hadn't missed a Derby in ten years, but this was the first time she had arrived in such style. In previous years she had travelled on foot, or by omnibus. She had joined the enormous encampment on the eve of Derby day which lit the downs in the evening twilight. Here the fairground folk set up their booths. Wrestlers and pugilists drew crowds to their rings. Mountebanks, tricksters, gypsies, pick-pockets and whores thrived amidst the drunken revelry.

Today, from her superior place in the open vehicle, Beatrice felt like a queen where once she had been amongst the rabble. Her euphoria vanished as she caught sight of Zach smiling tenderly at Kara. Her sister had given birth to another boy, Robert, last month. It was Kara's first outing after the birth and Zach could not stop fussing over her.

Beatrice's pleasure in the day dimmed. The old hatred for her sister burned like acid in her gut. All Beatrice had achieved in the last six years was nothing compared to the riches and social standing of her sister. Everything Kara touched seemed to turn to gold. The shops, her marriage; even the swelling nursery of children, whom Zach doted upon. Those brats were proof that Zach still found Kara attractive. To her further chagrin Zach would not hear a word said against his wife.

'Frowning, sweetheart,' Mountgibbons teased. 'What's displeased you? Tell Freddie, he'll put it right.'

'I was remembering other Derby days,' she said, squeezing his hand. 'I never arrived in such style before. I feel like a queen.'

'I can't give you a crown, but I can give you a coronet. Marry me, Bea. I can't bear sharing you with your other admirers.'

She smiled provocatively. Freddie was the youngest and most generous of her lovers. The only one who wasn't married. He could be petulant and sulky when he did not get his way, but she had so thoroughly seduced him during the last year that he had become besotted with her. And having taught him to make love in a way which made her pleasure equal his, she now found him a satisfactory lover. Of all her paramours, he was her favourite. He had come into his title and inheritance two years ago, when his father's yacht had capsized whilst cruising the Mediterranean, and both his parents had drowned.

More than a dozen times, Freddie had asked her to wed him. It had made her analyse her life. She had a fine house, and her gentlemen friends kept her in style, but for how much longer?

Already the viscount had found a younger mistress. At twenty-two Beatrice realised that her life with Fancy had taken its toll on her once fresh features. She also had a passion for champagne and chocolates, both of which had begun to show in her figure. In another year or two, her looks would start to fade. Then what would be her future? A downward slope. At least she had the house given to her by the viscount as an enticement to become his mistress. She could set herself up as a brothel madam. Florence would turn in her grave. But that wasn't what she really wanted. It still kept her at the mercy of men's whims. Perhaps she should marry Freddie. She probably wouldn't get a better offer. As Lady Mountgibbons, she would be socially superior to Kara.

'Freddie, one day you'll ask me to wed you and I just might accept,' she teased. 'What would you do then? It wouldn't do to have your ancient lineage tainted with my common blood.'

He guffawed, his voice slurred from the amount of champagne he had already consumed. 'We started on the wrong side of the blanket. The first Lord Mountgibbons was Charles II's by-blow by an actress. She was ousted in favour of Nell Gwynne. In recent times my grandfather, after Grandmama died, took her seamstress as his second wife. I love you, Bea. Say you'll marry me.'

She laughed, indicating their two companions. 'You're embarrassing Westman and Blackworth. I'm sure they disapprove.'

Westman blushed and looked away. Last night he had been propositioning her to ditch Mountgibbons and become his mistress. She had refused disdainfully. Westman was narrow-faced and unattractive; balding, with a smattering of mousy hair. But worse, in Beatrice's eyes, he was a clutchfist where money was concerned. He thought buying a woman a meal was enough to make her jump into bed with him. He was married to a stout, equally unattractive banker's daughter, whom he had married to save his own family from financial ruin.

Blackworth, who was befreckled and filled with bonhomie, waved a pale, slender hand as he preened his auburn moustache. 'Marry who you will and be damned, old boy,' he advised. 'I, poor soul, am about to be shackled to the Honourable Delia Fitzhumphrey-Blythe. A plainer, pikestaff-thin creature never graced our venerable shores. She's been my betrothed since the cradle, don't you know? Lucky blighter, Mountgibbons. No parents or guardian to insist you toe the line. Marry the wench. Marry and be damned, I say.'

'There, Bea, you have their approval. Say the word and we'll be married by special licence next week.'

'If I decide to marry you, Lord Mountgibbons, it will be no hole-in-the-corner affair. Westminster Abbey for the ceremony, and the reception at the Savoy. But I refuse to give you an answer here. You have no romance in your soul.'

Kara, who had never attended the Derby before, was overwhelmed by the noise and bustle of the crowd. Countless tents, and refreshment pavilions, and a huge fairground covered the fields. Hundreds of motor vehicles and carriages of every kind were spread over the Downs. Every year since her wedding, Zach had urged her to come. Until now she had either been too advanced in pregnancy, or too busy dealing with some crisis with the business, to join him. She suspected that, before he had opened his gaming club, he had used the race meeting to steal from the rich, and she had no wish to be any part of that side of his life.

At least the club had stopped him from risking his freedom in that manner – though owner of a gambling hall was hardly the most respectable of occupations. Zach had sworn to her that his income was now honestly come by and his criminal life was behind him. If only she could believe him. In her heart she knew Zach was not as innocent as he would have her think.

As they strolled amongst the booths, Zach held the twins' hands as they excitedly strained to run towards every new sight. Kara was amazed at the vast number of people. It seemed the whole of London had journeyed to Epsom. Clerks and shop girls dressed in their Sunday finery paraded amongst the nobility. Paupers mixed with wealthy merchants.

Twice she had seen the jovial figure of King Edward enjoying the day, his pleasure no less than the tattered urchins trying to turn a penny. The press of the crowd elbowed and jostled each other as they joined in the festivities. Sharp-faced, swaggering tipsters, coarse-visaged coster-mongers, mischievous apprentices and bandy-legged grooms swelled the revellers. Ragged organ-grinders with their monkeys played in competition with negro serenaders. Red-faced serving girls eyed broad-shouldered navvies.

Mountgibbons, encouraged by his companions, was in high spirits, and paid his shilling to cast sticks at the coconut shy.

'A wager, Morton,' he urged, rolling up his sleeve. 'Ten guineas says I knock down the first coconut.'

Laughing, Zach accepted. Mountgibbons threw first, skimming the top of the coconut, which wobbled, but remained firmly planted on its stand.

'Bad luck. Count out your guineas, your lordship,' Zach grinned. He tipped back his top hat, rolled back his cuffs and took aim. He scored a central hit. The coconut thudded to the ground amidst a round of cheers from the spectators. He chose a jack-in-the-box as a prize for the twins and, taking the ten guineas from Mountgibbons, declared, 'Double up your bet on the archery. Kara and myself, against you and Beatrice.'

'I've never used a bow,' Kara protested, laughing.

'Then this will be a day of new experiences,' Zach replied. 'Beatrice is quite a markswoman. Scored a bull's-eye last year and won me twenty sovereigns on a wager.'

'Then I'll take you on,' Mountgibbons said, laughing. 'It's a certainty Bea and I will win.'

'Three arrows each,' Zach insisted as they paid their money and took up the bows and arrows. 'And I get to give Kara instruction.'

The circular targets were small, to compensate for the short range, and were comprised of an outer blue ring, a red one in the middle, and a solid, gold-coloured centre. Beatrice fired first and got two arrows in the red and one in the gold. Zach scored two golds, and just clipped the dividing line into the red. Mountgibbons was weaving so tipsily that he missed the target completely with the first arrow.

Zach laughed. 'You've gone into the green, old boy. No points for that.'

Freddie eyed the arrow sticking up in the grass. 'Come here, Bea, and give us a kiss for good luck.'

Beatrice complied with such a resounding kiss that Westman hooted with glee. 'I say, Freddie, if that's what you get for missing the target, how will she reward you for scoring in the gold?'

'Ah, that will be Freddie's and my secret.' Beatrice winked at Mountgibbons. 'Don't be letting me down, Freddie love.'

Mountgibbons's hand was shaking as he pulled back the arrow. Then, shutting one eye, he drew a steadying breath. His arrow scored a perfect gold, as did the following one.

'I'm going to lose you your bet, Zach,' Kara said as she lifted the bow and fumbled to hold the arrow correctly between her fingers.

'Just relax. Take a deep breath as you bring up the bow and align the arrow with the centre of the target.' Zach stood behind her, his arms around her as he guided her arms into position. He was grinning, his teeth white against his tanned complexion. 'You can do anything you set your mind to, Kara.'

Beatrice flinched at the tenderness in his voice. His expression was loving as he leaned over Kara's shoulders with his cheek close to hers. Jealousy pierced her, making her add tartly, 'How about raising the bet, Zach? Five guineas on Kara not getting more than one arrow in the outer circle.'

'Bet taken,' he answered, without taking his eyes from Kara's profile, which was set in concentration. 'I've never known my wife to fail me yet.'

Beatrice willed the arrow to snaggle in the bowstring and fall to the ground a few feet away, as was usual with most beginners. Instead it hit the straw target with a thud in the outer circle.

'Get ready to pay up, Bea old girl,' Zach chuckled as he guided Kara's arm back to the correct tension.

The second arrow also struck the outer circle.

'You've lost your bet, Bea.' Mountgibbons hiccuped congenially. 'Never mind, I'll pay it for you.'

Beatrice was scowling, and her face was flushed red with anger at seeing Kara's third arrow land in the middle ring. Murder entered her eyes at witnessing Zach's delight.

Oblivious to the crowds, he crushed Kara to him and kissed her resoundingly on the cheek. 'Well done, my darling.'

Kara laughed and, as she stepped away from her husband, Beatrice saw her sister stiffen. Her gaze was on a man's figure in the crowd. For an instant, such yearning shone in Kara's eyes that Beatrice's interest quickened. Following her sister's glances, she saw Richard Tennent with a beautiful blonde-haired woman on his arm. She recognised her as Fenella Sommerfield, the music-hall star. Tennent had also been unable to conceal his feelings in the moment when he encountered Kara.

Beatrice's eyes narrowed. So there *was* something between him and Kara. She glanced at the twins. Their colouring, though dark, was lighter than Zach's. In the summer sunlight, they had the same reddish-brown lights in their locks, which duplicated the chestnut sheen of Richard Tennent's hair.

They were no seven-month babies. Zach would be furious when he learned the truth. He'd leave Kara for sure. Beatrice smiled slyly as she regarded her sister. As though aware she was being studied, Kara looked across at Beatrice. Lifting an auburn brow, Beatrice pointedly glanced from the twins to the departing figure of Richard Tennent. To her delight, Kara paled, confirming her suspicions.

At that moment, Zach scooped young Tim up on to his shoulders and gave a carefree laugh. He had never lost his military bearing, his straight-backed figure still slim and commanding. He had recently shaved off his moustache, keeping only the thick side-whiskers, and looked more handsome than ever.

'Come on, lads. Let's go and place a bet on the first race,' Zach suggested. 'What names do you fancy?'

Zach read out the list of runners, and the boys shouted their suggestions.

Beatrice turned away, her stomach sour at the sight of so much blissful domesticity. Mountgibbons and his companions had wandered over to the paddock to assess the runners parading in the ring. A gypsy fortune-teller in a black shawl and gaudy striped skirt was seated a short distance away outside her pavilion.

'I must have my fortune read,' Beatrice declared.

'It's all nonsense,' Zach scoffed. 'She's already seen you with Mountgibbons, and in those fine clothes she'll tell you you'll marry a rich man within the year.'

'It so happens I may do just that,' Beatrice said with a coquettish smile. 'It's not as though I haven't been asked.'

'You mean Freddie has asked you?' Kara said, delighted at her sister's good fortune.

'Actually, he begs me every week to be his bride.' Beatrice beamed with pride, whilst through her lashes she was watching Zach's reaction.

He laughed. 'Then snatch him up fast, old girl, whilst he's besotted. That's if you've a mind for a title. Lady Mountgibbons has a fine sound to it.'

Beatrice felt her smile freeze on her lips. Zach didn't care if she married Mountgibbons or not. His attention was all on those damned twins. They were his pride. Several times she'd seen the affectionate way he glanced down at Kara, who strolled on his arm. Jealousy ate into her. Mountgibbons might be a lord, but he was nowhere near the man Zach was. She didn't want to spend her life tied to a spoilt boy... Although to be Lady Mountgibbons would be something. It would put her above that haughty sister of hers. It would show the world how high she had risen from the gutter.

Zach raised a mocking brow, goading her anger. 'What's Mountgibbons worth?' he asked. 'He's lost thousands in the last few months at The Retreat.'

Beatrice shrugged, refusing to allow Zach to see that she had any misgivings about the prospective marriage. With a sly smile she fingered a large ruby ring that Freddie had given her last night. 'He's a lord, isn't he? Must be worth a mint. The estate runs to hundreds of acres, with a forty-room Georgian house in Staffordshire. Money comes from the coalmines on his land. I shall insist we live in the Kensington house. I've no intention of becoming a country mouse.'

'No chance of you becoming a mouse, Bea,' Zach said with a wink. 'Regular wildcat is what you'll always be.'

'Well, I'm having my fortune told,' she announced. 'Coming, Kara?'

'What does she need her fortune told for?' Zach taunted, slipping an arm possessively around his wife's waist. 'Hasn't she got what every woman dreams of? A handsome rogue who adores her for a husband; five healthy, beautiful children; and a successful business which exceeded her expectations. Besides, you make your own fortune in this life.'

'They do say pride cometh before a fall,' Beatrice returned. 'Perhaps Kara has led a secret life you know nothing about, Zach. No one ever learns everything about another person.'

Kara shivered in the heat. Beatrice was being deliberately vindictive. She didn't want her sister planting suspicions in Zach's mind.

'Not my Kara,' Zach said with an affectionate laugh. 'She's the most honest, unselfish, sweet innocent I ever met.'

Venom flashed in Beatrice's eyes. Before her sister could say anything, Kara said brightly, 'Yes, let's have our fortunes told. Come on, Bea. It will be fun to hear what the gypsy has to say.'

To her relief, Beatrice followed her, but her

triumph at getting her away from Zach was short-lived.

'You aren't so innocent as Zach believes, are you, Kara?' she taunted.

'I would not have succeeded in my business if I were.' She lightly turned the subject from dangerous ground.

Her conscience remained uneasy. She had been a fool to let her emotions show at unexpectedly seeing Richard. She had been unable to control her jealousy at the possessive way his companion clung to his arm. She had recognised Fenella Sommerfield, for she was a favourite performer of Zach's. Whenever he took her to the music hall, Fenella would be on the bill singing her bawdy songs. She was notorious for the number of lovers she'd had.

Kara's heart twisted painfully that Richard had fallen beneath the beautiful woman's spell. But what right had she to be jealous? Richard was a handsome widower, she could not expect him to live like a recluse.

It disturbed her that Beatrice appeared to have guessed the truth. Since the opening of The Gentleman's Retreat, Beatrice had worked there as its hostess. Kara suspected that her sister had a stronger loyalty to Zach than herself. She knew Beatrice still resented their different upbringings, and even the difference in their lives now. Everything Kara had set out to achieve she had accomplished. Beatrice was evasive about what she wanted for her future. She pursued pleasure with a recklessness which alarmed Kara.

They reached the fortune-teller's tent. The old

woman rose stiffly from her stool and held open the flap for one of them to enter.

'You first, Kara,' Beatrice insisted.

Kara wondered if Beatrice was going to return to Zach and taunt him with her suspicions about the twins. She glanced back to where he had been standing. He was further away, carrying Tim on his shoulders towards the donkey-rides. Relaxing, she stepped inside the musty-smelling tent and paid a half-crown to the gypsy. The close proximity of the gypsy's unwashed body on this hot day made Kara regret her hasty decision. Not unusually superstitious, she shivered with sudden unease.

She sat on a rickety chair opposite the gypsy, whose dark eyes stared into hers. The woman's hooked nose was covered in blackheads, and greasy strands of black hair snaked out of the scarlet and purple scarf which covered her head. Two large brass hoops dangled from her ears. With a grunt she passed the deck of Tarot cards to Kara.

'Shuffle the cards, then cut them,' she commanded in a deep, unexpectedly musical voice.

Kara did so. The gypsy picked them up and began to flick them over and place them before her.

She pointed to the first card. 'Six of Pentacles, or the Lord of Wealth and Success. This describes you. This second card is what crosses you. Ah, the Lovers. A possible romance is foretold. Or will wisdom battle against passion?' She stared at them for a long moment before continuing. 'Beware, for here is the Ten of Swords, a card of sudden misfortune, perhaps ruin. It is a warning. But you have the Daughter of the Flaming Sword to uphold you. It is a card of strength and the courage to triumph. That shows here again in the Nine of Swords, the Lord of Strength card. Fate will be kind to you. Difficulties lie ahead, but also great happiness.'

The gypsy stabbed a finger at the spread of cards. 'You have a favoured life. But nothing is achieved without paying the price. Great riches. Success in a venture. The reckoning must be made. You are steadfast of nature. But there is trouble. A warning. Hidden enemies.' She sighed and looked at Kara with a frown. 'Beware of those who wish you harm. There is danger. But there is joy. The Six of Cups which is the Lord of Pleasure is a card of wishes fulfilled. Harmony. The card of your future is the Seven of Wands – the Lord of Valour. Triumph over adversity. Strength and mastery. Your wishes achieved, but at a cost.'

She smiled, revealing only four teeth remaining in her mouth. 'Love will conquer in the end. You have a golden future ahead.'

Kara rose, disquieted by the prediction. The gypsy had come uncomfortably close to the truth on certain points. She shrugged off her unease, refusing to allow the gypsy's words to spoil her day. The woman must have spun a tale, guessing that Kara was too intelligent to be taken in by a prediction of too rosy a future.

'What did she predict?' Beatrice smirked. 'Riches? A good future? A long life and happiness?'

'Something like that.'

With a toss of her head, Beatrice sauntered into the tent, ready to mock any prediction given to her by the cards. As Zach said, you made your own future. After shuffling the deck with the expertise of a gamester, she put down the cards.

She saw the gypsy's hand tremble as it closed over them, and a closed expression set the swarthy features into a bland mask. As the gypsy laid out the pack she faltered before placing three of the cards in position. 'The Ace of Pentacles,' she said curtly. 'A change for the better. Financial security. It is crossed by the Five of Cups; a card of worry, regret and disappointment. There's a need to reconsider your values in life.' She fixed Beatrice with a cold stare as she pointed to the card with a Tower. 'A bad omen. Drastic changes. Conflict ahead. Guard against any rash action. It could have widespread repercussions. Yet there is good. The King of Wands, which represents the Prince of the Chariot of Fire, stands for an honest and just man who will take charge of your life. Heed him and you will be saved.'

'What man is this?' Beatrice snapped.

'That is for you to discover.'

'You've told me nothing. I didn't pay you to spout off about bad omens. Will I be rich? Will I marry the man I love?'

The gypsy sucked in her lips. 'The Two of Wands says you have power over others. You will succeed in your endeavours. Yet the path is not easy. The Nine of Swords foretells the loss of a loved one. And of deception and violence.' The gypsy sat back as though to place greater distance between them. 'Trouble is ahead if you stray on to the dark path. Yet to compensate there is the Ten of Pentacles – a card of security, wealth and family life. You cannot escape your ancestry.' She tapped the last card. 'Everything is governed by this card. The Fool. The card of obsession. Of gratification and lack of sensitivity. It shows recklessness. It is also a warning that you are approaching a crossroads. Consider before you act. It can lead to new beginnings. To happiness, or disaster.'

'I didn't pay my money to hear a lot of mumbo-jumbo. You're a fake. I'm about to wed a lord. What do you know?'

Beatrice flounced out. The old hag was supposed to have cheered her up, given her the usual old flannel about a husband and children which she could have mocked and made fun of. All she got was a lot of double meanings. A lot of hocus-pocus.

'What do I know indeed?' The gypsy shook her head as the woman left the tent. 'Trouble. Death. Betrayal. I see it all. The dark path lies ahead for that one, if she does not heed her conscience.'

Incensed by the gypsy's words, Beatrice brushed past Kara who was waiting. She could see Freddie and his friends chatting to a family party which included four attractive and well-dressed young women. On reached Freddie's side, she possessively took his arm and smiled invitingly up at him.

'My dear, may I present Lord and Lady Hetherington and their daughters.'

Beatrice inclined her head in acknowledgement, still disturbed by her encounter with the fortune-teller. Abruptly, she excused Freddie and herself, and pulled him away.

'Did you miss me?' she teased. 'I couldn't resist having my fortune told.'

The love in Freddie's eyes soothed her momentary panic. The prophecy had shaken her. And seeing Freddie engrossed in conversation with women of his own rank had filled her with alarm. The crossroads the gypsy had spoken of must be this one. Her obsession was Zach. That was the road to disaster. Zach would never marry her. Freddie could give her the wealth and security she craved.

'What did the old witch tell you?' he inquired.

'She said a new life awaited me.' Beatrice masked her disquiet. 'A happy family life.'

He grinned. 'Can I take it that you are accepting my proposal?'

'Yes, I will marry you, Freddie. Our wedding will be in Westminster Abbey. How's that for you, and a honeymoon in all the gayest capitals of Europe? Nothing less, mind.'

'You'll give up working at The Retreat?'

'My life will be devoted to you in future, dearest Freddie.'

When Kara, Zach and the children rejoined them, Freddie waved a bottle of champagne.

'We're celebrating. Beatrice has just agreed to become my wife.'

'Beatrice, that's wonderful,' Kara drew her sister into her embrace.

Zach saw the glitter in Beatrice's eyes. It wasn't the light of love, or even excitement, as she pulled herself from Kara's arms. It was a feral radiance, like a beacon warning of danger.

'Clear the course!' The cry went up.

Their bets were placed for the Derby. The Morton and Mountgibbons parties had just taken their places in the grandstand. Already the jockeys were riding the prancing horses to the starting post. Kara felt the buzz of excitement which began to ripple through the crowd. A stir of heads turned like ears of corn in the breeze towards the regal figures of King Edward VII and Queen Alexandra as they walked to the royal box. The king bowed graciously to people he recognised. In his sixties, he was still a commanding, if portly, figure. His full bearded face showed the excesses he had indulged in during the strain of the long years of waiting to claim his throne. On the far side of the course where the vehicles were lined up, men clambered on to the roofs of omnibuses better to view the race. The murmur of impatient voices became an exhilarated drone.

'They're off!'

Another shout broke like a wave through the crowd. All faces turned in one direction. The approaching runners were distorted by the shimmering heat. A low drumming of hooves built in the distance. Dark shapes with dots of bright colours swarmed like butterflies over the horses' straining backs. A low roar mounted in volume as the horses pounded closer. Shriller and faster rose the yells. Voices were scraped raw as the crowd surged closer to the rails. The bellowing was deafening.

Young Tim, sitting on Zach's shoulders, clapped his hands over his ears. Kara held Harry tightly as he perched on the wooden railing fronting their box, and felt the boy's figure trembling with excitement. The same excitement which pounded through her blood as the horses galloped closer. Restraint was gone. Men bellowed, women jumped up and down and indecorously screamed encouragement. Then, in a blur of thundering horseflesh, they were past the winning post. Groans from the losers were drowned by the cheers of the winners. Hats were tossed into the air, handkerchiefs waved wildly and, as the winning jockey pushed his horse through the milling crowd, bowlers and top hats were waved atop the owners' walking sticks in salute to his victory. Below in the betting ring, red-faced punters converged, the throng of bodies merging into a wild St Vitus's dance.

Zach's triumphant shout was the loudest in the box. He'd won two hundred guineas, and in his joy he scooped Kara into his arms. Harry and Tim chanted with glee. 'Papa's won. Papa's won.'

Mountgibbons was stony-faced. His horse had come in fourth.

'Never mind, my darling,' Beatrice said with tart satisfaction. 'Unlucky at gambling – lucky in love.' Her eyes were bright with enforced gaiety, her manner reckless. When she saw King Edward passing close, devilment prompted Beatrice's tongue. The king's horse had not been placed.

'Never mind, Yer Majesty. There's always another race, another filly.'

The startled king looked over the heads of the

crowd and saw Beatrice's vivacious face smiling mischievously. He tipped his hat in salute to her.

'Beatrice,' Mountgibbons voiced his dismay. 'You can't address His Majesty in that way. Too damned familiar by far.'

'He didn't look put out. He looked rather pleased, I thought.' She nudged Freddie in the ribs, her heart thudding wildly as she realised the king was coming in their direction.

He stiffly acknowledged Freddie and cast a curious eye at Zach. Mountgibbons bowed, his face reddening. 'May I present Captain Zach Morton, owner of The Gentleman's Retreat club in the Strand. And his wife, Kara.' He nodded briefly to Kara, who dropped a nervous curtsy. 'May I also present my fiancée–' his voice swelled with pride as he saw the king's interest sharpen – 'Miss Beatrice Kempe.'

'So you're to be married, Mountgibbons. Not seen reference to it in any of the court papers.'

Mountgibbons blushed even redder. 'The lady only agreed this afternoon.'

The king tipped his Homburg to Beatrice as she executed a shaky curtsy, and moved on. Her heart was racing so wildly that she felt it would burst through her ribcage. The king had smiled at her and, if she was not mistaken, that twinkle in his eyes had shown a deeper interest. It sealed her resolve to wed Freddie at the earliest opportunity. King Edward was a womaniser, but he never took as a mistress an unmarried woman. Too risky in promoting a scandal. Mistress to the king. Beatrice's hopes ran high. She knew men, and was confident that it was a distinct possibility.

Chapter Twenty-three

A month after Derby day the atmosphere in The Gentleman's Retreat abruptly changed.

Zach was upstairs mixing with the gamblers when Dipper Jones, without his usual caution, darted across the room, jostling several members. As Dipper whispered urgently in his ear, Zach stood to attention, his saturnine face alight with expectancy.

'Gentlemen, forgive me. A most important guest has arrived. I must greet him.' The laconic manner in which he usually patrolled his domain for once deserted him. On reaching the upper landing, he was aware of the reverent hush which had fallen over the guests in the hallway. He was half-way down the stairs when the portly figure entered with two companions a step behind him. As a liveried footman stepped forward to take the silk top hat, the man's evening cloak parted, revealing the blue sash across the barrelled chest, its diamond garter star glittering in the gaslight.

Zach was at the King of England's side as he relinquished his cloak. He bowed formally, his heels clicking together in military fashion. 'Welcome to our establishment, Your Majesty. We are deeply honoured.'

The king nodded affably. 'Heard favourable accounts of it. You're said to have the best French chef in London, and a cellar to tempt the most discerning palate. Not to mention the gaming. Partial to a hand or two at cards myself, Morton.'

Zach hid his amusement at the understatement. Since his early manhood, and as Prince of Wales, he had shocked his staid mother with his wild ways and gambling. His liaisons with the most beautiful actresses and music-hall stars were notorious.

'Will Your Majesty be dining here?' Zach asked.

The king's roving eye had been scanning the hallway as he walked slowly to the stairs accompanied by Zach. His stare widened, and Zach heard the king's satisfied sigh as his gaze lingered on a figure at the head of the stairs. Zach looked up and saw Beatrice, dressed in gold satin, the plunging neckline revealing her smooth, creamy shoulders and firm high breasts almost in their entirety.

'May I introduce you to Beatrice Kempe, my hostess for this evening?'

Beatrice sank into a deep curtsy, giving both Zach and the king a magnificent display of her half-naked breasts. Beatrice's cheeks were flushed with excitement, her bright eyes shimmering with enticement. She looked ravishing. Zach heard the king's sharp intake of breath at her sensual beauty, and felt his own body stir with desire. Tonight Beatrice was not for him.

'I will leave you in the care of Beatrice,' he said diplomatically. In this he knew Beatrice would not fail him. If the king approved of The Gentleman's Retreat Club, it would soon become the most popular in London.

Beatrice felt she was walking on air as she

accompanied the king into the gaming rooms. He insisted she remain at his side for good luck, and for the next half-hour he proceeded to win every hand.

When he rose from the table, Beatrice inclined her head towards the roulette wheel. 'Luck is with Your Majesty tonight. Would you like to try your hand at roulette, or something else?'

His heavy hooded eyes gleamed, and his voice dropped to an intimate whisper. 'What had you in mind, dear lady?'

For the first time in years, Beatrice blushed. She cursed herself for feeling as awkward as a prissy virgin with her first suitor. 'I am here to serve your pleasure, Your Majesty. Until recently I used to sing in the supper rooms, but my fiancé Lord Mountgibbons did not approve – as he does not approve of my remaining hostess here. After my marriage, I must leave.'

'And when do you become Lady Mountgibbons?'

'In two days.'

The king smiled. 'Mountgibbons is eager to make you his bride, and I cannot blame him. Will he be a possessive or an understanding husband?'

Beatrice was bathed in a flush of expectancy. 'I am my own woman. Freddie understands that.'

He lifted her hand to his lips and kissed it lightly. 'I am delighted to hear that. There are private parlours here, are there not?'

'For the use of members and their guests.' Beatrice knew the need to protect the reputation of the club so that it was not regarded as a bordello. She had never before entertained a member in one of the private rooms. But then she had never been propositioned by a king before.

'Would you join me as my guest, Miss Kempe?'

'I would be honoured.'

'And, as my guest, may I persuade you to sing to your world-weary king and give him comfort?'

She did not answer, but smiled in a way which assured him that he would not be disappointed in her company.

An hour later, she kissed her latest lover farewell and smiled as she leaned against the door which she had closed behind him. Mistress to the king. Who would have thought she would rise so high? And she had not disappointed him. Her discarded clothes, scattered across the floor, bore testament to the hour of unbridled passion and pleasure. For a man in his sixties, she had not expected so virile a lover. His parting words were that she must retain her own house after her marriage, where he would send word when he could visit her.

Of course Freddie would not be pleased. Beatrice shrugged. Not that it was considered a disgrace for the king's eyes to fall upon another man's wife. She could be discreet when it was worth her while. Besides, Freddie wouldn't know until after the wedding. And the king had made it clear that their continuing affair was only acceptable to him if she was married.

When Zach saw the king enter a private room with Beatrice, he smiled. She would keep him occupied for an hour or more. The king's arrival was doubly fortuitous. It assured the club's success, and what better alibi could he have – should any suspicion arise from his plans tonight – than to have the king vouch that he had been at the club all evening. His Majesty would not risk a scandal by confessing to spending an hour alone with an unmarried woman. An hour was ample time to complete the vendetta.

It was a good omen. Tonight it was arranged that he would be avenged upon the Gilbert brothers.

His spies had informed him that there was a meeting for a pay-off on a large opium deal. Zach was far from a moralist, but he abhorred the drug racket for the misery it inflicted on those who quickly became addicted. He had seen the horrors of the opium dens. The doped wretches sitting staring into space, their bodies gradually wasting as their addiction took hold. Every vestige of decency was gradually stripped from them in their need to find the money to pay for the drug. If there was a choice between buying food or the drug, they always chose the drug. When their wasted bodies were no longer capable of even petty crime to sustain their habit, they sold their hair, even the clothes on their backs, to lie naked in the stinking opium cellars. When the effects of the drug wore off, the creatures long addicted were pitiful to behold. They sweated, shaking as though smitten with the palsy, and eventually screamed in agony. With no money for further supplies, they were thrown into the streets to die.

The Gilbert brothers had seen the opium dens as a way to a quick fortune. Hundreds of pounds would exchange hands tonight. Zach intended to intercept the Gilbert brothers before they paid over the cash. The opium smugglers were a vicious Chinese gang who would then wreak their own punishment on the Gilberts.

Zach left the club by the back entrance. Dipper had procured him a ragged, calf-length frock coat and a battered top hat, and left them by the back gate. In the darkness, Zach pulled on his disguise and tugged the hat low over his eyes. The coat was buttoned high over his white evening shirt. In the warren of dimly lit alleyways, he would pass as one of its ragged inhabitants. He wrinkled his nose in disgust at the foul body odours rising from the coat. His men were waiting outside a tavern and he nodded approval that all were dressed in as nondescript a way as himself.

By his reckoning, the Gilbert brothers would be leaving their club with the money about now. They should pass the top of this unlit alley in less than ten minutes. No carriage could pass through the narrow twisting street. They would be on foot and easy to ambush, although Slasher and Fancy went nowhere without a half-dozen armed guards. He had a dozen of his best men with him, all ex-soldiers. They would strike before the enemy even knew they were upon them. He did not doubt the outcome. His men had never failed him in the past.

'Remember, I don't want the Gilbert brothers killed. They aren't worth any of you getting hanged for,' Zach instructed. 'Besides, death would be too quick and easy for them. I want those bastards to suffer. And they'll suffer when the opium smugglers discover they've no money to pay them. The men they deal with come from the race which invented torture. Lay all of them out cold if you can. I don't want any of them crying out. Neither do I want Slasher, or Fancy, dragged to safety by one of their men. Once we have the money we run for it.'

Zach nodded for them to get to their places and the army veterans slunk into the darkness. He leant against the wall of a darkened warehouse. High above his head, the pulley above the unloading bay creaked in the night breeze. Rats snuffled and squeaked over indeterminate piles of rubbish, and a tomcat nearby yeowed its satisfaction at taking a mate.

Even at this time of night few of the alleys and streets were deserted. The taverns echoed with the sounds of drunken revelry. Thirty yards away was a street where most doorways were filled with whores, beggars or orphans, looking to turn a last penny before finding a dingy hole to crawl into for the night. Sly-faced men with long greasy hair and hands thrust deep in pockets loitered on corners, ready for a fight, or eyeing passers-by as potential victims to rob. Aged drunks sprawled in the gutters. Old crones and bawds, their syphilitic faces covered with gauze, rummaged in competition with half-starved dogs amongst the discarded slops tossed on to the pavement. Dejected matchgirls and tinkers trudged with their wares-trays to linger hopefully outside taverns. A last sale would enable them to buy hot soup or a pie from the all-night bakehouse.

This grinding poverty and squalor was something Zach had never got used to. With the growing success of the club, he had donated large sums of money to Dr Barnado's, and to the home for unmarried mothers which Kara devoted so much time to. 'The Reform House for Fallen Women' was what he called it. He grinned wryly. He'd also had an interest in fallen women before his marriage; though it had been in the enjoyment of their company, not seeking to reform them. Kara was the voice of his conscience. Apart from Beatrice, or an occasional tumble with a serving maid, it was not often he strayed from his wife's bed. At thirty-four he had found himself strangely content with his home and family life. Marriage had mellowed the reprobate in him, without him realising it.

Not that he was *so* reformed. His vendetta tonight was proof of that. He concentrated on the task ahead, going over any scenario which could end in disaster, and planning how to counteract it. Waiting was the hard part. It was like before a battle. He was conscious of the heavy thud of his heartbeat, the trickle of sweat along his spine. His breathing was shallow, his body taut with nervous tension. In his pocket was his army revolver, though he had given instructions that guns were only to be used as a last resort. He had spent too long keeping a low profile over his underworld activities to blow it all in a mindless gang-killing of the Gilbert brothers.

Within a few minutes he heard the sound of advancing footsteps. He felt the rush of adrenaline through his blood. Then his mind was crystal clear, as it had been in every battle.

It was all over so quickly, even Zach was surprised. The heavy carpet bags were taken. Slasher's bodyguards were overpowered; daggers pressing into their necks, freezing their retaliation.

'Move and you get the same treatment Slasher gives all his enemies. A slit throat,' Zach rapped out. 'Fitting end for scum taking his pay.'

He bent over Slasher, who had been forced to his knees in the gutter. His hand was clamped over the villain's mouth to muffle his cries. The gangleader's eyes bulged with fear.

'There's no one to help you. You've got this coming, you bastard,' Zach snarled, and brought his knee up to slam into the man's fleshy chin. The neck cracked back with a sickening thud. Slasher groaned as his teeth ripped through his lip. As his head flopped forward, Zach drew back his foot and kicked him in the groin. 'That's for what you did to me before my wedding.'

Beneath Zach's hand over his mouth, he groaned in agony, then slumped over, half unconscious. Released by his captor, Slasher's legs and body twitched in spasms on the ground, his hands clutching his groin.

Zach rounded on Fancy. Two of his men, who had previously been beaten senseless by the Gilbert gang as a warning not to work their district, were hammering into him with their fists. His face was a bloody mask.

'That's for the beatings you gave Beatrice,' Zach declared. 'It's time you both got a taste of your own medicine. By now the Chinks should be looking for you. You're late with your pay-off.'

He nodded to his men to step back. Fancy was out cold. A quick survey showed him that all the Gilberts' men were unconscious.

'We'll leave the opium dealers to finish them off. Let's get out of here.'

Fancy was the first of his gang to regain consciousness. Beside him lay the groaning figure of his brother. Running footsteps and the excited jabber of Chinese voices were close to the turning. He shook his head and winced at the stabbing pain in his skull.

'Leg it, Slasher,' he croaked. 'The Chinks are here.'

He staggered to his knees and then upright. A couple of the bodyguards were beginning to stir. He didn't trouble with them. They'd failed to protect him and his brother. If the Chinks didn't finish them off – if he lived – then he would kill them. His fear was for Slasher, who was still squirming in the mire of the gutter making inarticulate sounds. He had just taken a step towards his brother to help him when the first of the Chinamen rounded the corner.

Fancy was still hidden by the shadows. If he tried to save Slasher, they'd both be dead meat. He retreated further into the blackness. He knew this district as well as he knew his own back yard. A dozen yards away was a cul-de-sac where there was a sewer cover. He hobbled to it, using his dagger to hook the iron lid out of the cobbles. As his feet slid into the aperture, the sound of the gushing water told him the sewer was full. He could hear the Chinamen gabbling as they found Slasher. Several footsteps ran past the cul-de-sac, which looked deserted as he lowered the sewer cover over his vanishing figure. It would only be seconds before they doubled back. He climbed down the iron rungs of a ladder set into the sewer wall, sliding the cover over his head and into place. Outside he heard the first screams from his brother.

The cover grated as it was repositioned. Darkness surrounded him, as cloaking as the grave. The acrid stench of excrement clawed at his nostrils and throat, making him gag.

'You'll pay for this, Morton. Yer should have done fer me when yer 'ad the chance. Yer'll pay for Slasher's death. Yer and that tart of mine yer took up wiv.'

A quarter of an hour later, Zach handed Dipper his disguise to dispose of, and strolled back into The Gentleman's Retreat. Placing the four heavy carpet bags on his desk, he tipped out their contents. He chuckled with delight as the pouches of golden sovereigns spilled across the green leather top.

Ten minutes later, the money locked in his safe, he was mixing with the supper guests. When he later ascended the stairs on his way to the gaming rooms, he saw the door to one of the private salons open. The king appeared, a satisfied smile on his bewhiskered face.

Zach inclined his head in deferential salute to the departing figure of the monarch. He drew contentedly on his large cigar. Beatrice had not failed him. Her success filled him with elation. A sister-in-law who was the king's mistress presented many possibilities for advancement.

A cloudburst made the small wedding party run from the steps of Westminster Abbey to the awaiting motor cavalcade, umbrellas raised to protect their finery. Beatrice was scowling as she looked down at her ivory silk and lace wedding gown, its long trailing train and hem sewn with seed pearls splashed with grey filth.

'It's ruined. My lovely gown is ruined,' Beatrice groaned.

Freddie laughed softly. 'Does it matter? You are Lady Mountgibbons now. You need never wear the same ballgown twice if you do not wish to.' He pulled her into his arms and kissed her. 'My darling. You have made me the happiest of men this day.'

Impatiently, she pulled back from him. 'Freddie, you're ruining my hair. How can I arrive at the Savoy looking all mussed up like a trollop?' She patted the upswept coiffure, pressing back into place several pins, and straightening the diamond tiara holding her veil.

'You never used to be so fussy,' he said peevishly. He reached for her and slid his hand up her calf beneath her petticoats to touch the bare flesh of her thigh above her garter.

Beatrice clamped her legs tightly shut. 'Not here, Freddie.' She pushed his hand away. 'People will see. I'm your wife. I should be treated with respect. For you, I've given up all my gentleman admirers. Yet you would still treat me like a whore.'

Freddie glowered at her. 'Changed your tune, haven't you? If I'd wanted a prude for a bride, I could have chosen from amongst a score of debutantes. I wanted a woman with fire in her blood. You're a whore, Bea. But you're my whore and no one else's. Remember that.'

The indolent lover she had ruled with ease was no longer apparent. Instead the arrogant manner he had displayed when they'd first met had returned. He was addressing her as a lord would his serf.

'I'm your wife and your lady,' she responded tartly.

'And I'm your lord and your master. You're my wife, but you're not my equal in birth.'

'This is 1909, not the dark ages!' she said, growing angry at his unexpected belligerence. Her devoted Freddie was at heart a tyrant. This was a side of him she had forgotten about. After their first night together, he had always since been pleading, eager to comply with all her wishes to keep her favours.

He took her breast in his hand and squeezed it. 'You've led me a merry dance for months.' The husky note of desire entered his voice, mellowing his anger. 'I love you, Beatrice, but I will not be made a fool of by you, or have my family name dishonoured.'

He kissed her with savage possession, his manner alarming her. She had underestimated him. She had been dazzled by the prospect of a title and the belief that he was a malleable young man. She had miscalculated. Five centuries of tyrannical rule ran in his veins. Arrogance glittered in his eyes as he regarded her.

'You are beautiful. You are the toast of London. And were elusive. Others offered you marriage and you refused them. Yet you chose me.' His voice harshened with possessive fervour. 'I saw the way the king looked at you on Derby day. Even His Majesty will envy me having you constantly at my side. You are mine – and mine alone. I was forced to share you as my mistress. As my wife you are solely mine. We leave tonight for Crownfield Hall.'

Beatrice was stunned. Freddie had deceived her. Tricked her. He had promised everything she desired would be hers when they wed. She had believed that he would complacently accept her becoming King Edward's mistress. Clearly he would not. Her grand illusions were stripped from her. How dare he presume to drag her off to moulder in the seclusion of his estate? Her temper flared dangerously. With an effort she controlled it. Two could play at deception. She was a past expert.

'Freddie, my love.' She touched his cheek with her gloved finger, provocatively trailing it across his lips. 'You sound so cross and grumpy. So suspicious of your loving Beatrice. Much as I'll adore being mistress of Crownfield Hall, I was so looking forward to a honeymoon in Europe. Then I'd assumed that we would spend the rest of the season in London. I'd be so proud to be seen on your arm as Lady Mountgibbons.'

'One cannot put personal pleasure before

family tradition, my dear. It is more fitting that a bride first visits her new home.'

A home, or a prison? She suppressed a shudder. Marriage was not the glittering prize she had envisioned. If she left London for Crownfield Hall, she had a premonition that it would be months before Freddie returned to London. Out of the king's sight, his interest in her would wane. He would forget her. His roving eye would soon alight upon another, more accessible beauty. She would not go.

Nothing of her rebellion showed in her face as she smiled at her husband. 'Freddie, darling, you sound so masterful. I want no one but you.'

'Then we shall get along very well, my dear.' He grinned boyishly, again reaching for her. When his hand again scooped up her hem and travelled along her leg to her thigh, she feigned pleasure. They were too close to the Savoy for him to demand she oblige him further.

Her voice was silky against his ear. 'I love you too much ever to deny you anything, Freddie my darling. But I want you to be proud of me. Treat me as a whore before your friends and I will become a laughing-stock. That will rebound upon you. Treat me with respect and, by my devotion and fidelity to you, men will envy the man who tamed Beatrice Kempe. Shut me away at Crownfield, and they will laugh at you behind your back. They will say you were not man enough to tame me, that you hid me away like the feudal barons who kept their wayward wives locked in a tower. I wouldn't want them to think that of you, my darling.'

Her hands moved to his groin, feeling his hardening response through the material. 'You are too much of a man for that.'

She kissed him passionately, drawing back with a regretful sigh as the Lanchester halted in front of the Savoy. He was breathing heavily, his eyes dark with desire.

'You will not be shut away at Crownfield Hall, my darling. We will entertain lavishly whilst we are there. You will be its finest jewel, and I shall shower you with riches and position. But deny, or fail me... Dare to follow your old ways and take another lover, no matter how elevated...' He paused significantly. Beatrice felt her palms break out in a cold sweat. He knew the king desired her. '...Then I will not hesitate to banish you. Not to Crownfield Hall, but to a smaller estate in Ireland. I shall say that you contracted the consumption which killed your mother, and are taking a cure in Switzerland.'

The door of the carriage was wrenched open by the Honourable James Westman and Lord Blackworth. There was a press of young noblemen behind them, all clamouring for sight of the bride.

Freddie stepped on to the kerb and, as they walked through the foyer of the Savoy to their private dining room, he possessively took her arm to keep her close by his side.

Beatrice bit her lips to stop her heated retort at his conduct. Her husband was a pompous braggart. Who did the little squirt think he was? She had wound Fancy Gilbert around her finger for years. He'd never tamed her by his brutality.

Neither would Freddie by his bullying threats. She would use all her wiles to stay in London. Before the month was out she intended to entertain the king in her bed again.

Chapter Twenty-four

At the same moment that the wedding party toasted the health of Lord and Lady Mount-gibbons, Bessie Brown stirred and cursed. She'd fallen asleep on a wooden bench, her head against the wall of the ratting cellar. Her temple ached from the gin she had drunk the previous evening. A dozen other snoring forms were sprawled on benches, tables and chairs, too in-ebriated to stagger to their homes. She rose stiffly, scratching at her hair, and expertly cracked a louse between her fingers. She licked her parched lips. God, she needed a drink. Where the hell was Fancy? He'd been supposed to meet her at the club two nights ago. The bastard hadn't showed up. Not that she was sorry. Her body was still bruised from his brutal assault on her earlier in the week.

She sauntered to the door. The club stank of stale drink, sweat and vomit. She needed fresh air. She wrenched open the basement door of the club. Her screams started the other occupants awake.

Bleary-eyed, they peered at Bessie's plump figure slumped on the ground, her hands covering her face as she screamed hysterically.

'Shut that bleedin' row.' A snarling villain lifted his hand to cuff her.

It froze in mid-air. He was staring past her to the open door. Hidden from passers-by, in the dark shadows of the basement staircase, was the headless corpse of Slasher Gilbert, suspended from the iron railings outside the door.

Throughout the wedding reception at the Savoy, Beatrice charmed all Freddie's friends. Play-acting the part of a devoted wife, she fussed over her husband. She was determined to dissuade him from taking her off to Crownfield Hall.

Zach leaned across the dining table and grinned at Mountgibbons. 'I've never seen Beatrice so considerate of a man's needs.'

'That's because Freddie is the only man I have ever considered marrying,' she retorted with an adoring smile at her husband.

'Watch out, old boy,' Blackworth chortled. 'I can see the old ball and chain rattling in the background now you're wed.'

The Honourable James Westman sniggered into his wine glass. 'Beatrice can crack a whip or two over me, if Freddie isn't up to muster.'

Beatrice parried the bawdry, her attention all for her husband. It wasn't until the hired musicians had struck up a waltz, and Freddie led her on to the floor, that her good intentions faltered. Zach was dancing with Kara. He was laughing at something she had said, and his expression was so tender that jealousy consumed her.

'You must dance with my sister, Freddie,' Beatrice insisted. 'It's time we mixed with our guests.'

'You're the only woman I want to hold in my arms, Bea.' He slurred his words. He had been drinking heavily throughout the meal.

'In an hour or two you will have me alone to command in all you will. Until then you must do your duty as groom and mix with our guests.'

His initial reluctance was fleeting. Beatrice was not amused when she saw how he smiled with pleasure as he led Kara away from her husband.

Beatrice approached Zach. 'Since Freddie is dancing with Kara, will you honour the bride with a dance?'

'My pleasure.'

'It was always mine to be held in your arms, Zach.'

His amber eyes narrowed. 'Mountgibbons adores you, but he's the jealous type.'

'True. He intends to take me straight to Crownfield Hall. I'm not going. The king will–'

'The king will not countenance a scandal,' Zach warned.

'I thought you'd see the advantage of my being His Majesty's mistress.'

'I also see the disadvantages of a scandal breaking. The Gentleman's Retreat would be abandoned by the Marlborough House set and their friends. I could be ruined.'

'So you'd see me rot in Staffordshire.' Red colour stained her cheeks. 'I thought you cared for me, Zach. After all we've shared…'

His expression hardened. 'By mutual agreement we shared some pleasurable hours in bed. You knew there was nothing more. You had your pleasure, as I had mine. That was all. Don't make more of it than what it was.'

'You bastard!' she spat through clenched teeth.

'Don't get angry, Bea. People are watching you.' He raised a dark, mocking brow. 'This is your wedding day. Be happy. Freddie adores you. He'll shower you with riches and jewels. Isn't that what you wanted? He made you a baroness, no less. You'll want for nothing.'

'I don't love Freddie. I love you, Zach. I always have. Even before you met Kara.'

'Then that's your misfortune. I don't love you.'

Pain slashed through her heart at his brutality. 'Do you love Kara?'

He tensed, standing stiffly to attention. He glanced towards his wife, who was nodding and smiling at she listened to Freddie praising her sister's beauty. Her body swayed sensuously to the rhythm of the waltz. Her figure, still slender after giving birth to five children, held him captivated. She was beautiful and graceful.

'Yes, I believe that I do. I had not fully realised it before.'

Beatrice closed her eyes. She didn't want Freddie Mountgibbons. She didn't even want the king. She wanted Zach. And if she couldn't have him, then no one would.

Fancy Gilbert had emerged cautiously from the sewers just before daybreak. He'd been fearful of returning to his rooms. The Chinks would be after him. And they were vicious bastards. He slunk away in the darkness, cursing the foul stench which clung to his clothes from the sewer.

He growled low in his throat and lashed out when he tripped over a drunk asleep in a doorway. Without compunction he clubbed him with his pistol butt and stripped him of his clothes. They were far from clean, but were dry and did not reek of shit. As he worked, he kept glancing over his shoulder, alert for any stalking figures. The dark alleys were never empty. Beggars and urchins crawled into any shelter they could find – an upturned barrel or a broken wooden crate.

As he tugged the ragged trousers from the bony legs, he realised that he had killed the man. He felt no remorse. Casting another furtive glance behind him, he thought he saw a figure slinking into a doorway. He gripped his pistol and froze, waiting to see if it moved. Nothing. Not even a rat scurried into the gutter. It must have been the moonlight playing tricks with his nerves.

Twice more he thought he heard a noise behind him. He trembled. The Chinese were dangerous enemies. Opium was a dirty trade and attracted the most ruthless villains. Whirling around, he scanned the street dappled in silvery moonlight. Again nothing.

'Yer losing yer nerve,' he muttered, unable to shut out Slasher's screams from his mind. He'd best lie low for a few days. There must be somewhere the Chinks would never find him.

He had prowled the streets for an hour. All the time the hairs at the back of his neck had sensed a stealthy presence behind him. But whenever he swivelled round to challenge it, the street was deserted. He was scared shitless and it showed. Twice he tripped over a sleeping form and cried out in alarm. A bat swooped down from a belfry in Ludgate and he fired his pistol in terror. The loud retort made him dart through the backstreets to the riverfront. He finally fell exhausted and trembling into an old bolt-hole in a disused warehouse near Billingsgate. He was miles from his usual haunts. He'd be safe here.

He did not dare leave his hiding place for two days. His battered and exhausted body needed sleep more than it needed food. Hunger awoke him. It was daylight and he was lying in a puddle of rain which had dripped from a leak in the roof. He sighed with relief. He'd shown the Chinks a clean pair of heels.

Rolling over, his leg brushed against something hard wrapped in sacking. His first thought was that one of his men had discovered his whereabouts and left him some food.

His stomach growled and he sat up, shaking his head to clear his wits. He had some serious thinking to do. His gaze fell upon the sacking bundle in contemplation of satisfying his hunger. His eyes widened in horror. Blood had seeped through the coarse hessian and dried. His stomach contracted with fear. Shaking violently, he kicked the repellent sack away. His boot hit a solid object. The cloth moved, the top opening. A brown, red and pink ball rolled to rest by his thigh.

Fancy sprang to his feet, vomit rushing from his throat. The bloodied face of Slasher, his lips twisted in an agonised death scream, lay on the floor. Both eyes had been gouged out. His ears had been cut off and his nose was slit.

The Chinks had followed him. This was their gruesome warning. That they had not seized him and tortured him already meant that they intended that he should sweat. At the sound of a footfall, his bladder emptied in terror. Four figures were advancing towards him.

In the weeks leading up to autumn, Kara immersed herself in work to blot Richard from her mind. Louise still remained in their house. She had been painfully shy with her father and begged not to be taken away from Harry and Tim. Kara had agreed she could stay until she felt ready to leave. Richard visited her twice a week, taking her to the zoological gardens, or to one of the parks. Kara ensured she was never at home on those days. On Sundays she took her own children to picnic by the river with Zach, or attended a garden party. In the first week of September, Richard sent a letter informing her that he would collect Louise the following Wednesday. He had now engaged a nanny and a housekeeper, so Louise would be living with him in Belgravia.

Expecting Richard to arrive after office hours, Kara returned early from an antique book auction to ensure that everything was in readiness for his daughter's departure. On entering the nursery, she froze in the doorway. Richard was already there with Louise. He was seated in a rocking chair. His daughter was curled on his lap as he read from Lewis Carroll's *Alice in*

Wonderland. The twins were at his feet listening raptly. As usual the boys were persistent with their questions.

Kara was about to leave before her presence was discovered, when Tim's curiosity brought a smile to her lips. She lingered upon hearing him ask, 'What made the Mad Hatter mad?'

'And why doesn't the king cut off the wicked queen's head?' Harry hugged his knees close to his chest, his violent eyes intense.

Richard laughed and ruffled Harry's curly cap of hair. 'What a bloodthirsty lad you are.'

'Anyway, it's just a story,' Tim declared. 'It's pretend. You went to a real wonderland didn't you, sir? Mama said you're an explorer. Did you have adventures? Did you kill monsters?'

'I wasn't that sort of explorer, Tim. Nothing so glamorous.'

'I want to be an explorer when I grow up.' Harry jumped to his feet and waved his arm about as though he was fighting with a sword. 'I want to discover new lands and slay dragons.'

'There aren't many dragons left,' Richard said gravely, humouring rather than patronising the boy. 'But there're always new discoveries to be made about this wonderful world of ours.'

Unwittingly, Kara made a small sound in her throat as she swallowed against a tight knot of emotion. Seeing Richard and their sons together made her love for him almost too painful to bear. The sound lifted Richard's gaze to hers. He and both the twins turned to face her. The similarity in their hair colouring and facial expressions was so strong that her heart jolted. Soon others would note the resemblance, and speculate as to whether Richard or Zach was their father.

Panic flooded through her. At some time in the future she would have to pay the price of her deception. Dear God, she fervently prayed, let it not be catastrophic.

Richard gently set Louise on the floor and stood up. 'I've come to take Louise. Nanny is collecting her things together. I wanted to thank you personally for all the love and care you've given her.'

'She's a very lovable child. I was honoured to be chosen.' Kara's voice was tight. They were standing as rigidly and formally as strangers. 'I shall miss her.'

'Louise is very fond of the twins.' Richard smiled fondly at the boys, who had taken Louise to one side. They were now kneeling on the floor playing tiddlywinks together. 'I'd like her to see them from time to time. Is that possible? They're good lads. Zach must be proud of them.'

Kara blinked aside a wayward tear. 'He is. Of course Louise must see them. The two nannies can arrange it.'

For a long moment they studied each other in silence. At last Richard said, 'Remember I will always be there for you, if you have need of me.'

'Perhaps Miss Fenella Sommerfield would object.' She could not hold her jealousy back. 'Do you love her, Richard?'

'You must know that I do not. She's a charming companion.'

'I had no right to ask.'

Nanny Cummins appeared at the door carrying

Louise's suitcase. A footman followed behind her with a trunk of toys and other possessions.

There was a shout of delight from Louise. 'I won, I won! Papa, Aunt Kara, I won. First time ever! I beat Tim and Harry.'

Kara saw the tell-tale glitter of tears in the twins' eyes, which they were manfully trying to hide. They didn't want this parting, and had let Louise win to make it easier for the girl. Kara's heart swelled with pride at such thoughtfulness in boys so young.

'Louise,' she said softly. 'It is time to leave with your Papa. Say goodbye to Tim and Harry. You will see them again soon.'

With the fickleness of the young, Louise jumped to her feet and ran to take her father's hand. ''Bye Tim. 'Bye Harry.' She stood shyly for a moment, then broke free of Richard's gasp and flung herself towards Kara.

Kara knelt and took her into her arms, tears streaming down her cheeks as she kissed the little girl. 'Be a good girl, Louise. You will still come and have tea with the boys, and I will visit you when I can.'

'I love you, Aunt Kara,' Louise said fiercely.

Kara held her away from her and ran her fingers through the blonde ringlets. 'I love you, too, Louise. You have your Papa to love now. Your place is with him.'

'I wish it could be with both of you. You, and Papa, Tim and Harry, are the people I love most in all the world.'

Richard and Kara held each other's gazes for a long moment over the child's head. Their own love for each other radiated between them. Then abruptly, and without another word, Richard hoisted Louise into his arms and walked quickly from the nursery. Kara did not follow. She dared not.

Beatrice fretted at Crownfield Hall for three boring months. No amount of pleading had prevented Freddie insisting that they spend their honeymoon on his estate. She had been tempted to refuse to go, and let the gossips think what they liked about her marriage. But scandal had to be avoided if she wanted to continue as the king's mistress. She checked her anger. The only way she would get Freddie to return to London was to make him believe there was no danger of her betraying him.

Not once had she complained of her imposed exile. Always she had acted the passionate and loving bride to win his trust. He had kept his promise, and they were never free of guests. Most of them bored Beatrice. They were snooty aristocrats, shallow and self-centred. She knew they looked down their haughty noses at her lowly birth, and she despised them for it.

As the leaves turned golden and began to fall, Beatrice's patience was at an end. She sought out Freddie in the study after he had finished his morning's business with his steward.

'My darling, I have such wonderful news.' She slid her arms around him and kissed his cheek.

He pulled her down on to his lap. 'You look adorable, Bea. What have you been up to?'

'It's what we've both been up to, my darling. I

do believe I'm pregnant. Though I would like to see a doctor to confirm it.'

'Pregnant so soon, Bea?' Freddie beamed at her. 'I say, that calls for a celebration. Of course, you must have the best care. Midwife Hughes is still on the estate. She delivered me. I'll get her to examine you. Today.'

'No, Freddie.' Beatrice stood up. This was not at all what she had planned. She was not pregnant and had begun to suspect that she was barren after her abortions and miscarriages, but Freddie must never suspect that. He often spoke of an heir for Crownfield. She had decided that a phantom pregnancy was the only way to get back to London.

'I don't want a country midwife to bring the heir to Crownfield into the world,' she flared. 'I want the finest London doctor.'

'Hughes was good enough for my mother,' Freddie began, a petulant scowl marring his good looks.

'I'm frightened, Freddie. Didn't Kara's best friend die in childbirth?' Beatrice burst into theatrical tears. 'I don't want to die, Freddie. I don't want a country midwife.'

Instantly, Freddie took her sobbing figure into his arms. 'My darling, you mustn't be frightened. What is more natural than giving birth?'

She wept more loudly. 'You're a man – what would you know? Mama always said that if woman had produced the first child and man the second, there would never have been a third. If you love me, you won't let me suffer. Oh, Freddie, I'm so frightened.'

'It's your condition which is making you fanciful. You're a strapping strong woman, Beatrice, I'm amazed you can act so irrationally.'

Realising that her tactics were not working, she wrenched away from him. 'I won't endanger the life of myself, or my child. It's my duty to give you a healthy heir. I want to be assured that everything is well with this baby.' She paused, looking suitably stricken and repentant. 'I never told you, but I miscarried some years ago. I was so ill I nearly died.'

'Why didn't you tell me?' His tone was guarded, his stance becoming arrogant.

When he struck that pose she actively disliked him. He was so remote, so supercilious. Only two hours earlier he had awoken her with fervent kisses, his lovemaking more tender and fulfilling than that of any of her other lovers. If only he didn't act so much of a gaoler, she could have been happy with him.

'It was some years ago. You know I hate talking about my past – what I endured when Fancy Gilbert was my lover. He beat me and I lost the child. I have nightmares about it still.'

The nightmares were true. Rarely a week passed when the images of the last years with Fancy did not return to terrorise her. Freddie always comforted her, and they would make love to banish her fears.

She eyed him defiantly. 'I made no secret about my life. You know what I was before I became hostess at The Gentleman's Retreat. You promised me you would never reprove me for my past. I've tried so hard to be a good wife to you and to entertain your friends. Although I know they all despise me.'

'That's nonsense! Westman and Blackworth adore you, as do Harman and Carrington.'

Beatrice did not tell Freddie that each of those so-called friends had propositioned her since her marriage. She had refused them. She might resent being forced to stay at Crownfield Hall, but in every other way Freddie pandered to her wishes. She had fine clothes, and jewels beyond her wildest dreams. Since horses terrified her, he had even indulged her by teaching her to drive the Lanchester, and had promised to buy her a car of her own.

She wrung her hands. A tantrum would only make him turn from her in disgust. 'I am frightened, Freddie. So frightened. Do I ask so much?'

The arrogance left his face, replaced by tender concern. 'Then you shall be reassured by a London doctor.' He took her back into his arms. 'I can refuse you nothing, especially now.'

Beatrice kissed him on the lips and immediately he responded by drawing her down on to the tiger skin which lay on the Indian carpet.

'I love you so much, Bea,' he murmured as he pressed kisses along her neck and began to unfasten the buttons on her lace blouse. 'I can't bear the thought of so many men admiring you in London. I'd kill anyone who ever tried to take you from me.'

'There's no danger of that, my darling,' Beatrice answered throatily. His hand slid beneath her skirts to caress the silken skin of her bare thighs above her stockings. His ardour roused her passion. Her fingers were impatient at the fastening of his trousers, her breathing quickening as she felt his arousal, hard and swollen, in her hands. To her surprise she no longer feigned her pleasure when he made love to her. Freddie knew how to set her blood on fire.

Drawing her blouse down to her waist, he buried his face in her breasts, sucking at each hardened nipple. With an impassioned moan, she reared up and hooked her legs over his shoulders.

'I love you, Bea. But you are mine,' he groaned as he thrust with gathering momentum into her. 'Only mine.' His words were muffled as his desire made his breathing ragged. When he finally laid his head on her breasts, his body replete and slick with sweat, he murmured, 'You are mine. No other man shall have you.'

Zach returned early from The Gentleman's Retreat to spend an afternoon with Kara as it was her half-day. Dilys, their maid, bobbed a curtsy as he entered the house.

'Mrs Morton was called away, sir. There was a phone call from the manager in the Leytonstone shop. It was broken into last night. The police needed an inventory of stock. The mistress has gone there.'

The maid eyed him speculatively, her expression saucy and inviting. Zach smiled at her. She was as black-haired as a gypsy, with sultry grey eyes. Plump and pretty, she was an obliging wench who had whiled away the odd hour when he had been at a loose end. He was usually discreet with any of the maids in their employment, but Dilys was so keen to please, so eager to learn all there was about the sexual act, that she had tempted him to stray more than most. Like others before her, when he became bored with her, she would be paid off with a handsome recompense and reference.

'Bring me tea in my study,' he ordered. He was annoyed with Kara for not being here, and the maid's bold stare had roused his ardour.

Ten minutes later she placed the tea-tray on a side table and waited, her eyes wide and expectant, her breathing already erratic.

'Lock the door, Dilys. We don't want the housekeeper coming upon us.'

As she ran back into his arms, he twisted her around until she was lying across the desk. Then, with a deft flick of her long skirts and petticoats, he exposed her legs which were clad in thick black stockings with a red garter above each knee. The garters had been his last present to her, and he was delighted that she was wearing them.

He opened his trousers and entered her swiftly, his excitement rising as she moaned in ecstasy against his cheek.

'Oh that's good – so good. Ooooh!' Dilys gasped as she writhed beneath him.

Her fingers clawed his back. Zach shifted, unwilling to be marked by her nails. Her heels were drumming into his buttocks as he drove into her; then, with a sharp cry, he collapsed on to her soft flesh.

'You really are quite something, Dilys,' he said, easing back on to his elbows. Her face was flushed, tiny tendrils of black hair corkscrewing damply to her temple where they had escaped her maid's cap.

'Each time it gets more wonderful. Did I please you, sir?'

'As always you pleased me very much, Dilys.' Zach grinned, wickedly.

She dimpled with pleasure. 'I want to please you so much. I live for these moments when we can be together.'

Zach frowned. He heard the possessive note in her voice and disliked it. The girl was fresh up from the country in Dagenham, and a little too gauche for his taste. It was time she was given notice. He was about to caution her about getting too involved when he heard Beatrice's voice in the hallway.

'Straighten your clothes. Be quick, girl,' he snapped as he adjusted his own clothing and stepped in front of the mirror over the fireplace to smooth down his hair and realign his necktie. He unlocked the door and held it open for Dilys to pass through.

'Beatrice,' he greeted. 'What a surprise. I was just about to take tea.' He turned to the maid, annoyed to see that she was looking rather mussed, her cheeks still flushed. 'Bring another cup for Lady Mountgibbons. We will take tea in the parlour now, Dilys.'

Beatrice raised an auburn brow as she sauntered past him along the hall to enter the parlour. 'Up to your old tricks again, Zach. I thought you had more sense than to dip your wick on your own doorstep.'

He didn't reply, but his lips thinned with annoyance at being caught out.

Beatrice paced for some moments before taking a seat. The room had a double glass door which opened into a large glass conservatory filled with exotic ferns. Beyond that the lawn with its several weeping willows ran down to the riverbank. It was a beautiful house and garden. But not a patch on Crownfield, Beatrice reflected with satisfaction.

As Zach entered behind her, she turned to stand on tiptoe and kiss his cheek. She was piqued that he did not hold her close.

Peevishly she retorted. 'Ugh, I can smell her on you. Just as well it was me who arrived and not Kara.'

Zach returned with equal sarcasm, 'So Freddie has finally allowed you the freedom of London, to return to your old tricks?'

'For all Crownfield's forty-room splendour, it's no joking matter to be incarcerated there. Subterfuge was the only way I could get back to London.'

'And how did you do that?'

'I told him I was pregnant.'

'Congratulations.'

She glared impatiently at him. 'I'm not actually. I was desperate, but not that desperate. I've no intention of being saddled with a horde of screaming kids. Besides, Freddie doesn't know, but I think I'm barren.'

'That was a cruel trick, even for you, Bea.' Zach stopped smiling. 'I daresay, by now, Freddie is spreading the news of his impending heir all round his London clubs. He'll look a fool when the truth comes out. He's a good chap, Mountgibbons. You're an idiot to deceive him. I'd have thought you had the sense to realise when you're well off.'

'I'll take to my bed for a week with a feigned miscarriage if I have to.' She dismissed his derogatory remarks. 'I couldn't stay in the country, and you know why? Has the king been to the club? Did he ask after me?'

Zach looked at her in astonishment. 'That path will only lead to ruin, Bea. You can't mean to risk your marriage to become another of the king's light-o'-loves. Freddie isn't the green boy you seem to think him. He's proud. I've met many of his sort in the army. Honour is everything to them. He'll divorce you. Or possibly have you locked up as insane. You wouldn't be the first unfaithful wife to be committed to an asylum.'

'Are you trying to protect me, or your wife's reputation? It wouldn't do her precious business any good if her sister was involved in a scandal, would it? Though I suspect having Lady Mountgibbons as her sister had increased her prestige.'

'I was thinking of you, Bea,' Zach answered stiffly.

She regarded his tall, slim figure through narrowed eyes. 'I doubt it. You always were a selfish bastard. You are looking to protect the reputation of The Retreat. You don't care about me. You never did.'

Zach saw the flush in Beatrice's cheeks. Her temper was up and at such times she could be unpredictable and dangerous. He had hoped that, once married to Mountgibbons, she'd cease to be a problem. Clearly not. Her ambitions were too high. A scandal would not only end her marriage, but it would ruin him and Kara too. She had to be made to see reason.

'You have the world at your feet,' he reasoned. 'And more wealth than you could have dreamed possible two years ago. Mountgibbons adores you.'

'He's so possessive. I'm a prisoner. I can't live like that,' she raged.

'Just give him time. He knows your past. He loves you. He's frightened of losing you. He has to learn to trust you. Prove to him there's no one else. Then he'll loosen the leading reins. He'll want to show you off as a prize. He won't be able to refuse you anything. You're Lady Mountgibbons now. He's faced ridicule to make you his. Doesn't he deserve your respect? You've come a long way from the life you led with Fancy Gilbert.'

'Thank God both those perverted, murdering bastards are dead.'

Zach did not remind her that only Slasher's body had been found. His own men had searched for Fancy. There had been no sign of him in the underworld haunts. His body had probably been thrown in the Thames and carried far away by the current. Sometimes it was months before a corpse resurfaced: by then the fishes and decay had rendered the body unidentifiable.

'Be reasonable, Bea,' Zach advised. 'Do you really want to throw away so much for so little?'

'Being the king's mistress is not such a little matter.'

'But he's no longer young and he's far from well.'

'So you won't help me,' she blazed, shooting out an accusing finger to jab at his chest. 'You owe me, Zach. I know what went on that night the king came to me at the club. You shopped the Gilberts to the Chinks. What if they were to learn that you stole their money?'

'Don't try and blackmail me, Bea. Mountgibbons won't save you if word gets out you shopped me.'

She regarded him through narrowed eyes, then slowly smiled. It sent a shiver of disquiet through him.

'I reckon we've been through too much together to talk of betrayal,' she said, sweetly. 'All I want is a bit of help. Is that so unreasonable?'

He did not respond. Beatrice was up to something and he didn't trust her. When her hand spread out across his chest, her fingers sliding beneath a shirt button to scratch lightly at his skin, he caught her wrist.

'No games, Bea,' he warned.

She pouted. 'It's been five years since The Retreat opened. We've been partners a long time. Why not have a dinner party at the club to celebrate the anniversary of its opening? It comes up in a few weeks. Kara will give the proceedings an air of respectability. I, as past hostess, would naturally be expected to be there. Freddie won't complain at that. And if His Majesty should receive an invitation...'

'I won't have Kara involved,' Zach snapped. 'She's worked hard to get her shops established. She's a remarkable woman. She'd be hurt to learn what you're planning. She's so proud you married well.'

'I'm not doing this for her, but for me.'

'Exactly. I won't have Kara shamed by your behaviour. She's so good and kind. She never saw you for the scheming baggage you are. She's never guessed how you've hated her all these years. You're not fit to tread the same floor as her. Ruin your life if you must, but don't involve my wife.'

Something snapped in Beatrice. She had spent three miserable months in the country. She still loved Zach and he had shown no warmth at their meeting. Her hatred for Kara erupted into white-hot fury.

'Always Kara must be protected! Nothing must harm her! You delude yourself if you believe your dear wife is sweet and innocent. She's played you for a fool all along.'

Zach closed in on her, his amber eyes slitted with anger. 'What would a scheming whore know of decency? Kara is a perfect wife. She spares herself nothing in bringing up our children, or working on her charities for unmarried mothers. Not to mention the success of her shops. I think you had better leave. We have nothing more to say to each other.'

'Don't we?' She rounded on him, her face tense with malice. 'For years all I've heard is how perfect dear sister Kara is. She's not so bloody perfect. For all her airs and graces, she's no better than a whore. Those precious twins you boast so proudly of aren't even yours! Seven-month babes, my arse! She married you so fast because she was carrying another man's bastard. Another man's twin bastards, to be exact.'

At seeing his face pale, she laughed cruelly. Ruthlessly, she pressed her advantage, wanting to hurt him as he had hurt her. 'You're so full of your own conceit, you can't see that they're the image of their father. Richard Tennent. Two months before you wed Kara, she was at the opera with him, wasn't she? I was so sick of having her held up as a paragon of virtue that I made a few inquiries some years ago. They didn't go straight home that night. They went to a private room in a restaurant.'

A stinging slap across her cheeks stunned her into silence. Zach never raised his hand to any woman. But then she had never seen him looking so murderous before. Holding her cheek, she backed away.

'Get out!' he raged. 'Get out of this house before I kill you.'

She regarded him malevolently. His proud shoulders had stooped and his swarthy skin was ashen. Only his eyes showed any life. What she saw in their depths was the look of a man who would sell his soul to the devil to wreak his revenge.

'I'm leaving. But I weren't the one who took you for a sucker.' She twisted the knife that she knew would be tearing his guts apart. It was obvious Zach loved Kara. For that she could never forgive him. Again she was second-best to her sister. 'I weren't the one who foisted two bastards on you and let you believe they were your own. Your dear wife ain't so sweet and innocent, is she?'

Chapter Twenty-five

'Who is the father of Harry and Tim?' Zach demanded the moment Kara stepped into the parlour. He was standing by the fireplace, a brandy glass in his hand, his face pale and menacing. From the slurring of his voice it was obvious that he had been drinking heavily.

'Zach, what are you talking about?' Kara strove to appear calm, though her heart was pounding.

'You know very well what I'm saying.' His amber eyes were like a wolf's assessing its prey. 'Were the twins seven-month babies, or full-term? Am I the twins' father? Or is it Tennent? You were at the opera alone with him nine months before they were born.'

It felt as though every drop of blood had drained from her heart. With slow, controlled movements, she drew the hatpins from her hat, removed it and laid it on a side table, then peeled off her gloves. 'I can only believe it is the drink talking. Who can be spreading such evil mischief?'

'Don't twist the blame.' Zach drained his brandy glass. 'I always wondered why you wed me so fast.'

'Have you forgotten how ardent a suitor you were? After the Gilbert brothers threatened me, you were the one who insisted on an immediate marriage.'

'Aye, I played into your hands, didn't I?'

'Is it so inconceivable that I fell under your charm? You were determined to get your hands on my fortune, if I remember. I thought we had resolved all that. I thought we were happy together, Zach.'

'Your supposed fortune did attract me. I don't deny that. But if you've lied to me about the boys…' The tense lines of his face showed his pain. 'Have you taken me for a fool all along? You were alone with Tennent at the opera. I could not take my eyes off you in the box that night, you looked so ravishing. There were some very tender exchanges between the two of you.'

Kara clasped her hands tightly together and willed her heart to stop its frantic pumping. Zach's mood was dangerous, but she must appear calm and counter his accusations with cool assurance. 'I made no secret that Richard and I were friends. We had many interests in common. That was the first time I had been to the opera. Was it so surprising that I was excited? The only reason I was alone with Richard that evening was because his wife was taken ill at the last moment. I was a guest in their house, remember?'

'But you did not return straight home from the opera, did you?'

'A table had been booked at a restaurant. Elizabeth Tennent insisted that we did not curtail our evening on her account. She would have been upset if we had done so.'

His lip curled back derisively. 'And she wouldn't have been upset to learn that you and her husband became lovers that night?' Zach raised his voice, his jealousy causing his temper to soar.

Kara fought to maintain her composure. His amber eyes bored into her, missing nothing. Her cheeks stung with shame, then drained to a deadly pallor. 'I will not stay here to be insulted in this manner. You adore the twins and they worship you. If gossip is more important to you than–'

'Not so fast.' He bounded across the room and gripped her arms. For the first time in his presence she felt fear. Those golden lupine eyes bored into her, searching the depths of her mind to probe her darkest secret.

'You're lying. You always were a bad liar. Hell! To think I trusted you. I revered you as so innocent, so worthy a woman. You're a whore like your sister. At least she's honest about her morals. How many other lovers have you had behind my back?'

'I have never been unfaithful to you. I took my wedding vows seriously, even if you did not.' She dared not allow her fear to show. But this murderous anger was a side of her husband she had never seen before, although his handpicked bunch of ex-army men were familiar with it. How else could he have risen so high in the underworld hierarchy?

His hands moved to her neck, his thumbs

pressing into her throat. 'You can't clever-talk your way out of this. I can see the fear in your eyes. It's true. The twins aren't my sons. No one plays me for a fool. You'll pay for this humiliation. I'll divorce you. The scandal will destroy you. You'll lose the shops. No one will patronise a business owned by a notorious woman. You'll be ruined. And no judge in the land will give you custody of my children.'

Outside the parlour door, Dilys Hills paused with the tea-tray. Her face was pink with embarrassment on hearing the mistress accuse the master of infidelity. She had become his mistress three months ago when he had come upon her unexpectedly making up the bed in their bedchamber. Since then at least twice a week he had sought her out. Her body still tingled from him making love to her earlier that afternoon. She wanted him again already. She just couldn't get enough of him. From the day he had taken her virginity in his wife's bed, she had wanted him with an all-consuming hunger. She was seventeen and besottedly in love with Zach. She believed his words of seduction. Had he not sworn that she was a temptress who drove him wild with desire? When he caressed her breasts, he told her they were beautiful, her body a heavenly perfection he could drown in. When he possessed her writhing body, his moans of pleasure were proof he must love her. He would not seek her out so frequently if he did not. Her romantic dreams for weeks had been of eventually becoming mistress of this fine house. And wasn't he now about to divorce his wife?

Dilys's heart raced. That could only mean that Zach intended to wed *her*. She pressed her ear closer to the door so as not to miss a single word.

'You will never take my children,' Kara screamed, and began to hit out at Zach. It was her worst nightmare. Even losing the shops and all she had worked for was unimportant against this greater threat. The loneliness of her childhood rushed in on her. The years of misery at being separated from her mother made her desperate. She knew how Florence had suffered. She would not let history repeat itself.

'There's guilt written all over your face,' Zach raged. 'I trusted you, Kara. I thought you were something special. Is Tennent the twins' father?'

'Zach, stop torturing yourself.' Kara tried one last attempt to reason with him. 'What's brought all this about? Who told you such evil things?'

'Beatrice. Your loving sister. She never trusted you. She suspected there was something between you and Tennent. She made inquiries about your stay in his house. You'll be surprised what you can learn if you pay a servant well enough.'

Kara sagged against him with shock. Beatrice had betrayed her. She had thought they had become close. What a fool she had been. Finally she realised how deep was her sister's resentment.

'Beatrice has never forgiven me for marrying you. She loves you, doesn't she? Has she been your mistress as well, Zach?'

'For several years,' he declared, enjoying her pain and seeing the disillusion. She did not deserve any mercy. She'd lied to him about the twins. He could never forgive her that. If only he had not loved her so much. The other women weren't important. They were just minor diversions. He had believed her so innocent. So pure. This betrayal was more than he could bear, and he was not a man to suffer pain without retribution.

'Tennent will pay as well,' he ground out. 'Don't think he won't.'

'You can't just ruin Richard's career because of malicious hearsay.'

'You've got guilt written all over your treacherous face.'

He thrust her from him and marched to the door.

'Where are you going?'

'First to consult a lawyer. Then to see Tennent.'

'You can't mean to destroy us all. The scandal will ruin you as well, Zach.'

'You forget I'm the injured party. Men's infidelities may be frowned upon, but they are glossed over. When a woman blatantly tricks a man into marrying her to give a name to her bastards, society reviles her. Especially when that woman sets herself up as some holier-than-thou matron. No wonder your charity work was with fallen women. But for tricking me into marriage, you'd be one of them. The gossips will have a field day.'

'I won't let you do it, Zach,' Kara shouted. 'You will not destroy Richard because Beatrice spoke out of spite.'

'And just how do you intend to stop me?'

Dilys Hills gripped the tea-tray tightly. The pot

had long since gone cold.

The mistress's voice carried clearly to her. 'I will do whatever it takes to stop you.'

The door was wrenched open, and Dilys hastily stepped back. Zach strode angrily past her. His body was tense with fury. He did not glance in her direction, though his shoulder rammed into her own. The tea-cups rattled in their saucers and the milk slopped on to the embroidered cloth. Dilys opened her mouth to speak, but the front door slammed before she could utter a word of comfort. She had to side-step rapidly to avoid being knocked into by the mistress.

'Damn you, Zach Morton,' Kara Wyse muttered as she ran blindly past the maid. She jammed her hat on to her head as she hurried to the door. 'You won't ruin us all. I mean it, I'll see you in hell first.'

The door banged a second time, as Kara fled out of the house to warn Richard of Zach's vendetta.

Kara walked to the end of the road and hailed a hansom. She had deliberately not taken the chauffeur-driven Daimler, fearing that Zach would question the driver as to her destination.

'Tennent & Finnemore offices in Chancery Lane,' she instructed.

She felt sick with apprehension at the slow progress of the cab through the busy London traffic. It was five-thirty when she finally reached the solicitor's. What if Richard had left? What if he was away on a case? Her palms broke into a nervous sweat at the thought of not being able to warn him. She didn't want Zach to be the one to tell him the twins were his. That would be too cruel. The years of guilt at keeping her secret flooded through her, and she pressed a shaking hand to her temple.

'Are you all right, ma'am?' the cab driver asked with concern as he opened the door for her to alight.

'Yes, thank you,' she quickly assured him. She glanced along the street and, seeing a youth leaning against the wall, his hands thrust deep in his pockets as he spoke to the vendor, she said, 'Would you ask that lad to run an errand for me? I'll pay him a florin.'

The cab driver nodded and emitted a shrill whistle. 'You lad. Here. There's a florin in it fer yer.'

The youth ran across the road, and Kara pulled a pocket notebook and pen from her bag – something she never left home without as she was constantly making notes on the shops and stock when she toured her business. She wrote a brief note.

Richard,
Imperative I see you at once.
I'm outside in a hansom.
Kara

She folded the paper over. 'This is to be given to Mr Richard Tennent and no one else. Tell whoever asks that it's extremely urgent. If Mr Tennent is not there, bring it back to me. Or any message he may have if he's delayed. There'll be another shilling for you when you return with his reply.'

The youth tugged the peak of his large cloth cap in acknowledgement and ran into the offices. Fifteen minutes later he still had not returned. Kara began to feel panic sweeping over her in waves. Normally so calm and in control, the shock of Zach's accusation and threats had unnerved her. Never had she needed Richard more. She leaned back against the cab's seat, closing her eyes as she swallowed to control the nausea brought on by her fear.

The door opened, making her start violently. The youth was grinning at her. 'Mr Tennent says yer to go straight in. His last client 'as just left.'

Kara paid him the promised money and settled with the hansom driver.

'Kara, you look like death,' Richard said worriedly as she entered his office. The clerks had already left. 'Why all this secrecy?'

'Are any of your employees still here, or Finnemore? I don't want to risk being overheard.'

'We are quite alone.' He smiled in a way that made her heart turn over with yearning. Then, to her horror, she burst into tears.

Immediately she was taken into his arms. 'Kara, my darling. Whatever is wrong? I've never seen you so upset.'

She breathed deeply to stem her sobs. 'I'm sorry. I never meant to embarrass you like this.'

'You could never do that,' he said, his breath fanning her cheek through the thin veiling of her hat which was tied under her chin. 'I welcome the chance to hold and comfort you. What's wrong?'

'Everything. Zach's going to divorce me. He's so angry – so vengeful. He wants to see us both ruined.'

'Us both?' Richard queried. 'You mean he learnt we were lovers? But that was nearly seven years ago. Before you married him.'

Kara nodded. The feel of Richard's arms around her was comforting, but it was also a danger. The ghost of their desire was between them, unforgotten, awaiting resurrection. Her emotions were too raw; she didn't dare complicate matters by allowing them to flame into passion.

Reluctantly she pulled away. 'I mustn't stay long. I had to warn you. Zach has threatened to seek you out once he's spoken to his solicitor.'

'I would have been offended if you had turned to anyone else.'

'I knew you would not fail me. But I don't deserve your kindness. I've... Oh, Richard, I'm so ashamed.' Her violet-blue eyes widened, beseeching him to understand. 'You'll hate me when you hear what I have to say.'

'I could never hate you, Kara.'

She stared into his rugged face, her love for him as fierce as ever.

'Don't look at me that way, Kara–' he forced a lightness into his husky voice – 'or it won't be talking we'll be doing. Have you any idea how much I've missed you?'

'Richard, how can you talk that way? Don't you understand? Zach wants to ruin your reputation and mine.'

'He can't prove anything. You are worrying needlessly.'

When she did not smile, he took her trembling hands and squeezed them. 'There's more than the divorce which is troubling you.'

She could not look at him. She loved him too much to see the hurt appear in his eyes. Pulling off her gloves, she clenched her hands and walked over to the window. The street below was crammed with vehicles and pedestrians hurrying to their homes after their work. They were an indistinct blur through the tears which she held in check.

'I've wronged you, my love,' she finally said. 'Tim and Harry are not Zach's sons. They are yours.'

She heard his harsh expulsion of breath. She glanced across at him, but he had turned away. One hand rested on his slim hips as he came to terms with her news.

Fearful that he would now despise her for keeping the truth from him, she rushed on. 'I've hated myself and felt so guilty keeping the truth from you. My pregnancy was why I married Zach. I couldn't tell you. You were married to Elizabeth and were trapped by duty to your family. Also I feared you'd never go to South America if you learned the truth. I didn't want you blaming yourself for my lost reputation. I took a coward's way out rather than face the shame of disgrace. I could never have remained Sophia's partner. She would have been horrified. So I married Zach. He had no reason to believe that they were other than seven-month babies. He accepted them and loved them. That's why he's so angry. I've hurt him terribly. If he did not love the boys so well…'

She broke off. Tears were again streaming down her face. 'I had meant to tell you the truth when you returned from Peru, but what good would it have done whilst the boys are so young? You at least were seeing them when they visited Louise. They look upon you as a hero for your work in the jungle. I should have told you the truth. You had a right to know.'

She wiped at her tears, and raced on, not letting him interrupt until she had finished. 'Now Zach wants to destroy you as well as me. He's threatened to unleash the scandal. I don't care that I shall lose my good name and possibly the shops. What frightens me is that he's threatened to take the children from me. I can't live without them. I know how Florence suffered. They are more important than anything. And I don't want you to suffer because of my foolishness. You don't deserve that. This mess is all my doing.'

'Oh, Kara, Kara.' The words were torn from him in an agonised groan. 'I'm the one to blame. I'm the despicable cad who made you pregnant.'

She went to him, seeing the pain of self-recrimination in his eyes. She reached for his hands. Their warmth pervaded the chill which had settled over her heart. 'I wanted you to make love to me that night. You're not a cad. You're the only man I have ever loved. I was proud to bear your sons. I wanted to tell you the truth, but felt trapped. I thought I had acted for the best. Yet to deny you was wrong.'

When he gazed down at her she expected to see condemnation in his eyes. She was unprepared for the love which blazed in their depths. It was love laced with torment – desire curbed by agonised restraint.

'My sons. It takes some getting used to. What right have I to blame you for keeping the truth from me? They are fine boys. I envied Morton such sons.' He swallowed, clearly fighting his own emotion which was threatening to unman him. 'Morton has no grounds to divorce you,' he stated. 'Unless you have been unfaithful since your marriage.'

'I have not. But Zach has had many mistresses. Beatrice was one of them, and so were several of the maids we employed.'

'Then it is you who must divorce him.'

'There'll be a scandal. I would not have the children face the ridicule of it. It's the only reason I've stayed with him. Somehow his infidelities did not matter. Was I not disloyal to him by loving you? But Beatrice's betrayal is what hurts. She's the one who told him. I thought I had won her friendship. She hates me. She's always hated me. She'll never forgive me for having such a different childhood to hers.'

Richard took her into his arms. 'You must be strong, Kara. Divorce Morton. You are the wronged party. He was a fortune-hunter who married you for your money. They can have no proof that we were lovers, only servants' gossip at best. You are a respectable business woman and are renowned for your charity work. Morton runs a gambling house, although it's a prestigious one, nevertheless the Church frowns upon such establishments. I also suspect there's more to his background than the outside world knows. I'll employ some men to look into his affairs. I wouldn't be surprised to find that Morton has links with the underworld. They will be his downfall.'

'But I don't want to see Zach destroyed, or imprisoned. In his way he's been a caring husband, if an adulterous one. He loves the children.'

'If he's involved with the underworld there's bound to be trouble sooner or later. What if his enemies attacked the children? They'd stop at nothing to get revenge upon one of their number.'

Kara blanched. 'If that is true, I couldn't risk the children being put in danger.'

'You must be strong, my love. Morton can prove nothing.'

He lifted her palm to his lips and kissed it; his eyes, heavy-lidded and dark with promise, devoured her. He caught her chin in his fingers and tilted it up as he gravely regarded her. His lips slanted across hers and she swayed against him. She had forgotten how deliciously sweet was the magic he could weave upon her senses.

With a muffled groan Richard drew back. 'Nothing must compromise your divorce. You must return to your house. I'll deal with Morton. If he so much as insinuates that I was your lover, I'll issue a writ for slander. I won't allow your name to be dragged through the dirt.'

'I don't want to go back there. But I must for the children's sake.'

He ran the back of his hand tenderly along her

cheek. 'That's my brave love. You must maintain your innocence at all costs. You don't believe yourself to be in any physical danger from Morton, do you?'

'I don't think so. Though there is a dangerous side to his temper, I don't think he would harm a woman. He was shocked and upset when we quarrelled. He will have cooled down – and I hope be more reasonable – when I return.'

'If he lays a finger on you, he'll answer to me,' Richard said darkly, 'and it won't be in a law-court.'

Lord Mountgibbons dismissed the man before him. His eyes were glacial. So Beatrice had tricked him. She hadn't gone to see a doctor. She'd gone straight to Morton. And had been with him for over an hour. The man he had paid to follow her had done his work well. He'd also learned from making inquiries at The Gentleman's Retreat that the staff believed Beatrice and Morton were lovers. They were frequently alone together in his office for hours on end. He'd been in Morton's office. There was a small room leading off it with a double bed. It was supposed to be for when Morton stayed so late at the club that he thought it wiser not to return home and disturb his wife.

Rage boiled in Freddie. He unlocked a glass-fronted cabinet and took out the brass-inlaid walnut box. A pulse throbbed in his temple as he raised the lid. His mouth was compressed into a grim line. His hand clasped the pearl handle of one of his grandfather's duelling pistols as he lifted it from its velvet bed. Five times his grandfather had used these pistols to defend his honour, and five times his opponents had been grievously wounded. One had later died when gangrene had set in. Freddie had been brought up on tales of avenging honour. Now it was his turn.

He was still cleaning the second pistol when Beatrice entered the room. She kissed his cheek and wrinkled her nose with distaste at the guns on the table.

'I thought you'd be at your club, my dear.'

'How was your visit to the doctor?' Freddie drawled. 'When is our child to be born?'

'Early summer,' Beatrice answered airily.

'Which doctor did you see? I'm concerned for your health, my dear. I would consult him myself as to how to safeguard you from miscarriage.' There was no warmth in his voice as he regarded her.

Icy fingers of dread clenched around Beatrice's heart. Freddie sounded cold and suspicious. 'There's no need for you to see the doctor. He says I'm well. I was being foolish to be so frightened at Crownfield.'

'His name, Beatrice,' he rapped out in an imperious tone he had never used to her before.

'Freddie, it isn't necessary to put yourself to so much trouble.' Her heart thudded with growing alarm.

He smiled. It did not reach his eyes. 'But I think there is. You never went to a doctor, did you? You went straight to Morton.' He picked up a pistol and broke it open to squint inside its barrel. 'He's your lover. Is it his child you're carrying? Or perhaps you aren't even expecting. I wouldn't put it past you to lie through your teeth about anything to get your own way.'

The change in Freddie, from the tender lover to cold, hostile accuser, smote Beatrice. Her only defence was anger. 'That's a wicked thing to say.'

'Not if the man who followed you spoke the truth!'

'You had me followed!' Her anger flared. 'I'm your wife and you treat me like a criminal.'

His glare was frosty. He continued cleaning and then priming the pistol as he spoke. 'You betrayed me. I was prepared to forget and forgive you your past. It isn't just me you've made a fool of. It's seven generations of my ancestors' good name. That I cannot tolerate. Others of my kin may have married beneath them, but their wives knew their place. They knew the importance of upholding one's honour. Not so yourself.'

He poured the gunpowder into the barrel, then a round shot, and rammed it home. Raising the pistol, he levelled it at Beatrice.

For several seconds she stared down the barrel, her spine coated in an icy sweat of fear, her heart hammering wildly.

'Freddie. Dear God, you don't mean to...?'

Horrified, she watched him pull back the firing pin with his thumb, his forefinger tightening over the trigger.

'No. Freddie. No!'

At the last moment he moved the pistol slightly and the shot whizzed past Beatrice's ear to shatter a tall Chinese vase on a pedestal. With a

sob, Beatrice flew at her husband.
'You bastard! You scared the shit out of me.'
'Language, my dear.' Freddie caught her wrists as she lashed out at his chest. 'If I'd meant to kill you, you would now be dead. I'm a crack shot. We will be returning to Crownfield tomorrow.'
'I'm not going,' she seethed, struggling to free herself from his bruising grip.
'Oh, but you are, dear wife. Besides, there will be nothing to keep you in London after tonight. I'm calling Morton out.'
Beatrice stared at the duelling pistols with returning horror. 'But duelling is illegal – and barbaric.'
'It's how a gentleman settles an affair of honour. Did you think I'd complacently raise another man's bastard?'
'I'm not carrying another man's child. Damn you, Freddie! I'm not even pregnant.' She laughed harshly. 'I'm very likely barren. I just had to get away from Crownfield. You were treating me like a prisoner.'
'Barren!' His face bleached of all colour. 'You mean I faced the ridicule of my peers in marrying beneath me, and you can't even give me an heir?'
'I thought you loved me, Freddie.' Beatrice was unexpectedly hurt by his accusation. 'I thought it was me you wanted – not a brood mare for bloody Crownfield.'
'I have the responsibility to continue my line,' he sneered. 'As a commoner you would not understand that. I gave you everything I could to make you happy. And you have flung it back in my face. You're a heartless bitch. How could I

ever have thought I loved you? Stay in London if you wish. I shall be calling on my lawyer tomorrow to start divorce proceedings. First I shall deal with Morton.'

He placed the pistol back in the box and, closing the lid, tucked the walnut case under his arm. Striding to the door, he paused to look back at her stunned figure. 'Goodbye, Beatrice. Have your possessions moved out of here immediately. You can move in with your sister. Help to console the grieving widow. I shall stay at my club until you leave.'

The door closed, and Beatrice heard him cross the marble floor of the hall, then silence as he passed into the street. She stood frozen on the spot. Pain was tearing through her heart. She felt sick, devastated, totally immobilised with shock. She could not believe the speed with which events had changed her life. Freddie loved her. He had worshipped her. It was true, he had given her everything. He was the only man who had ever really shown her loving tenderness. She had taken it as her due. Like a fool she had allowed her obsession with Zach to blind her to the love which enveloped and protected her.

Under her tuition he had become a skilled master in sexually satisfying her. And in bed he did give her enormous pleasure. She had taken his devotion for granted.

A wretched cry was torn from her lips. The pain in her heart was relentless. A deeper fear now spread through her than when Freddie had pointed the pistol at her. She had thrown away everything in her petty need for revenge upon her sister. Damn it all! She was a titled lady. Freddie had done that for her. He had faced ridicule in his love for her. She had seemingly unlimited wealth and jewels at her disposal. All because Freddie adored her. And though Crownfield was not in the London she loved, it was a magnificent house. If she had not been taken there feeling like an exiled prisoner, she would have been proud to be its mistress. Freddie had given her so much. How little he had asked in return.

Belatedly, she realised he was not the weak fool she had taken him for. If he had a weakness, it was his love for her.

Despair brought her hand to her mouth. 'What have I done?' she groaned. 'What did Zach ever do for me, except use me for his own selfish ends?'

And Freddie was about to challenge Zach to a duel. Freddie may think himself a crack shot, but he had never killed a man. As a soldier, Zach was not only deadly with a pistol, but he had killed many men. And not only during wartime. He was still a ruthless bastard. Didn't the way he had manipulated the deaths of the Gilbert brothers prove that?

Freddie was the only man who had been truly kind to her. She did not want him to die. The pain tearing through her told her it was him she loved, not Zach. Freddie would be no match against Zach with a pistol. She must save him.

Fear for her husband galvanised her into action. It was nearly dark, but she would go to Zach and beg him not to take up Freddie's challenge.

Kara paced her study for hours awaiting Zach's return. When she heard his footsteps in the hall, she rushed out to confront him. He was swaying slightly as he handed his top hat and cane to their butler, Ferring.

He glowered at her and turned his back on her to walk into his own study. He'd been drinking and was in a dangerous mood. She ran after him.

'Zach, we have to talk.'

His mouth set into a cruel line as he regarded her with hostility.

'We have nothing to say to each other.'

'I won't let you take my children. I won't let you ruin Richard Tennent's career upon unfounded jealousy.'

He lifted a dark brow sardonically. 'You went to see him this afternoon. You couldn't stay away.'

She realised that Zach had put a spy on her. She decided to continue with her bluff. 'I went to warn him. He deserved that much.'

'Ah, yes, I forgot how loyal you can be. When it suits you.' His voice was abrasive. His gaze swept disparagingly over her figure. 'And how did Tennent receive you? With affection? I expect it was a touching, tender scene. He wouldn't want you getting suspicious. After all, your guilty secret is his guilty secret.'

'There is no secret. If you don't trust me, how can you believe that a man as honourable as Richard would seduce a client under his own wife's roof?'

He laughed. A sound without mirth, just cruelty. 'Love blinds you, Kara. Obviously you didn't know that Tennent had a mistress while he was married. He'd set her up in Kensington – visited her regularly during his wife invalidity. About the time you moved into his house, his mistress was dismissed.'

Kara stood rigid, fighting to hide her pain. Richard had been so tender, so caring this afternoon. She had not doubted that he still loved her. It was a shock to discover that he had betrayed Elizabeth with another woman.

Zach saw Kara's shock. To him it marked her guilt. 'You didn't know about his women, did you?' he persisted. 'There've been several. You weren't the only one. He's seen more of Fenella Sommerfield than most. Gossip is rife about them. Fenella was at the club last week with a party of friends. She declined the attentions of Lord Witterham, pronouncing that she would soon be giving up the stage for marriage.'

Jealousy speared Kara. Her face lost all colour, her lip trembled as he compounded the pain. Was Richard another womaniser like Zach? Had she allowed her love to blind her? Until she sought him out this afternoon, she had not seen or heard from Richard in months. He had wasted little time in taking up with Fenella Sommerfield. And yet this afternoon he had been so tender... Or was it an act of an accomplished seducer? Telling him of the twins would have evoked memories of the night they were conceived. His kiss had been brief and restrained.

Suspicion, once roused, developed many heads. His persuasive coercion had lulled her into false security. She had obeyed him without question.

But had it been in her interests, or his, that he had been protecting? If word of their affair broke, it could ruin him. Fenella Sommerfield was beautiful. Ravishingly beautiful. How could any man resist her? Her ideals crumbled. Richard was no different from Zach. He'd been unfaithful to Elizabeth and all these years she had felt so guilty at that betrayal. How could she trust him?

Fury took hold of her. Her voice rose to a scream as she fell prey to Zach's cruel goading. He responded in kind, sparing her nothing in his abuse and contempt. Finally, with a sob, she ran from the room. She hated Zach. She no longer trusted Richard. Her life was about to crumble in ruins. A red mist formed before her eyes as she was overtaken by a murderous rage.

Beatrice was nearly frantic. She had gone to the club, but Zach had not been there. Apparently he had been drinking heavily and the staff had been relieved when he had left an hour ago with Dipper. The ex-sergeant-major who served as a doorman had looked concerned.

'Cap'n were in a right temper. Never seen 'im like it. Anyone who so much as looked at 'im got their head barked off. Dipper was taking him home. But the captain were having none of it. Though I reckon once 'e hit the fresh air, the whisky he'd been putting back all afternoon would have hit 'im. I'd try 'is 'ouse. Likely 'e'll be sleeping it off by now.'

Beatrice's toe beat an impatient tattoo as she waited for the door of the Morton house to be opened to her. The butler, Ferring, regarded her with the stiff formality of an automaton.

'The master and mistress are not receiving,' Ferring announced. 'I will tell them you called.'

'You can't stop me seeing my own sister,' Beatrice demanded, though it was Zach she needed to warn.

'Madam is indisposed and not receiving anyone.'

'I am sure she will see me.'

The butler looked down his long hooked nose. 'Her instructions were she would see no one.'

She was about to give him the benefit of her gutter expletives and push past the officious squirt, but thought better of it. She had become conscious of passers-by and thought better of creating a scene in public.

Retracing her steps to the pavement, she turned sharply right and hurried towards the side alleyway which led to the back of the house. Strangely, neither of the gaslamps which usually illuminated it were alight. A moment's unease made her pause. It was a common thieves' trick to douse a gaslamp and lie in ambush for an unsuspecting victim. There was enough moonlight to show her that the alley leading up to the side-gate appeared empty. She must take the risk.

With her heart racing, she covered the short distance. To her relief the side-gate was open. It made her entry easier, for she was getting too old to be climbing over gates, but at the same time her disquiet deepened. Zach was too aware of the possibilities of burglaries not to order the gate locked at dusk.

Silently she slipped into the garden. Rhododendron bushes shielded the back of the house from her view as she crossed to the open door of the glass conservatory which opened into the darkened parlour. An orb of light shone through the lace curtains in Zach's downstairs study. Rather than risk running into the officious Ferring again, she decided to tap on the study window to attract Zach's attention.

She was half-way across the lawn when she heard the first gunshot.

Chapter Twenty-six

'She's done for the master. She's killed 'im!' a maid screamed hysterically as Beatrice came upon the scene.

Kara sat on the floor, her cream gown drenched in blood. Zach's head was in her lap, his eyes staring and sightless. The front of his tan summer suit and white shirt were scarlet; blood still oozed from the six bullet holes. A pistol lay by Kara's right hand, a thin spiral of smoke still trailing from the barrel.

Beatrice took in the frozen tableau of Zach's and Kara's figures, her mind working furiously. She darted forward and slapped the hysterical maid on the cheek. 'Be quiet, girl.'

'She's done for 'im, I tell yer,' the maid accused, her eyes wide with horror. 'She said she'd seen him rot in 'ell. Now she's killed 'im.'

Ferring appeared in the doorway, puffing from

his fast ascent of the stairs from the servants' quarters.

'Good God. The master!' he declared, his face turning ashen. Quickly he recovered himself. 'Stop snivelling, Dilys.' He turned on the maid. 'Go and get the constable who patrols the road. It must have been an accident.'

'Six shots ain't no accident,' Dilys stated. 'I 'eard the mistress threaten 'im when 'e said 'e were going to divorce 'er.'

The butler glanced at the maid. 'That's enough of such talk. It is a matter for the police.' He then noticed Beatrice and raised a grey eyebrow.

She saw the suspicion in his eyes. The pompous squirt thought she'd done for Zach.

'I came in by the side-gate. I told you it was urgent I spoke to my sister.' She gave him a quelling glare to stop any further questioning. 'Clearly Mrs Morton is in a state of shock. Send for the doctor.'

'Shocked at being caught red-handed,' the maid spat out between wild sobs of grief. 'She shot 'im. The gun's at her feet.' Another glare from Ferring had her scurrying from the room to fetch the policeman.

Beatrice glanced at Zach. No question about it, he was dead. The bullets had slammed into his heart and lungs. Kara was absently stroking back a lock of his dark hair, her eyes wide with shock, a tremor every now and again shaking her rigid body.

'Kara, the police are coming.' She put her hand on her sister's shoulder and could feel her violent trembling. 'They will want to speak with you.'

There was no response.

'Kara, you can't sit there,' she insisted. Taking her sister's arm, she attempted to pull her to her feet.

'He's dead. Dead.' Kara's glazed eyes cleared and she stared down at Zach's bloody chest. 'I never wanted this.'

'Hush,' Beatrice warned. 'Careful what you say. You don't want the peelers twisting your words.'

The maid's high-pitched voice carried from the hallway. 'Master's body is in the study, constable. The mistress is there with 'im. She did it. The gun's at 'er side. She did for 'im, the jealous bitch. 'E were going to divorce 'er. They've bin quarrelling all day.'

From the rooms at the top of the house came the sound of a baby crying, and Tim called from the top of the stairs. 'What were those bangs, Mama?'

The sound of his feet running down the stairs made Kara clutch at Beatrice's hand with her bloodied fingers. 'Don't let the boys see,' she hissed urgently.

Beatrice nodded. She passed the policeman at the door and hurried out to catch Tim before he ran into the study. For a moment she contemplated lying to him, but when the seven-year-old looked at her with his dark, piercing eyes, she said softly, 'Your Papa's dead.'

'Papa, Papa!' Tim began to shout, struggling to be free of Beatrice's hold to run into the study.

'Tim, no.' Beatrice held him tight against her as he began to sob. 'Remember your Papa as he was. You've got to be brave for your Mama's sake.'

The tall thin figure of Nanny Cummins was on the stairs. In her navy skirt and high-necked white blouse she was a demure figure. She looked close to fainting. She was probably another of Zach's conquests, though Beatrice thought that with her large nose and prim mouth she was not Zach's type. The thirty-year-old spinster probably worshipped him from afar. Zach had that effect on many women.

'Cummins,' Beatrice said sternly. 'See to your charge.'

The woman's eyelids fluttered as she countered her fainting spell. Beatrice ordered sharply, 'Take Tim back to his bedroom. Better give him a few drops of laudanum to help him sleep. Your mistress won't be needing the children wailing through the house. Or the staff.'

'The poor master,' Nanny Cummins sniffed into a handkerchief as she took Tim's hand and led him up the stairs.

Further along the hall, Ferring held the stem of the telephone in one hand, the earpiece shaking in his fingers. 'That's right, sergeant,' he said. 'It's murder. The constable asks that you send an inspector at once.'

Behind Ferring she saw Dipper Jones sneaking towards the back door, a hastily packed carpet bag in his hand. Dipper wasn't about to hang around for any nosy inspector to question the staff. He had his own criminal past to flee from.

Watching Dipper dash down the servants' stairs, she saw the housekeeper and a young, rather simple-looking kitchen maid looking shocked and uncertain. 'Best brew up some strong tea,' she addressed them. 'Bring it into the parlour. Mrs Morton could do with a shot of brandy to steady her.'

'I can't believe the mistress killed the captain.' The kitchen maid burst into fresh tears.

The housekeeper kept an impassive expression. 'They do say still waters run deep. She had cause enough. The dear woman was too innocent to know the half of what went on in this house.' She glared at Dilys, who had stationed herself by the front door, clearly intent on confronting the inspector with her accusations the moment he appeared. She had never liked the maid, who had an uppity manner, probably because Zach was bedding her.

'Have you no work to do, Dilys?' Beatrice demanded.

'I quit. I ain't working for no murderess. But I've a right to have my say. I was 'ere, wasn't I? I'm an important witness. The captain was a good man. She'd tricked him. She foisted her bastard twins on him. There were the mother and father of all rows 'ere this afternoon.' She crossed her arms over her heavy breasts to combat the sobs which threatened to destroy her speech. 'I'll see she pays. I'll see she hangs. She didn't want him, but she couldn't stand to see him happy with another woman.' Tears streamed from the maid's eyes.

Zach Morton, you really were a prime bastard! But God rest your whoring soul, you were certainly a charmer. What did I see in you? Blind, obsessive passion, that's what. I was no different from that snivelling slut of a maid. You betrayed us all.

Beatrice inhaled sharply. Her own grief lay like lead upon her heart. Who'd have guessed Zach would get his come-uppance in such a manner?

She returned to the study where the thickset policeman stood like a guard over Kara's stunned figure.

'Could we not await the inspector in the parlour?' Beatrice suggested. 'It will be less upsetting for my sister.'

The policeman brushed his bushy brown moustache with his forefinger. His manner showed that he believed Kara was the murderess and deserved no compassion.

'Aye, I suppose so,' he conceded reluctantly.

Kara's gaze remained on the bloodied figure of her husband. Her face was devoid of colour, her violet-blue eyes wide with shock. Beatrice had to admit that Kara's behaviour made her look as though she had killed Zach. Didn't the French have a phrase for it? A 'crime of passion'. Or so Zach had once mentioned, when the newspapers reported that a courtesan had stabbed her paramour when he had ditched her for a younger woman. Zach had joked over it. This weren't no joking matter.

Surprisingly, she felt removed from the grief and horror of Zach's death. If her heart ached, her eyes were dry of tears. The bastard had used her as his whore without caring for her. Because of her obsession with him – or rather her need to be avenged upon her sister in any way she could – she had jeopardised her marriage.

Thoughts of Freddie made her heart beat

faster. When she had heard the shots, her fear had been that he was here. That he was dead, or had shot Zach and would then face trial for murder. Her relief that it was not Freddie had been short-lived. Then a deeper fear had hit her, and she had dived back into the shrubbery to conceal herself. She had still been trembling when she'd entered the study and found Kara bent over Zach, the smoking pistol at her side.

At last revenge was at hand. Kara in prison would face the deprivation she had suffered as a child. She would be stripped of her dignity and wealth and treated like scum. Decent folks would revile her, as Beatrice had been reviled when Able Wyse's abandonment had consigned Florence and herself to life in a rookery. Revenge was sweet.

The prison door clanked shut and Kara was in total darkness. She remained in the centre of the tiny cell, clutching her hands to her breast. The darkness could not blot out the image of Zach's bloody form. Or the rasping, gurgling gasps of his breath as his body twitched in its dying spasm. The smell of gunpowder, blood and death clung to her nostrils, her body still in the grip of uncontrollable shaking.

Sightlessly, she stared up at the tiny barred window above her head. A square of grey light forewarned of the approaching dawn. What had happened to the hours since Zach's death? There was a blur of faces in her memory. Voices spoke, but words did not penetrate her dazed mind. The voices became angry, shouting, abusive. Hard fingers had pinched and bruised her flesh as she had been hauled into a hansom, then brought here. Faces thrust close to her: shouting, menacing.

Nothing had really registered. It was like a disjointed nightmare. All her mind centred upon was the horror of Zach lying dead in her lap.

Her trembling turned to violent shivers as cold bit deep into her bones. Still Kara did not move. Her unfocused stare fixed on the tiny square of light above her head as the window lightened to reveal a grey leaden sky. The hiss of a steady downpour of rain was drowned by the gathering rush of blood to her head.

She fell in a faint to the cold flagstones. Her head gashed open as it struck the wooden corner of the pallet bed.

Consciousness returned slowly. Pain registered first. In her temple, fiery arrows winged through her skull. She stirred. Cramp gripped her chilled limbs in an agonising vice. There was a repetitive shaft of pain shooting through her back and side.

'Wake up, Murderess.' A harsh voice grated as again agony exploded through her back. Groggily, she realised that she was being kicked.

With a groan she rolled on to her side, fighting to shake the mists of exhaustion and horror from her dazed mind. A slap stung her cheek, tearing her lip against her teeth. The iron taste of blood ran down her throat and she coughed.

Opening her eyes, she saw a heavy-jowled woman, her upper lip covered in black hair, bending over her. 'Get up, yer filthy, murdering whore. Inspector Urquhart is waiting ter interview yer again. Must be soft in the head. He always did 'ave a weakness for a pretty woman. Just looking at yer dress says yer guilty as 'ell. And that's where yer'll burn after they've hanged yer.'

Kara rolled on to her knees to push herself upright. Straggles of hair fell over her face from her dishevelled coiffure. As she lifted her hand to brush the strands back, she saw the dried blood in her long fingernails. Then her gaze fell upon the blood-encrusted front of her cream skirt. All the horror of last night crowded back. The dirty whitewashed walls of the cell spun crazily.

Another vicious slap to her face sent her spinning round on to the bed. 'Oh no yer don't. I'm not having yer fainting agin.' Brutal fingers grabbed her shoulders, shaking her violently. 'No good putting on your fine airs and graces here. Yer a bloody murderess. Smith, get in 'ere and give us a 'and with this vermin.'

Another large woman appeared and, snatching Kara's arm in a painful grip, the two women dragged her half-swooning figure out of the cell.

Kara stumbled, her feet twisting under her as they half dragged her along a corridor. The indignity of it roused her pride and anger.

'Why am I here? Where are you taking me?' Her dulled mind was beginning to clear. Yet still she could not believe what was happening to her. Why were they treating her this way?

Her plea was ignored. Her shins slammed painfully against stone steps as she tripped on the first one and fell headlong. Unable to recover her footing, her shins hammered against each stair until she was hauled upright at the top of the flight. She fought for breath and for clarity of mind through the foggy mists of pain stabbing through her temple and legs. The warders halted by a closed door. It gave Kara the chance to straighten her back and lift her head to confront whatever awaited her.

She was walking normally as she was thrust into a room where a short, portly, bewhiskered man in a brown suit looked at her with acute distaste. There was only one chair. He sat down on it and signalled to one of the women to leave.

'Now, Mrs Morton, I want the truth,' he fired out in a thick Scottish accent. 'It's nae use playing dumb like ye did last night. All the evidence is against ye. Ye murdered yer husband. Admit it.'

The last of the numbness which had settled over her drained, to be replaced by gut-churning fear. The hostile glare of the man regarding her filled her with terror. He really believed that she had murdered Zach. Panic momentarily overwhelmed her. She began to pant like a cornered vixen about to be seized by a pack of hounds.

'I want my solicitor here,' she croaked. 'I will say nothing until I have spoken to him.'

Kara remained in the interrogation room, refusing to answer the questions shouted at her. Her head ached abominably from the cut on her temple, making it difficult to think clearly. Zach was dead. Shot. Murdered. They thought she had done it. The same thoughts revolved through her mind. Resolutely she remained silent, though her insides had begun to quake at Inspector Urquhart's bullying tactics to wear down her resistance.

'Confess!' he shouted. 'The gun was beside ye, woman. Ye murdered yer husband!'

Pride made her keep her head high. When she tried to tidy her unkempt hair, the wardress slapped down her hands. The blood-stiffened petticoats beneath her skirt were repulsive against her skin. She could feel her lip was swollen from her rough treatment, and being forced to remain standing was torture. Her bruised body throbbed from the kicks she had received, but she refused to slump. She kept her shoulders squared, her spine straight, and her gaze fixed on a point above Urquhart's bald head. It was the only way she could stop herself breaking down beneath the humiliation she was subjected to.

The door opened and Richard stepped into the room. Shame and embarrassment flooded her as she saw his shocked expression at her dishevelled state. She must look like a street drab arrested for fighting.

'Why has this prisoner been beaten?' he demanded fiercely.

'She fell over in her cell,' the wardress grunted.

'Did you fall, Kara?'

She touched the throbbing lump on her brow and nodded. Her finger went to the swollen cut on her lip and she glared at the wardress without speaking. She could feel Richard's strength reaching protectively across the room to her. He looked so strong and handsome. She pulled her thoughts up. Zach's taunts had destroyed her faith in Richard's love. Had he been protecting his own reputation when advising her?

He was another womaniser like Zach, using flattery and tenderness to lull her fears. Yet all the time he was planning to marry Fenella Sommerfield. Like a fool she had believed him when he said that he did not love the singer. That was what her heart had wanted to believe.

She did not want to think of Richard's betrayal now. She dared not. She had no one else to turn to. Didn't he have as much to lose as herself if a scandal broke about their affair? The beautiful Fenella would probably leave him.

Richard was talking in his cool authoritative way, drawing her thoughts back to the present. 'Mrs Morton has also been beaten.' His eyes flashed with anger.

'We had to restrain her,' the wardress barked.

'Help me, Richard,' Kara cried out, near to breaking point. 'They think I killed Zach. I didn't. I didn't.'

'Anyone who knows you would never believe you capable of murder.' The assurance in his voice brought a resurgence of hope. Richard would not fail her. She could see he was fighting to control his emotions. His face was haggard. For a moment she could almost believe that he loved her. But that was foolish romantic dreaming. Why should a man of Richard's sensuality love a woman he had made love to only once. It was a bond between them, nothing more. And now he knew she was the mother of his sons, he would do everything in his power to free her. For their sake, if not his.

'Am I not permitted to speak in private with my client?' Richard demanded.

'Mrs Morton canna be yer client, Mr Tennent,' Inspector Urquhart coldly informed him. 'Ye're here yeself tae answer questions raised by statements given by Mrs Morton's staff. Ye were her lover. For all we know, ye were part of the plot to murder Morton. It's alleged that ye are the father of two of her children. Morton had threatened to expose ye. Such a scandal would ruin your career.'

Richard turned on Urquhart, his face tense with contempt. 'These accusations are false and slanderous. Mrs Morton is incapable of murdering anyone, as I shall prove.'

'Ye first have tae prove your innocence, Mr Tennent,' the inspector snarled. He walked to the open door, 'We'll take your statement in another room. Ye'll have no chance to collaborate on a story with the accused.'

'I didn't kill Zach,' Kara cried. 'I swear I didn't.'

The inspector regarded her contemptuously. His short legs were planted arrogantly apart and he patted his vast stomach with complacency. 'All the evidence points to your guilt.'

Richard's eyes glittered with fervour as he stared across at her. 'I know you're innocent, Kara. I shall prove it.'

He was led away for questioning. Kara was marched back to her cell. The inspector had only allowed her to see him to show her how the odds were stacked against her.

'Better if yer come clean with it.' The wardress

eyed her malevolently. 'Ain't no point in lying. Yer guilty as 'ell. Yer maid saw it all. 'Er evidence will see yer 'anged.'

'The maid, like many others in our household before her, was probably my husband's mistress. She's in love with him. They all fall for his charm.'

The wardress smirked. 'Jealousy is the most common reason for a woman to murder a man.'

Fear drenched Kara in a cold sweat. 'I did not murder my husband.'

'Save yer pleas of innocence fer the judge. But 'e won't be fooled by them, any more than I am.'

Beatrice had given her statement to the police and returned to the Mountgibbons' house. Freddie, true to his word, stayed away. She sent a message to his club, begging him to see her. Tomorrow the newspapers would be running the story of Zach's death. She needed to talk with Freddie. He ignored her message. He also ignored the seven other notes she sent.

On the second morning of Freddie's absence, Beatrice awoke feeling ill and shaken. She couldn't keep any food down. She had to see Freddie. The nausea churning her stomach made her shaky; but, determined to speak with Freddie, she called for the Lanchester. To her dismay the pavement outside her house was filled with reporters. News of Zach's murder was spread all across the headlines.

'That's her. She's Morton's sister-in-law. Lady Mountgibbons, can you tell us–'

Beatrice ran into the car, refusing to look at the

reporters as they pressed around the windows. Their shouts became abusive when she refused to answer their questions.

'Drive on,' she ordered. 'Just get me away from here. And make sure no one follows.'

When, ten minutes later, they appeared to have lost the last of the trailing reporters, Beatrice ordered the chauffeur to drive her to the houses of Freddie's friends. Westman was not at home. Neither was Blackworth. Both houses were shut up with only skeleton staff. At another old friend's, Lord Harman's house, the butler announced, 'His Lordship is not at home.'

'That's a lie. I just saw him looking out of an upstairs window as my car pulled up.'

The butler cleared his throat. 'His Lordship is not at home to you, Lady Mountgibbons.'

Anger gouged through her at the way she was being treated. She was about to shove the pompous butler out of the way when the doorway began to swirl and dip crazily about her. For the first time in Beatrice's life, she fainted.

Smelling salts thrust under her nose made her breath snatch and she came to, finding herself slumped in a hardback chair in the hallway. A maid was bending over her.

'If you are recovered, Lady Mountgibbons,' the butler announced, 'I must ask you to leave.'

It was on the tip of her tongue to give the butler a dressing-down. Then she remembered the duty she owed to Freddie. She had vowed, on returning to their empty house in Mayfair, that she would never give Freddie cause to feel ashamed of her. She meant to be a good wife. She loved him and wanted to make up with him before it was too late.

Eating humble pie did not come easily to Beatrice. She swallowed and asked softly, 'Could you at least tell me if Lord Mountgibbons is staying here?'

'He is not, Lady Mountgibbons.'

Disheartened, Beatrice left, her step heavy as she moved towards the car. A legless beggar, propelling himself along the pavement on a board with small wheels, stopped in front of her.

'Sixpence, ma'am. For a soldier who lost 'is legs serving 'is country.'

Beatrice glared at him. She was sick of being treated like scum by Freddie's snotty friends. Her temper raw, she snapped, 'Yer lost yer bleeding legs lying drunk in the gutter, Bert Scroggins. A cart run over them.'

The man's mouth gaped open. 'Gawd blimey if it ain't Bea Kempe. And all dressed up like a toff.'

'That's because I am one,' she announced proudly, loudly enough for the snooty butler to hear. 'I married Lord Mountgibbons, who will not be pleased to learn that his wife has been treated in this manner.'

'Mountgibbons, is it? He were here couple of days ago. Gave me 'alf-a-crown. Decent chap, 'is Lordship. If yer wed to 'im, wot yer doin' 'ere, and not wiv 'im in France. That's where he were off ter. Heard him say so to his mate.'

Beatrice mellowed and gave the beggar her most disarming smile. She held out a gold sovereign. 'Did he say where in France, Bert?'

'Aye he did.' Bert winked and pocketed the sovereign. 'Nice.'

Kara lost track of the passage of time. She knew it was only hours since her arrest – probably less than a day. Each hour dragged like a week. She was never alone. Shock and exhaustion was beginning to tell on her. Whenever her eyes closed with sleep, the wardresses ensured she was kept awake. She was not even granted a moment's privacy to use the slops pail in the corner of her cell. They were trying to break her down to win a confession.

The numbness and shock of Zach's death had left her. With it came pain and remorse. His death had been so sudden – so unjust and cowardly. There was an emptiness in her. She had been fond of Zach, fonder than she had realised. Their marriage had been happier than those of many acquaintances she knew. And in his selfish way Zach had loved her.

Together with her grief, she had to come to terms with her feelings for Richard. There had been no further word from him. She was plagued by doubts. By jealous visions of him with Fenella. She trusted him to free her, for he was a brilliant lawyer. Any other feelings for him were carefully battened down.

She remained adamant under the inspector's questioning.

'I will say nothing until I have spoken with my solicitor. Why has that right been denied me? I am innocent.'

Later that morning, when her eyes were

scratchy from lack of sleep, and her head ached so that she could barely think straight, she was taken to the interrogation room. A man who was not Inspector Urquhart stood with his back to the window. For a moment her heart leapt, thinking it was Richard. When he turned to greet her, her disappointment was acute.

'Mr Finnemore,' she said hollowly.

He cleared his throat in embarrassment. 'As matters stand, Mr Tennent has asked that I represent you. I am here to take your statement.'

Kara glanced at a table and two chairs which had been placed in the room. A wardress led her to one chair and she sat down. The woman then positioned herself by the door.

'Are we not to be alone?'

'It appears not,' Mr Finnemore said, sitting down and producing some blank paper. 'Tell me what happened.'

'I thought Mr Tennent would represent me.' Her voice cracked.

'He is, indirectly,' Finnemore whispered. He had a round, homely face. His greying hair had already far receded, giving him a kindly, fatherly air. 'He doesn't want to give any fuel to a scandal at the moment by coming here.'

'Speak up, man,' the wardress ordered. 'Don't want no plotting 'ere. Take her statement and have done wiv it.'

Kara told him all she could remember. Since her arrest she had gone very carefully over her last conversation with Richard. Every word she said had to be carefully weighed, so that it could not be twisted against her.

'Zach and I had been quarrelling. I'd had enough of his infidelity. I wanted a separation. He'd been drinking and became abusive. Divorce was mentioned. He threatened to take my children from me if I left him. We resolved nothing and I had gone to my study. I was upset. It was impossible to work on my books, but I stayed in my study needing peace to think. I knew I could not stay with my husband any more. But I did not want to risk the scandal of a divorce. About an hour after I had retired to my study, I heard the first shot.'

She paused, pain flickering across her face as the memories crowded her mind.

'I know this is difficult, Mrs Morton, but I must have all the details,' Finnemore gently urged.

She nodded and steeled herself to continue. 'I ran into my husband's study as the last of the shots were fired. There were two black and bloody holes in Zach's tan jacket where the bullets had passed through his body. He had fallen back against his desk, gripping hold of it for support. I saw the flash of the final shot from the darkness of the conservatory. Zach collapsed on the floor. Blood was everywhere. His face was contorted with pain. I ran to him. Tried to help. It was useless. He was dying…'

She broke off, reliving the horror of Zach's death. She wrapped her arms about her shivering figure, her voice strangled. 'All I could do was hold him in my arms. I've tried to recall exact details, but so much after that became a blur. All I can remember is the awful death rattle in his throat, the life fading in his eyes. He was trying to speak. Only a gurgle and a rush of blood came from his lips. He had seen who shot him. He was trying to name his murderer. He died before he could speak.'

'How did the gun come to be by your side, Mrs Morton?'

'I don't know. I never saw it. Perhaps the murderer had tossed it into the room before he ran off.'

'A maid says you had threatened to kill Zach before.'

Kara looked startled. 'Never!'

'Her exact words were that you said, "I'll never let you take my children. I'll do whatever it takes to stop you. I'll see you in hell first." Did you say those words?'

Kara's heart clenched with fear. 'I suppose I must have. I was hurt and angry. They were said in the heat of an argument. I never meant I would kill him. I did not kill my husband, Mr Finnemore.'

'Unfortunately your words condemn you as they stand. It is why the police are still holding you. Unless a witness saw the murderer running off, I fear you will be put on trial for Mr Morton's murder.'

Kara shivered and hugged her arms protectively across her chest. 'I didn't shoot Zach, I swear I didn't.'

'Richard believes you. But he needs to find witnesses. He's also making inquiries about Zach's life. To see if he has enemies.'

Kara digested this. She felt sick with fear. Her throat was tight as though the noose was already about her neck. She swallowed painfully and strove to keep calm.

'Zach must have enemies. The Gentleman's Retreat was a front for his underworld activities. He never spoke of them. But I learned he was a thief shortly after we were married. The men he hired all had the same hard look in their eyes. They were ex-army veterans. I suspected most had criminal backgrounds.'

'What about the maid, Dilys?' Finnemore asked as he furiously wrote down Kara's words.

'She was probably in love with Zach. He made a habit of seducing the maids.' She paused, waiting for him to catch up with his writing. Then pursued, 'What about Beatrice? She was there. I don't know when she arrived, but I remember her in the study.'

Arnold Finnemore blushed and no longer seemed able to hold Kara's stare. 'Your sister's statement also points to your guilt.'

Kara flinched. She had not expected that. Her voice cracked as she asked, 'What did she say?'

He briefly outlined her sister's statement. With each word, Kara saw her freedom vanishing. Beatrice had described only what she had seen as she entered the study. She had been in the garden. How was it she had not seen the murderer? Or had she?

Finally Kara accepted the depth of her sister's hatred. Did she hate her so much that she would see her hanged for a murder she did not commit? Kate slumped in the chair. Her pride was crushed. It was the final betrayal.

'Someone must have seen who fired the gun.

They must have escaped through the garden. Zach lived a double life. I'm sure he still had links with the underworld. Ask his valet, Dipper Jones. They'd been together for years.'

'Jones has disappeared. Of course, he could have done it.'

Kara shook her head. 'Jones was totally loyal to Zach; though it's likely that he had a criminal record, and wanted to avoid any awkward questions...'

Her mind raced. Was the murderer someone Beatrice knew? Did they have some hold over her? Even now she refused to acknowledge that her sister could so wickedly wish her destroyed.

'Time's up,' the wardress grunted. Stepping forward, she took Kara's arm.

Mr Finnemore collected his papers. Kara looked back over her shoulder. Finnemore looked worried and haggard. Obviously the evidence against her was damning. She clung to her faith in Richard.

'I think Beatrice knows more than she's telling, Mr Finnemore.'

Chapter Twenty-seven

Richard was released after two hours of questioning. He was determined that Kara would be freed before the scandal broke. He knew Kara was innocent and he would prove it. To Inspector Urquhart he had forcefully denied that Kara was his mistress. He was adamant that their close association over the years had been that of solicitor and client, and of friendship. He reminded the inspector that Kara had been his wife's friend, and that she was godmother to his daughter.

Eventually he convinced Inspector Urquhart that the accusations that Tim and Harry were his sons were just malicious gossip. Not only did Richard want Kara's name cleared, he did not want any scandal attached to the children.

The maid, Dilys, under further questioning, had broken down in her grief, revealing that she believed Morton would marry her. Reluctantly she conceded that, despite his liaison with herself, he did continue to share his wife's bed. The other servants confirmed that, apart from the last two days of quarrelling, the Mortons appeared to have had a contented marriage.

So far Kara's name had been kept out of the papers which had reported Morton's murder. She had not yet been formally charged. Yet still Richard was unable to secure her release from police custody. Beatrice's evidence was damning when coupled with that of the maid. Unless a witness came forward to state they had seen someone fleeing from the garden on that night, on the evidence available, Kara would face trial for her husband's murder.

Richard hoped that the method of taking fingerprints, in use for the last seven years, would prove that Kara had not used the pistol. There were no prints on the weapon. The murderer must have worn gloves.

Beatrice was the key to Kara's release. Richard had never trusted her. He remembered the hostility and jealousy in her eyes in the first months of the sisters' reunion. He also suspected that Beatrice was in love with Morton. And Beatrice was capable of bearing a grudge. Since his return from Peru, he was not convinced that she had changed towards Kara. Beatrice had just become more proficient at hiding her jealousy and resentment.

On his release he went to the Mountgibbons' house.

'Lord and Lady Mountgibbons are not at home,' the butler informed him.

'It is to Lady Mountgibbons that I wish to speak. It is extremely urgent. Where can I find her?'

The butler hesitated. The authoritative and forceful look in Richard's eyes, and his determined stance, prompted a reluctant answer from a man trained for years in discretion.

'Lady Mountgibbons left for Dover this morning. She's travelling to France to join His Lordship.'

Richard's heart sank. If he missed her, there could be a delay of weeks before he could procure Kara's release.

He made Dover in record time by automobile. Another half-hour was wasted on gaining information about Lady Mountgibbons' ship. As he marched up the gangplank, there was only half an hour before it sailed. He rapped on Beatrice's cabin door. There was no answer.

He swore beneath his breath and banged

louder. Again no response. Trying the handle, he found it turned.

A woman's figure was lying prone on the small bed. 'Lady Mountgibbons, I have to speak with you.'

'Go away.' Her voice was watery with tears.

'Beatrice, Kara is in police custody under suspicion of a murder she did not commit. I can't believe you want her to suffer as she is.'

'Go away,' she sobbed. 'I've problems of my own.'

Her obvious misery made him control his mounting anger, though he rapped out, 'You never have cared about anyone but yourself, have you?'

'Sod off!'

'That's it, resort to the guttersnipe when you can't get your own way. You can't shock me into leaving. I don't believe you're as evil as you act. You must feel something for Kara.'

'Kara. Kara! It's always what's best for Kara.' Beatrice rolled on to her side to glare at him belligerently. 'What about me? She's had everything. It all comes so easily for her. What I've achieved I've had to fight for. Everything just fell into place for Kara. Zach. Her business. Even you. You'll fight for her because you love her. What do I ever get but abuse and rejection?'

He saw her pain and vulnerability. The hurt and suffering of her childhood was visible in the strained set of her mouth and the bleak defiance in her eyes.

'Kara loves you. Florence loved you. And Mountgibbons...'

'Freddie's left me,' she cried. 'I've got nothing. Not even my pride. I'm going to beg him to take me back.'

He hadn't expected that. No wonder the woman was distraught. He wished time was not so short. He disliked bullying tactics, but in this he had little choice if he was to get Beatrice's help before the ship sailed. 'Mountgibbons is besotted with you,' he reasoned. 'If he left you, you must have hurt him deeply. A man in love, as he was in love with you, will forgive you, if you are truly contrite. If you show yourself worthy of his love and respect.' His hazel stare challenged her pouting glare. 'Make Mountgibbons proud of you. Pettiness is so unworthy. So you wanted revenge upon your sister for having a more comfortable childhood than your own. Does she deserve what she is now facing in prison?'

She laughed bitterly. 'Did I deserve to be born in the workhouse? I was, you know. Who ever gave a toss about me?'

He changed tactics. 'You were so jealous of Kara's wealth you could never see that she envied you many things. You may have been poor, but you had your mother's love and devotion. What did Kara have? A father who despised her for not being a son. A man incapable of affection. She was isolated and lonely, permitted no friends. Do you envy her that?'

Beatrice sniffed back her tears, her expression stony. Richard looked at his watch. There were only twenty minutes before he must leave the ship. 'You know Kara did not kill Morton. Yet your statement was worded in a way which made her appear guilty.'

'I only said what I saw.'

'It's what you didn't say that I want to know. What else did you see that night?'

'I told the police everything.'

'No, you didn't. Whom did you see in the garden?'

The colour drained from her face and her eyes were dark with fear. She would not look at him. 'I saw nothing.'

His tone sharpened. 'Kara believes you to be someone very special. You can't forgive her for having an easier childhood than yourself. How petty. How vindictive. What harm has Kara ever done to you?' He turned away in disgust. 'I'm not surprised Mountgibbons has left you. You've a meanness in you which no amount of love can reach. You're selfish to the core. Why must you hurt those who love you? *Really* love you.'

Beatrice gasped, holding the back of her hand to her mouth as though he had struck her. 'What do you know of my life? What I suffered?'

'All I know is that, because of Kara, you were able to put that life behind you.' The earlier pity he had felt for her evaporated at her spite. 'Is this how you repay her? You've betrayed her. You deserve all you get from life. At this rate you'll end up a bitter, twisted, lonely woman.'

Beneath his contempt, Beatrice broke down. It was the final straw. Yet even so, any show of weakness was unlike her. Even when Fancy had beaten her, she had always remained defiant, never weak and weepy. She had been feeling ill ever since Freddie had left her. Richard Tennent made her sound so horrible. That wasn't how she was. Was it? Was that how Freddie now saw her?

'Crying won't get your husband back.' Richard was merciless now, hardened against her tears. 'Kara will face ruin if she goes to trial. She'll be a notorious woman, even if she is eventually proved innocent. Everything about her life will become public knowledge, and that will include your life as well. Have you considered that? Mountgibbons may love you. He may choose to ignore your past life when it is not widely known. Once it is spread across the national papers, his family pride could swamp all other emotion. He will also be held up to ridicule. Is that what you want? If you want to continue to live in luxury as Lady Mountgibbons, then you had better put honour before personal vengeance.'

'I don't care about the luxury,' Beatrice screamed at him. 'That's no longer important. It's Freddie I want. He's the only man who's ever treated me decently. I love him. I've been such a fool.'

She burst into fresh weeping.

Richard sighed, his pity for her returning. Her body shook with the force of her sobs. He put a hand on her shoulder and spoke more gently. 'Then be worthy of him. Tell the police everything. Save your sister who also loves you.'

She raised red-rimmed eyes to him. 'You don't know what you're asking. If I spoke I'd be the next victim.'

Richard's heart pounded with expectancy. 'Was the murderer someone you recognised from the underworld?'

She nodded. 'He didn't see me. I ducked back in the bushes.' Fear was stark in her grey eyes. It was as though she had seen a ghost. 'You don't know what he's like. If I grassed on him, I'm dead meat.' She began to shake with terror. 'Even Freddie couldn't save me.'

'You'd have protection, Beatrice. You'd be safe. Freddie would take you away until it blew over.'

She looked at him, her lips curling back with derision. 'It will never blow over. Not for them. No matter how long it took, they'd get me ... I'm not about to spend the rest of my life looking over my shoulder – awaiting the assassin's bullet, or knife.'

'So you'd let Kara be hanged because of your own cowardice. You'd rather risk losing the man you love. Can you live with yourself, if you do that?'

Her throat worked as she stared at him. 'You're a hard bastard, Tennent.'

He understood her fear and sympathised with her, but he dared not relent. Kara's life depended on it. Ruthlessly, he pursued his line of questioning. 'Who did it, Beatrice? Do you really want to see Kara hanged? What did she ever do to harm you? She loved you. You betrayed her. You've betrayed Florence. For once in your life do something for someone else, not just yourself.'

The ship's whistle blew, warning Richard he must leave the ship as it was about to sail.

'For God's sake, Beatrice.' His voice was gruff with pain. His anguished stare pinioned her. 'You can't mean to let Kara die!'

She shuddered. Terror for her own safety made

icy fingers claw at her spine and innards. The nausea of the last few days increased. Her head swam, as it had once when she had climbed the steps of the Monument near the Thames and looked down on the streets below. She swallowed hard, fighting to control it. The solicitor's words shamed her.

Her feelings for Zach had been an obsession. A destructive force. Since Freddie had left her she had come to see many things differently. Now she recalled the kindnesses Kara had shown her. Her generosity. Her trust. At the time she had scoffed at them. She had thought her sister a fool for throwing her money away. She'd never have sought out a brat of a lost sister – especially on learning she'd led a life such as Beatrice had done. Yet Kara had never condemned her, or judged her. She had accepted her without recrimination. Loved her. Without Kara she'd still be in the gutter. Kara had paid Fancy to allow her to leave the rookery. It had been the start of the years of rivalry between the Gilberts and Zach Morton, with Zach triumphing over them. Until…

She shuddered again, her voice crackling with fear. 'All right. I'll tell you what I saw. Just let's get off this ship before it sails. I'll catch the next one to Boulogne.' She forced a weak smile. 'Might not do Freddie any harm to calm down a bit. You never know, he might even miss me.'

After the police received Beatrice's revised statement, Kara was released. The next day was Zach's funeral. The press was waiting outside the cemetery shouting questions, demanding a statement. Kara was pale in her widow's weeds, grateful for Richard's supporting arm as he raised a hand to halt the questions. 'Mrs Morton is still shocked by the murder of her husband. I am sure the murderer will soon be apprehended.'

'Was Morton a leading figure in the underworld, Mrs Morton?' a persistent reporter yelled. 'Did his fortune come from prostitution and thieving as well as his gaming house?'

Kara blocked her ears from the shouts. Her eyes lowered behind her black veil as the car drove away through the reporters. More reporters waited outside the house. Kara put a hand on Richard's arm. 'Take me away from London, Richard. The children are at Crownfield Hall. When Lord Mountgibbons learned of Zach's death from an English newspaper, he telephoned to offer his home as a sanctuary for the children. He invited me to join them. I suppose he thought Beatrice would be there.'

'Mountgibbons has left Beatrice,' Richard said after ordering the chauffeur to drive to Staffordshire. 'That's why Beatrice has followed him to France. She should be safe there from any retribution from the Gilbert gang. Though as yet the police have had no luck in tracing Fancy. That villain seems to lead a charmed life.'

'I thought all that was far behind us. The Gilbert brothers have cast a long shadow over my family. Hasn't Beatrice suffered enough at their hands?' Her eyes blurred with tears of love and pride. 'She risked her life to save me. There were times when I thought she hated me. I tried so hard to win her love. But the diversity of our childhood is always there between us. Resented by her.'

'Beatrice has changed,' Richard advised. 'She's no longer so self-centred. Or resentful. Why should she be? Is she not Lady Mountgibbons? She finally realises that she has obligations to that title. At last she feels she is your equal.'

'She was always like that. It is more important that she is in love with her husband. I wrote to His Lordship telling him how Beatrice had risked her life to save mine. I hope she finds happiness with him. She deserves it.'

'As you deserve happiness, Kara.' His voice was rusty with emotion. 'You've sacrificed so much to protect others.' He lifted a hand to push away her black veil. For a long moment he stared into her eyes. Neither spoke. Kara felt the magnetism of his charm and knew she was succumbing to it. With an effort she drew back. Richard was in love with Fenella Sommerfield. It was the memory of one single night of passion which wove its magic around them.

A cauldron of memories simmered in her mind. She had cherished that night of love for seven years. It had been fed by the constant reminder of the twins, who grew daily more like Richard. For years Richard's invasive shadow had coloured her life. To forget him, she had worked hard expanding her business. It had stopped her loving Zach. Her deepest regret was that he died with so much ill-feeling between them. Zach had been good to her in his way. Perhaps he had even loved her. But that had not kept him faithful. His infidelities had hurt her more than she admitted. They scored her pride. Lacerated her self-esteem. Belittled her as a woman and wife.

She was haunted by the promise in Richard's eyes. But he had betrayed her innocence. As both Beatrice and Zach had done. She did not want to be hurt again. Though an unquenchable longing in her did not want to lose his friendship.

Her stare refocused on the thinning houses. With a start she turned to Richard. 'We are leaving London. Are you not returning to your office? Your home. It is thoughtless of me to expect you to accompany me. Staffordshire is several hours' drive away.'

'This is not a time for you to be alone. But if my company is intrusive upon your grief...?'

She shook her head, but could not look at him. 'It is a great comfort, as it has always been. But won't Miss Sommerfield be concerned at your absence?'

He frowned. A finger lifted her chin so that she was forced to meet his penetrating gaze. 'You once said that, if we have a time for loving, it was not then. This is our time, Kara, I've waited seven years.'

His voice, beguiled, tempted. Suspicion challenged, defied.

'Is it me you want, Richard, or the twins? Elizabeth told me how much you had craved a son. This way you get two. And what about Miss Sommerfield? She's expecting marriage from you, I hear. Am I expected to tolerate her as a mistress, as Elizabeth endured the woman you kept in Kensington?'

Richard paled, his face stiff with affront. He drew back; his eyes snapping fire. 'I never claimed to be a saint. I didn't love Elizabeth. Why should I deny myself the comfort of a woman because my wife denied me her bed? Was I supposed to pine for you like a love-sick fool whilst you bore Morton three children? I even thought the twins were his. You denied being pregnant when I asked you if there had been any consequences from our night together. You must already have been planning tricking Morton into marriage then.'

'He was always there when I needed him,' Kara threw at him in her hurt at his accusation. 'And he never fed me a barrelful of lies to seduce me into his bed. You're a philanderer – just like Zach. At least I was true to my marriage vows.'

Richard glared at her, his expression incredulous. Abruptly, he rapped on the window dividing them from the chauffeur. 'I'm getting out here. We've just passed a station. I'll get a train back to London.'

He stepped on to the street. She was too angry and hurt to stop him.

'Goodbye, Kara.'

She looked away without answering. For seven years she had carried a false image of the man she loved. What did she truly know of him? In many ways he was a stranger to her. Jealousy made it hard to accept that he had kept a mistress, although she knew Elizabeth played upon her illness to deny him her bed. She had thought Richard so perfect. Yet who in this world was ever perfect? Her gaze fixed on the passing hedgerows which had replaced the houses. Where her heart had beaten so vibrantly, there was now an aching void.

As dusk fell, a stout man weaved drunkenly along the gutter of a London backstreet. A brandy bottle was frequently raised to his lips, and his bowler hat was tipped jauntily to one side. The brandy bolstered his confidence. He leaned against the iron post of the gaslamp and whistled tunelessly, an inane grin on his lips. He'd just returned from observing Morton's funeral. The bastard had been sent off in style. The wealthy widow on the arm of her lawyer; members of parliament rubbing shoulders with thieves at the graveside. The man hiccuped. Morton had been given a grand send-off all right. And no hint in the papers of who had murdered him.

The brandy bottle was raised in silent salute to himself. A job well done. He sniggered. He continued whistling as two short figures materialised out of a side alley. Recognising them, he staggered forward.

'Morton's in 'is grave. Like yer ordered. Yer got yer revenge on that thieving bastard. Honour intact, and all that crap.'

'Not quite,' the shorter of the two said, in a voice which turned the man's innards to water. 'Still a small matter of incompetence to settle.'

Sobered by the icy dousing of fear gripping his vitals, he edged away. 'It were agreed bygones were bygones. I told yer it were Morton who stole yer money for the opium. I agreed to kill 'im fer yer. For that I was ter go free.'

The Chinamen regarded him with flashing

brown eyes. 'A man who shops one of his own kind is not a man to be trusted.'

Panic ground through Fancy Gilbert. He relived again the moment of terror when the four Chinese had found him in the warehouse. Slasher's head had been held up before his pain-crazed eyes as they tortured him until he had screamed for mercy.

'You said if I killed Morton, I'd live.'

'You have lived for many days longer than you would have done. Days when you have eaten well, bedded beautiful ladies and boys. Tasted the finest wines. These days we granted you. Now you die.'

Beatrice knew she was on a wild-goose chase. At Nice she learned Freddie and his companions had travelled to Monte Carlo. At Monte Carlo she had missed them by a day: they had left for the Italian lakes. Disheartened, she took to her bed. She had never felt so wretched. She feared Freddie lost to her. Once it was learned that she had informed on Fancy, her days would be numbered. And on top of that she had picked up some damned illness which made her body drag with weariness and nothing she ate would stay down.

The prospect of continuing to chase Freddie was all too much. She would return to Crownfield Hall. At least there, if he still wanted her to leave, he would have to confront her in person. She lay back on her pillows, an English newspaper unread by her side.

'My Lady,' her maid, Tilly, hovered by the foot

of the bed. 'You haven't touched your breakfast.'

'I don't feel like eating. Take it away.'

'You haven't eaten a proper meal for days, Your Ladyship,' Tilly said with concern.

Beatrice glared at her, about to remark that what she did was not her maid's concern. The look on Tilly's face stopped her. They had been together for six years. Tilly was ten years older than Beatrice: plain, plump but maternal. At least Tilly cared that she felt so ill and wretched.

'I'll get up later. We shall return to Crownfield.'

'Are you sure you're strong enough to travel, My Lady?'

'Perfectly.' A wave of nausea churned through her. 'Perhaps not. I feel so weak. So sick all the time.'

'Let me summon a doctor. Perhaps you need a tonic. The last weeks have not been easy for you, My Lady.'

Beatrice turned her head away. She saw her reflection in the dressing-table mirror. Her face was waxen, dark shadows hollowed her eyes, and her auburn hair looked dull and lifeless where it lay spread across the pillow. She pulled a face. 'I look awful. How can I win Freddie back looking like this? I'll see a doctor, Tilly. If I can just shake off this tiredness and nausea, make-up will hide the ravages to my face.'

When the maid left the room, Beatrice picked up the discarded newspaper and flicked through the pages. Idly, she glanced at the headlines. Her reading was too slow to bother with any of the longer items. About to throw it aside, she turned another page, and her gaze was riveted on the central column. 'LONDON VILLAIN FOUND HANGING FROM LAMPPOST. GANG WARFARE SUSPECTED.'

It went on to say that Fancy Gilbert, a known criminal gang leader, had been found hanged from a lamppost in Covent Garden.

Beatrice sighed with relief. Since Fancy had been murdered by a rival gang and not arrested by the police, it looked as though she was safe.

There was a tap on the door and a doctor was announced. 'What ails Your Ladyship?' He bent his tall, thin frame to peer through horn-rimmed spectacles at her. His English was flavoured with a thick French accent she had trouble understanding.

She explained briefly, and answered his questions as he examined her eyes and tongue.

'Is there pain in your stomach?' he asked.

'No. Just the constant nausea.'

He continued his examination and straightened to regard her sternly. 'You rest one week in bed. You are foolish woman to travel. You are *enceinte*. With baby. Could lose baby if travel sooner.'

Beatrice stared at him incredulously. She never kept track of her monthly courses, believing herself barren. Her mind scanned back across the weeks. Ten weeks. Could she truly be pregnant? She did not know whether to laugh, cry, or shout with joy.

Her mind raced with plans. She would rest, then return to Crownfield. Her home. Her child's inheritance. For the first time in her life she was ecstatically happy.

Freddie would never divorce her now. And she

knew how to reclaim his love. She no longer wanted his enslavement, she wanted his respect. That might take longer to achieve, but she would win it. She wanted Freddie to be proud of her.

She grimaced with dismay at the creature she had been in the past. Bitter. Vengeful. Bent upon retribution. Ruthless in achieving her aims at the cost of others. She was ashamed. She had so much to be grateful for. It was time to make her peace with Kara. Her jealousy mellowed. They might never be close friends, but they were sisters. Now that her envy had ebbed, she realised how much she owed to her sister. How much she would miss Kara, if she was no longer part of her life.

Kara spent three weeks at Crownfield with her children. She was restless and unhappy. She mourned Zach. For all he had been a rogue, he had been a charming and irresistible one. And despite loving Richard, she had been charmed by Zach.

Yet her unhappiness stemmed not from Zach's death, but from missing Richard. As the shock faded from Zach's murder and her arrest, she saw things more clearly. She feared she had misjudged Richard. Yesterday there had been an item in *The Times* announcing the wedding of Fenella Sommerfield to the wealthy industrialist, Arthur Jacobs. It had prompted a letter by special delivery to Richard's home. It read simply:

Forgive me,
Kara

It wasn't very romantic, and it didn't touch upon the complexity of her feelings. If Richard truly cared he would respond. Each time the phone rang she held her breath in expectation, her heart thudding wildly. It was never Richard.

Beatrice had arrived last night, glowing and joyous in her pregnancy. Freddie, tender and loving, had been at her side. They had been reunited in London after Freddie had returned there from Monte Carlo instead of travelling to Italy with his companions. He had been too wretched to continue his journey. He had missed Beatrice and wanted a reconciliation.

Kara was enfolded in her sister's arms.

'I've been such a bitch to you.' Beatrice was hugging her close. 'Forgive me. I want more than anything for us to be friends.'

Kara had readily forgiven her. But her words had echoed the plea in her letter to Richard. It remained unanswered. Heavy of heart, she excused herself from Beatrice and Freddie's company. They were so in love, unable to stop smiling or touching each other, so that watching them together became a torment. It was too harsh a reminder of the emptiness of her life.

Kara strolled aimlessly through the grounds. She could hear the excited laughter of the twins as they played tennis on the court. It was past their bedtime, but it was a warm evening and she left them to their play. She stopped by a stone bench which overlooked a lake overhung with willows, and sat down.

The sun sank lower. Purple and apricot

streaked the sky, a light breeze ruffling her hair and making her cross her hands to her upper arms to instil some warmth through the thin silk of her white blouse. It was a glorious sunset. Since she had made her vow to Richard before he left for Mexico, she had rarely seen a more magnificent one. Its beauty accentuated the void which filled her heart.

Heartache bent her head as she braced herself to face the future without the man she loved at her side.

'Forgive me.' The words whispered through the rustling willow branches.

The husky male voice made her start.

'Forgive me, Kara. I lost you once. I could not bear to do so a second time.'

It was her imagination playing tricks. No, the voice was real. She turned slowly, still fearful lest her mind had deceived her.

Richard stood beside the willow tree. 'That damned tongue of yours always was brutally honest. I should never have allowed my anger to get the better of me. You sounded like you hated me. When I returned to my office an urgent case awaited me. It took me to Devon. I was going to write, but words appeared so inadequate on the page. I'd been back in London just a few hours when your letter arrived. I left immediately. I'd have been here last night if I hadn't got a double puncture miles from anywhere.'

The passionate intensity of her love for him overwhelmed her. The apricot hues of the sunset bathed them in its healing light. It had always been their special time of the day. The reforging of the bonds of their passion.

'I was a jealous fool,' she said, drawn irresistibly towards him. 'Fenella Sommerfield was so beautiful and young. She could give you so much more than I.'

'You are all I ever wanted.'

He held out his arms and she ran into them. She could feel his tension, the muscles coiled against her rejection. Then, with a heartfelt sigh, he clasped her to him.

'This is our time for loving, Kara. From now until eternity.'

The publishers hope that this book has given you enjoyable reading. Large Print Books are especially designed to be as easy to see and hold as possible. If you wish a complete list of our books please ask at your local library or write directly to:

Magna Large Print Books
Magna House, Long Preston,
Skipton, North Yorkshire.
BD23 4ND

This Large Print Book for the partially sighted, who cannot read normal print, is published under the auspices of

THE ULVERSCROFT FOUNDATION